HERITAGE BUILDERS

To Mary
A special lady and a wonderful sister-in-law
I hope you enjoy my book
"Love Ya"

EXTENDING SHADOWS

Billy Parker

Wishing you winter sun and summer shade
Billy Parker
May 21, 2016

HERITAGE BUILDERS PUBLISHING
MONTEREY, CLOVIS CALIFORNIA

This is a work of fiction.

People, places, and events portrayed here exist
only in the mind of the author.
Any relative similarities found herein are purely coincidental.

FOREWORD

By Charlene Montgomery, Author of The Legend of George Jones

From the humble town of Tremont, Mississippi just south of Red Bay, Alabama, a vibrant accession of artistic aptitude has embedded its roots to progressively extend its branches through the boundless fields of music and literature. From country music superstar Tammy Wynette to song writer Agnes Wilson, Tremont is teeming with extensive talent, including and certainly not limited to the creative mind of Billy Parker.

Billy's inspired literary style is sure to extend his namesake beyond the borders of his hometown, and into the homes and hearts of American and international readers alike.

Billy's own infectiously good-humored and genuinely authentic personality come to life in his writing, and he expertly captures the reader's mind, entrapping them in a tense cover - to - cover journey whose suspenseful flair will keep you guessing at every turn. It is the sign of a truly remarkable book that can take you from this world through text and into a new world of life and excitement.

This, as I see and do truly hope, is only the beginning of Billy Parker's incursion into the world of literature.

PROLOGUE

Sergeant Mitchell Simmons has spent the last eight years in Afghanistan, and today he is hitchhiking to visit his Army buddy. A pretty girl offers him a ride, but a blonde in a red Ferrari takes his boots from atop his duffel bag. What Simmons does not know is that one is his buddy's sister, the other his buddy's fiancée, and his buddy is dead.

People say he killed himself, but Simmons knows better. They had seen too much death in Afghanistan, and his buddy hated dead bodies. If he were going to kill himself, it would be where his body would never be found. Simmons would bet his life on that, and vows to find out what really happened.

As a boy who grew up in an orphanage, the Army being the only family he has ever known, Simmons soon finds himself in the world of the ultra-wealthy—luxury jets, private helicopters, diamonds, drugs, and murder. Now someone is trying to kill him, but they are finding that it's not so easy. The Taliban had been trying for the last eight years.

HERITAGE BUILDERS PUBLISHING
© 2015

All rights reserved. No part of this publication may be reproduced, stored in a retrieval system, or transmitted in any form by any means, electronic, mechanical, photocopy, recording, or otherwise, without the prior permission of the publisher, except as provided by USA copyright law.

First Edition 2015

Contributing Editor, Christina Raines
Cover Design, Ashley Dondlinger
Book Design, Nord Compo
Published by Heritage Builders Publishing
Clovis, Monterey California 93619
www.HeritageBuilders.com   1-888-898-9563

ISBN 978-1-942603-39-9

Printed and bound in United States of America

TABLE OF CONTENTS

CHAPTER 1	Simmons	13
CHAPTER 2	Penny	29
CHAPTER 3	Anna	43
CHAPTER 4	Robert 1980	55
CHAPTER 5	Gaither (Gee) Gilmore 1773	65
CHAPTER 6	JMA 1999	77
CHAPTER 7	Mina 1773	99
CHAPTER 8	Elaine	109
CHAPTER 9	Gilsan Oil 1980	121
CHAPTER 10	Sam Stewart 1773	133
CHAPTER 11	Investigation	151
CHAPTER 12	Pump Some Oil 1980	161

CHAPTER 13	Amos & Marie	169
CHAPTER 14	Leaving Home 1774	187
CHAPTER 15	Chief Bates	207
CHAPTER 16	The Cherokee 1794	227
CHAPTER 17	Diamonds	247
CHAPTER 18	Tall Grass 1774	263
CHAPTER 19	Booby-Trap	279
CHAPTER 20	Mules 1775	295
CHAPTER 21	FBI	305
CHAPTER 22	Ambush	327
CHAPTER 23	Ears 1779	347
CHAPTER 24	Davis	359
CHAPTER 25	Diamonds	369
CHAPTER 26	Gold 1793	381
CHAPTER 27	Search	395
CHAPTER 28	Bones 1797	411
CHAPTER 29	Suspects	429
CHAPTER 30	The Truth	445

CHAPTER ONE

SIMMONS

Twenty-Ten

Autumn leaves of red, yellow, brown, and gold glistened on the hardwoods, mixed with the dark green colors of pine needles. *It is beautiful. Makes a person feel secure and self-confident, just like Jeanie*, she thought, admiring the fall colors. As she drove, her mind drifted back to her morning history class at Mallory Middle School. At the end of her third period class, Jeanie Lester, a cute little girl with her long blonde hair tied in a ponytail with a yellow ribbon, had walked up to her and said,

"Miss Simpson, I'm going to marry David Butler. He's so cute." Her blue eyes were gleaming with as much self-confidence as any twelve-year-old could possibly have.

As she thought about Jeanie, her mind wandered back to the days when she was in the sixth grade. Those memories were a little vague, and there were not a lot of them. However, she did remember one cute little boy, Steven Jackson, though she could not remember if she had wanted to marry him. Her mind continued to drift to her high school years. The basketball years were what she remembered most because they had won back-to-back state championships, something almost unheard of in Texas. After high school she had accepted a scholarship from the University of Arkansas at Pine Bluff and was proud to have graduated with honors, both there and in grad school.

She remembered dating a few boys in high school, one or two in college, but none had she wanted to marry.

Oh well, I am happy the way I am. I guess I'll just be an old maid school teacher.

She continued to daydream as she drove, listening to soft music playing on the satellite radio, her mind now on the girls basketball team she coached. She wondered if this year's team would be as good as last's.

Maybe. . . I only lost two girls from last year's team, but one of those girls will be hard to replace. She is a very good player and will no doubt play high school and college ball.

Oh no! This is my turn. She braked the Honda hard before turning right onto Texas State Highway 155, a narrow two-lane road running through the Hill Country of East Texas. Halfway through her turn, an Army duffel bag on the left side of the intersection caught her attention. It was sitting upright with U. S. Army stenciled above a white star. On top of the bag was a pair of brown cowboy boots. Beyond the bag, under the shade of an oak tree, a U. S. soldier in dress uniform stood holding out his thumb. She did not know why she stopped except maybe it was because her brother had been in the Army.

She rolled her window half-way down and watched the soldier stroll across the highway holding out his hands, palms upward, letting her see there was nothing in them. She saw a grateful smile on his fairly good-looking and deeply-tanned face. He was about six two, trim, and broad shouldered with brown eyes glistening with gratitude. His brown hair was cut short, Army style. He wore a slightly wrinkled uniform with a sergeant emblem on the shoulder.

He stopped a few feet from her car and asked in a low, soothing voice with a trace of a southern accent, "Are you going as far as Longview? If you are, could you give me a lift?"

Yeah, why not? she thought and was about to say yes, when she heard screeching brakes and saw a red car slide to a stop next to his duffel bag. A hand reached out, grabbed the boots, and a split second later, sped away, tires spinning, one leaving a long black streak on the pavement, the other slinging rocks and dirt. Some hit the duffel bag so hard it toppled over and was now lying on the ground, the white star almost hidden beneath the dirt.

She watched the soldier turn toward his duffel bag just in time to see a hand grab his boots. He heard the screaming tires, saw the smoke, the flying rocks, and the red car that roared off down the highway.

"That mother fu...!" He stopped, remembering he was no longer on an Army base where these words were common. Turning, he faced the girl, and yelled, "Did you see that? They... she took my boots." Pointing first toward his bag, then down the highway, "She... she stole my boots." His voice trailed off as he stared down the highway, still not believing what had just happened. He turned to face the girl and saw she was doubled over with laughter, her body rocking back and forth, her hands pounding the steering wheel and tears streaming down her face.

"It's not funny. She took my boots," he protested. She continued to laugh and pound the steering wheel. He turned and stared down the highway, running over in his mind what had just happened. Still staring in disbelief and not knowing what else to do, he said to no one in particular, "Well... nothing I can do about it now."

Finally, the girl managed to control her laughter and looked closely at him. His face reminded her of someone she had seen before, but she could not remember who or where. "Where are you from?"

"I..." he mumbled, "I've been in Afghanistan. I rode the bus from Frisco to Little Rock, then hitchhiked to here." He paused, looked down the highway, and added in a slightly sarcastic voice, "To here—the boot theft capitol of the world." He shrugged his shoulders and turned to face her. "Could you give me a lift?"

"Get your bag. And make sure you knock some of the dirt off. This is a new car."

She was giggling as she pushed the trunk release button. "That was so funny."

The solider walked to the other side of the road, kicked his bag, and watched the dirt fly. He set the bag upright, brushing it with the palm of his hand as he looked down the highway. He picked it up, walked to the back of her car, and threw it into the trunk. He walked to the passenger side and saw her removing some books and papers from the passenger seat. He waited until she laid them on the back seat, then opened the door and sat down.

The seat was leather, and the car had a new car smell, plus the light aroma of nice smelling perfume. The radio was playing soft classical music he did not recognize, but it was nice and had a soothing effect on him.

I need that, he thought.

He looked at the leather dashboard, the built-in GPS, the satellite radio, the sun roof, and a can of diet Dr. Pepper sitting in one console cup holder. In the other was a small bottle of hand sanitizer and a pack of Doublemint.

"Nice car. I haven't been in an American car in over eight years. Yeah, nice car," he said to himself.

He looked at the girl who appeared to be in her mid-twenties. She was very attractive and reminded him of Princess Diana, except this girl had auburn hair, cut short. She had the same warm and charming personality that Princess Diana had displayed when he had seen her on television. Her skin was soft, smooth, and lightly tanned. Her lips were full, turning slightly upwards at the corners, giving the impression that she was smiling—and maybe she was. Her smile revealed perfect white teeth. Her eyes were sea-green with lighter shades of green mixed with black, blue, and white. They reminded him of gentle ocean waves, streaked with sunlight and breaking onto a white sandy beach. The kind of eyes that make you think you are looking out through the galaxy, seeing soft starlight, twinkling and inviting.

They were beautiful, even though they were still a little red from the tears of laughter. Silver crosses hung from her ears, reflecting streaks of sunlight onto the dashboard.

She reminded him of someone he had seen before, but he decided that could not be since he had never been in Texas until today. Still, something about her reminded him of someone. She wore a loose-fitting, light green dress with a yellow sash tied around a slender waist. Her breasts were full and, from where he sat, he could see nice, long, tanned legs and imagined that under the dress would also be a nice figure. Even with her sitting behind the steering wheel, he could see she was tall, five-eleven, maybe more. *Nice*, he thought. He looked at her hands. They were soft; her long nails were well-manicured. *Nice!* And she was not wearing a wedding ring.

Funny how that word "nice" just keeps reverberating through my mind. He looked at her and wondered if it was because he had spent the last eight years in Afghanistan, where there were no girls to look at. The few you saw wore loose-fitting clothes and burkas, which covered their bodies, revealing only their eyes. They also wore gloves to cover their hands and could not be seen in public unless escorted by a man.

No, it is not because I haven't seen a girl in a long time; this girl is nice, he reasoned.

"My name is Simmons, Mitchell Simmons," he said, offering her his hand. "I'm Elaine," she said, shaking his hand gently with a warm, but firm grip. *Nice*, he thought.

"It's nice to meet you, Elaine. Thanks for giving me a ride."

"How long have you been in the Army?" she asked as she pulled back onto the highway. Her voice was soft, and each word was spoken distinctly, but with slight authority.

"Almost ten years. I have been in Afghanistan the last eight. I guess that's why I was admiring your car so much. I haven't seen anything but a Humvee in a long time." He paused, wondering if she would be interested in hearing about the Humvee, but as they topped a hill, there on the shoulder of the road was a red Ferrari 599 GTO. A girl in short shorts stood behind it, holding a pair of cowboy boots at arm's length in front of her.

Elaine began laughing and almost ran off the road as she pulled behind the Ferrari.

The girl walked to the passenger side of the car, clutching the boots tightly against her chest and looking at him with sparkling blue eyes and a sensuous smile. "What could I get for a pair of cowboy boots?" she teased. She waited for him to answer, and when he did not, she handed him the boots.

He opened his mouth, but could not say a word as he took the boots. He sat staring at her, not fully understanding what was happening. The girl was not as tall as Elaine, but well built with long tan legs, beautiful blue eyes, and long blonde hair.

Wow! This is one good-looking girl, Simmons thought. He sat in the car, not knowing what to do. He was vaguely aware of Elaine telling the girl what he had said and how he had acted when she took his boots. They sat down on the shoulder of the road, both doubled over with laughter.

Finally, he opened the door, got out, and stood by the car, still holding the boots and continuing to stare. It was a few minutes before they stopped laughing. Elaine looked at him and said, "This is Penny, the boot thief. She's also my best friend."

"I'm Simmons," he said after a brief pause, adding, "Mitchell Simmons," in a voice he did not recognize as his own.

The girl looked up at him and smiled for a brief moment, but an instant later her face went blank. Her blue eyes narrowed, lost their sparkle, and were no longer friendly. Her body stiffened, her shoulders slumped, and deep lines of concern formed on her forehead. She covered her mouth with both hands, drew in a deep breath, and did not exhale for a long moment.

Simmons

She continued to stare at him, a look of shock on her face. She did not say another word, just got up, walked to her car and opened the door. She looked back at Elaine and in a cold and demanding voice said, "When you drop him off, come on over. I'll order us a pizza." She glared at him, with a strong emphasis on the word *us*. She started the Ferrari and drove away.

"Whew! That was cold. What did I do? All I did was tell her my name." Simmons looked at Elaine and saw a puzzled look on her face as well. He could see that she was also wondering what that was about.

After a few awkward seconds, they got into Elaine's Honda and rode a few miles in silence before she turned and looked at him, long and hard. "You have family in Longview?"

"No, not really. I came here to visit an old Army buddy who lives just outside of town. We were in the service together, though I haven't seen him since he left Afghanistan four years ago. His name is Lanny Simpson. Maybe you know him?"

He saw her body stiffen. Her hands gripped the steering wheel so tight her knuckles were turning white. She shot a cold glance at him. So cold, he could feel the icicles slam into his face. She frowned, and her face hardened as she slumped in the seat. She turned to stare at the road, not saying another word.

So much for her knowing him, Simmons thought as he sat thinking of Lanny.

Lanny had left the Army while they were in Afghanistan. They were in the mountains on search detail when word came that Lanny's father had died. Lanny's tour of duty was up in three weeks, so the Army granted him an early hardship release. He had returned to the States to take care of his mother, and Simmons had volunteered for another tour. The last time he had spoken to Lanny was almost four years ago. He had tried to call him several times since then, but his phone was no longer a working number.

A lot can change in four years, Simmons thought, and wondered how this girl fit into the picture. Probably she had dated him, possibly becoming serious about him. Lanny had always been a ladies man. Not only was he handsome and charming, he had a personality that seemed to say, "I am your best friend and I've known you all my life," even if you had just met him. No matter where they went, the girls were always falling for Lanny, Simmons remembered.

They never paid much attention to me when we went out; it was always Lanny, he thought. *Yep, I bet he had dated this girl, broke it off, and she did not like it.* He looked at the girl, still thinking of Lanny. *Well, Lanny, you may be handsome and charming, but you're not very smart. This girl is nice.* There was that word again. *Is it the only word I know?* he asked himself and vowed not to use it again.

He did not say anything for a long time as he waited for her to say something. She said nothing, only looked straight ahead, never once looking at him. Finally, he broke the silence. "I guess because our names were so close together, spelling-wise I mean, we were always grouped together. We were in the same training camps, on the same mountain tops, same foxholes, same everything. Over time, we became like brothers. It'll be good to see him again."

She said nothing, just gripped the wheel and continued to stare at the road.

Oh well, I like him, even if she doesn't, he said to himself.

Simmons could see she did not want to talk, so he said nothing more, just gazed out the window at the rolling hills of oak and pine trees, seeing a few farm houses, some pastures, but mostly timber land, all in beautiful fall colors. It was good to see something with colors, especially since all he had seen in the last eight years were rocks and sand—and a lot of both.

Before Lanny left Afghanistan he made Simmons promise when he came back stateside, he would drop by for a visit. Lanny had given him photos and directions on how to find his place, so now Simmons watched the left side of the highway looking for two red silos sitting side-by-side next to a white house and a red barn.

Elaine did not talk or even look his way, so he laid his head back against the seat and admired the fall colors while the memories of Lanny danced through his head. Simmons was surprised when she slowed and turned off the highway onto a gravel road. He did not know what was happening until he saw two silos, a red barn, and a white house. This is where Lanny lives... His heart began to pound a little.

It will be good to see him, Simmons thought.

Around a curve, up and over a small hill, the car stopped in front of an old Southern-style house which once had a breezeway through the middle, but was now enclosed. A porch ran the width of the front with a shorter one on the left side. He could see two rooms on either side of the enclosed breezeway, one with a chimney and each with a door and a window.

Simmons immediately recognized it from the pictures Lanny had shown him, but in the pictures, the grass was neatly mowed and the painted house glowed in sparkling white. Simmons was shocked to see the house was now ragged and run down; the paint was peeling and the yard was waist high in weeds. One of the posts on the front porch was loose at the top and leaned inward. The door on the left side of the house was open, and a window was broken out, sash and all.

Wonder what's wrong? he asked himself. *Lanny was always so neat, so orderly. Why would he let his house look like this? Does he even live here? If not, why did the girl bring him here?*

Elaine got out of the car and closed her door. Simmons knew this is where Lanny lived, or had lived, but why bring me here? The thought kept racing through his mind.

He looked around, realizing no one had lived here for quite a long time. There were no animals in the barn, no dogs, no cats, no chickens, no nothing, except a blue jay that flew away as they drove up. Still, he could not understand why she had brought him to an abandoned house.

Simmons stared at the house, watching as Elaine walked to the front fender and slumped against it. She was sobbing softly. He got out of the car, looked at Elaine over the top, and asked, "What gives? I don't understand."

She said nothing for a long time. He asked again, and still she did not answer. He wondered if he should just walk away until she turned to face him and said in a low, quivering voice, "He was my brother, and he killed himself." She looked back toward the house and screamed, "I hate you, Lanny! I hate you! You left me with this—all of this. It's falling down, and there's nothing I can to do about it." She was sobbing harder now, tears streaming down her face.

Simmons' mind was racing. . . *Lanny's dead? Killed himself? Her brother!* He stared intently at her and then it hit him. *Of course, this is Lanny's sister. She has the same warm and charming personality.* He remembered all the things Lanny had told him about her. *Yes, this is Lain,* and a million thoughts raced through his mind, all in one millisecond. As he looked at her, he remembered pictures and newspaper clippings Lanny had shown him. *This is why she reminded me of someone*, he thought.

This is the Lain that Lanny was so proud of. . . the All-State basketball player, the captain who had averaged more than twenty points a game as her high school won back-to-back State Championships. The Lain who had numerous scholarship offers to play college basketball and had made the starting lineup as a freshman. The Lain who was captain of her team as a sophomore and was well on her way to playing ladies professional ball before she blew out her knee.

He stood there, stunned, staring at the house and at the girl, unable to say a word.

Elaine turned, looked at him, and shouted, "Get out of here. I don't want you here. I should have never picked you up.

Go away!" She slumped to the ground and sat against the left front wheel, wiping tears from her eyes.

He walked around the front of the car and uttered more to himself than to anyone else, "No way. Lanny would not kill himself. He hated dead bodies and valued life too much. No way would he kill himself. No way!"

Elaine sat with her head nestled in arms wrapped around her knees and continued to sob. He sat down beside her and saw her body stiffen as she tried to push him away. "Get out of here. He's dead. Dead! Don't you understand? Dead," she shouted, as long, hard sobs raked her body and uncontrollable tears streamed down her face.

Simmons sat there, stunned and not knowing what to do. He thought of the million things Lanny and he had done, of all the things they had gone through. All those days in training camps, all those days in Afghanistan, the endless days in the mountains where death was all around them, as close as the next step. Of the days some of his buddies had made that next step and stepped no more. Days they piled bodies into a net to be lifted out by helicopter, or days they picked up body parts and put them in a bag. He would be dead himself if not for Lanny.

Lanny's memory screamed at him, and his mind went back to the day he had knelt beside a fallen solider. He had intended to raise the body to look for a name tag when he heard Lanny screaming, "Don't touch him! Don't touch him. There's a bomb. Get away from him."

Lanny had noticed the fresh earth under the body and knew there was a bomb beneath it. Simmons had not seen this himself, but he knew what would have happened had he rolled the body over. He remembered thinking there would be a family who would miss this soldier, and he wondered why it was not him instead of this man. He had no family. No one would miss him. Yes, this man would be missed by someone, and his heart ached for all of those who had died. They were gone, and now Lanny was gone. The emotions built up inside him, and for the first time since the day he was sent to the orphanage, tears trickled down his face.

They sat side by side for a long time, neither saying a word. Finally, she looked at him and said softly, "I am sorry. I had no right to yell at you."

Simmons could think of nothing to say. He sat head down, staring at the ground. They were sitting, slumped against the front wheel, when he heard the sound of an automobile and a car door slam. He looked up and saw the girl who had taken his boots staring at them. He could see that she, too, was crying.

"Come on," she said to Elaine, her voice shaky, barely above a whisper. "The pizza will be there any minute. Bring him with you." She got back into the car and drove away. Simmons and Elaine only sat in silence, too emotional to move.

A couple of minutes later, Simmons heard another car drive up. This time there was a short blast of a siren. Simmons stood and watched a deputy sheriff walk up to the passenger side of the car and look inside. He walked around the front and stopped, his hand resting on the butt of his service revolver. He looked at Simmons and then down at Elaine, whose head was buried in arms folded around her knees.

"What are y'all doing here, smoking pot?" he demanded in a rough voice.

All Simmons could do was shake his head. Elaine looked up at the deputy and nodded at Simmons.

"This is Lanny's Army buddy." She paused and added, "He did not know Lanny was dead."

The deputy's face softened when he recognized Elaine. He lowered his head, and after a brief pause, said softly, "I saw a red car leaving here real fast so I thought I would check things out." He hesitated, looked at Simmons, and said, "I'm sorry about Lanny. He was a friend of mine, too." He paused, looked around, and added, "Don't y'all stay here too long. It's not the safest place in Hardin County. Lots of transients come through here." He tipped his cap to Elaine, walked slowly back to his cruiser, and drove off.

Simmons looked down at Elaine and saw her looking up at him. He took her by the hand and helped her to her feet. She swayed on unsteady legs and laid her head against his chest. He put an arm softly around her shoulder, and they stood a long time, leaning on each other, seeing only extending shadows as the sun began to sink below the trees. Somewhere in the distance a dove cooed a mournful coo of regret.

Just like life, he thought. *The shadows get longer and longer, and then they are gone. Gone like Lanny. Gone like so many of my Army buddies. Gone! Forever gone. Why?* he asked himself over and over as he fought to control his tears.

"Do you want to come to Penny's with me?" Elaine asked. Her voice was barely above a whisper. "You don't hate him? I don't know what happened; I just know he would not kill himself."

"I don't hate him; I was just upset." She looked at him, wiping at the tears.

"Lain, believe me; Lanny would never kill himself. He saw too much death in Afghanistan. . ."

She interrupted. "Lanny always called me Lain," she paused, and without looking at him, continued, "but please call me Elaine." She looked at him and asked, almost pleading, "Are you coming with me?"

"Elaine, he did not take his own life. I knew him too well. I don't know what happened; I just know he would not kill himself."

"Penny doesn't think so either. They were engaged." She paused, looked at him, and added, "Are you coming with me?"

He turned and looked at the house. He thought of Lanny and of the girl who had taken his boots. The girl Lanny was supposed to marry. *What had happened?* He looked at the house, staring at it for a long time, before asking himself, *Why not go with her? I have nowhere else to go.*

There were a million questions burning in his mind as they rode in silence. *What had happened?* He knew this question would not bring Lanny back, but he could not get it out of his mind. *I know Lanny would not kill himself. I have two weeks leave, and I swear I will find out. I will find out what happened,* he told himself again, as the anger burned inside him, just as it had many times when he lost one of his buddies in Afghanistan. He stared out the windshield, not really aware of anything as Elaine drove.

He laid his head against the back of the seat, his mind still racing, and was aware of nothing until he noticed a ten-foot-high fence of gray and tan rock on one side of the road. They followed the fence quite a ways before Elaine turned into a driveway with heavy, steel gates that opened on her command. As the gates swung wide, Simmons saw a long, tree-lined concrete driveway leading up a small hill. On top of the hill he saw numerous buildings, all nestled among huge oak trees. Each building had well-manicured lawns, adorned with shrubs and flowers. Lots of flowers!

He was awestruck as he gazed at an enormous house overlooking a large lake. It was three stories high, built with the same light gray and tan rocks as the fence with gray slate tiles on the many gabled roofs. Parts of the walls on each side of the house were covered with ivy, and all the windows had window boxes filled with beautiful blooming flowers, even this late in the year. There were several balconies on each floor, each with bay windows.

Elaine drove to the front entrance under a huge double archway supported by four rock columns, then circled around the house to a three-car garage. Across a large concrete parking area was another three-car garage.

Next to the house was a huge patio with marble floors and a stainless steel grill at least six feet in length. Built into the gray and tan rocks was a refrigerator and a wet bar with a marble top. A round glass table with six chairs plus numerous other chairs stood next to a stainless steel rail. Next to the patio were an Olympic-style swimming pool and two hot tubs. Just beyond these was a large bathhouse. Standing next to it was an outside shower enclosed with stained glass walls, all covered with slate tile roofs. The evening sun highlighted a brilliant white barn with tile roof, a riding arena, and several other buildings all built with gray and tan rocks. One building appeared to be a large ranch-style dwelling while another one was probably a stable, though Simmons knew absolutely nothing about stables or horses.

Beyond the stable, he saw a pasture enclosed with a white, three-rail fence, which disappeared over a hill. Even this late in the year, the green grass glistened in the setting sun. Several horses and some Texas Longhorns were grazing peacefully on the rolling hills.

About 200 yards downhill and slightly in back of the barn was a ranch house with a concrete driveway circling from somewhere behind the house. In front of a two-car garage was a 4x4 pickup truck with *Sanderson Ranch* painted on the doors. Two saddled horses were tied to a hitching rail in front of the house, patiently awaiting the return of their riders, he decided.

There were other buildings—he had no idea what they were—but all were built with the same pattern of gray and tan rocks and tile roofs. All windows, shutters, and doors on every building were neatly painted, and the lawns were meticulously groomed with a variety of trees, shrubs, and flowers arranged in perfect harmony. *No doubt, this is the work of a professional gardener,* Simmons thought. As he gazed at all this luxury, one thought kept spinning through his mind: *Lanny would have been a part of all this. More reasons to believe he did not kill himself.*

CHAPTER TWO

PENNY
Twenty Ten

Earlier that day, Penny had driven to Little Rock for a business meeting and to pick up tickets for a Clint Black concert next Saturday. Afterwards, she met Elaine at the Waffle House in Texarkana to discuss their plans for the weekend.

"We can go to my apartment, spend a quiet and comfortable weekend, and you can forget the rigors of your business," Elaine suggested. However, Penny insisted that they go to her house that night, then on to Dallas tomorrow.

"We can do some shopping and stay for a Cowboys game on Sunday."

Her family always purchased season tickets, but she had not attended a game this year. A Cowboys game was all right with Elaine, but she would have much preferred to see the Mavericks. Elaine shook her head and insisted she could not go. "I have to prepare Monday's test papers."

"Aww. . . come on, let's go to Dallas. You can do your school work tonight," Penny insisted, and Elaine reluctantly agreed.

"I will need to go to my apartment to get some school supplies."

"Okay, I've got to stop by the plant and pick up some paper work. Mother has gone to Houston for a Ladies Club convention, and our housekeeper has probably left. So, if you get there before I do, you know the combination. Go in and mix us a drink," Penny said as they walked to their cars.

Penny drove to the Texarkana Bottling Company and held a brief meeting with her plant manager, picked up some papers, and left. As she drove towards Longview, she thought of how their businesses had come about and how lucky she was. She admired the fall colors and mentally relived the events that had made her family well-respected and very wealthy.

Her ancestors had found gold on their property in North Carolina back in the 1700s, and her family had prospered ever since. Her great-grandparents founded the Gilmore Bottling Company in Tyler in 1904, then another one in Longview in 1908. After their deaths in 1951, her grandparents, Amos and Marie Gilmore, operated the plants until 1989. Penny's parents ran the plants until her father was killed in a plane crash in 1999. She remembered how devastated she was after her father's death and all that transpired afterward.

For a while her mother managed both plants, but it soon became too much for her, so she hired Arnold Bradley, a manager of a Pepsi plant in Houston, to manage the plant in Tyler. Her grandfather was still president and Anna was the CEO, but she gave Bradley the authority to run the Tyler plant as he saw fit. Neither of Penny's grandparents agreed with her mother, but they did not interfere.

Penny was away at college when her mother married Bradley in 2003. The lived together fewer than three months and divorced soon afterward. He moved to Tyler and continued to manage the Tyler plant, per a prenuptial agreement. Soon afterward, her mother founded the Texarkana plant. Her mother was the CEO of all three bottling plants, though for the past two years, Penny had taken on most of the responsibilities of running both the Longview and Texarkana plants.

Her grandfather remained president of the Gilmore Bottling Company and the Gilsan Oil Company, which her mother and father formed after her father found oil on her grandfather's ranch.

We are wealthy; we've traveled the world and want for nothing, but are we really happy? She did not think they were... and knew she was not. *I'm just going through the motions, pretending to be happy.*

As she approached the intersection of U S Highway 59 and Texas Highway 155, she saw Elaine's car pulled to the side of the road. On the other side of the road was a duffel bag with a pair of cowboy boots sitting on top of it. A solider was speaking with Elaine and had his back to the boots.

Penny thought how funny it would be to take his boots. She knew Elaine would probably give him a ride and she could give them back to him, or if Elaine did not give the guy a ride, she would bring the boots back. She rolled her window down, reached out and snatched the boots, then sped away. She drove a short way before pulling to the side of the road. She got out of the car, picked up the boots, and walked to the rear of her Ferrari, waiting for Elaine and the soldier.

A few minutes later Elaine came over the hill and stopped. Penny teased the soldier about his boots. Elaine told her how he had acted, the utter disbelief on his face, and what he had said. They sat on the ground and laughed hilariously as the solider watched. Finally, he got out of the car and came over.

As he came closer, Penny thought his face looked familiar. When she saw Simmons on his uniform, she realized that this was Lanny's Army buddy, Mitchell Simmons. Lanny had shown her photos of the two of them in both the States and in Afghanistan.

She felt a chill race through her body, a cold and numbing chill. Her mind went blank, and her body began to shake. She could not speak, just stared at him in shock; her body like a statue. *What is he doing here?* she asked herself. *I do not need to be reminded of all those memories of Lanny. Why did Elaine stop? Does she know who he is?* She did not think so and wanted to tell her to leave him right there, but was unable to say a word. She hardly remembered leaving and did not remember what she had said or even if she had said anything.

She drove home in a daze, her body cold and shaking, her mind remembering Lanny. They were meant for each other. Both were funny, full of life, full of desires, full of adventure, and after three months, they were deeply in love. She did not believe—would never believe—that Lanny had committed suicide. She had tried to tell people, but no one would listen, not even her own family. People told her he was under so much grief when he came home after his father's death, and, three weeks later, the added pain when his mother died. All that and the scarred emotions of war—it was just more than he could handle. That was what people kept telling her, and after a time she began to doubt it herself.

"Doesn't matter. . . After all, nothing will bring Lanny back." Penny had convinced herself. . . she had thought. . . maybe, just maybe, time would erase the memories of him, heal the hurt, and until today, some of that hurt *had* healed. But seeing Simmons brought back so many painful memories, so much hurt, now her body ached all over.

"Why did he have to come here?" she asked over and over. She turned off the road onto the driveway and stopped. With shaking hands she looked up Pizza Hut's number on her cell phone and ordered a sausage pizza. She drove up to the house and spoke "Open Garage" into a black box attached to the sun visor. The garage door opened; she pulled inside and sat for a long time, thinking of Lanny as she waited for Elaine.

She should have been here by now, Penny thought, but remembered where Lanny had lived. *So, Elaine does know who he is and has taken him by Lanny's house. That is why she is not here. I have got to get her away from him. I have got to get him out of our lives. I don't need him here to remind me of Lanny—and neither does Elaine.*

Penny

We are now just getting our lives back in order! her mind screamed as she backed out of the garage and headed to Lanny's house. Anger emanated from every nerve in her body as she backed out of the garage and drove towards Lanny's house.

When she arrived, she saw Elaine and Simmons sitting beside the car, tears on both of their faces. Her body began to shake uncontrollably, and her heart seemed to explode. The anger left, replaced by emotions that had built up inside her. Tears streamed down her face, and she could not stop crying. She cried for Lanny, for Elaine, for herself, and for a very unhappy life.

She remembered saying something to them and driving back to her house, totally unaware of everything around her. She reached her house, a huge, cold, empty, old house, and could not find the courage to go inside or even to pull into the garage. She knew her housekeeper had left, so she laid her head on the steering wheel and waited outside.

Two hours ago we were laughing hysterically, and now we're crying. She continued to sob, letting her mind drift back to Lanny, remembering his love, his touch, and his arms around her. She remembered him making love to her and how her body ached for him. With tears still streaming down her face, she relived every moment they had spent together. She had loved him so much. They would have been so happy. She closed her eyes and could almost feel Lanny sitting beside her.

"Oh Lanny. . .Why? Why?" She closed her eyes and asked again, "Why? Why?"

Her mind was jolted back to reality by the closing of car doors. Elaine and Simmons came up to her car. She said nothing as she wiped the tears from her eyes and somehow managed to get out of the car.

"I could not bring myself to go inside. Mother's not here, and our housekeeper has left. The house is. . . is so cold, so empty, so lonely." She shrugged. "First it was Daddy, then Judy, and then Lanny. . ." Her voice trailed off.

"It's been a bad day," Elaine said and put her arms around her.

"I'm sorry I ruined your day," Simmons said. "Maybe I should go. . .," knowing that the only place he could go was back to the Army base. He did not want to do that. Not yet. No, he did not want to go until he found out what had happened to Lanny. He promised himself he would find out and would stay somewhere, anywhere, until he found the truth.

They stood in awkward silence until the pizza delivery boy drove up and snapped them back to real life. Penny gave him two twenty-dollar bills. He held out the pizza and tried to give one of the twenties back to her.

"It's only fourteen bucks."

"You keep the money and the pizza, too, or give it to someone. Someone who can eat! I can't. I need a drink. A strong one."

The pizza boy looked puzzled, standing for a long moment, contemplating what to do. "You sure?" He looked at Penny, reluctantly put the money in his pocket, placed the pizza on the back seat, got into his car, and drove away.

Penny looked at her Ferrari. "Elaine, Mother's car is at the airport, and mine has only two seats. We could call for the chopper, but I don't want to wait for it. I'd love it if you would drive us to Manny's."

Penny called Manny's as they rode in silence through Longview and turned south onto Texas 31. They crossed the Sabine River just as the last rays of the setting sun disappeared below the horizon. The sky was aglow with colors of red, green, orange, and gold, and streaked with different shades of brown, gray, and black. The sunset exploded with color, but even this was not enough to cheer them up. Each stared out the windshield, seeing only white dotted lines coming at them.

No one said a word, even when Elaine slowed and turned off the highway by a sign that read, "Manny's: Members Only."

Penny

She drove up a driveway that wound its way through oaks and cottonwoods, past numerous tennis courts, a gymnasium, and two large swimming pools, one enclosed in glass. A number of Jacuzzis and several other buildings were scattered over the grounds.

Elaine stopped under the veranda of a sprawling, southern plantation-style building, supported by four huge columns. The bright lights embedded in the ceiling sparkled in the windows, off-black shutters and white paint. A red carpet led from the curb to the entrance way with "Manny's" written above it in wrought iron letters. Simmons noticed there was a golf course on one side of the building and on the other a lighted driving range, two putting greens, and several tennis courts. *Some place*, he thought.

Two parking attendants opened the car doors. Penny got out and spoke to one in Spanish. He smiled; it was obvious he knew Penny as he looked at Elaine and Simmons, nodding his head in agreement as she spoke. He escorted them to the entrance where a doorman greeted them with a smile. Penny returned his smile as he led them inside a huge lobby. Three suede couches, several chairs, lots of green plants, and a monstrous widescreen TV sat below a massive chandelier. The doorman signaled a porter, who led them to a private dining area and seated each of them.

The room was large; the walls were lined with paintings and artwork. A chandelier glowed softly, casting small delicate shadows upon the walls. Beneath the chandelier was a large wooden table, shined to such a shine the chandelier's reflection was like a photograph. Six chairs sat on each side of the long table and one on each end. At the other end of the dining area were an elegant suede couch, two matching recliners, and a large flat screen TV. Along one side of the room, partially-opened red velvet curtains hung from ceiling to floor, revealing the main dining room, filled with well-dressed men and women. On the far side of the main dining room a five-piece band stood on a stage, highlighted by blue and red lights, and played classical music. In front of the stage was a dance floor where three couples danced slowly to a soft melody.

Penny asked Simmons as a waiter approached, "What is your choice? Scotch, bourbon, wine?" She forced a wry smile and before he could answer, added, "You can also have a beer."

"I'll have a glass of wine," Elaine said.

Maybe she's taking a cue so as not to embarrass me, Simmons thought. "Me too," he said, grateful to Elaine for the concern.

A waiter dressed in a tuxedo arrived, nodded, and bowed gracefully to each. Penny spoke to him in a language he presumed was Spanish. He left and returned shortly with a bottle of Parker Heritage bourbon, a bottle of wine on ice, two wine glasses, a shot glass, and a tray of appetizers. He filled the wine glasses and poured Penny a shot of bourbon. She thanked him; he bowed slightly and walked to the far end of the room where he stepped behind a curtain.

They toasted their glasses, but said nothing as Penny gulped down the shot of bourbon while Elaine and Simmons sipped their wine. Penny poured a second shot and downed it.

Simmons looked at Penny. She was indeed a beautiful woman with a warm, inviting smile. Her face, though still saddened, was soft and warm. Her long blonde hair was tied in a ponytail, and she had dark blue eyes. She wore a light blue designer shirt with the top two buttons unfastened, revealing a lot of her breasts. She did not have on a bra and from where he sat, he knew she did not need one. The next two buttons were fastened, but the others were undone, leaving the shirt tails tied around her small waist. She wore short-shorts which revealed shapely, tanned legs. Around her neck was a gold chain with a diamond-studded cross; her ears were adorned with diamond earrings. The diamonds, and the fact they were in a private dining room in a private club, spoke of someone with money. Simmons only knew Penny's first name, that she drove a Ferrari, and lived in a monstrous house. He knew she was wealthy and so he kept thinking of the name on the truck—"Sanderson Ranch"—but it did not ring a bell.

Simmons looked at the people in the main dining room. The men were dressed in suits and the ladies in expensive clothing. *There is probably not one lady here who would not trade her attire for Penny's, especially if she could look as good in it as Penny does,* he thought and stole a quick glance at Penny, comparing how she was dressed with what others were wearing. He wondered if this was the reason they were in a private dining room. Somehow he knew it was not—this girl knew who she was and she answered to no one. She was a rich woman and a woman in charge, but a woman who carried a deep hurt inside. Simmons was sure of that.

"I am glad you are driving," Penny said to Elaine as she downed a shot and poured herself another. Elaine said nothing, just glanced at Simmons. Elaine and Simmons sipped their wine, and the waiter returned and refilled their glasses. He offered to refill Penny's shot glass, but Penny spoke to him and he left, returning with three glasses, a bucket of ice, and sodas. He mixed Penny a bourbon and coke and offered one to Elaine and Simmons. When they declined, he bowed and retreated behind the curtain. Simmons wondered how he had known he was being paged, until he saw a small black clip lying on the table.

They drank in silence. When the silence became awkward, Penny looked at Simmons and asked, "Do you mind if I call you Mitchell or Mitch?'

"Either one will be fine," he said, although his Army buddies just called him Simmons.

"Where are you from?" she asked politely.

Simmons really did not care to tell them he was raised in an orphanage. . . that the Army was his only family. He thought of just saying Mobile, and letting it go at that, but decided she was only trying to break the awkward silence. He hesitated, and then decided he might have to tell them later, so why not get it over with.

"I was born in Mobile and lived with my aunt until I was about four. When she could no longer take care of me, I was sent to an orphanage in Montgomery. I lived there until I joined the Army." He spoke softly, his head down, looking at the table.

There was a long silence. . . a silence that made him uneasy. He continued, "Well, I know a little about Elaine—Lanny talked about her all the time—but what about you?" he asked, looking at Penny.

"I was a rich kid, a brat, a. . .," she paused, and Simmons got the feeling she was about to tell him about a troubled past, but saw Elaine's look that said, *don't tell him that*, so she changed the subject and continued, "I was wild and spoiled, and I always got what I wanted," she paused again, and it was a long time before she continued, "until I met Lanny." Now it was her turn to drop her head and stare at the table.

Simmons could feel the hurt as they sat in silence for a few seconds. Penny broke the silence by saying, "Let's order! I'm starved." She pushed the button to summons the waiter and asked him to close the curtains. When the curtains were closed, she looked at Simmons. "They have some wonderful steaks! I would suggest the Porterhouse if you like steaks."

Simmons had heard of it, but never eaten one. They didn't serve them in the orphanage or in the Army. "That will be fine with me," he said.

"Make mine medium," Elaine said. Her voice was soft and low.

"Rare," said Simmons

"Mine too!" Penny added.

No one said anything as they ate their salads and waited for their steaks. Simmons poured another glass of wine, offering one to Penny and Elaine. Both declined. Simmons had the uneasy feeling that he might be the reason for the silence, but decided it was about Lanny. They were all hurting. Simmons sat across the table from the two women and could feel them staring intently at him when he was not looking. He knew they wanted to know more about him, but it seemed no one wanted to start a conversation. Even though no one was talking, everyone seemed to be considerably more relaxed, including him. Maybe it was the alcohol, but he felt there was the beginning of a trust or a bond forming between them.

Or maybe it is just my wishful thinking. He looked at Elaine and saw her looking at him. There were questions in her beautiful, sea-green eyes. What was she thinking? Was she thinking the same thing? He wished he knew as his thoughts began to relive the day's events, all of which seemed like ages ago.

His thoughts were suddenly interrupted, as the curtains between them and the dining room were ripped open. A man of about fifty stormed into their room. His face was flushed with anger, his eyes red, and his hands shaking. He confronted Penny, pointing a finger at her, and glared at Simmons. The man stepped closer to Penny, and Simmons started to rise, but Elaine took hold of his arm and pulled him down gently. She said nothing, but shook her head slightly, as if to say, *she can take care of herself.*

The man was in Penny's face, his body heaving and his voice hissing, not yelling, but loud enough that the people near them could hear. The waiter came from behind the curtain, not knowing if he should intervene. He saw Elaine holding on to Simmons' arm and decided to wait and see what happened, although Simmons could tell he was more than ready to come to Penny's aid, if need be.

The man screamed at Penny, loudly enough now for everyone in the dining room to hear. *That is what he wants. I don't know who he is, but he wants to show his authority,* Simmons thought as the man yelled.

"You bitch! How dare you come in here looking like a two-bit whore and dragging that golddigger in with you!" He looked at Simmons, livid hate in his eyes, and continued, "Embarrassing me in front of my friends? Get him out of here before I have all of you thrown out. Get out and don't come back until you get some decent clothes on, and. . . and ditch that. . . that sonofa . . ."

Before the man could finish, Simmons was on his feet and grabbed the man by coat and tie, picking him up and slinging him through the curtains into the main dining room. The man skidded between a couple sitting at a nearby table, knocking it over, their plates and wine glasses crashing to the floor. One side of the red velvet curtain ripped from the ceiling and fell on top of him. The collision was heard throughout the dining room, and people stared in disbelief. The band stopped playing; the only sound audible in the dining room was a low moan from the man lying on the floor.

People began to scatter as Simmons pulled the curtain off of him and was about to kick him in the gut, but in a flash, Penny was between them. In a voice that was both low and fierce, she said to the man, "Get up and get out of here before I let him beat the hell out of you, you stinking bag of scum. You don't tell me where I can go, who I can bring, or what I can wear. I'll go anywhere I please, with whom I please, wear what I please, and there's not a thing you can do about it. If I came in here with nothing on but a frigging G-string, these people would be happier to see me than you. You came into *my* dining room, threatening me and calling him names. I'm surprised he didn't kill you."

She was pointing her finger at him, her rising voice easily heard throughout the dining room. "And by the way, on your way out you might want to read the by-laws. But because you are so stupid, I will tell you what they say. They say, 'If one guest harasses another guest, he or she will be barred from this club.' Now get out of here before I change my mind and let him

Penny

kill you." Her eyes were like lightning bolts, her voice loud and demanding.

The man climbed to his feet, and Simmons stepped in front of Penny, ready to take him out if he made any move toward her. Knowing this, the man just hissed at her, "You will regret this. I will see to it that you never get a cent from my company."

Before Simmons knew it, Penny stepped around him and slapped the man so hard his head jerked back sharply, and his body staggered. "The company is not yours; it is my mother's," she screamed. Before he could recover, she slapped him again, this time bringing blood to the corner of his mouth.

He lunged at her, but Simmons grabbed him. In one swift and savage motion, Simmons twisted the man around, and with one arm around the man's neck, he placed his knee in the man's lower back and violently slammed him to the floor. The back of the man's head hit the floor with a loud thud, and Simmons jammed his foot on the man's neck just below his chin, pressing down hard. The man went limp, and, for a moment, Simmons feared he had broken his neck, but he stood over him, putting more pressure on the man's neck when he tried to move. Soon the man moaned and lay still.

Two men appeared, and one of them said to Simmons, his voice stern but definitely amused, "Stand down, solider!"

Simmons was accustomed to taking orders and instinctively took his foot off the man's neck. Penny looked at one of the security men and said, "Gregg, get him out of here before I kill him myself." Simmons decided most of the people in the dining room knew she meant it.

The man was barely conscious as they lifted him onto wobbly legs. Taking hold of his arms, one of them said, "Sir, would you please come with us?"

"You will pay for this," the man wheezed, glaring at Simmons.

"Get him out of my sight," Penny demanded. The security men led him over the downed curtains and out of the dining room as the guests watched in silence. A few may have seemed concerned, but as Simmons scanned the dining room, he felt that most looked pleased.

"That was my ex-stepfather," Penny murmured. Anger was still raging inside of her, but after several seconds, she relaxed a little, looked at Simmons, and added, "Thanks."

CHAPTER THREE

ANNA
Nineteen Eighty

Robert Sanderson and Anna Gilmore met in a sociology class at the University of Houston. He was a senior and a second-string linebacker on the football team. She was a sophomore and a majorette in the Cougars marching band. She had a beautiful face, large, sparkling brown eyes, and long black hair. Her skin was dark and silky smooth with beautiful, long legs and a gorgeous body.

There seemed to be an immediate attraction between them. Still, he was a little surprised when she agreed to have an ice cream sundae with him. After all, she was so attractive, she could have had even the quarterback eating out of her hand, and he was only a second-string linebacker.

As they ate their ice cream, he was amazed at how witty and charming she was, so relaxed and easy to talk to. After their first few dates, there were no doubts that they were falling in love.

Maybe I was in love the first time I saw her, he thought. She was more than anything in his dreams, and now she was all he could think of. There could never be anyone but her; he was certain of that.

She told him she lived in her parents' home, and a couple of weeks later brought him to their house on Galveston Bay. The house was a huge, two-story dwelling located in an exclusive neighborhood in southwest Galveston with a private beach on the Gulf of Mexico. Erected on forty concrete pilings ten feet above the ground, the house had a walkway that led out into the water. A porch ran the length of the first floor, facing the water.

There was a large den on the first level of the building with expensive paintings and a six-foot statue of a man wearing a buckskin shirt, a black overcoat, and a black hat. A long flintlock rifle stood by his side. The statue mesmerized Robert. It was definitely meant to be outdoors, and he wondered why it was inside.

There was a bathroom in the den, with another one in the hallway leading to a study. In the center of the kitchen was a long counter with a cooktop and double oven. A sink next to a window looked out at the blue water of the Gulf. A huge chandelier hung above a beautiful walnut table in the large dining room. Adjacent to this was a large game room with a pool table and wet bar. Across the hallway from the bar was a larger room containing a leather couch, two leather recliners, a love seat, and six luxurious theater-style seats sitting in front of a giant TV with speakers built into soundproof walls.

Upstairs was a spacious master bedroom with king-sized bed, two elegant leather chairs, a zebra-wood table, two walk-in closets, and a large bath, complete with Jacuzzi, a marble vanity, and a private balcony with one-way vision glass panels that opened to catch the salty breeze of the Gulf. There were three other bedrooms upstairs, each with private baths. Another bedroom included a balcony, also enclosed with sliding glass panels. Anna's touch could be seen inside this room. The walls were pale blue, with color-coordinated blue curtains and a queen-sized bed. Band photos and trophies sat on marble top tables; art and other personal photographs adorned the walls.

As Anna continued to show him the house, she thought how nice it would be for Robert to live here with her, but she knew her parents would strongly disapprove. In fact, they expected their daughter to save her virginity for her wedding night. Thus far, she had done that, but with Robert she sometimes wondered if she could wait that long.

When they first met, Robert did not know her family was wealthy, although he knew she drove a new Corvette convertible. She never acted like she was wealthier than anyone else, so he was surprised when he learned she was the daughter of Amos Gilmore, the owner of Gilmore Bottling Company.

He was from a middle-income family in Odessa. His mother was a nurse, and his father worked the off-shore oil fields. Robert had a small academic scholarship, half of a football scholarship, and drove an ancient Chevy Nova. His parents paid the rest of his tuition, and he worked a part-time job at a Farm and Ranch store after his classes on Friday and all day Saturday, earning a little extra money. Lately, most of what he earned went to pay for his dates with Anna. He refused to let Anna pay because a man was supposed to pay; this was a man's thing. That was the way he had been taught.

After a couple of months, they were deeply in love and spent every possible second together. Tonight they walked along the beach, holding hands and listening to water splash upon the sand. The night was warm with a gentle breeze blowing in from the Gulf. They walked to a secluded spot on the beach where they had laid many times. They snuggled close, enjoying each other's company and watching the stars, which seemed so close it was as if they could reach out and touch them.

"I want to ask you about the statue in the den. It is an amazing statue! I've wondered if it is just decoration or does it have a special meaning?"

"That is a long story. I am not sure you would be interested." "I love long stories, especially if you are telling them."

"Okay, but I warn you, it is a long story." She waited for him to say "Never mind," and when he did not, she rose upon one elbow and laid her other arm around him.

"The statue is of Gaither Gilmore, but I think most people back then called him Gee. He was my five times great-grandfather, and I guess the beginning of my family's success. The story has been passed down through the generations about how he found an Indian girl, who had been beaten and raped. This was a time of intense tension between the settlers and the Indians, and he knew taking her in would mean trouble, but he could not leave her in the woods to die. The story is they were forced to leave their home and go live with the Indians, who later gave them several thousand acres of land in a remote valley. They found gold on this property.

"Later, he founded the Gilmore Tobacco Company, which employed a lot of workers. They wanted to move closer to the company, so since he owned the entire valley, he sold them land on which to build. Soon it became a community, and later, a town was built and named Gilmore. After several prosperous years, the townspeople erected a statue—the one you see in the den—to honor him for the things he did for the town and for the people of Gilmore.

"About twenty years later, with so many people raising tobacco, he purchased more tobacco from the people in the valley than he could sell, simply to provide an income for them. With his warehouses full of tobacco and no one buying, he had to lay off most of his employees. Later, he sold the company to the Salem Tobacco Company, who promised to keep the company in Gilmore. However, the next year they moved it to Salem. Most of the people worked for the tobacco company, so when it moved, they lost their jobs. One merchant after the other closed or moved elsewhere, and the townspeople blamed him for that.

"Also, this was a time of intense racial hatred. Because his wife was full-blooded Cherokee, the people began to harass them. He eventually sold his farm and moved to Georgia, where his son and daughter had purchased two huge plantations. The town of Gilmore soon became a ghost town, and someone purchased,

Anna

or stole, the statue, which by now was badly defaced. My grandfather, Jones Gilmore, who founded the Gilmore Bottling Company, had heard stories about the statue so after an extensive search, he found it in an antique shop in Charlotte. He purchased it, had it restored, and erected in front of the Bottling Company in downtown Tyler. When the company moved to its present location, he brought the statue here to Galveston."

"See... I told you it was a long story." She laughed.

"Like I said, I love long stories, and I love you, too." He kissed her, and they lay there until the chill of the night cooled their almost naked bodies. They walked back into the house, stripping off swimwear as they climbed the stairs to her bedroom.

As they lay there, Robert's mind wandered back to the first time they had made love. They had abstained for a long time, lying on the beach many times, almost naked, exploring each other's body, kissing and touching. Anna said she was a virgin and that was what her parents expected her to be until her wedding night. She did not want to disappoint them, and, thus far, they had managed to stop before going all the way. They loved each other enough not to press the issue. However, the more they were together, the more their passions burned. He would forever remember the night Anna moaned and said, "Robert, I can't stand this any longer. Please take me to bed."

The phone rang, shocking him back into reality. Anna considered not answering, but was afraid it might be her parents. She always feared they would come in and catch her in bed with Robert. After all, it was their house so they could walk in unannounced if they pleased. She did not think they would, but it worried her. Tonight, she had taken a little comfort knowing they never came down except on the weekends, and today was Thursday. However, a call at one in the morning... something might be wrong. She answered the phone.

"Hey, sweetheart. We're at the little service station down the street and wanted to come over, but since it was so late, thought we had better call first. We didn't want to alarm you. We'll be there in a couple of minutes, if that's okay."

"Ah, yes. . . sure. Of course. . . I would be hurt if you came through, and I didn't get to see you." She was shocked; terror shot through her as she turned to Robert.

"That was my parents. They will be here in a couple of minutes." Her mind was racing, trying to think of what to do. Knowing Robert did not have time to dress and leave, she said, "Robert, go. . . uh. . . go to the guest bedroom. No wait! We've got to get our clothes from downstairs."

She remembered that every time they came inside, they would begin stripping off their swimsuits as they raced up the stairs before jumping into bed. They raced down the stairs, picking up clothing as they went, and hurried back up the stairs. At the top of the stairs she stopped, out of breath, but laughing,

"Go in there," she said, pointing to the guest room. "But don't turn on the lights. A little bit after they arrive, come downstairs and tell them you heard voices. Act as though you just woke up. I will tell them we studied late, and you slept in the guest room." *That is not a bad plan*, she thought. *Not a bad plan at all on such short notice. I hope it works!*

Robert made his way to the quest room just as a car turned into the driveway. Anna tried to look sleepy as she greeted her parents at the door. They embraced.

"Our flight was delayed in San Antonio and caused us to miss our connecting flight to Tyler. We were kind of glad because we wanted to see you, even though it is late."

Her mother interrupted, "Anna, you look. . . you look exhausted. Is everything okay?"

Before Anna could reply, Robert called from the top of the stairs. "Is everything alright? I thought I heard the phone and then voices?" he asked, looking at Anna's parents while rubbing the fake sleep from his eyes. He made his way down the stairs in bare feet, buttoning the last button on his shirt.

Anna

Anna saw the questions on her parents' faces as they looked at Robert and at her. "Yes, Robert, everything is fine. These are my parents!" She pointed at Amos and Marie.

"Mom, Dad, this is Robert, my friend I told you about. We studied late, and I convinced him to stay rather than drive back to Houston."

Her father looked at her with suspicion, but turned and faced Robert, extending his hand. "Robert, it is nice to meet you," he said in a slow, Texas drawl.

Penny's mother offered Robert her hand and added, "Yes," then paused. It seemed to Robert that she was selecting her words carefully. "Yes, Anna talks a lot about you. We had hoped that you would come up for a visit so we could meet you. Anna said she had asked you, but you have to work on weekends. You must take some time off and come for a visit."

Robert rubbed his eyes again as if he were trying to wake up. "It is my pleasure to meet you; I promise I will visit."

"Well, it's late, and we are tired so I think we'll turn in and let you two get back to sleep. We can talk more in the morning," Mr. Gilmore said. He looked at Robert and added, "Sorry we disturbed you."

"Yes, we are. Good night," Mrs. Gilmore said and headed up the stairs to the master bedroom.

About half way up the stairs, Robert saw her pause and look at his swimming trunks lying on the stairs. "Oh! That's mine! Must have been clinging to my pants when I came down," he added, pretending to be amused, but glancing at Anna. She was horrified.

He noticed Mrs. Gilmore had a touch of a smile on her face that seemed to say, "Do you think I'm that dumb?"

The next morning Robert called the feed store and asked if he could come in at noon, explaining about Anna's parents. They loaded into Mr. Gilmore's rental car and drove to Cracker Barrel for breakfast. They drank coffee and waited for ham and eggs to arrive. Robert could feel they were judging him, and, though it did make him a little uncomfortable, he figured they were entitled to that. Still, he could not help but wonder if they approved, and he said a short prayer. He was in love with their daughter and planned to marry her, though he had not yet asked her. *Not yet, but soon,* he thought.

He found that both Mr. and Mrs. Gilmore had warm and soft-spoken personalities. They did not act like two wealthy people, just down to earth, and he had no trouble deciding he liked them. Mrs. Gilmore had a warm smile and dark brown eyes. Her skin was dark, darker than Anna's. *Maybe of Spanish descent,* Robert thought. Her hair was long and black, with just a hint of gray. She wore brown slacks and a matching blouse, long gemstone earrings, and a matching necklace. The only make-up she wore was very light red lipstick.

Robert guessed she was in her early forties and thought her very attractive. Perhaps twenty years ago, she would have looked just like Anna. He both liked and admired her. He decided she was a gentle and fun woman who could be trusted.

Mr. Gilmore, or Amos, as he suggested (though Robert could not call him that) was tall, with broad shoulders, brown eyes, and dark brown hair, graying at his temples. He was probably in his mid-forties and was dressed in blue slacks, a white shirt, a white Stetson, and alligator boots. The only clue that he was a wealthy man, other than the boots, was a large diamond ring and a Rolex with diamonds studs mounted for each hour. He was friendly, yet business-like, a man who was in control of his surroundings, not arrogant, just in control. He was friendly enough, but distant in a kind of distrustful sort of way.

Mr. Gilmore talked about the weather and their flight from San Antonio. Rather slyly, he tried to get Robert to tell about himself and his family. From Anna's body language, Robert could tell she was a little annoyed at her father's questions, and more than once, she gave her father a stern look, as if to say, *he is not on trial here.* It wasn't long before Mr. Gilmore realized he was irritating Anna and changed the subject. Anna excused herself and went to the powder room, leaving Robert alone with her parents. He was uncomfortable, but this was the time.

He had promised himself that the first time he met Anna's parents, he would ask if they approved of him marrying Anna. He was scared stiff and though he had practiced the words many times with stern and convincing authority, he was now as nervous as he had ever been, his voice quivering and squeaky.

"Mr. and Mrs. Gilmore, this is something I have been waiting to ask you, and I swore I would ask the first time I met you." This is not the way he had rehearsed it, he thought, but he continued, "I know you don't know much about me, and I know that I am not good enough for Anna, but I'll do everything under God's green earth to make her happy and treat her right, and. . . so. . . so. . .," he stuttered.

This is terrible. This is definitely not how I intended to ask them. Where was the speech I practiced? He was horrified and wondered what he would do if they said "no"? After the way he had messed this up, he knew they probably would. *Well, I can't stop now.* He took a deep breath, looked at them and asked, "I want to ask if you would approve of me asking Anna to marry me?" There, he had done it. He held his breath, knowing this was not how he had rehearsed it, and that he had really messed it up big time.

Mr. Gilmore looked at him intently, and with a slightly disapproving voice, said, "No offense, Robert, but yes, we do know very little about you, and I think it would be wise. . ." his voice trailed off when Mrs. Gilmore cleared her throat.

Robert's heart stopped beating. He realized Mrs. Gilmore had not yet said a single word. It seemed like an eternity before Mr. Gilmore continued, "Well, Marie, how do you feel about it? After all, it is a decision both of us should make because we both want what is best for our daughter." He paused and looked at Marie, "However, Anna is an intelligent woman and is free to make up her own mind. We trust her to make the right decisions."

Robert could tell that Mrs. Gilmore was giving her answer careful consideration. It seemed like an eternity before she said, "I think you would make Anna a wonderful husband, but I wish you would please wait until she graduates."

Robert could hardly hold back the tears, but he managed to say, "I. . . we will do that, that is, if Anna even agrees to marry me. We have talked about it, but I haven't officially asked her yet. I mean we are not engaged; I haven't asked. I mean. . . I wanted to wait and see if you approved." *How could I have messed this up any more than I did is beyond me!* At last he managed to say, "I was so afraid you would not approve."

"But we didn't." Mrs. Gilmore smiled at him with a warm and understanding smile.

Mr. Gilmore looked at him for a long moment while Robert waited. Finally he said, "If she says yes, you have our blessing." He grinned, knowing Anna would say yes. He had seen how they looked at each other. It was only then that Robert's heart began to beat again.

The next day Robert went shopping for a ring. That night he was on his knees, asking Anna to marry him. His heart stopped when he saw the frown on her face. He knew her well enough to know she was wondering about her parents.

"I asked them yesterday, and we have their blessing. They only want us to wait until you graduate. I told them I would if you said 'yes.'" He reached up, ready to take her hand and place the ring on her finger.

"Well, I will have to give that some thought," she said, putting her hand behind her back. She studied him carefully, as if she were giving it great consideration. Robert's heart was not beating, and she made him wait a little longer before saying excitedly, "Yes! Oh yes, Robert, yes!" She jumped on him, knocking him backward, and fell on top of him as they rolled on to the floor. She held him very tightly and told him, "As long as I know I can have you, I can do that." She paused, looked at him, and asked, "But, how did you know I would say yes?"

"I didn't believe you would want me to die," Robert said. Finally placing the ring on her finger as they laughed, they kissed each other passionately and lay on the floor a long time, holding each other very close.

CHAPTER FOUR
....

ROBERT
Nineteen Eighty

During the Thanksgiving holidays, Robert visited his parents in Odessa while Anna went to her parents in Tyler. Robert was pleased to see his family, especially his sister, whom he had not seen in almost a year. She had been away at nursing school, and he was at the university. He enjoyed the time they spent together, but could hardly wait to get back to Houston.

Two weeks later, Anna and Robert left Galveston a little after three in the morning, stopping long enough to grab a sausage and biscuit just north of Houston. Three hours later and a little south of Tyler, they turned off Highway 37 onto Farmers Market 22. After about three miles, Anna turned into a cattle gap between a white rail fence and drove up a driveway lined with elm trees to a modest ranch house overlooking a lake. The place had an inviting and comfortable feel, a farm any upper middle class occupant might own. The only clues to wealth were the two Mercedes parked inside an open garage.

"Welcome to our house," Anna said, looking at him as she drove up the driveway. Seeing how tense he was, she said, "Relax. They won't bite you. They won't, but I might!" she teased, biting his lip as she kissed him and drove past the front entrance to the back of the house

Mr. and Mrs. Gilmore met them on the patio. They both embraced Anna, and Mrs. Gilmore gave Robert a big hug and said, "Welcome, Robert! Our house is your house. We are pleased you could visit." She put one arm around Anna and the other around Robert as they walked towards two French doors. Mr. Gilmore trailed behind.

They entered a large den with floor to ceiling windows on the side of the room overlooking the lake. The den was richly furnished with a leather couch, a love seat, and two matching recliners sitting on either side of a fireplace with gas-burning logs. An oil painting of a man wearing buckskin clothing and holding a flintlock hung above the leather couch. Family photos, paintings, and other artwork lined one wall. Along another wall were a television and wet bar. Wine glasses hung upside down from a rack above the bar. *Nothing elaborate, just warm and comfortable*, Robert thought.

"Would you like a glass of wine? I am sorry we don't have whiskey, just never acquired a taste for it, I guess." Mr. Gilmore motioned them towards the love seat and started to speak, but stopped when a woman came hurriedly into the room, squealing with joy. She rushed over, grabbed Anna, picked her up, and swung her around.

"Oh! It's so good to see you! I have missed you so much," the woman said, gleaming with pure delight.

She sat Anna down and turned to face Robert, holding her arms open wide. "Robert, Anna has told me so much about you! I love you already. My name is Kaysa."

"Kaysa. . . what a beautiful name! It is nice to meet you, Kaysa. Anna said you were her second mom, and now I can see why she likes you so much."

"Second mom, huh," she shot a glance at Anna while wrinkling her nose. "The only reason I am not her first mom is because I could never get Amos in the bed with me." She looked at Mrs. Gilmore with twinkling eyes that said, *I'm kidding,* and added, "Anna said you liked ice tea, so I made some for you. Can I get you a glass?" She smiled, looking approvingly at Robert.

"I would love that."

Robert

Mrs. Gilmore smiled at Robert and said, "This is her house," nodding towards the kitchen. "We do as she says so please have a seat," she continued as she gestured toward the couch, "and tell us what you two have been doing, besides studying." She smiled mischievously, her brown eyes saying she knew the answer to that question.

They sat down, and Kaysa returned with tea. "We are your guests, too, you know. Would you bring us a glass of wine?" Mr. Gilmore said jokingly.

Kaysa stared at him and walked to the front of the bar, holding her arms wide, shielding the bar. "You have had two already; you cannot have another one till lunch."

"She is also our boss," Mr. Gilmore said, winking at Robert. Kaysa threw her head back and muttered, "Ha!"

About sixty years old, Kaysa was tall and big-boned, but not heavy. She had dark brown skin and big brown eyes, with short hair that was almost entirely gray. She had a tantalizing smile and a lively personality. Robert liked her immediately.

Robert sipped his tea and began to relax a little. Now he understood why Anna had never flaunted her wealth. Neither did her parents.

"How was the drive up from Houston? Nice fall colors I bet. I was in Atlanta last week, and the colors were fantastic, even from the air!" Mr. Gilmore said.

"Yes, it's beautiful. . . all different colors. I never get tired of looking at them. We don't have trees in Pecos, just lots of sand and cactus."

"Does your family live in Pecos?"

"No, sir, I grew up in Pecos, but my parents live in Odessa. There are not a lot of trees there, either, as I'm sure you know."

"Well, I guess when you graduate, you will be going back there. Oh. . . by the way, what is you major?""Daddy! Robert is not applying for a job, you know." Anna shot him a demanding stare, visibly upset. "That's okay," Robert said, trying to think of something that would ease the tension between the two of them, though nothing came to mind.

"Anna, I think Dusty knows you are here," Mrs. Gilmore interrupted. "That's Anna's horse." She turned to Anna, "Why don't you take Robert to the barn and maybe go for a ride? We have some pretty colors here, too, you know."

"That's a great idea," Anna said, pulling Robert off the couch and slipping her arm around him, giving her mother a grateful smile while scowling at her father.

When Robert and Anna left the room, Mrs. Gilmore looked at her husband, slightly annoyed. "Amos, I am shocked! What has gotten into you? This is your future son-in-law. He is not here to be interviewed."

"Well, Marie, if he is going to take our little girl, I think I am entitled to know a little about him. He will not mind me asking if he has nothing to hide, will he?"

She walked over, put her arm around his neck, and kissed him lightly on the forehead. "Amos, Anna is not your little girl any more. She is almost twenty-one, and I think she has chosen Robert to be her husband. He is not 'taking' her. They are taking each other, just as you and I did when I was in Lafayette. Speaking of which, they are already sleeping together and have been for quite a while, even before that late night visit we paid them in Galveston." She smiled knowingly.

"What!" Amos blurted out. "She is not pregnant, is she?" he yelled, with a look of horror on his face.

"Nooo, but if you will look at the two of them together, not just at Robert, you will see. If you still have doubts, wait until they come to spend a night with us and watch their reaction when I tell them they can sleep in Anna's room or in the guest room. I can't wait to see the look on their faces."

"Marie, you wouldn't!"

Robert

"Yes, I would! And Amos, it's not any more than you and I did, now is it? And I don't regret it, do you?" He smiled, put his arm around her, patted her backside, and said, "Not right now." He picked her up and carried her toward the bedroom.

"Amos, we have company." But she threw her arms around his neck, laid her head on his shoulder, and giggled.

Robert felt uneasy as they walked arm in arm to the barn. "I never rode a horse in my life."

"That's okay. We have one we call High Moon; that's because he bucks so high. That is, until you show him who is boss. The way you boss me around, I am sure you won't have any trouble. I'll saddle him for you," Anna offered.

"Maybe we could take that," he said, pointing to a Kawasaki four-wheeler sitting in a shed beside the barn. "Chicken!" She put her hands in her armpits and began flapping her elbows up and down. "Cluck, cluck," she teased and hugged him tight. "I love it when I get the best of you."

They walked into the barn, and he saw a horse's ears perk up when he saw Anna. She patted him on the neck. "This is Dusty." She rubbed his ears and gave him a sugar cube. "Did you miss me?" she asked as he nuzzled her hair. She put a bridle on him, led him to the tack room, and gave him another sugar cube.

Anna saddled Dusty and another horse for Robert. She helped Robert to mount, adjusted the stirrups, and gave him a quick verbal lesson on how to ride, how to keep his feet in the stirrups for balance, and how to use the reins to guide him.

"What gear do I start off in?' Robert teased.

Anna smiled, mounted Dusty, and walked out of the corral, leading Robert's horse. They walked the horses slowly through the pasture. After a little bit, Robert began to feel slightly more comfortable and decided this could be fun. He asked what his horse's real name was since he did not think it was High Moon. Anna replied that it was not a horse, but a mare, and her name was Roxi. They walked Dusty and Roxi close together along a fence not far from the timberline, admiring the fall colors. Anna looked at him and asked, "Do you want to gallop?"

"Isn't that in New Mexico?" He laughed and slapped Roxi on the hip. She bolted forward so quickly he almost fell backward, but regained his balance as they blasted past Anna and Dusty. The race was on, but his lead was short-lived as Dusty flew past him with Anna waving her arms in a circle, saying, "come on." After about a quarter mile, she slowed to a canter and let him catch up.

They walked their horses to the top of a high hill and dismounted. Anna took his arm and led him to a log bench sitting beneath a big white oak. Robert stared at a big valley, seeing green pastures with patches of trees, mixed with every color imaginable. From atop this hill he could see miles of rolling hills, pastures, and, in the far distance, a single farm house, almost hidden by trees. He put his arm around Anna and said, "It is beautiful." He was thinking of her father's question about him going to Odessa. *I think that question has just been answered,* and he knew Anna was probably thinking the same thing.

"I love this place," she said and kissed him. Holding on to him, Anna slid down to the ground and pulled him off the bench beside her. They lay there for a long time, admiring the view and listening to the birds, the wind in the trees, and the cry of a hawk as it circled above. They watched golden leaves glistening in the sunlight, some drifting downward and falling around them. They lay among the leaves for a long time, neither saying a word.

"Nothing could be better than this," Robert thought.

After a while Anna suggested they go back; Kaysa would have lunch waiting for them. As they reached the house, Anna saw her parents' horses saddled and tied to the hitching rail next to the patio. Mr. and Mrs. Gilmore came out of the house with Mrs. Gilmore carrying a picnic basket.

"Kaysa made us a picnic basket—fried chicken, French fries, potato pie. And, of course, iced tea," she smiled, looking at Robert as Mr. Gilmore beamed triumphantly, raising a bucket of ice and a bottle of wine. They mounted their horses and rode a trail that wound its way through the timber, down into a valley, and to a lake almost hidden among the trees. A gazebo stood not far from a small pond with dark green, almost black water running from a spring at the base of a hill. Robert looked at the black water with interest. *This is the same kind of place in which my grandfather had drilled his only big well,* he thought. The more he looked, the more interested he became. His father believed places like this contained oil. Now, if the water is warm and slightly toxic, there could be oil here. Since he majored in geology, he was especially interesting in finding oil. After all, his family once lived and breathed oil. They drilled a lot of wells, had one that did okay, but never found the gusher. His grandfather had died trying to find the big one when a chain broke and almost decapitated him.

They sat on the gazebo, ate their picnic lunch, and made small talk for a while. Finally, Robert could stand it no longer. He had to see the spring. "Anna, would you mind showing me the spring?"

Anna gave him a puzzled look, but arose and took his hand as they walked towards the pond. When they reached the pond, Robert walked to the upper side where the water trickled out of the base of a hill. He knelt down, dipped some water in his hand, and smelled it.

"The water is not good to drink. It is hot and smells bad. Even the animals will not drink from the spring or the lake. I don't think there are any fish in it, either," he heard Anna say.

The water was indeed warm and smelled somewhat like a mixture of cough syrup, peanut oil, and vinegar. He scooped up some water, rubbed his hands together, and looked at them. The water left a light, greasy residue on them. Showing his hands to Anna, he asked if her father realized that there might be oil here.

Anna was surprised. She stared at Robert and shook her head. Robert knew of the oil wells that were around Lufkin and asked Anna if she knew of any wells close to here. She shook her head again as Robert dipped more water from the spring and tasted it. It tasted like dead and rotten trees mixed with a sour blend of something that resembled soy sauce. Robert remembered that taste from a well his grandfather had drilled. No doubt about it; there was oil residue in the water.

As they walked back to the gazebo, all Robert could think of was how he should go about telling Mr. Gilmore there might be oil on his land. *Maybe I should wait,* he thought, but he was so excited, he could not.

Back at the gazebo, he could think of nothing but oil. "Mr. Gilmore, I am majoring in geology, and one of my specialties is finding locations where there might be oil. Have you ever considered that there might be oil here on your land?"

Both Mr. and Mrs. Gilmore stopped sipping their wine and looked at him. Robert continued, "My father and grandfather were wildcatters, drilling a few wells that turned a little profit, but never hit a big one. However, it was their belief that springs like the one over there come from deep within the earth, probably close to an oil reserve. From the studies I have done, I think that is possible. As you know, there are wells south of here and up in Oklahoma, so there might be oil here, also. From what I have seen at the spring, I think here could be a lot of oil here—I mean a lot."

Mr. Gilmore studied him, contemplating his answer for quite some time before he spoke. "Robert, I don't want you to think that I am not grateful for what you've told me, and I don't mean to brag, because not bragging is something our family takes great pride in not doing." He paused, looking at both Robert and

Anna, and waited a full minute before adding, "Like I said, I don't mean for you to think I am not grateful, but I really don't need the oil. It would bring destruction to this beautiful land."

Robert was kicking himself for not consulting with Anna before bringing up the subject. Mr. Gilmore continued to study him. "However, I am a pretty good judge of character, and it is my belief that you are not the type of person who would marry Anna only for money." He waited, looking off into the distance before continuing. "Since you and Anna are just beginning your lives together, and I believe that you would not accept charity should I offer it. . ." He paused again and looked at the distant hills. "From what Anna has said about you not letting her pay for anything you two did, it is my opinion that you consider it your responsibly to provide for her. I think that you would choose to pursue your own goals in life."

He looked at Marie for a long moment, and with what seemed to be great anguish, he added, "Therefore, if Marie agrees, we could give you permission to explore this further, the one condition being, if you do find oil, that you will be very careful to disturb the environment as little as possible. We love this place and would hate to see it ruined." He turned and faced Marie, "Would that be agreeable to you?" Slowly, she nodded her head.

Robert did not know what to say and looked to Anna for help. She shrugged her shoulders, her body language saying, *You are on your own here*. He had the gut feeling her parents were doing this so as not to disappoint him, or maybe as a way to voice their approval of him. Finally, he managed to say, "It was only my belief and not a known fact. A lot of testing, geological surveys, the filing for mineral rights, and numerous other things must be done before we can be sure."

He paused, and seeing the concerned look on their faces, he knew the more he said, the worse it got. He tried to find a way out by saying, "I am really sorry. It is your land and your decision. I had no right to suggest that, and, of course, there is no hurry. Again, I am sorry that I brought this up. I got excited when I saw the potential for oil. I guess there is more of my father and grandfather in me than I thought." He gazed at each disappointed face, knowing he had put them in an uncomfortable situation.

CHAPTER FIVE

GAITHER GILMORE
Seventeen seventy-three

Gaither Gilmore was born in Pennsylvania in 1757, but lived his childhood in Virginia. A few days after his fourteenth birthday, his father was killed by a Shawnee raiding party, and he quickly became the man of the house, doing the farming and all the things a father would do. His little brother, Jimmie, died not long after his father was killed. He was ten, but had never grown up. He looked like he was only four or five and had barely learned to talk before he died. His mother had been devastated and could not watch as Gaither dug the grave next to the ones of his father and his grandparents. The small cemetery stood on a slight hill beneath a big oak tree not far from the back of their house at the foothills of the Appalachian mountains. Three poles tied together like a teepee stood on each corner of the graveyard with a larger pole lying in the cross on top. A smaller pole was tied to the outside of each corner, making a fence strong enough to keep out the farm animals.

Gaither remembered how hard it had been to dig that grave because of the many roots he had to chop through, along with the deep hurt in his heart. He had made a box out of small timbers, notching them to fit, the same way a friend had done when they buried his father. His mother gave him a quilt in which to wrap Jimmie's body. Gaither laid the body in the box and put two layers of tree limbs and a layer of rock over the box and covered it up. He drove a wooden cross into the ground with *Jimmie Gilmore, 1763-1773* carved into the wood. Gaither removed his old black hat and stood looking at the graves.

Jimmie had always been so loving, so kind, with his big blue eyes and a ready smile on his face. He had never learned to say *Gaither*, but for some reason no one could understand had called him *Gee*. Now everyone, including his mother, called him Gee.

Today as Gaither stood looking at the graves, he reminded himself, *This is where I will lie someday* . He turned and strolled slowly towards the cabin, his head down, still holding the black hat in his hand, thinking of his grandfather who had purchased, traded, or took the land, according to whom you asked, from the Indians and built a ten-by-twenty log cabin a short distance from a small stream that flowed from the hills.

The cabin had one shutter covering an opening for a window, a door on the front, and a rock chimney on the side. The door was the only entrance to the cabin. Inside the cabin was a fireplace with cooking bars reaching from side to side. Two wood barrels containing flour and corn meal were supports for a log table made of split logs, hewed smooth with a drawknife. Another split log, fitted onto two blocks of timbers, was used for seats.

On the other side of the cabin were two beds, each made of split logs sitting upon four log posts, cut in two-foot lengths. Each bed had a burlap bag mattress stuffed with cotton and quilts made from flour sacks. A wooden rocker sat in front of the fireplace beside two chairs made from small branches tied together with strips of rawhide. The seats bottoms were made of hickory wood split into narrow strips and woven together. Burlap bags filled with cotton were used for seat cushions by day and for pillows at night. Between the beds and the fireplace was a ladder leading to the loft, where two cotton mattresses lay on a split log floor. The loft had a cutout for a window on each end, with shutters that could be opened or closed.

A short distance from the left side of the cabin, spring water ran into a log box with burlap bags stretched over the top. This was not only where they got their water, but was also used to cool their milk and butter. A small stream of water flowed from the spring through the corral and into the hog lot. It emptied into a creek a short distance from the house. Between the house and the spring stood a smokehouse where they salted and smoked their meat. On one side of the smokehouse a lean-to was used for a woodshed and was filled with firewood.

Not far from the cabin, close to the stream, was a log barn with a corn crib on one side of a wide hallway and a stall for the cows. On the other side of the hallway, two stalls for the horses stood with wood poles across the door to keep the horses inside. A steel tired wagon sat in the hallway beneath a loft used to store hay. The barn, like the house, was covered with split wood shingles. A split rail fence circled the barn, the corral, and the hog lot. It crossed the small stream, ran up to the side of a hill, and back to the barn.

The house and barn sat in the corner of ten acres of farmland which had been cleared by Gee's father and grandfather. His father was clearing two more acres next to the stream when he was killed by Indians who slipped down the stream and jumped him as he chopped down a tree. They took his musket and his horse. Gee was somewhat surprised, but very grateful they did not scalp him.

Trying to farm with one horse was very hard on Gee. He had hoped they could buy another horse this year, but because of a severe drought, their crops of tobacco and corn were very small. It would take most of their profit to buy salt and flour for the winter. Still, he considered them lucky because they grew most of their vegetables, and he hunted deer and turkey for their meat.

Today, as he walked his horse with a sack of flour tied behind his saddle and a bag of salt hanging from the saddle horn, he was thinking of how they could get a horse. It was early

October, and he was returning home from a trip to the trading post. He was alert, looking and listening for anything out of the ordinary. There were still Indians around, and he hated the Indians. After all, they had killed his father and that gave him reason to hate them, although, as his mother had said, not all Indians are bad. He thought about this and admitted to himself he really did not know any Indians. He had seen them, but never been around them. In his mind, he decided he did not hate all the Indians, just the ones that killed his father.

Gee was tall, broad-shouldered, well built, and looked older than his sixteen years. He had large blue eyes and long blonde hair cut straight across at the top of his shoulders. He had the makings of a stubble beard on a strong jaw and a slightly rounded, but not overly large, nose. He wore overalls, a buckskin shirt, a black duster, and his father's old, black hat that was about two sizes too big for him. Around his waist was a handmade leather belt with gun holster and knife sheath. Inside the holster was a Lyman flintlock pistol, and inside the knife sheath was a long hunting knife, honed to a razor's edge, which he used for skinning animals and for shaving. A flintlock musket fit snugly inside a leather boot on the right side of his saddle across from the bag of salt. The saddle had belonged to his grandfather, and it squeaked as he rode. The squeak was as loud as the hoofs of the horse, and the sound probably carried much farther. He had greased it with lard and mink oil several times, but had not been able to stop the squeak. They were on the edge of Indian country and the squeak bothered him. He decided that next time he would ride bareback to the trading post.

He walked his horse slowly, scanning the woods ahead. He was alert, but still thinking of how badly they needed a horse. Maybe he could trap enough beaver, mink, and otter this winter to buy a horse come spring. Someway, they had to have another horse.

Suddenly his horse stopped, ears perked and nostrils flared. About 300 yards ahead, in a grove of cedars on the side of the road, he saw movement. He watched as a man with long red hair, wearing a black coat, got off the ground and quickly mounted a chestnut horse. He pulled a black hat down over his head, spurred the horse hard, and galloped hurriedly through the timbers. In a short time the sounds of the hoof beats faded away.

Gee was puzzled. Something was not right. He scanned the wood and listened for a few seconds before dismounting. He knew a man on a horse made a huge target. He stood beside the horse and lifted the musket from the boot with his left hand, then reached into his saddlebag and withdrew a powder horn and hung it over his neck and shoulder. Reaching into his saddlebag again, he lifted out a small leather bag containing wadding and bullets. He held these between his teeth and drew his revolver as he listened for sounds. He heard nothing.

Both his revolver and rifle were single shot flintlocks, so if there were more than one rider, two shots were not a lot of firepower. He had practiced reloading the pistol and knew he was fast enough to get off another shot if needed. Gee stood on the opposite side of his horse from the direction in which the rider had gone and continued to wait. Remembering the way the rider had acted, he fully expected the rider, especially if there were more than one of them, to return or try to ambush him, so he waited, watched, and listened.

I'm not going down without a fight. I'll be ready for him. . .or them, he thought. *I can probably take three of them, but if there are more than that, maybe my horse can outrun them*, he told himself and waited for several minutes before slipping slowly along the road for about twenty yards, putting a group of large oak trees between him and the way the rider had gone. He waited a few more minutes and slipped a little farther along the old road. The only sounds were the *clip clop* of his horse's hoofs on a road beaten hard by the hoofs of Indian horses for many years, lately by the horses and wagons of settlers looking for more land.

He thought of how the settlers were always pushing the Indians off their ancestral lands, either by trading them cheap whiskey or just taking it by force. He could understand why the Indians were hostile and did not blame them for fighting to protect their land, but why kill his father for a horse and a musket? They could have just taken them, but again, he was thankful they did not scalp his father. He would hate to know that his father's scalp was hanging on a pole or tied to some Indian's horse.

He waited as the sounds of the forest returned to normal. He looked intently for any movement, either in front of him, to each side, or behind him. He watched for the flushing of birds, listened for insects that suddenly stopped chirping, a squirrel that barked at an intruder—anything that was not the natural sound of the forest. He walked his horse a few more steps, stopped again, and waited. He was sure something was not right, so he waited a long time, looking and listening.

From somewhere behind him, he heard the sound of a galloping horse. He turned quickly, ready to fire, but saw the chestnut horse and rider emerge from the woods about 400 yards behind him and gallop away, heading toward the trading post. He stood and waited until he could no longer hear the sound of hoof beats. He waited before walking his horse to within a couple of hundred yards of where he first saw the rider. He had acted strangely so there could be more than one of them. A man who was not cautious was a man who did not live long, his father once told him.

He eased forward again and stopped again, watching and listening. Finally when he was satisfied it was safe, he mounted his horse. He put the musket back into the scabbard and continued slowly up the wagon trail, still holding his revolver. He had gone maybe a hundred yards when his horse stopped again, his head high, his ears perked, looking intently ahead. Gee dismounted quickly, grabbed the musket from its scabbard, and knelt on the ground. He scanned the road ahead and at about seventy yards, he saw something lying on the ground, just off the road. From this distance it looked like an animal. He stared at it for several minutes, trying to decide what to do. Remembering what his father had said, he crawled forward, every nerve in his young body alert. At about forty yards, he could see that it was not an animal, but a body, curled into a tight knot and almost naked.

"Hey you!" he yelled, but the body did not move.

He yelled again and saw a leg move. He belly flopped to the ground, placed the musket to his shoulder, and aimed it at the body. He lay there a long time, waiting for the body to stand, but it did not move again. He waited a few more minutes, looking and listening, then crawled another twenty yards, watched and waited. He was in pistol range now, so he laid his musket on the ground and pointed the pistol at the body, yelling again. When the body did not move, he belly crawled forward, dragging the musket beside him, all the time keeping the pistol aimed at the body. Still cautious, he looked around him, swinging the pistol as he looked. He crawled forward a little more, stopping at about twenty yards.

"Hey you!" he yelled a third time and saw the body sit up.

It was an Indian girl.

Probably a Cherokee, he thought, as she moaned *tla, tla, tla* over and over. He did not know what she was saying, but saw her head shake from side to side. She sat with arms wrapped around knees that were drawn tight against her chest. She clutched a torn and soiled buckskin dress to her chest, still repeating *tla, tla,* over and over. She was mostly naked from the waist down and he could see blood on her shoulder and on her legs. She looked at him with both hate and fear in her eyes and jumped to her feet. She tried to run, but fell after a few steps. She tried to crawl away, but collapsed on the ground and coiled tightly.

Tla, tla, tla! she pleaded.

Extending Shadows

Gee stared at her and at the surrounding woods, looking for more Indians, but saw nothing. He waited, scanned the scene once more and saw nothing but a moccasin lying a short distance from where she lay. He waited, still pointing his pistol at her.

The normal sounds of the woods returned, and he was pretty much satisfied that all was safe. He relaxed a little, let go of the musket, and stood up, still pointing the pistol in her general direction. He could see she was too weak to fight and had no weapons. He walked to within a few feet of where she was laying on her side, coiled tightly, her face hidden between her knees, not looking at him. He holstered his pistol, took off his coat, and laid it over her. He walked over and picked up her moccasin. When he turned around, he saw the girl sitting upright, looking at him, but clutching his coat tightly around herself, covering herself as best as she could.

"Put this back on." Gee held out the moccasin, but realized she did not know what he had said so he motioned to his feet. She looked at him and pulled the coat tighter while trying to cover her legs and thighs with the torn dress. Unable to do so, she dropped her head and stared at the ground. He took a couple of steps and tossed her the moccasin. She eyed the moccasin for a bit, hesitated, but finally picked it up and put it on her foot, still staring at him with fear in her dark brown eyes.

He did not know what to do. She watched him closely as he sat down a little ways from her. He looked at her and was shocked at how pretty she was. She had long black hair and bronze skin that was smooth as silk. She was pretty—very pretty, even with red, swollen eyes. Her face was bruised and bleeding from a busted lip. Blood ran down her arm from a cut on her shoulder. She was probably thirteen or fourteen, he thought, but he did not know. He knew very little about girls, especially Indian girls, but he knew enough to know she was pretty.

"What happened? Can I help?"

Seeing that she did not understand, he tried to make sign language, but failed miserably. He smiled at her, something all people knew and understood. She did not smile back, although she did seem to relax a little. He could not take his eyes off her. She had a beautiful face, even with a busted lip. He could see her lips were full, and she had perfect white teeth. Though he had never kissed a girl, he wondered what it would be like to kiss her. Their eyes met; he smiled and got a funny feeling inside, one he had never felt before. They stared at each other, and he noticed some of the fear had faded from her eyes. He smiled again, but still she did not return his smile. He pointed up and down the trail, making his fingers into a walking figure.

She shrugged. He lifted one hand, making a small circle and lifted both hands upwards and raised his shoulders. She shook her head. *She doesn't understand or does not know where she is*, he thought, and raked his mind trying to think of a way to communicate with her. He laid his head on his hands, trying to make the sign of someone sleeping. He saw her eyes brighten, but again she shook her head, and yet he knew she had understood. He tried to ask her where her family was, but could not make her understand these signs. Finally, he made a sign of holding and rocking a baby, the way his mother used to rock Jimmie, and pointed around in a circle. She understood, but again, shook her head.

"What am I going to do? She's an Indian!" he said aloud.

The fact she was an Indian girl ran over and over in his mind. Finally he decided; I cannot leave her here, Indian or not. Maybe if I can get her to my house, Mother will know what to do with her. He motioned towards his horse and made a sign of someone riding. She understood, but shook her head and said, *Tla*. He motioned around the woods, pointed to the sun, and made a sign of it going down, then rubbed his stomach. She looked at him, but did not try to move. He contemplated picking her up, but knew this would only frighten her more. So he walked over, mounted his horse, and walked it close to her. His horse was a little skittish as it approached her, but calmed when he sensed that Gee was not alarmed. He removed the bag of flour from behind the saddle, laid it across the saddle in front of him, and patted the empty spot behind him. He could see she was still afraid and was trying to decide whether to go with him or stay.

As she looked around, Gee could see she was thinking of the red-haired man and figured she might be dead, had this rider not came along. Also, the red-haired man might come back; going with this white man might be better. She did not know what to do. She could not make herself rise, so she just sat there, still coiled, very uncertain of what to do. He pointed at the sun once more, making a sign of it setting and leaned out of the saddle, offering her his hand. She looked at him and around the woods once more and slowly got to her feet. She stood on unsteady legs, uncertain whether to try to run again or go with him. After a long pause she lifted her hand. He took it and lifted her gently onto the horse behind him. His horse was calm, accustomed to having Gee and his little brother on his back. She put her arms softly around his waist as he walked his horse cautiously toward home.

He was still a little scared... scared of what would happen if the Indians found him and scared about what his mother might do when he brought an Indian home. *But what else can I do?* he asked himself as he walked his horse slowly, turning off the wagon road on to a trail that ran through the trees leading to his house.

About a mile later, they emerged from the timber. Gee saw his mother walking from the chicken pen with eggs in an apron she held by the corners. She stopped and stared when she saw a girl jump from the horse and run back into the edge of the timber before stopping to look at them. Gee could see the girl was horrified. He sat on his horse and decided the girl must have thought he was taking her to her village. Now she was scared of another person she did not know.

His mother walked up to him and demanded, "What have you done? Who is that Indian girl?"

Gee dismounted and told his mother how he had found the girl and about the red-haired man. He said the girl did not know where her village was, and he did not know what to do with her, but knew he could not leave her in the woods to die.

"I thought you might know what to do with her," he said to his mother as they turned and looked at the girl sitting on the ground, her body bent over, holding her head in her hands. Both Gee and his mother could hear her sobbing.

His mother untied her apron, holding the corners so the eggs did not fall and handed them to Gee. She walked slowly toward the girl, calling to her in a soft voice, and held out her hand. The girl raised her head, looked at his mother, and then at him. He smiled, nodded his head and made a sign of holding and rocking a baby. This, he hoped, would let the girl know that this was his mother. The girl looked first at him, then at his mother, and slowly got to her feet, but did not run. His mother walked slowly up to the girl, smiled softly, and offered the girl her hand. She hesitated, but took his mother's hand, and they walked slowly toward the house, each of them uncertain about what to do next.

CHAPTER SIX

JMA

Nineteen ninety-nine

The day Penny was born, her father Robert Sanderson was, by far, the happiest man in the state of Texas. He watched as Anna held the baby and could not take his eyes off them, looking from Anna to his daughter and back again. He recalled he had unconsciously wished for a boy, but now, just looking at his daughter, he knew he had been wrong. Now he was happy she was a girl. He was very happy.

"She's so beautiful; I'd give a pretty penny just to hold her!" Robert had a wide smile on his face, and his eyes sparkled. Pride emanated from him like rays of sunlight.

Anna smiled at him. "Give a pretty penny, huh?" After a brief pause, she said, "How about we name her Penny because she is as pretty as a penny?" They looked at each other and knew her name would be Penny Marie, not Julian Marie, as they had planned—Julian after Anna's grandmother and Marie after her mother.

As Robert stared at his wife and baby, his thoughts wandered back to the day they first met. It seemed they were in love the first time they saw each other. His mind wandered to the house on Galveston Bay and the first time they made love. He remembered their wedding and the wrenching heartbreak of losing their first born, a little boy who never drew a breath. *But now, we have a living child. We have a beautiful baby girl! We have influential friends, a big house, and a successful business. . . everything we could possibly want. Life is great.*

Penny grew up loving the outdoors and spent many happy hours with her father. She was his little shadow, always tagging along after him. He taught her to fish, to shoot, to ride, to help mend fences, and to feed the cattle and horses. He taught her to call the turkeys, to hunt deer, to make a campfire—all the things a father might teach his son. Maybe even before she was born, she could sense that her father had wanted a boy, and since she could not be that, she would do things a boy might do. As far back as she could remember, she had loved being a tomboy. She loved her father; she adored him. She worshiped him!

The early memories of her mother were a little different. She remembered her mother taking her shopping, taking her to school, washing and combing her hair, and teaching her to speak Spanish so she could communicate with their maid. She remembered her mother was a gentle lady, and Penny could feel her mother's love for her. Many nights she would sing Penny to sleep. She loved her mother, but she was absolutely a daddy's girl.

Penny was about eight years old when she began to realize she never wanted for anything. When she had wanted a horse, she got the best horse; when she wanted a bike, she got one. . . a tree house, a rifle, a dog. . . in fact all her life she could not remember ever wanting for something she did not get. She wanted a car for her sixteenth birthday, and they gave her a new Chevrolet Camaro.

They had vacationed in the U. S. and traveled to Paris, the French Alps, London, Madrid, Rome, Japan, and a lot of other places she could not remember. She lived in a very big house, and her parents owned a condo in St. Thomas and a big house in Galveston Bay. By the time she was a teenager, she knew they were wealthy, and her life was a fairy tale. Nothing could hurt her.

All of that changed on June 1, 1999, when an airplane ran off the end of a runway in Little Rock. There were 150 people on board the plane and eleven died. Out of 150, why did one of the eleven have to be her father? Penny could not understand. She was emotionally devastated and went into shock. She was admitted into the hospital, but she would not eat or drink for more than a week, being fed intravenously. She lay in the hospital bed and stared at the ceiling, hardly moving. A lot of friends and loved ones came by to see her, but she said nothing and acknowledged no one. Anna enlisted the help of numerous doctors, even brought in a noted psychologist from Houston, but no one helped. Penny lay as if she were in a coma, only occasionally moving her eyes.

On the tenth day in the hospital, she got out of bed, pulled the IV out of her arm, walked to the window, and tried to open it. When she could not, she began banging her head hard against the glass. Anna tried to calm her and when she could not, she buzzed a nurse for help. When the nurse came, Penny began cursing her, throwing trays and water cups, tossing pillows and bed clothes onto the floor. The nurse called for help. Two more nurses arrived, and it took all three of them to hold Penny down while one nurse gave her a sedative, continuing to hold her until the medication took effect. Penny collapsed and began to cry before drifting off to sleep. When the medication wore off, she became enraged again, throwing the flowers she had been given from the vase onto the floor, stomping on them, and screaming uncontrollably. The nurses came, strapped her to the bed, and gave her another sedative. Anna hired private nurses to stay with her daughter around the clock. Several days later, Penny began to eat, yet still would not speak and was filled with rage when not sedated.

Three weeks later Penny returned home from the hospital accompanied by two nurses. She would not speak, and Anna feared that seeing the house without her father would send her deeper into shock. The nurses led her inside. She stared straight ahead, then suddenly broke away from them, ran to her room, and locked the door. She did not notice the bars, which Anna had had a workman install on all upstairs windows, fearing Penny might try to jump.

A week later, still very thin and hollow-eyed, Penny went to the barn and saddled her horse. She rode, but stayed clear of the fences she had ridden many times with her father. Later that day she spoke for the first time since her father's death, asking Anna to take her to see her father's grave. Anna was excited and believed she was finally getting better. At the cemetery, Penny stood and stared at her father's grave, showing no emotion until she began screaming.

"You didn't care about us. You cared more about your stupid oil company. You didn't care if you got killed. Out of 150 people, you let yourself get killed. You didn't even try to survive. You just wanted to punish me for not being a boy." She kicked dirt and grass on to the grave. "Well, I don't care about you either, and I didn't need you to care for me. I'll care for myself and I'll do what I please, and no one is going to stop me. I hope you rot in hell." She screamed again and spit on his grave.

Anna tried to calm her, but she screamed, "Leave me alone. You don't care either. No one cares." Penny ran stiff legged back to the car, got into the back seat, slammed the door, and slumped onto the seat. Anna tried to console her, but she lashed out at Anna, screaming and cursing, "Go to hell. You can go and get yourself killed, too, for all I care."

Anna was shocked. Penny had never talked to her like that before. *Lord, what am I going to do?* When they reached their home, Penny did not say a word, but went straight to her bedroom. Later, she slipped into the wine cellar and drank almost an entire bottle of wine before getting sick and passing out. Anna sat in the den and cried for a long time before going upstairs to check on her.

As she passed the stairs leading to the basement, she noticed the door was open. She took a few steps down the stairway and saw the open wine cellar door. She found Penny lying unconscious in a corner of the wine cellar. Fearing the worst, she called for the nurses. The nurses quickly came to the wine cellar, and, seeing that Penny was only drunk and passed out, carried her to her room.

Penny was vaguely aware of Anna and the nurse helping her back to her room. She knew her mother was sitting by her bedside as she drifted off to sleep and spent another restless night. . . the nightmares of seeing her father being killed in a plane crash playing over and over in her mind.

The next week she continued to sulk, never leaving her room. She had lost so much weight, she was skin and bones, and white as a ghost. A week later she slipped out of the house just after dark without telling anyone. Anna heard her car leave and checked her room to make sure it was she. She was pleased Penny had left the house, but was concerned about where she was going and why she did not tell anyone.

Anna was waiting up when Penny came home a little after 3 a. m., drunk and smelling like marijuana. Anna tried to talk to her, but Penny was very belligerent and refused to say a word. She staggered up the stairs, cursed, then slammed and locked the door. Anna called her parents to tell them what had taken place. She was upset and asked her parents to come and spend some time with her.

The next day, the nurses and her grandparents attempted to talk to Penny, but she only glared at them and would not say a word. That night Penny left again and came home the next day, drunk again. Her eyes were bloodshot and glazed, her hair wet and tangled. Her skirt was wrinkled and soiled; her blouse was fastened with only one button, and she did not have on a bra. She would not talk, but pushed Anna away, refusing her mother's attempts to talk to her, then ran to her room and locked the door.

Anna asked her parents if there was some way to keep Penny from going out, at least until they could find a way to help her. Amos said he would have a mechanic disable Penny's car. That evening when Penny realized her car would not start, she screamed and cursed Anna and her grandparents, turning away angrily and running back to her room. Later, she tried to open the wine cellar, but found it padlocked.

The next morning, Penny demanded they fix her car. Anna said they would fix her car when she returned to school. Anna was optimistic since school would start on Monday, and Penny had always enjoyed school. Anna hoped it would help her get her mind straight. But Penny retorted that she was not going to school, and they could not make her. "If you are not going to school, you cannot have your car," Anna told her sternly.

That night, Penny slipped from the house and rode her horse to a gravel road that ran along the back side of the ranch. She tied her horse to a fence post and got into a car that was waiting for her.

It was after sun up when she rode her horse to the barn, left him saddled, and staggered up to the house. Her mother and her grandparents confronted her. They pleaded with her, but soon realized they could not talk to a drunk and let her go to her room.

Later, after Penny had gone to asleep, Anna slipped into her room, and took the phone and all Penny's clothes from the closet. Amos and Marie agreed to stay to make sure she did not get violent or leave the house again. After three days of being confined to her room, Penny said she would go to school. Satisfied she was getting better and happy she was going back to school, the mechanic repaired her car, and Amos and Marie went back to Tyler.

The next day Penny left the house, but instead of going to school, she went downtown and paid someone to buy her a six-pack of beer. She drank four bottles on her way to school. Staggering into her classroom, she verbally abused her teacher, who took her directly to the principal's office. Anna was called to pick her up, but before Anna arrived, Penny bolted from school. She wrecked her car and would probably have been arrested for DUI were it not for her prominent family name. Instead she only received a stern lecture from the policeman. Since her car was still drivable, she drove to a cheap motel and called some boys, who brought more beer. They spent the next two days stoned—drinking beer and smoking pot.

There was nothing Penny would not do, yet somehow she managed not to get hooked on any hard drugs. Maybe deep down, the memory of her vigorous father was the only reason she didn't. In the innermost part of her being, Penny knew her father would not approve of the way she was living, but she convinced herself he did not care what she did and neither did her mother. All she ever did was sit and cry. Only two days into Penny's junior year, the honor roll student she had once been had become a student suspended—wild and out of control.

When Penny bolted from the school and did not come home for two days, Amos knew he had seen enough. He knew they had to do something; if they did not, Penny would probably be dead within a month. They discussed what they should do and concluded that the only reasonable answer was to send her away to a reform school, which they had already threatened to do. Now they had no other choice.

Amos called the sheriff and the state troopers, instructing them to either pick Penny up if they found her or to let him know. Later in the day, the deputy sheriff spotted her car at a cheap motel and called Amos. He asked the deputy if he would have two female deputies bring a strait jacket and meet him, Marie, and Anna at the motel.

They obtained a key from the front desk and found Penny naked and passed out on the bed. They dressed her and wrapped her in a strait jacket, and Amos carried her to a patrol car. They followed the two deputies to the airport where a doctor and a nurse were waiting. They transferred Penny to the company's Gulfstream G3 and strapped her into a seat. When she began to wake, the roar of jet engines made her realize she was in an airplane and that she was strapped into a seat. She could not move her arms, so she began cursing and screaming for them to turn her loose. They completely ignored her. Her head hurt so badly, she soon sat quietly and vaguely remembered that her mother and grandfather had threatened to send her to a reform school.

As the plane taxied to the end of the runway, she feared that was what they were doing. She had not believed they would follow though on their threat, but now she told herself she did not care. "I'll show them . . . I'll show them all." She cursed her mother and grandparents, vowing to get even with them and to make life miserable for the people who would be at her future destination, wherever that was.

Less than an hour later, the plane touched down at Williams Regional Airport, on the south side of San Antonio, and taxied to a hangar. The doctor unfastened her seat belt, helped her to her feet and down the steps to a light blue van with Julia Martin Academy on the door. A tall, slender, black man stepped out and opened the rear passenger door. Penny was now wide awake and thought about making a big scene, but decided to wait until she got to wherever they were taking her.

"Can you take this thing off?" Penny asked, nodding her head towards the strait jacket.

"No, I am sorry; they will take it off once you reach the Academy," the doctor said, and then added, "I wish you the best." Penny did not answer.

The man helped her into the van. Penny noticed there were no door handles or window controls on the doors, and the glass partition between her and the driver was closed. For the first time in her life, she felt fear building inside her. She did not know where she was or where they were taking her, but managed to convince herself that she did not care. She would show them. . . show them all. As the van pulled away, she saw the doctor and nurse wave to her. She did not wave back.

The van headed south on I-37 and exited onto Texas 24 fifteen minutes later. After a few miles, it slowed alongside a high wire fence, turned off the road, and stopped at a security gate. A guard presented the driver a clipboard. He signed it and drove slowly up a tree-lined drive.

Penny could not help but notice the place was impressive, with flowers, rock gardens, and gazebos scattered over the grounds. The grass was thick and green, the shrubs well-trimmed, the walkways neatly edged and adorned with flowers. Some girls in light blue jumpsuits waved as the van passed. She ignored them.

The van soon reached a U-shaped building with verandas across the front and down each side. A balcony covered all of the verandas. An Olympic-sized swimming pool was between the two wings of the house. On one side of the house were two tennis courts and a nine-hole golf course. A putting green and a driving range were on the other side. About twenty yards behind the main house was a building as wide as the wings of the house. It was connected to each wing of the main house by covered walkways. All buildings were made of gray brick and had light blue shutters.

Penny saw a barn about 300 yards in back of this building with a dozen horses grazing in a picturesque pasture. The van stopped under the awning of a large two-story building. The driver opened Penny's door, unbuckled her seatbelt, and said in soft, pleasant voice, "Please lean forward." He untied the straitjacket, took it off her, and held her hand as she stepped out. "Please follow me."

She thought of running, but decided he was only the hired help, so she followed him into a lobby. The first thing she noticed was a huge portrait of a girl dressed in light blue riding clothes and standing beside a beautiful palomino horse. The painting hung on the wall directly in front of the entrance way.

The driver led her through the rotunda, down a hallway, stopped at on open door, and knocked on the door jam. On the door was a sign that read, "Director." A woman of about fifty sat behind the desk and looked up from a folder she was holding. "Hello. I am Betty Witherspoon, and you are?" She offered her hand.

"Can't you read?" Penny said in a snotty voice and did not take her hand, but stared at her in contempt. The woman smiled, picked up another folder from her desk, and looked it over before commenting, "Yes, Penny Marie Sanderson. You will be in room 211. Daria will show you the way." She motioned to a girl Penny had not noticed standing in the back of the room. She smiled and continued, but with some authority. "She will show you where to get your necessities, and someone in the fitting room will help you get fitted. All our girls wear uniforms, as I do. Everything is furnished by the Academy. The only personal item you are allowed to keep is your bra. Some of our girls choose to wear our sports bra. If you decide against the sports bra and need others, we will FedEx them to you. You will put the rest of your clothes and personal belongings, including shoes, in the lockbox in your room, then lock it and bring the key to me. You cannot leave your room unless you conform to our clothing regulations. I want you to understand that we are. . ."

"You can keep your crap. I don't need it," Penny interrupted.

Mrs. Witherspoon did not seem annoyed. In fact, Penny thought she could detect a slight smile on her face. She continued in a firm tone, "As I was saying, we are here to help, but if you do not cooperate, we still have your straitjacket."

She nodded to Daria, who stepped up to her and said, "I'm Daria. Will you come with me?"

"I'm not going anywhere with you or anybody else."

"If you do not go, we will put you in the straitjacket and carry you," Mrs. Witherspoon said sternly. Penny shrugged and followed Daria down the hallway and into a large recreation room. Several girls were lounging on couches watching TV. Some were playing ping pong, others pool, and some sat at tables looking at laptops, reading or just talking. The room also had another large painting of the girl in blue, this time standing beside a red Porsche convertible. They walked past a dining room, up a flight of stairs, turned right for a short way, then left into the right wing of the building. About halfway down the hallway, they entered room 211. The door was open, and Daria did not close it behind them. The room was divided by a folding wood partition that slid from wall to wall, providing separate living quarters for two people. With the partition opened, it made one large room.

"That side is yours. Everything you need is in there," Daria explained, pointing to the bathroom, "including new toothbrushes, hair brushes, and tampons. When you are ready to get your uniform, let me know, and I will go with you."

"I don't need anything," Penny said defiantly. Daria said nothing, just turned and left the room.

Penny looked around the room; there was a closet, a full-sized bed next to a window, a recliner, a dresser, a chair, and a desk with a picture frame lying face down on top of it. The private bathroom was small, with a commode, an enclosed shower, and a vanity. Penny walked to a door beside the folding room divider, opened it, and stepped out onto a balcony. She looked at the setting sun, which reflected off the blue-green waters of a lake with two piers where three girls sat watching the sunset. *It is pretty, but I am not staying. I will not eat or drink, nor leave my room. And when I do that, Miss Witterpoon, or whatever her name is, will call my mother, and she will come get me.* She closed the divider between the two beds.

With that plan in mind, Penny refused to eat or leave her room. However, she quickly learned that no one seemed to care. Penny said nothing to her roommate and never opened the partition between them. Penny hated them all, and she would show them. She was rich and always got what she wanted.

On the third day, Penny realized no one seemed to care. She was essentially confined to her room. She was locked behind a wire fence and definitely could not come and go as she pleased. Since she refused to leave her room, she got one meal a day, brought to her by Daria, who would set the meal on the table and leave without saying a word. This was real. Penny was a prisoner and soon realized that in here, she was not rich and no more important than her roommate or anyone else. She sat on her bed, staring at a picture lying face down on the table.

"No one wants to see me, either. No one cares! No one!" Never in her life had she felt so alone. She lay down on the bed; it was the first time in her life she could remember crying. She cried for a long time, but did not know why she kept staring at the picture lying face down on the table. Finally, she picked the picture up and turned it over. It was a photo of the girl in blue, only this time instead of standing beside a beautiful horse, she wore a blue dress and was in a casket. Penny inhaled a violent gasp and with shaking hands, she quickly laid it face down again. She was still crying when the buzzer went off.

Penny had noticed that a buzzer sounded fifteen minutes before the lights went out at 10 p. m. and after that, everything was quiet. She was still crying when she heard Daria come in. The partition was drawn across the room, but she could hear Daria getting ready for bed. She waited untul Daria had gone to bed before opening the divider a little and saying, "Daria, can I talk to you?"

"Sure, I wondered when you would ask," Daria said, getting out of bed and opening the divider.

"Come in and sit with me," she said, pointing to a place on the bed. Daria had dark skin, dark brown eyes, and long black hair. She had a pretty face with a warm smile and full lips. She was taller than Penny and had a very nice figure. Penny knew she was Mexican, but she spoke perfect English and had a warm personality, which made her easy to talk to.

"Could you tell me where I am and what is this place?" Penny asked.

"Well, you are in Lakewood, Texas, just south of San Antonio, and this place is the Julia Martin Academy for Troubled Girls or JMA for short."

"How do I get out of here?'

Daria held back her laughter and only smiled, "You don't. You are here for at least six months from the day they checked you in. After that, if you are no longer, as they say, 'troubled,' you will be released, but monitored closely. If you cannot adapt to life outside, then you will be sent to a reform school. . . and believe me, you don't want to go there. I was there before I came here."

"Six months!" Penny said in disbelief.

"I noticed your shoes and clothing when you came in, and I'm guessing this place is probably not what you've been accustomed to, but it is not bad. It's a million times better than reform school, so I have to say again, do anything to stay out of there."

"What do I do? I mean, I can't stay for six months with nothing to do. I'll go crazy."

"You go to school, which is in the building beside the cafeteria. You follow the rules, keep your room clean, and do some chores. Let me explain how things work. Each girl has chores—some call it a job—however, each chore is rotated once a week; that way we all learn different skills. A list of the available chores and where to start the rotation is posted in our classrooms each week. There are a number of chores you can choose, like housekeeping, cooking, gardening, animal care, and numerous others. You can swap a chore with someone else, but eventually you will get the kitchen duty, which almost no one wants." She paused, making sure Penny was still listening.

"You also get paid, so to speak, for doing your chores satisfactorily. The grades you receive are from the students—one of us who is in charge. We call that 'Sargent Duty,' and that is also rotated. You get a token a day, the same as everyone else. The tokens are deposited into your account and are used to pay fines for failing to conform to the rules. When you leave here, the tokens you have in your account are worth ten dollars each. To some of us, that is more money than we have ever seen. If you think you are unjustly accused, there is a court system here, made up of the students, each taking turns to serve as a judge or on a jury. They hear the cases and appeals. Most of us look forward to the time we can serve again. However, we find that the longer a girl is here, the less likely she is to wind up in court."

Daria continued, "You will find that everyone is treated the same—rich kids, poor kids, blacks, whites, brown, or whoever. No one is better, and no one is worse. Eventually we all accept this, and we adjust, as JMA calls it. This is how we learn to interact with others, learn different skills, and learn to work with different people. We learn to obey the rules, take responsibility for our actions, and have compassion for others.

"We have group sessions twice a week where we learn that no matter who we are or where we grew up, each of us has her problems. We learn to talk about them, accept them, and learn to live with them. If we don't, we know that sooner or later, we will be another girl in a blue dress." Daria nodded toward the photo lying face down on her table. "Have you looked at it?"

"No!" Penny gasped, looking at the photo. "I mean 'yes.' It's creepy. What is it?"

"It's not a what; it's a girl, and her name was Julia Martin. The Academy was established in 1981 in her honor. Her father owns a big ranch in South Texas with hundreds of oil wells. She had everything a girl could want—fancy clothes, horses, cars—but got hooked on drugs and died of an overdose. He built this place in her honor and set up a trust fund of ten million dollars, I'm told. The interest from the fund pays the tuition for poor and unfortunate girls, while the others pay their own way. Julia's father said if a place like this had been available for her, she would probably be alive today." Daria paused and watched Penny's reaction to what she was saying.

"The JMA is operated by the state, and the enrollment is split in half: half for the wealthy and half for the less fortunate. The less fortunate is what the courts calls girls like me, and it is how I got out of reform school to come here. The theory is that both the rich and the poor of all nationalities can benefit from the interactions between one another. The group sessions are a way for us to share our feelings with other girls, and a way for us to get to know everyone better. It's worked for me."

"Where are you from?" Penny asked as the lights went out.

Daria lowered her voice to just above a whisper and said, "I was born in Mexico. I came to El Paso when I was four years old, but did not start school until I was eight. I was two years older than the other kids in my class and spoke little English. It seemed like I was always in trouble with both the teachers and my classmates. I quit school in the fifth grade, got a fake green card saying I was eighteen, and found a job working in a garment factory. My step-daddy had abused me from as far back as I can remember so I was a tough kid with a chip on my shoulder. Two months later, I was fired for slapping a supervisor. I did a few other odd jobs, but soon wound up on the streets. Later, I was arrested for selling drugs and for prostitution. When the authorities found out what my real age was, I was sent to a reform school. The things that went on in there, I don't like to talk about, but being abused was not as bad as the gangs, drugs, and sex that are in there. Working the streets was a picnic compared to that, so I decided to be a model prisoner and get paroled as soon as possible. That may be the reason I was transferred here... I don't know. I do know that this place has changed my outlook on life. How about you?" she whispered and waited for Penny to volunteer her story.

"Daria, you are very nice, and I thank you, but can I talk to you later? I just need time to sort all this out."

"Penny, everyone here knows how you feel. Most of us were like you when we came here, and the first thing we learned is that we must follow the rules. Some learn it quicker than others, so the quicker you decide to obey the rules, the quicker you can get on with your life."

"Daria, I can't go on like this. Where do I start?"

"We will get you what you need in the morning, and I think you need to start with an apology to Ms. Betty. You were very rude to her. You will find that she is a good person who cares deeply for us."

Penny did not go to sleep for a long time, but lay in her bed thinking of what Daria had said. It made a lot of sense. *The girl in the blue dress was not unlike me,* she thought. *She had everything, same as me, and she is dead.* She thought back to the way she had been living and realized that it could have been her in the picture, lying face down on a table.

Early the next morning after Daria finished her chores, she came and asked Penny if she had changed her mind. Penny nodded her head, and they went to get her a uniform, shoes, and the other articles she needed. She was surprised that everyone seemed nice and friendly. She was also surprised to find out how comfortable the jumpsuit was, especially with the sports bra Daria suggested she wear.

They spent the next hour as Daria showed her around the JMA and introduced her to every girl they met. All seemed genuinely pleased to meet her, and most offered to help. *This is strange*, Penny thought, *a stranger offering to help. Was this just a big put-on or were they sincere?* Penny could not explain it, but deep down inside, she believed they really meant it.

Penny overheard one girl talking about the horses and began a conversation with her. Two other girls joined them as they talked. A little later Penny was aware that Daria had slipped away. Now Penny was on her own, but she did not feel threatened. She felt as if she were among friends.

A little later Penny excused herself and made her way to Mrs. Witherspoon's office. The door was open; in fact, she could not remember a door that was not opened. She knocked softly on the door jam, and without looking up, Mrs. Witherspoon said, "Please come in." She looked up to see Penny standing in the doorway and seemed pleasantly surprised.

"Mrs. Witherspoon, I came to apologize for being so rude," Penny said and waited for her to respond. Mrs. Witherspoon looked at Penny, smiled, but said nothing. Penny waited, but Mrs. Witherspoon just stared at her. A deep hurt begin to build inside Penny, and she said, "Mrs. Witherspoon, I am sorry." Her voice was almost breaking as she turned to go.

"Thank you, Miss Sanderson. Please wait," she said in a soft and forgiving voice. She arose, came to Penny, and held out her hand. Penny took one of her hands, but Mrs. Witherspoon held onto one hand and grasped the other. "Penny, a lesson in life is that almost anyone can apologize for their actions, but it takes a person who really means it to say they are sorry. Saying they are sorry shows a person is sincere and honest and that they do, in fact, really mean it. I accept your apology because I know you mean it."

She walked back to her desk, motioned to a chair, and said, "Penny, will you please have a seat?"

Penny sat down and Mrs. Witherspoon continued. "I want you to know that my door is always open. If there is anything I can help you with, please ask. In fact, I live here on the grounds, and my house is also open. You will also notice that not one door here at JMA is ever closed. Everyone is available to help you make the transition from a bad situation to a productive one. I believe you are now on the way towards that, and I think you will learn to enjoy your stay with us."

She sat on the side of her desk and continued, "Penny, once a student conforms to our dress code, she is allowed to leave her room. Now that you are properly dressed, you are invited to attend an orientation meeting this afternoon. Here student counselors will explain the numerous rules and regulations, some you will think unnecessary, but we have been observed by presidents, diplomats, professors, and many others. What we do here is a model for other institutions. All of our regulations are to help our students, not discipline them, and if there is discipline involved, your fellow students will be the ones that discipline you." She paused, looked intently at Penny, and continued, "There are numerous activities our students enjoy and are free to participate in after they finish their classwork and chores. Your classwork is basically the same as what you had in your own school and is approved by the Texas State Board of Education. Dell has graciously given us computers programmed for grades one through twelve for each student. A class on how to use the computer is available for anyone who needs it. Each computer is password protected, and you are free to keep a personal diary or other personal information on it. Also, certain programs are available from the Internet, but, as of now, you will be denied access to some. However, as you progress through our programs, more will be granted until you have full access. All this will be explained to you in more detail this afternoon. Also, when you leave JMA, the laptop is yours to take with you."

She walked around her desk and sat down. "Do you have any question?"

"Mrs. Witherspoon, Daria and I talked a lot last night. She filled me in on a lot of things and said one of my chores might be with the horses. I love horses. Would that be possible?"

"It certainly would. In fact, our new arrivals always get their first choice of chores. Of course, you will have to rotate your duties, but once your classwork and chores are complete, you are free to spend as much time with the horses as you like. You can go riding any time there is a horse available."

She paused and studied Penny for a long moment before adding, "Penny, you have a special girl for a roommate. Daria has had a rough life, but has adjusted to life here. I hope you will confide in her. Her time here is almost up, but she has petitioned the board to stay another six months to counsel other girls. I think the board will agree to let her stay."

"Mrs. Witherspoon, I agree with you about Daria. Even though we had only a short conversation last night, I like her, and I believe we will become close friends."

Penny thanked Mrs. Witherspoon and left her office. *This place might not be so bad after all,* she thought, and realized she felt better now than at any time since the news of her father's death. She could hardly wait to tell Daria her own story.

Daria's petition to stay another six months was approved, and during the next two months Daria and Penny became very close friends. Penny studied hard, did her chores, even the kitchen chores, and never complained. She soon learned to enjoy life at JMA and looked forward to the group sessions, although she was sometimes shocked at the stories she heard. Some girls had sheltered lives, like hers, and some were used and abused, like Daria. She learned it did not matter if a person was rich or poor; each had problems and was learning to accept them.

After three months her conduct and attitude were such that Amos, Marie, and her mother came for a visit. Penny cried and apologized numerous times for what she had done. She could not believe she had once forgotten just how much she loved them, and she deeply regretted that she had caused them so much grief.

Penny introduced them to Mrs. Witherspoon and to a lot more of the friends she had made. She told them how her roommate Daria had been abused as a child, and how she taken Penny in and cared for her when she first came here. "She is my best friend and like a big sister to me, even though she is younger than I am."

Penny's mother and grandparents were impressed, not only with her other friends and Mrs. Witherspoon, but also with JMA. So much so, Penny knew her mother and grandparents would contribute heavily to the operation of JMA in the future.

It was then she decided to ask her mother and grandparents to sponsor Daria to finish high school and college, and on to medical school since Daria's dream was to be a pediatrician. This way they could say thanks to JMA and to Daria; each had changed her life, probably even saved it. Immediately, they agreed and went to tell Daria of their decision.

They found Daria sitting on a pier by the lake; she was alone. It was then that Penny realized this was Visitors Day, and no one had come to visit Daria. As Daria looked out across the dark green water in the lake, Penny knew it must have seemed sad to Daria. Penny embraced her, saying she would always be her friend and would never let her be alone again.

After Penny introduced Daria to her mother and her grandparents, Penny told her about the scholarship they had agreed to give her. Daria stood in shock, looking first at each of Penny's relatives, then back at Penny, not knowing what to say.

"You're kidding! No one would do that!" Daria stared in disbelief as they nodded their heads. Knowing it was not a joke, she burst into tears, tears that flowed down her cheeks and fell to the ground. A lot of tears. . . happy tears. Penny and her family embraced Daria and promised not only to be her friends, but her family. She would come and live with them when she was released from JMA. Penny explained to her family that Daria was staying here only because she wanted to help the other kids and that she received no pay for doing it.

The next three months flew by in a flash. Mrs. Witherspoon arranged for Daria to leave JMA when Penny did. They came home to Longview, and Daria stood in awe of the big house, the barn, all the other buildings, even a heliport. Daria was treated no differently than Penny and was an equal member of the family. She finished both high school and college. After college, Penny went to grad school at the University of Texas, and Daria to Baylor College of Medicine. Although one was in Austin and the other in Waco, they spent almost every weekend with each other. They were the closest of friends, always thankful for their devotion to each other.

Daria could hardly believe it—from an abused child to this lavish lifestyle—yet she tried not to allow this to lessen her desire to help others. She was constantly reminding herself, *you are just Daria, no better and no worse than anyone else.*

CHAPTER SEVEN

MINA
Seventeen seventy-three

Gee watched his mother and the girl walk to the house. At the door the girl stopped, unsure whether to go farther. Gee could only think what must be going through her mind and how afraid she must be. This was probably the first time she had seen a white person's house; he could understand her fear of going inside one. He heard his mother speaking softly to the girl, not loud enough for him to hear what she was saying. For whatever the reason, the girl reluctantly nodded her head and entered the house, stopping in the doorway to look back at him. He smiled at her.

As Gee walked his horse to the barn, he wondered what the neighbors would say when they learned an Indian girl lived with them. After all, his father had been killed by the Indians, and he had heard the saying, "The only good Indian is a dead Indian." Why, then, did he bring her home with him? Why had he not just ridden on by and left her? He did not know the reason. He only knew he could not have done that.

He removed the saddle from his horse and rubbed him down with an old curry comb and gave him some corn and hay. He patted the horse on the neck as it nuzzled his ears. He stood combing the horse's mane, but his mind was on the Indian girl and his mother. There was so much they needed, and they barely had enough food to last through the winter. They had a little corn, which they could crush into meal, some dried peas, beans, a few potatoes, and a milk cow. They had no meat, but that would not be a problem. He could hunt for deer, rabbit, and turkey, but still they would have little to eat, especially if the winter was severe. Why then, did he bring home another mouth to feed? *And what are we going to do with her? Maybe we can find her village, or maybe we can find someone else who will take care of her.*

Gee asked himself these questions, but had no answers. The more he thought about it, the more confused he became. He was torn between whether he should have left her or brought her here, as he had finally decided. Maybe if he had left her, someone—one of her family, perhaps, or someone else—would have found her. Deep down inside, however, he knew this was not true. She had been so weak she could not have defended herself, especially without a weapon. He knew if he had not brought her with him, the wolves would have torn her to pieces before morning.

I guess I did the right thing, Gee convinced himself as he gave the cows some corn, picked up the milk bucket, and began to milk one of them. The other one did not need to be milked; she was going to have a calf soon. Gee hoped it would be a heifer because they could sell a heifer for more money than a bull. With the money from a heifer and the money he planned to make trapping, maybe this spring they could buy a horse. *Or, maybe we can trade the girl for a horse.* Even as he thought that, he felt a deep shame inside for even thinking such a thing and did not understand the feeling he got when he thought of the girl. He also knew his mother would not stand for it. They would starve before she would allow him to do that. So, to rid his thoughts of the girl, he wished for a lot of snow high up in the mountains. That would force the animals to come down and make hunting and trapping much easier. *Yes, a lot of snow is what we need to help us get a horse.*

Gee realized he had stopped milking when the cow switched her tail and lashed him across the face. He placed her tail in the bend of his knee and began milking again, but his mind was still on a horse. They had to have a horse; their existence depended on it. No way could they make another crop with only one horse. They had tried this year; it had almost worked them to death and they had little to show for it. One horse could pull the turning plow, but he had to plow shallow and turn the earth in small strips of dirt, so it took him twice as long to plow the field. The wagon and other equipment—a middle buster, a disk, and harrow—were for two horses and were of no use with a single horse. Without another horse to pull the wagon, all their crops and firewood had to be carried by hand, which was backbreaking labor and time consuming. Even the supplies from the trading post had to be carried on horseback, which meant two or three trips compared to one trip with the wagon.

    He finished milking and made his way towards the house as the sun slid slowly behind the mountains. The sounds of whippoorwills, katydids, and frogs sang as a few cotton candy clouds drifted leisurely overhead. A full moon was rising above the treetops. Gee thought how peaceful everything was, but couldn't stop wondering how long it would last. He had an uneasy feeling that the events of today would forever change their lives.

    He hesitated at the cabin door when he heard his mother talking in a low, soothing voice, but not loud enough for him to understand what she was saying. He opened the door and saw the Indian girl sitting on the side of the bed. She was wearing a pair of his overalls with a blanket draped over one shoulder and around her chest, the ends tied together at her waist. She held a cloth over one side of her face, covering a split lip and a black eye. His mother was patiently cleaning the wound on her shoulder with a white cloth and warm, soapy water.

    The girl watched him as he set the pail of milk on a table. He saw her gazing intently at it, and he knew she was either thirsty or hungry, maybe both, but was too afraid or too proud to ask. He reached into a box at the end of the table, took out a glass, filled it, and offered it to her. She looked at the glass, at his mother, and back at him, and shook her head. Gee put the glass close to his mouth, pretended to drink, offered it to her once more, pointed a finger at her, and nodded his head. The girl looked at him and then at his mother. When his mother smiled and nodded her head, the girl took the glass, smiled faintly, and drank until the glass was empty. Gee took the glass and intended to pour her another one, but his mother shook her head and said, "Maybe you should wait until supper."

The girl, not understanding what his mother had said, dropped her head, probably thinking she had done something wrong by drinking the milk. It was very plain that she was grateful and that she did not want to do anything that would displease them. He wondered how long it had been since she had eaten or had anything to drink. His mother had also seen the girl's reaction and motioned for Gee to give her another glass of milk. She drank this glass a little slower, looked at Gee and at his mother, and smiled, "*Wado.*" Gee and his mother could only speculate, but knew it probably meant, "Thank you."

His mother finished cleaning the three-inch long cut that ran from the back of her shoulder to her collarbone. It was not a deep cut, but would probably leave a scar. When his mother finished with the bandage, she asked the girl if she was hungry. The girl looked at her with questions in her eyes. His mother, realizing the girl did not understand, pointed at the table. The girl did not move, and his mother walked to the table and patted the log bench. The girl got up, pulled the blanket tightly over her wounded shoulder, came and sat down on the bench.

A fire was burning in the fireplace with two black, iron kettles hanging on a steel rod about a foot above the flames. The rod extended from one side of the fireplace to the other. A frying pan sat on two metal rods anchored about six inches beneath the kettles. Another pan and a fire poker hung on nails besides the hearth.

Mrs. Gilmore walked to the fireplace and removed the lid from one of the kettles. With a large wooden spoon she dipped beans into a wooden bowl and set it in front of the girl. She filled two more bowls, took a plate of cornbread from the top of the mantel, and set it on the table with three glasses of milk. She said a short prayer and crumbled cornbread into her bowl as the girl watched.

She motioned for the girl to eat, but the girl did not move, just stared at the bowl for a few seconds, still watching Mrs. Gilmore carefully. After watching Gee crumble cornbread into his bowl, she slowly crumbled cornbread into her bowl and began eating with her fingers. She looked at Gee and at his mother and saw they were both using a spoon. Gee realized that this embarrassed her. She picked up a spoon and turned it over and over as she studied it. She began eating with the spoon, awkwardly at first, but soon managed to finish her bowl and drink her milk. She looked at the kettle, and Mrs. Gilmore refilled her bowl again. "*Wado*," the girl said, which they would later learn, was, indeed, "Thank you" in her language. Gee and his mother knew she had been very hungry and wondered how long it had been since she last ate.

After supper Mrs. Gilmore washed the bowls and spoons in a pan of water sitting on a table near the fireplace. She took the kettle of beans, placed a cast iron lid on top, and asked Gee to take it outside and hang it up on the side of the house where the bears could not reach it. "It is cool enough that the beans will not spoil, and we can have them tomorrow," his mother told him.

Gee walked outside, took a long stick standing next to the house, lifted the kettle up, and hung it on a nail about three feet above his head, hoping the bears would not climb the wall to reach it. He walked over and sat down on a log bench next to the hitching post. He listened to the whippoorwills' chant of '*chip-fell-outta-white-oak*', and thought of the girl, still wondering if she would cause them trouble with their neighbors. Also, he feared that the Cherokee might think he had kidnapped her if they found out she was there. He only hoped they would inquire about her before they attacked; then the girl could tell them the truth.

He watched a falling star light up the darkening sky and wondered if this was a good omen or a bad one. *Well, whichever, we'll just have to deal with it.* He was startled when his mother laid her hand on his shoulder.

"I guess you have lost your bed. You will have to sleep in the loft until we find her people." She stood looking at the distant mountains, as if wondering where the girl's people might be. "I hope we can find them. I just don't think it would be wise for us to let her stay here. Our neighbors will be furious with us, not to mention what the Indians might do when they find out."

"I know, Mom. I have been thinking the same thing, but we will figure something out. I just couldn't leave her," he said as he heard the cabin door open. In the lamplight they saw the girl looking at them, the blanket wrapped tightly around her and fear once again in her eyes. Both realized the girl thought they were planning to send her away.

Mrs. Gilmore waved for the girl to come and patted the log for her to sit. The girl came over, sat down between them, and pointed to another falling star, saying only, "*Nvda.*"

Mrs. Gilmore did not know what she had said, but decided it must mean falling star. She put her arms around her and said to no one in particular, "I feel so sorry for her. She has been thrown into a world she knows nothing about. We are strangers, and she cannot understand what we are saying. I just can't imagine how scared she must be." They sat outside until darkness forced them inside.

Mrs. Gilmore turned the bed covers down on the bed across from her own, pointed to the girl and to the bed. She smiled and gave the girl a sign by laying her head on her arms and closing her eyes. The girl understood, came over and sat on the side of the bed. Mrs. Gilmore took off her moccasins, gently pushed the girl onto her side and covered her with a blanket. Gee climbed the ladder to the loft and lay down on the burlap mattress as his mother blew out the candle and called good-night.

He lay in the darkness, his mind cluttered with the events of the day. From the floor below him he heard the girl sobbing softly, and a short time later, his mother's soft and tender voice soothing her. He decided he liked to sleep up here and was proud to let the girl have his bed. It had been a long and stressful day; soon Gee fell asleep.

It seemed as if he had just gone to sleep when the rooster crowed, and he remembered how he had once hated the rooster. He arose and climbed down only to find the girl not in her bed. He feared she had left during the night. *If she has, that would solve a lot of our problems,* he thought, but immediately regretted it. He knew he did not want her to leave. He opened the door, walked outside, and was relieved to see her sitting on the bench. Walking over to where she was, he sat down beside her. She looked at him with a faint smile on her face. Even in the dim light of dawn, he was reminded of how pretty she was and how good it was to see she was not afraid of him anymore. He held out his hand and smiled at her. She hesitated, but laid her hand in his. They sat without talking until the sun began peeking through the trees. They watched the sunrise until his mother came to the door and summoned them inside to eat flapjacks and red-eye gravy.

It was a little after sun up when Gee finished his breakfast and went to the barn to do his chores. He fed the horse and gave the cows some hay and a little corn. He was milking the cow when he got the feeling someone was watching him. He turned and saw the girl.

"Do you want to?" but he did not finish for he knew she did not understand. *We have got to learn to communicate with her,* and he began thinking of ways to do it. He patted the cow on the flank, and, pointing to the cow and then to his mouth, he said,

"Cow." He said it again, pointing to the cow. "Cow," he said once more.

She looked at him, pointed to the cow, and said, "*Wa-ga.*" "*Wa-ga. . .* cow," Gee repeated.

"Kow." She pointed to the cow again and smiled.

After he finished milking, they did the same with the horse, the pigs, and the chickens. She was amused, and Gee could tell she was eager to continue. They took the milk to the spring and began with it, continuing with the barn, wagon, smokehouse, house, and even the outdoor toilet.

"This is the toilet. Toil-et," he said again.

She was curious about the toilet, a small structure made with split logs leaning against a tree. They went inside, and Gee had trouble conveying its purpose to her. Finally, he sat down on the two logs lying next to each other with a portion of the log chopped away to make a hole. He sat down and strained as if to do his thing, removed some cotton from a bucket, and pretended to wipe his rear.

"Totltet." She blushed and walked away, giggling softly.

During the next few days they explored more words—beans, potatoes, corn, pots and pans—anything he could make reference to. She was learning English, and he was learning Cherokee. Mrs. Gilmore soon joined them, and each of them had fun learning to speak a new language. It wasn't long before they could communicate with each other in a mixture of English and Cherokee. They learned that her name was *Mina*, and that it meant "precious stone."

Within a short time Mina became comfortable with them and seemed to enjoy her new way of life. The interaction between Mina and his mother was good, especially for his mother. Since the deaths of his father and Jimmie, Gee knew his mother had been hurting. She needed time to get her mind off what had happened, and Mina was filling a big hole in their lives. It was good to come home to the laughter of his mother and

Mina

Mina exploring new words. He especially looked forward to the mornings when they sat outside on the bench and held hands as they watched the sunrise. These were happy times—the best times he could remember since the deaths of his father and Jimmie. The only thing that could make it better was for them to get a horse.

The snows came early, and Gee did well with his trap line. He had taken deer and turkey for their meat, and mink and otter to trade. They had plenty to eat, and the cow gave birth to a heifer. Now, he was sure they had enough to trade for a horse, and he needed to do that before the winter was over. Afterward, the price of a horse would be much higher. Not having horses to pull the wagon was a big problem. He had no way to get the calf or the furs to the trading post. Maybe he could explain this, and the trader might lend him a horse to bring in his goods. If not, he would have to get the trader to come here, but that would mean he would get less for the furs and the calf.

Maybe their neighbor, Coleman Grimes, who lived about a half mile away, would lend him a horse. Gee expected he would, but really did not want to ask. He was a grouchy old man who lived alone, and he would be Gee's last choice. However, he decided that one way or the other they would have a horse before spring. Yes, everything was looking good, really good. It seemed that Mina had brought them good luck. Little did he know how much their lives were going to change because of her.

CHAPTER EIGHT

ELAINE
Twenty Ten

Before Penny, Elaine, and Simmons finished their meal, a waiter handed Penny a note. She looked at it and said, "Of course." Seconds later two people came into the dining room. Simmons could see they were concerned about Penny. After hugs, Penny introduced them to Simmons.

"My grandfather and grandmother, Amos and Marie Gilmore." She pointed to each as she spoke. "This is Mitchell Simmons, Lanny's Army buddy."

"It is a pleasure to meet you. We came in after the excitement, sorry to say. Thank you for standing up for her. It seems like she is always finding ways to entertain the guests, so to speak," Amos said as they shook hands. He turned to Penny and asked what had happened.

"Bradley said he didn't like the way I was dressed, but I think the real reason was Mitchell. I believe he hates anyone in a military uniform."

"From what I hear, I bet he hates them more now," Amos chuckled. "We will discuss Bradley later." He acknowledged Elaine, who was chatting with Mrs. Gilmore, and put his hand on Simmons' shoulder. "Why don't you and the girls come to our house after we finish?"

Simmons wondered if this was an invitation or an order. He looked at Penny, who looked at Elaine and said, "We are riding with Elaine, so it's up to her." Elaine nodded in agreement.

As they drove towards Mr. Gilmore's house, Simmons was questioning himself about getting involved in all of this. All he had wanted to do was visit Lanny and go back to the base. Life at the orphanage and at the Army was all he had ever known. He did not understand family ties, especially rich families. As he thought about this, he realized he had known these people fewer than eight hours, yet for some reason he was drawn to them—and it had nothing to do with Penny and the Gilmores being wealthy. He did not understand how Elaine fit into their circle until he remembered Elaine had told him Lanny and Penny had been engaged. Still, his gut feeling told him he was getting into something he knew nothing about, that things were moving much too fast. He felt he owed it to Lanny to find out what had happened. *At least I will try*, he vowed to himself.

They turned into a driveway which he presumed was the Gilmores, and he saw two oil well rigs, neatly enclosed by white picket fences, their long arms rising and falling. He fully expected to see a mansion, maybe even more elaborate than Penny's house in Longview, but even in the light of a half moon, all he saw was a modest ranch house.

The Gilmores pulled in behind Elaine's car, walked them to the door, and welcomed him to their home. They did not mention Elaine, which meant that she had been here before. Mr. Gilmore offered him a glass of wine, which he accepted. They thanked him again for aiding Penny, and made small talk about where he was stationed and how long he had been in the Army. The conversation eventually drifted to Arnold Bradley and the events of that night. Simmons listened as Penny recounted the details, and it was easy to see Mr. Gilmore was enraged, even though he tried to hide his emotions. They agreed they would meet with Penny's mother on Monday and decide what to do about Bradley. There was more small talk which Simmons felt was largely intended to make him feel at ease—and, to his surprise, he was.

Elaine

About forty-five minutes later they said goodnight, and Mr. and Mrs. Gilmore made Simmons promise he would visit again. As they drove back to Penny's house, Simmons asked if they could drop him off at a motel. To which, Penny replied with mild indignation, "No way! Our house has seven bedrooms, and there is a guest house, too."

They drove without saying very much. It seemed as if each of them was entranced by their own thoughts. Simmons knew he was. After arriving at Penny's, they had a couple of drinks and. . . maybe the alcohol had taken some of the edge off. . . because they relaxed and discussed the events of the night. They had a good laugh when Penny described the look on Bradley's face as he skidded across the dining room floor.

Later, Simmons was led up a beautiful spiral stairway with magnificent teak wood handrails to a lavish bedroom at the top of the stairs. He had just gotten out of the shower when he heard a light tap on his door. He opened the door, and Elaine quickly slipped past him into the room. He was shocked and stood staring at her as he closed the door behind her. Her hair was wet, and she wore a white robe tied tightly around her waist.

He stood in disbelief, his mouth open. He had not expected this, not in a million years. He looked at her and noted how nice she looked. *There is that word again*, he thought.

"Oh! I did not come in here to crawl into your bed, so you can relax." She smiled, knowing that he was wondering if that was the reason she was here. "I wanted to talk to you earlier, but never found the chance." She walked over and sat down on the side of the bed. He could not move; she was not only nice, she was gorgeous. She was sensuous, and he could tell she was so very much a woman, a beautiful woman with wet hair. He wanted to tell her that in less than a day, he was in love with her, but he could only stare.

"Could I call you Mitch? I will let you call me Lain," she teased.

He nodded, still unable to talk, his mind exploding with thoughts of holding her in his arms, or maybe just touching her, seeing if she was really sitting on his bed. Never before had he felt this way. In fact, sometimes he had wondered if something was wrong with him. He had never been really interested in girls, but the fact that he was not interested in boys made him feel a little better. He had seen a lot of gays in the military and did not understand why someone preferred a person of the same sex.

"This was some day. Laughter, tears, fighting. . . What do you think?" she asked.

He looked at her and finally managed to say, "I think Lanny was right. You are a special girl, very nice and very pretty. I can see why Lanny is,. . ." he paused, "*was* so proud of you. He had every right to be."

"I am not talking about me. I want to know what you think of all this. I mean, I think you are getting involved in something you know nothing about, and I wonder if you really want to do that. What do you think you can accomplish?" There was a little sarcasm in her voice as she continued. "Lanny is gone, and nothing will bring him back. I think there are some powerful people here and things simmering just below the surface, about ready to explode. I think Lanny tried to find out what those things were, and I believe that is the reason he is dead. In the morning, why don't you just head back to your Army, and I'll go back to my classroom? I am afraid something will happen to you—to us—if you stay." She looked at him, and he could see a little displeasure in her sea green eyes.

Simmons thought about what she had said, and after a long silence, he replied, "I like Elaine better than Lain." He looked at her and wished he could take her in his arms and assure her that everything will be fine. Instead he said, "Elaine, Lanny once saved my life, and I cannot tuck my tail between my legs and run simply because I might get hurt. I've faced getting hurt the last eight years of my life, and my life would not be worth living if I ran. Maybe I am getting into something I know nothing about, and maybe I will get hurt, or hurt someone else, but I owe it to Lanny to find the truth. I promise, though, that I will do everything I can to see that nothing happens to you, to Penny, or her family." He paused and looked at the door. "I have two weeks of leave, and I am not heading back to 'my Army' until I get some answers."

"Have it your way. I had to try, but don't worry about me. I've been taking care of myself for a long time." She stood and walked toward the door.

"You can stay a while longer."

"Oookay," she smiled, stepped outside, and quietly closed the door.

Simmons slumped onto the bed; he was shaking. Never before had a girl made him feel so weak. . . so, so, something, he really didn't know what. He sat staring at the door. *What has happened to me? Is this real or am I dreaming?* He laid his head on the pillow, trying to understand his feelings. Hours later he drifted off to sleep with images of a girl with wet hair and wearing a white robe, swirling in his head.

His internal clock woke him at 6 a.m. He showered and shaved, decided he would wear civilian clothes today, but remembered his duffel bag was still in the trunk of Elaine's car. He dressed in yesterday's slightly wrinkled uniform, slipped downstairs, and followed the sound of voices. He found Penny sitting at a bar in the kitchen, talking to the housekeeper. She introduced him to Rosa and motioned for him to join her.

He acknowledged Rosa, who smiled and asked if he would like some coffee. He nodded and sat down at the table.

"Yesterday was quite a day, wasn't it?" Penny said, and smiled.

Rosa arrived with the coffee; Simmons thanked her, turned to Penny, and nodded, "Yes, it's like Elaine said—laughter, tears, and fighting."

He saw that Penny was trying to recall when Elaine had said that so he told her they had talked a little when they went upstairs. Penny looked at him, and he felt she could sense that he was interested in Elaine. After several long seconds she continued, "Elaine is a great person; she is intelligent, rational, and does not get flustered easily. She was the most popular girl in school, but even though we were in the same grade, we were not friends. I admit that I was jealous of her because she was always in the news, on TV, or in the papers. Even for a town as big as Longview, everyone knew who she was. She was Miss Longview, the homecoming queen, Miss Longview High. Miss Everything, yet she never let it go to her head. All the boys wanted to date her, but her life was basketball."

Penny sipped her coffee. "Mitchell, I wish you could have seen her play. She was a Lisa Leslie and a Michael Jordan in one package. She was quick as a cat and could run like a deer. She played in college until she got hurt, but went on to get her masters and is now teaching history and coaching girls basketball in Texarkana." She sipped her coffee once more and studied Simmons. "Elaine and I became friends when Lanny and I began seeing each other.

Now we are close friends. No, we are closer than that; we are like sisters. She has helped me get through some bad times." She paused, and Simmons could see the hurt in her eyes. He watched as she pushed memories aside, and her mood lightened. "We are going to Dallas today and to the Cowboys game tomorrow. Will you come with us? To protect us, of course. Maybe we can find some more fights and laughter, but we'll leave the tears here." She paused, "I would love for you to come with us, and I am sure Elaine would also."

Simmons shook his head slowly and said, "Penny, I am just a member of the Armed Forces, and I make Armed Forces wages. I accepted your hospitality last night and never really got the chance to thank you, so I'm thanking you now, but I have always paid my way or I did not go." He looked around the kitchen at the double oven stove, stainless steel refrigerator, marble counter tops with gold-plated faucets, and teak wood cabinets, as if to make a point. "I have saved most of my paychecks, and one day, since I have no family, I plan to retire and sit on some isolated beach in the South Pacific watching the sun rise and set. The only thing I plan to do is turn my chair around at noon." He smiled and looked at Penny. "So, I do thank you for the offer, but I can't go."

Penny considered this, changed the subject, and asked him how many days he had on leave.

"Twelve days, but I have some duty-free time built up, if needed." He thought about this and added, "Before I go back, I want to see if I can find out what really happened to Lanny. It's like I told Elaine, I don't believe he killed himself. We were close, and he saved my life once. I feel I owe it to him to find the truth."

They heard footsteps on the stairway, and soon Elaine came into the kitchen. She had a towel wrapped around her wet hair and was wearing white, knee-high walking shorts with a pale green blouse.

Simmons caught his breath. She was one sexy woman, tall with a beautiful figure. How was a woman this special still single? The only thing he could think of was there must be a bunch of dumb and blind Texans around here.

Penny saw how he was looking at Elaine and said to herself, *If Elaine wants him to go to Dallas, he will go. In fact, I think no matter what Elaine wants, he'll do it. He doesn't know it yet, but he belongs to Elaine—that is, if she wants him to, and I hope she does. I think it would be good to have him around.*

Penny and Simmons said good morning, and Rosa brought more coffee. Elaine thanked her and smiled at Simmons and at Penny. Simmons could not utter a single word. *What is wrong with me*? he asked himself.

When his head finally cleared, and he was able to comprehend what was happening, he heard Penny and Elaine discussing the trip to Dallas. Penny suggested they take the company plane, but Elaine was trying to convince her they would enjoy driving since the fall colors were so pretty. Penny finally agreed and said she had invited Mitchell, but he had given her some poor excuse for not going. "He thinks he is excess baggage, Elaine. Why don't you try and convince him to come with us?"

"Oh, come on, Mitchell, we can't be that bad, can we?" Elaine teased.

"Elaine, Penny will tell you why I cannot go." He waited a few seconds for Penny to fill her in. When she did not, he continued, "I would like for you to take me into town so I can rent a car. Look, I am convinced that Lanny did not kill himself, so that means someone killed him. If I can find out why, then I will be more likely to find out who.

I'm no detective, but in the Army I've learned if you start asking questions, people get nervous, and nervous people tend to make mistakes."

Penny and Elaine looked at each other and back at him. They said nothing for a long time. Penny finally asked, "Why do you think someone killed Lanny?"

"It's like I told Elaine. I just know it; I would bet my life on it. We saw too much death in Afghanistan. We picked up bodies and body parts, and Lanny hated it. He would never kill himself and leave his body for someone to take care of it. If he were going to kill himself, he would have done it where his body would never be found. We were together almost every minute for four years, and I know him. He did not take his own life. He didn't."

There was a long silence as Penny and Elaine thought about what he said. It was Elaine who broke the silence. "Lanny was very happy and was looking forward to marrying Penny. Lanny and I were pretty close and if something had been troubling him, he would have confided in me. Neither Penny nor

I believed he killed himself, but I guess we were in so much grief, we took everyone's word for it and did not question them."

She brushed a tear from her eye, shook her head, and sat for a long time looking out an open window. No one said a word. Finally Elaine turned and faced Simmons. "You said you were going to find out about Lanny. Did you really mean it?"

Simmons nodded, and neither said a word as they contemplated what to say.

"My uncle, Johnny Bates, is Chief of Police here in Longview. He told me if I ever needed anything, just let him know." She looked at Simmons and Penny for a long moment before continuing. "I know Lanny's case was handled by the sheriff's department, but I can still ask him to help you. And there is Greg Davis, the deputy we saw yesterday. He was a friend of Lanny's, and I really think both of them had doubts about Lanny's death."

"My grandfather thought it was strange that there were no autopsy," Penny added, looking from Simmons to Elaine.

"Sheriff Otis Green handled the case and said there was no doubt Lanny killed himself. He said there was a note saying he intended to kill himself, but no one saw the note and no gun was ever found. The sheriff said some transits probably came by and took the note and the gun. Maybe a gun, but why would someone take a note? The sheriff had been in office for ages, and no one would dare question his authority. Doesn't matter I guess, because he was killed in a car accident up in Arkansas. Our new sheriff, Joe Evans, has been in office only a couple of years, so he would not know anything and would probably be no help." Penny got up and walked to the window. She stood staring out it a long time before she continued.

"My grandfather knows Judge Caldwell, and the sheriff is the judge's son-in-law. He might help us. I think my grandparents and my mother will also help. My mother is a regular Scooby-Doo."

"Whoa... whoa. I am not getting you two involved. If someone killed Lanny, he would not hesitate to kill again," Simmons said strongly.

"We can take care of ourselves," the two women said, almost in unison. Simmons could see how determined they were.

"Look! You two go on to Dallas. I will ask around and let you know what I find out when you get back."

"We are not going to Dallas," Penny offered sternly as she looked at Elaine for confirmation. Elaine nodded in agreement. "We are going to find out what happened to Lanny. Elaine and I have talked about this many times. We just needed someone to get it started," Penny continued.

"I'm with her. All we needed was a little push."

"But, what about Dallas? Look, go to the game and have fun. We can talk about this later," Simmons advised.

"We will go to Dallas when we find Lanny's killer," they replied, again almost in unison.

It was a long time before anyone said another word. Finally, seeing they were not going to Dallas, Simmons began searching mentally for a place he could start. He stared out the window and sipped his coffee. Finally he said, "Penny, I need to know who the two security men were at Manny's last night. One of them had a military background, and I would like to talk to him."

"The one that asked you to 'stand down' was Scott McTune. I know he was in the service. The other one was Carl. I don't know his last name, but my grandfather will. I will ask him when we meet Monday to discuss Bradley." She paused, "In fact, I am not waiting until Monday. I'm going to see my grandparents today."

"And I'm going to see Uncle Johnny," Elaine added.

Penny told Simmons there was a pick-up truck in the other garage, and it was his to use for as long as he wanted. Penny asked if he had a cell phone, but knew the minute she asked that he did not. Why would he? He has no family.

"I will pick up one on the way to see my grandfather; that way we can keep in touch. Elaine says she has to go back to Texarkana tomorrow night, but you can stay in the guest house. I will call Mother and give her a heads up that a good-looking man is living here," she said and smiled at Elaine.

"Well, I don't know about the good-looking man," Simmons said, and tried once more to persuade them to go to Dallas, realizing soon it was useless. They had their minds made up, and nothing was going to change them.

Well, the investigation into the death of Lanny Simpson has just begun, and I think it's long overdue, he thought. He didn't have a clue as to what would happen.

CHAPTER NINE

GILSAN OIL
Year: Nineteen Eighty

Amos, Marie, Anna, and Robert mounted their horses and rode slowly back to the house. When they arrived, Anna said that Robert and she would take care of the horses. She rubbed them down, fed them, and walked over to where Robert was sitting on a bale of hay. She sat down beside him, put her arms around him, and laid her head on his shoulders. Neither said anything for a long while. Finally, Anna spoke,

"Robert, you had no way of knowing that my father would probably rather be broke that to have this ranch ruined. He loves this place and has instructed us to bury him on that hill over there." She pointed to a high hill on the other side of the valley.

"Thanks Anna, but I should have confided in you before I said anything. The only excuse is that I got carried away thinking of oil, thinking of how my grandfather had given his life searching for oil. 'It's down there somewhere, and I'm going to find it,' he always said. And here I am, stumbling upon what could be the biggest oil boom in Texas history. I believe that. Everything I know, and everything I have been taught points to it." Robert paused and watched the horses make their way out to the pasture.

"Anna, I promise you, though, I will never ask, and I will never drill here unless your parents give me the okay. No. . . unless they want me to. But the point is, if there is oil here, here in this part of the country, someone will find it sooner or later."

"But Robert," Anna protested, but Robert cut her off.

"Anna, please hear me out. I think there is a fortune to be made here. I suppose it doesn't excite you, but I have been poor all my life and dreamed, I guess, along with my father and grandfather of hitting the big one, wondering why others had their wells come in, but we never did. Now I have a chance to hit my well, a chance to make it on my own, and if I don't, people will always wonder if I married you for your money." He stared at the hills Penny had pointed to and continued. "Now, like I said, I don't have to drill on your father's land, but I need financial help to purchase the drilling rights from the farms and ranches around here. If there is oil here on your father's land, there will be oil on other farms and ranches as well, maybe a lot of ranches. Like I said, if I don't find it, someone else will."

Anna did not say anything, but Robert could tell she was thinking about what he had said.

"Robert, what you said, 'If I don't, someone else will,' makes a lot of sense. I will talk to Mother, and she can talk to Daddy. If he is not interested, then I will help. I will receive a rather large endowment when I turn twenty-one."

Robert interrupted, "Anna, I couldn't. What if I am wrong and there is no oil? I cannot waste your money!"

"When we are married, Robert, it will be *us*. Not me, nor you. Not my money or your money, but *our* money.

So what if you are wrong? It will not be the end of the world. We will still have each other, and who knows? I might even like being blue collar. It seems to have made a good person out of you."

They sat on the bale of hay, not saying a word, just watching the horses as they grazed on the grass, just beginning to turn brown. They sat for a long time, each one deep in thoughts of what they should do before walking back to the house. As they came in, Mr. Gilmore greeted them with a smile and a glass of wine. "This is my water. Even Jesus thought wine was better than water, because he turned the water into wine," he said, trying to imitate Johnny Cash, and doing a pretty good rendition of it.

"Robert, Marie and I were thinking of going to Manny's. It is a private club that Manny Martinez and I built a few years ago. He has done a great job with it. He has a good live band and serves the best steaks in Texas." Holding up his glass and winking at Robert, he added, "And the wine is not bad either."

Robert appreciated his light mood and knew Mr. Gilmore was trying to cheer him up. *But I don't think he has completely forgiven me,* he thought. He looked at Anna, who nodded her head agreeably.

They went to Manny's where they ate, drank, and enjoyed the live music. Robert danced with Anna, but after a few dances, Mrs. Gilmore broke in, saying, "Anna, you will have to dance with your father. It is my turn to dance with Robert."

After the dance ended, Mrs. Gilmore kept Robert on the floor, saying she wanted to make Anna jealous. They danced to two more songs, one of which was a lively number which Robert thoroughly enjoyed. Mrs. Gilmore was a great dancer; she moved across the floor with amazing ease, as if she were on a carpet of warm, flowing air. He was not a very good dancer, but felt no one was watching him, only Mrs. Gilmore.

Later, when Amos and Marie got on the dance floor, he watched in awe, as did many other people. The other dancers and almost everyone in the dining room stopped to watch. It seemed every step was choreographed; they moved as one person, gliding across the floor like two people on ice. The lights dimmed and a spotlight illuminated Marie as she whirled, her long black hair, deep bronze skin, and dazzling white dress sparkling in the light. Soon, the entire dining room was applauding. Most had seen this before, but Robert had not and he was speechless.

They arrived home a little after midnight. As they walked into the den, Mrs. Gilmore put her arm around Amos. She looked knowingly at him, and he knew in an instant what she was going to say.

"It is late, and I think Amos and I will call it a night." She paused and turned to Anna, "Anna, you and Robert can sleep in your room or in the guest bedroom, whichever you prefer."

It was all she could do not to laugh as she watched them stop in their tracks and stare at her with open mouths. Neither knew what to say and only stared at her in disbelief. She slipped her arm around Amos's waist, gave him an inviting smile, and said, "And I will sleep with you." They walked down the hallway toward the bedroom.

Robert and Anna stood like statues and watched as she turned and smiled at them, then wiggled her hips as they made their way to the bedroom. Both Robert and Anna watched the bedroom door, as if thinking she might come back out and say she was joking. Finally Anna shrugged. "That was quite a performance," Anna said, looking at Robert.

"Was she serious?" Robert asked, still not believing what he had just heard. Anna pulled his head down and kissed him.

"I don't know about her, but I am," and led Robert to her bedroom.

At breakfast the next morning, Mr. Gilmore said, "Robert, Marie and I discussed the prospects of oil being found on our land, and since you will soon be a member of our family, we have decided to give you permission to pursue the matter as you see fit. Any capital you may need will be available. We will work out the details later."

Robert sat in disbelief. He was thrilled, but decided there were many things Mr. Gilmore should be made aware of. He hardly knew where to begin. He got to his feet and began by telling Mr. and Mrs. Gilmore he was flattered, but there were other ranches nearby that probably had oil. He did not want them to offer their land if they had any doubts whatsoever, and especially did not want them to offer it if they were doing it only for him.

"We have decided," Mr. Gilmore said, rather sternly.

Robert told them again how grateful he was and informed them that if at any time they were not pleased, they had the right to change their minds.

"Robert, we gave our word; we are with you all the way," Mr. Gilmore said, slightly annoyed.

"Okay," was Robert's only reply. He wondered how to tell them that his father would know what should be done, and he would love to have him there to help. He waited, choosing his words carefully.

"Before we began, I would like to ask if you would object if I had my father confirm what I suspect. He has a lot more experience in this than I do. If he agrees, I would like to have him do the preliminary work. He will know what equipment we will need, at least for now. There will be geological maps and surveys and some seismometer tests, which would require a little capital. After this, if things still look favorable, we can proceed, but we will need a sizable investment or credit line for the actual drilling."

He looked at each of them, making sure they were still in agreement. They were.

"Let's not get the cart before the horse because there are certain things that must be done first. Most importantly, we must keep a lid on this until we can acquire drilling rights. That's usually easy as long as the property owner understands we are only getting the right to drill. If we should find oil, he will be paid a percentage of what the well produces." He paused and looked at them. "Also, if we fail to get at least a third of the drilling rights, including some large tracts of property, a big oil company will gobble up all the leases and force us out as soon as they learn we have found oil. Also, we must know if the property owner owns the mineral rights to his property. In some cases, the mineral rights are separate from property ownership."

He paused, and looking earnestly at Mr. Gilmore, said, "Sir, again I am sorry that I brought this up, and again, I don't want you to think you must do this because of me. If you had rather not include your property, I will understand."

"Robert, I have included my property, but what if I had not? What would you have done then?"

"Sir. . ."

Before he could say another word, Amos interrupted, "Call me Amos or at least Mr. Gilmore. I hate the word sir."

"Yes, sir. . . I mean, yes, Mr. Gilmore." He paused and looked at Anna for help. She only shrugged her shoulders. "Okay, I don't mean to be blunt, but whether you did or did not include your property, I believe there is a lot of money to be made here. I think it is my duty to provide Anna with as much financial security as possible. I would not want her to think otherwise."

He hesitated and glanced toward Anna before continuing, "I think if Anna approved, I would proceed with obtaining the drilling rights for as many ranches as I could sign. If she did not approve, I would respect her wishes and offer the entire project to my father. Mr. Gilmore, if there is oil here, someone will find it sooner or later. I am sorry, but that is just the way it is." He sat down, and Anna slipped her hand into his, squeezing it hard.

Mrs. Gilmore broke the long silence that followed. "Amos, I think Robert is right. Someone will do it. I also believe that Robert thinks he should be the one in order to provide for Anna. I would think less of him if he did not strive to do that."

Mr. Gilmore was slightly annoyed by being cast as the only negative vote and said, "Robert, like I said, you have my permission, and I will provide the capital you need. I also welcome your father as a member of this. . . this adventure. I am sure his involvement will be useful. We will discuss the details later." To make sure the conversation was over, he said, "Now, I would like for you and Anna to attend church with us."

Robert searched his mind for an answer and finally came up with, "I would love to, but I did not bring anything suitable to wear to church."

"We go to a small church, and our dress is casual. I do not wear a suit myself."

"We have some men that wear blue jeans, and a lot of women who wear slacks," Mrs. Gilmore added.

After church they ate lunch, and before Robert knew it, it was time for him and Anna to leave. They said their good-byes, and Mr. Gilmore asked to be kept informed.

As they drove to Galveston, Robert wondered if he had made a huge mistake. *Maybe it would have been better if I had not come. What if we drill a bunch of dry holes? What if my father says I am wrong or that he will not help us? What will Anna think of me if all this blows up in our faces? If that happens, Mr. and Mrs. Gilmore will think I am some kind of nut.* All these concerns weighed heavily on him. Anna sensed this, but really did not know what to say. She snuggled close to him as he drove.

Once they reached Galveston, Robert called his parents. He talked with his mother, who informed him his dad was on an oil rig in the Gulf and would not be home until Friday. He explained to his mother about visiting Anna's parents and his belief there was oil there. He wanted his dad to take a look, and if he thought there was oil, to do the preliminary work so they could drill. He asked his mother to have his dad call if she talked to him before Friday.

Robert also asked about his sister, and his mother said she would be home for Christmas. "Why don't you bring Anna and join us?" she asked.

"We have talked about coming for either Thanksgiving or Christmas, so we will plan for Christmas, if Anna has no objection. We will be in touch. I love you." He hung up the phone.

"I guess you heard that. Do you think we could make it to Odessa for Christmas?'

"I think that would be wonderful. I will book us a flight, tomorrow."

They ordered a pizza and beer, watched a little television, and studied a while, but both were worn out and went to bed early.

Robert had a stressful night; he could not get the events of the past weekend out of his mind. It seemed too good to be true, and he kept thinking of that old saying "If it's too good to be true, it usually is." He awoke in the morning, feeling Anna snuggled very close to him, making him feel a little more certain of himself.

At school, he managed to get an appointment with one of his professors to discuss what he had found and how to create a company should they strike oil. There were so many questions he did not have the answers to, but his father would. He could hardly wait to speak to his father.

It was Friday afternoon before his father called, and Robert knew his mother had told him about the oil. He could tell his dad was excited. They talked for over an hour, mostly about oil wells, and agreed that his father should fly in tonight. They could take a look at the property tomorrow. Robert suggested that his mother also come since Anna would love to meet them and introduce them to her parents. His father said he would call and let him know when their flight would arrive in Houston.

Twenty minutes later he called to say they would be on Southwest flight 246, due to arrive at Hobby at 9:03. Anna called her parents and gave them a heads up that all of them would be in Tyler in the morning.

Robert and Anna picked up his parents at the airport, and Anna was attracted to them immediately, especially to Robert's father, Everett. He was tall, deeply tanned, and handsome. He had an easygoing personality and was joking with a fellow passenger when she first saw him. When he saw them, he did not wait for Robert to introduce her, but pulled her to him, hugged her tightly, then pushed her away at arm's length and said, "So this is what my granddaughter will look like. I love you already." He pulled her back into his arms and turned her to face Robert's mother. "This is Judy, the only woman I ever loved, except you." He squeezed her tightly. "Robert and I are the luckiest two men in the world. We have two beautiful women in our lives."

Anna extended her hand, but Judy brushed it aside and embraced her saying, "Anna, you are even prettier than Robert said you were. I think you are the girl I always envisioned that Robert would pick for his wife. Thank you for choosing him."

Judy was tall and trim, with blonde hair cut very short. She could have passed for a man, except for her pointed breasts that stretched the yellow sweater she wore. She had a small waist, and hips that perfectly fit her black Capri jeans. She was warm and friendly and had a pleasant, soothing voice. Anna could see a lot of Robert in her. Anna remembered other girls who said they despised their mother-in-law, but quickly decided she already loved hers.

They left the airport and drove toward Galveston. Robert and Everett sat in the front seat, talking non-stop about oil. Anna and Judy carried on a number of different conversations ranging from childhood, college, and nursing school to what they should wear tomorrow. Anna was amazed at how easy and interesting Judy was to talk to. Robert's parents were fantastic, but she worried about what they might think of her family. She knew her mother would like them and be overly nice, but was not so sure of her father. He could be a little difficult at times.

Anna felt very alone lying in bed by herself. She had convinced Robert they should sleep in separate rooms. It would make her more comfortable, at least until she became better acquainted with his parents. It was a long night, and she soon regretted making that request.

They left Galveston early the next morning, stopping at Hardee's to pick up a bacon, egg, and cheese biscuit. They arrived at the Gilmores' a little after ten and were greeted warmly by Anna's parents. It took only a short time before she knew Robert's parents and hers were going to enjoy each other. They had stopped before reaching Tyler, and Everett bought flowers for Marie. Anna did not know where her father had gotten the long-stemmed red rose he gave to Judy, but she was proud of her parents and of Robert's. They were getting along so nicely even Amos seemed pleased.

Kaysa came in and was introduced as the "Boss." She blushed slightly and turned on the charm for her guests, insisting she make breakfast for them. They convinced her they did not want breakfast, so she went into the kitchen, soon returning with a tray of appetizers, a bottle of wine on ice, and, of course, a glass of ice tea, even though it was still morning,

"This is for my boyfriend, Robert," she teased and winked at Judy. She informed them that lunch would be ready at noon. Everett kidded her about her needing his help because he was such a good cook and went into a monologue about how he could boil water without scorching it.

Marie and Judy were seriously discussing their flower gardens and soon Amos and Elliot were chatting about the Cowboys. In a whisper Anna suggested to Robert that they give their parents some time alone. They slipped outside and went to the barn.

Anna said hello to Dusty. Robert patted Roxio on the neck and gave her a sugar cube, an idea he had stolen from Anna the week before. They saddled the horses, led them to the house, and tied them to the hitching rail. They walked to the back of the barn where there was a Jeep Cherokee 4X4 under a shed, which Robert had not noticed before. Anna drove the Jeep to the house, parked it, went inside, and found both her parents and Robert's thoroughly enjoying each other.

After lunch Anna said she and Robert would ride their horses to the lake with the oily spring while the others took the

Jeep. She suggested that the ladies could inspect the wildflowers while the men looked at the spring, even though it was late fall and most of the flowers were dropping their leaves. She could not help but notice how excited Everett was to hear about the spring, and she could tell he was itching to go.

At the gazebo they chatted awhile before the men walked to the spring. Everett looked around with interest, knelt down, smelled the water, and rubbed it between his hands. He tasted it and said excitedly, "From what I see, I would bet my britches there is oil down there. I have no way of knowing for sure until we do more tests and drill a few holes." He asked Amos if he knew of other lakes like this one. Amos said there were two smaller ones on his property, and that he had seen some from the air that looked dark like this one, but could not remember exactly where they were.

Everett kidded Robert about sending him to school for years to learn how to find oil, and here he had stumbled upon a place that required no schooling. "Look at all that money I wasted," he said as they walked back to the gazebo.

Amos called for the ladies, who were looking at the wildflowers, and asked them to join them. He told them what Everett had said about "betting his britches that there was oil here."

"And that is his last pair of britches. He's already lost the others," Judy teased, prompting a laugh.

Back at the house, they began making plans to obtain drilling rights on other properties, each knowing they were embarking on something that, if successful, would forever change their lives. Everyone seemed excited except Amos, who still had reservations, though he would never admit it.

CHAPTER TEN

SAM STEWART
Seventeen seventy-three

It was late afternoon; the wind was howling, and it was snowing so hard Gee could see no more than thirty yards. He had no choice but to let his horse find his way home. The bandana tied around his head was frozen where his breath blew through it. He was thankful when he rode out of the timbers, knowing his cabin was near and he would soon be out of this bone-chilling cold.

As he neared the cabin, Mina came running out to greet him. She was waving her arms over her head, and he could see she was very excited. She stopped by his horse's side, pulled on his leg, and pointed toward the barn. She had a big smile on her face and flashed her big brown eyes.

"*So qui li,*" she said in Cherokee, and Gee knew it meant "horse." He looked at her and asked, "Where?"

She pointed at the barn again and said, "Barn." This time she spoke in English.

Gee dismounted, and Mina rushed to him, jumping up and down, and began brushing the snow from his clothes. She took him by the arm still jumping up and down, saying "*So qui li, So qui li,*" over and over. She pulled at him, wanting him to come quickly to see the horse.

Gee led his horse to the barn and put him in a stall. He looked at the other stall, and there before him was the worst looking horse he had ever seen. It looked like it had not eaten in a month. Gee could count every rib, and his hip bones protruded like cypress knees. The horse was devouring ears of corn, cobs and all, and paid no attention to Gee.

Mina slipped her arm around his waist and said excitingly, "Good *so qui li*, him hunge. Me give him *se-lu*. okay?" She looked at Gee for his approval. He put his arms on her shoulder and nodded his head as he continued to stare at the horse.

"Where did you get him?"

"I look; him stand by barn. *E tsi* say him no ours. That we no keep, but why we no keep? You talk to *E tsi*. We keep." Gee thought about what she had said, but knew his mother would not agree. He understood Mina knew how badly they needed a horse and why she could not understand why he was not our horse. It did not matter to her that it might belong to someone else. The horse was here, and in her culture it would be hers because she was the one who found it.

Gee inspected the animal and found no brand or earmarks. Some of the farmers branded their horses because the split rail fences were not very reliable. If they got out and wandered to another farm, the farmer would know whom the horse belonged to.

The horse had on a bridle, and Gee could tell he had worn a saddle a long time before it came off as almost all the hair was missing from its back. Gee saw shoes on his hoofs, so this was definitely a white man's horse, but where did he come from and why was he so underfed? A horse was a man's prize possession, and people usually kept them well-fed. Gee removed the bridle from the hungry animal and patted him on the neck. The horse was more interested in the corn, but seemed to be relieved to have the bit removed.

Gee unsaddled his own horse and rubbed the snow off. He gave him corn and hay and threw hay into the stall for the other horse, who he never stopped eating the corn.

Mina stood watching him. "*So qui li get Ga li tso hi da.*" Gee looked at her and asked, "What is *go lee tosh I da*?"

She thought about this, held her arms wide, and said, "Him get fat." Gee laughed and nodded his head. He took her hand and helped her through the knee-deep snow to the house. Gee's mother opened the door for them, and Mina looked at her and inquired, "*E tsi, we keep so-qui-li?*"

Gee's mother looked at Gee, shook her head, and said, "We will see. If someone comes and claims him, we will have to let him go."

"*So-qui-li*; we feed," Mina protested.

Gee and his mother looked at each other, knowing what she said was true. Each knew they agreed with her. It was only fair if someone claimed the horse that they should pay for the corn and hay it had eaten.

Gee took off his hat and duster, shook the snow off, and hung them on a wooden peg next to the door. He stood by the fireplace and warmed his hands, then turned his back and held his feet close to the fire, one at a time.

Mina brought a blanket, put it over his shoulders, and stood beside him. He could tell she was waiting for him to say they could keep the horse.

"*So qui li be me and U ni tsi* . We ride." Both Gee and his mother smiled, knowing that she wanted the horse because she knew how badly they needed one.

After supper Gee and his mother discussed the horse and what they should do about it. They agreed the next time Gee went to the trading post, he would ask if anyone was missing a horse.

"When you go to the trading post, I would like to come along. I think we should trade some of our furs so Mina can have some clothes, a coat, and a pair of shoes. She has been walking around in the snow wearing only moccasins and a pair of your overalls. She does enough work around here that I think she deserves them. I'd like to get them as soon as the snow melts."

Gee agreed, but said they would have to wait until the horse was strong enough to hitch to the wagon. His mother wanted to know when he thought that might be, and he realized how eager his mother was to get Mina some suitable clothing.

"Maybe in a couple of weeks, if we feed him well."

Mina was staring at them, not fully understanding what they were saying, but understood enough to know they were talking about her. Fearing they were talking about sending her away, she walked close and said,

"Me *a li he le s di*," she paused, seeing that they did not understand, so she tried again in English. "Me hoppee; no go way."

Gee's mother pulled her close, hugged her, and told her that she was not going away, and that they were going to buy her some clothes and shoes. Mina dropped her head, and Mrs. Gilmore could see the girl was thinking they did not approve of how she looked.

"You need to wear some girl clothes, a coat, and some shoes. As soon as the horse is able to pull the wagon, we will go to the trading post and get them for you," Mrs. Gilmore said and hugged her.

"Me hopee." Mrs. Gilmore explained to her that the right word was happy, and Mina said, "Me hapee."

Two weeks later, the snow was gone, the day was warm, and the sun was shining from a bright blue sky. They had named the other horse *So qui li* and had fed him twice a day. Now he was strong enough to pull the wagon.

When Gee tried to hook him to the wagon, he could tell the horse had never been hitched to a wagon before and did not like the collar or the harness. It took half an hour before the horse understood what he should do. Finally, he learned to walk beside the other horse and help pull the wagon. Gee made several circles around the barn getting So qui li accustomed to the wagon before loading mink pelts.

Mina sat on the wagon seat between Gee and his mother as they set out towards the trading post. Gee was nervous about using the horse. He was afraid someone might claim him or accuse Gee of stealing him. If the horse did belong to someone at the trading post, how would they get the wagon back home?

Well, I guess I'll deal with that when it happens, he said to himself.

They rode in silence, watching the birds and a deer that waved her tail up and down, stomped her foot, and snorted as they passed, but did not run away. When they reached the place where he had found Mina, he wondered if the red-haired man might be at the trading post.

If he is and tries to hurt Mina, I am going to beat the hell out of him. . . maybe even kill him, Gee thought.

Mina was sitting on the seat between them and, recognizing where they were, stood up and said, "Gi ga gel U s di ye gv man." Gee understood the word "red" and knew the other word must mean "hair." Mina made a motion like she was holding a knife and slashing his throat. Gee's mother put her arm around Mina and held her close, running her fingers through her long black hair.

"It's okay. No one will hurt you anymore."

They reached the trading post a little before noon. As they drew near, Gee saw two men watching them. He stopped the wagon in front of the store and watched as the two men walked toward the wagon. Gee did not know why, but he could see the hatred in their eyes and knew they wanted a confrontation. Both men were armed, so Gee laid a hand on his pistol.

"What ya doing with that squaw?" one of them jeered.

"She is not a squaw; she is just a child," Gee's mother said angrily.

"Well, ye'll git your squaw child outta here if'n ye know what's good fer ya. She's a stinking Injun, and no one wants to smell'em, or ya'll neither." He jeered and spit tobacco juice onto the ground.

"Yeh, take yore child and get outta here before we make a good squaw outta her," the second man said and both laughed.

"Yeh, dah only good Injun is a dead Injun," the first man added, and they both slapped their pants legs, laughing loudly.

"Did you think of that all on your own? If you did, you sure are one smart fellow," Gee asked, his voice ice cold.

The man stepped close to the wagon and sneered. "Are you making fun of me, boy? You damn squaw lover." He reached for Gee's leg to pull him from the wagon, but in one swift motion, Gee kicked him in the face.

Blood splattered over his boots as the man screamed and hit the ground hard on his back. He grabbed his face and rolled onto his stomach, moaning, blood gushing through his fingers from a busted nose and a broken jaw. Gee drew and cocked his pistol as it came from the holster and aimed it at the other man who was trying to get his pistol out of his belt. The man's hand froze when he heard the gun cock. Gee saw the fear in his eyes as he pointed the pistol between them and said, "Go ahead and try it."

The man glanced at the man on the ground and then all around him, as if looking for help. He had his hand on his pistol, but only glared at Gee and did not move. "Try it and you're dead." Gee said, briefly pointing his pistol at the man's hand and back at his chest.

The man took his hand off his pistol and slowly raised both hands above his head. "Pick him up and get out of here," Gee demanded

"Ye'll pay fer this. Ya shor gonna pay," the man said, his body shaking.

"If I do, you won't be around to see it. Now get outta here before I pull the trigger," Gee ordered and again aimed the pistol on a spot between the man's eyes. "I said get him up, and get out of here."

Gee's voice was icy cold, and the man knew he meant it. He quickly helped the other man to his feet and onto his horse. "Ya damned sho gonna regret this," and pointed his finger at Gee before riding away.

Gee told his mother to get what she needed from the store and tell Mr. Randolph to come and get the furs he needed for payment. "Right now, I will stay with the wagon." He picked up the musket and got down from the wagon, watching the two men to make sure they rode away from the trading post.

Gee's mother and Mina got down from the wagon and walked up on the porch of the trading post. Gee was surprised when Mr. Randolph, who had been standing on the porch, turned, went inside, and closed the door. Gee heard the door bar slide into place.

"I am closed!' Randolph yelled.

"Mr. Randolph, this is Audie Gilmore, and we need some things." "I am closed! Now go," he shouted from behind the door.

Mrs. Gilmore stood shocked, not believing he would not sell them anything and not quite knowing what to do. Gee was also confused and wondered why he had locked the door. Anger rushed over him, and he shouted, "Come on, Momma. We will go to Mooresville when the horse gets stronger. We don't need nothing he's got, anyway." But he knew it was a twenty-mile trip to Mooresville and back.

They rode home in silence, and he could feel the tension in Mina. He was aware that she knew she was the reason they did not get what they wanted from the trading post, and that she did not understand why. Other than the red-haired man, Gee and his mother were the only white people she had ever known, and they had been good to her. She remembered her parents did not like the white man, but that was because they took land from the Indians and claimed it for themselves. She had never harmed those two men or taken anything from them, so why did they not like her?

Mrs. Gilmore, sensing that Mina was upset, pulled her close. "It will be okay, child," she said, and bent down and kissed the top of her head.

The fact that Mr. Randolph would not trade with them bothered Gee. The man had always been friendly and treated them with respect. Gee had liked him, and never heard the man complain about the Indians. A lot of the Indians traded at his store, so Gee did not think this was the reason Mr. Randolph would not to trade with them. It did not make any sense, unless he was afraid of the two men who were there. The more he thought about this, the more convinced he was that this was the reason.

Early the next morning, Gee saddled his horse, tied a dozen mink pelts to the saddle horn, and rode to the trading post. He did not tell his mother he was not going to run his trap lines because he knew she would worry. He was extremely alert as he rode, especially as he neared the trading post. He pulled the musket from the scabbard and laid it across the saddle. *If the two men are there, I may have to kill them,* he thought.

At the trading post, Gee dismounted and tied his horse to the hitching rail. He stood watching the store for a long while before walking inside, where he found Mr. Randolph alone. He could see that Mr. Randolph was afraid of what he might do, but in spite of that, he seemed glad to see him. Mr. Randolph came out from behind the counter and offered his hand to Gee, apologizing over and over for what had happened.

Somewhat reluctantly, Gee shook the man's hand and listened to what he had to say. Mr. Randolph explained he had nothing against Gee or the Indian girl and was ashamed of having to tell Mrs. Gilmore to leave. He had no doubt that the two men would have burned his store had he not done what he did.

"They came back just before dark and said they would burn me out if they found out that I traded with you. They'd been hanging around here all week, bragging about killing Indians. They said Cain Johnston was supposed to meet them two months ago in Mooresville. Since he had not shown up, they came here hoping to find him. They bragged to everyone who came in that they'd been killing Indians so they could take their kids and sell them as slaves."

Mr. Randolph paused to catch his breath and said, "Gee, they will kill you, too, if they get a chance. Not only do they hate you for what you did to them, but now they think you are the one who took the Indian girl from Cain."

"What do you mean?" Gee asked.

"Cain was here a couple of months ago. He told some people he had taken an Indian girl from a tribe close to Willard Creek. Said he was camped not far from here when a stranger rode into his camp. He said he gave the stranger some food, but when his back was turned, the stranger hit him in the head. When he came to, the man had taken the girl and run away like a dog."

"That's a lie," Gee said hotly. "Wasn't that the day I bought flour and salt?" Mr. Randolph nodded his head. "I was on my way home when I saw a red-haired man get up from the side of the road and run away. I found a girl where he had. . . where he. . . where he had hurt her. Her clothes were almost all torn off, and she was too weak to run. She had a cut on her shoulder, a busted lip, and a black eye from where he had beaten her. I knew if I left her there, the wolves would kill her. I did not know what to do so I carried her home with me. We took her in because she did not know where her village was."

He paused and asked, "Is Cain red-headed and wears a long, black coat?" "Yeh, that's him, and he's no good. . . and neither are the two you sent packing."

"Where are the two men now?"

"Like I said, they were here yesterday evening, and said they were going to Mooresville. They said maybe Cain was there by now, and if he was, then they were coming back to get you and Cain's Indian girl. Said they were going to cut the skin off you and hang it from a tree in front of your house."

He looked at Gee, his eyes pleading. "I hope you understand I had to do what I did. You can have anything you want today, and you won't have to pay for it. I am sorry," he said again, and Gee could see he truly was.

"I understand, Mr. Randolph, and I don't hold it against you. You probably did what was best, but I have a dozen mink pelts out there, and I will pay for what I get. I need a pair of shoes for the girl, a dress, and a coat."

"What size?"

"Her feet are about this long, and you saw how big she is." He held his hands apart showing how long her feet were. "Mother would know what size, but I did not tell her I was coming here."

Mr. Randolph searched through some boxes and handed him a pair of shoes. "These are the best women's shoes I have. If they do not fit, you can bring them back, and I will exchange them. Or you can bring her with you, if you like. I would like to meet her. I have nothing against the Indians, and right now, I'm so ashamed, I'd rather get burned out than not do what is right."

Mr. Randolph picked out a dress he thought would fit the girl while Gee selected some yellow and white cloth. He asked Mr. Randolph to cut off enough so his mother could make Mina a dress. His mother made all of her own dresses so he knew she could make one for Mina. He found a brown coat with a fur collar and laid everything on the counter.

Gee walked outside, got the furs, and gave them to Mr. Randolph, who counted out six of them. Gee said what he had bought was worth more than that and for Randolph to keep them all. If these were not enough, Gee said he would bring more.

Mr. Randolph asked him to wait a minute and went to the back of the store. He came back with a wool sweater and scarf, saying they were for Mrs. Gilmore. He picked up a peppermint stick and a pair of gloves and gave them to Gee and explained, "These are for the girl. I think this is now a fair trade." Randolph paused a moment before adding, "Gee, those men are no good.

There is no telling what they might do." He hesitated and looked out the door. "And Gee, there are others around here that will not like it when word gets around that you have taken in an Indian girl. Those two men already told Dorsey Evans, and if you know him, that's like telling the whole colony, so you be careful."

Gee looked at him for a long time before he spoke softly, "You tell the men, or anyone else, that if they come and bother the girl, they had better plan on staying. Yeah, plan on staying for a long time because they'll not be leaving." He rode home with a hand on his pistol, the musket unstrapped in the rifle boot, the powder horn around his neck, and a coat pocket full of musket balls.

When he arrived home, he gave Mina the presents and gave his mother the sweater and scarf Mr. Randolph had sent to her. Mrs. Gilmore wanted to know why he had gone to the trading post without telling her and why Mr. Randolph had treated them so rudely, but held up her hand for him not to answer when she saw how excited Mina was.

Mina was trying to put on the shoes with the buckles still fastened. Mrs. Gilmore showed her how to unbuckle the shoes and helped her put them on. Amazingly, they were a perfect fit. Mina looked at the shoes, jumped up, and hugged Gee, almost knocking him over backwards. She looked at the dress and began to unstrap her overalls.

Abruptly, she thought about what she was doing and pointed to the corner of the house, "*Go, no ha ga ta,*" she said, putting her hand over her eyes. Gee understood that he was not supposed to look at her.

She put on the dress, walked over to him, and told him to look. He did and was surprised to see how well she filled out the top of the dress, even though it was a little too big for her, something he had not noticed when she wore his overalls. He stared, unable to take his eyes off of her; she was beautiful. He got that strange feeling again and wanted to take her in his arms and hold her. She put the coat on, and though it, too, was a little large, she whirled around for Gee to see. *Wow!* he thought, and vowed that he would never let anything bad happen to her again.

He was watching the girl so intently, he did not see his mother looking at him and Mina or the big smile on his mother's face. Mrs. Gilmore loved Mina like a daughter and hoped they would continue to look at each other the way they were looking now. That way she would have a son and a daughter.

During supper, Gee told them what Mr. Randolph had said about Cain and the two men. Mrs. Gilmore looked concerned as Gee walked to the door and took down his dad's old musket hanging above it. He picked up a jar and removed a handful of nails that his father had cut into one-quarter inch lengths. He loaded these into the musket and placed it back above the door. He cleaned and reloaded his own musket with fresh powder and sat it beside the fireplace.

"Soon, we've got to teach Mina how to shoot."

Two day later, he returned from running his trap lines and was warming by the fire when Mina said suspiciously, "Horse come." Gee picked up his dad's old musket and walked to the window. He watched as a lone rider rode slowly up to the house and called, rather loudly, "Mrs. Gilmore, you home?"

Gee looked at him. He had never seen this man before. He looked at the edge of the timber, but saw no one else. He saw the rider had a pistol, but it was in his holster and both of his hands were lying on the saddle horn.

"Who are you and what do you want?" Gee asked.

"My name is Sam Stewart. I have been talking to Randolph at the trading post and would like to talk to you and your mother."

"About what?"

"I would rather talk to both you and your mother, if you don't mine."

Gee studying the man. He was in his middle to late thirties, a little heavy, but not fat. He wore a white shirt, a heavy green coat, brown pants, a brown hat and a gray duster. He did not appear to be angry or threatening, but Gee was taking no chances. He told the man to get down, take the pistol from the holster real slow and lay it on the ground with his left hand. The man did not hesitate and slowly removed the pistol from its holster and laid it on the ground. Gee instructed him to step away from it.

"Now open the duster and the coat so I can see what's under them," Gee demanded.

The man slowly opened his duster and coat with the fingers of his left hand. Gee could see no other weapons, but watched him for a short time. Gee moved quickly and opened the door, holding the scattergun by his side, pointing it at the ground, but ready to use it.

"I have no other weapon on me and would like to come in out of the cold, if I could." Gee was staring at him and was unaware that his mother had walked up beside him. "Mr. Stewart, I am Audie Gilmore. Won't you please come in?"

"Thank you Mrs. Gilmore." He said, taking off his hat.

Mrs. Gilmore turned and went inside. Gee stepped aside to let Stewart pass and walked out into the yard, picked up the man's pistol, stuck it in his belt and went inside. Mr. Stewart was standing beside the fireplace, warming his hands. He looked at both Gee and his mother and said.

"Look, I know you have no way of knowing if I am telling the truth or not, but why would I brave weather like this just to tell you a lie. The truth is, I live up south of Mooresville and a couple of men are in town stirring up trouble. They are trying to form a vigilante group to come down here and burn you out. They said you stole an Indian girl from them and they intend to get her back. I didn't know who they were talking about until Mr. Randolph told me about the Indian girl and what you said.

I believe you told the truth, but the trouble is, it does not matter if you stole the girl or not, a lot of people don't like the Indians and will do just about anything to get revenge for something the Indians may or may not have done. I am afraid that sooner or later they will come, and I wanted to warn you. Now the other reason I am here is that I buy and sell land."

"We ain't selling," Gee interrupted.

Stewart added politely, "I knew you would say that, but listen to me, if it ever comes to the point that you need to sell, just contact Randolph at the trading post. He can pass the word to me. I will give you a fair price, and you can start over somewhere else, maybe in a place where the people are friendlier towards the Indians."

Gee was steaming and was ready to ask him to leave, but his mother said, "Thank you, Mr. Stewart, for your concern for us, but I feel confident that we can manage. However, we will keep you in mind should we decide to sell. Now, I am afraid all I can offer you right now is a glass of milk or some water, but you are welcome to that."

Stewart looked at her and saw she was a woman with a warm smile and a pretty face. Her hair was chestnut brown, rolled into a ball, and she wore a simple, loose-fitting dress. She was a strong woman, well-built, a woman who had worked hard all her life for her family. He admired her and replied politely, "Thank you, Mrs. Gilmore. That would be nice of you."

He looked at Gee and then at the Indian girl who was sitting on the floor in the corner. Her legs were crossed, arms on her knees, and her head rested in her hands. She was staring at him; he smiled at her. She smiled back and said, "Me name Mina."

"*A yv* am Sam," he said, partly in Cherokee.

Mina's eyes lit up and she said, "*O s dv* meet you, Sam." Her voice was gentle and warm, her words spoken gracefully, which surprised him, but also brought back some painful memories.

Mrs. Gilmore returned with a glass of milk. He drank most of it, set the glass down, and pointed to Mina. "Mrs. Gilmore, she is a nice girl, and I can see why you want to protect her, but I sincerely believe that the only way you can do that is to find her folks or leave here. Hatred tends to build, and when someone stirs it, it boils over."

"We ain't leaving. And that's that," Gee interrupted. "Mr. Gilmore, I understand your feeling, but. . ."

"The name's Gee," he interrupted again.

"Okay, Gee, it is nice to meet you." Mr. Stewart studied him for a long while before he continued, speaking softly.

"Now, if you will permit me, I want to tell you a story, a true story. Before I came to Mooresville, my wife and I lived in Pennsylvania. She was Shawnee, and the people up there made our lives miserable beyond description. They burned our crops just before harvest, then our barn, and then our house. No one would help or even speak to us. I was nineteen and had no family. When they burned our house, the only place we had to go was to the Shawnee. They made us work like slaves, I guess, because she was married to me and not to an Indian. We were there two years before we had a son, who was stillborn. Shortly after that, my wife died with a fever. Sometimes I wonder if she died from the fever or from a broken heart."

He turned his hat around and around in his hands, staring at the fire for a long time before he spoke. "Anyway, after she died, the Shawnee told me to leave. According to them I was a bad spirit. I left with nothing but a buckskin shirt and a pair of pants. I wandered for days, not caring where I was heading. I just wanted to die, and probably would have had it not been for a man who found me in a barn that I didn't even remember entering. I was so weak I could barely walk, so he took me in, nursed me back to health, and raised me like his son, even after he found out that I had been married to a Shawnee woman. Why was that so important? His wife had been killed by the Shawnee.

He was the kindest man I have ever known, and he is the reason I am what I am today. I lived with him, and when he died, he left a will that gave me his farm and everything he owned.

No one said a word. In a voice that was soft and sincere, Stewart continued, "I don't want what happened to me to happen to you. I will help you relocate, if and when you choose to do so."

They looked at him, knowing he was sincere, that he really did care, but they could not imagine leaving this place. This was home. And where could they go?

Stewart got to his feet and said he must be going. He opened the door and saw it was snowing hard. Already big wet flakes covered the ground, and the wind was blowing hard. "When I left the trading post, I was afraid it was going to snow. It looks like I was right. But I felt I must warn you."

Mrs. Gilmore came to the door and took his arm. "I wouldn't think of letting you leave in weather like this. We may be in for a blizzard, and you would die out there. Gee will put your horse in the barn, and you will spend the night here. We have another bed in the loft, and I will fix supper. It won't be much, just some fatback, beans, and cornbread, but you are welcome to that."

She nodded for Gee to take care of Stewart's horse, knowing he had to feed their animals as well. Gee handed Mr. Stewart's pistol back to him and said, "We don't argue with Mamma."

Mr. Steward protested, saying he really should be going, but realized she was right. "Maybe you are right, but I won't put you out. I will pay you for your trouble."

"You will do no such thing. You would not have been out in weather like this, if not for us. Please take your coat off. I am sure Mina can entertain you while I cook."

After supper they talked at length about Mrs. Gilmore's family. Even Mina thought of telling about her parents,

Sam Stewart

something she had never mentioned to them, even when Gee and his mother had encouraged her to do so. Remembering her family brought back a flood of memories, but she said nothing as they sat by the warm fire, not knowing how soon and how drastically their lives were going to change.

CHAPTER ELEVEN

INVESTIGATION
Twenty Ten

Penny and Elaine finished their coffee and talked of going to Cracker Barrel for breakfast, but decided that they could not waste any time; they had to get this investigation underway. Elaine would meet with Johnny Bates, and Penny would have the chopper take her to Tyler to meet with her grandparents.

"Maybe we can meet at Cracker Barrel for lunch."

Simmons asked if he could use the truck to go to Manny's and also to drop by the sheriff's department. Penny said there was a GPS in the pick-up, so he should have no trouble finding his way around. Simmons found the truck and followed Elaine toward town, leaving Penny to wait on the chopper. The GPS showed the sheriff's department was closer than Manny's, so he decided to drive there first.

He found only two people in the office, a young deputy on the desk and a dispatcher. Simmons introduced himself to the deputy and said he would like to ask him a few question about Lanny Simpson. The deputy said he was relatively new in the department, and though he had heard about the Simpson case, he knew little about it. He suggested that Simmons talk to the dispatcher because she had been in the department longer than he and should be able to help.

Simmons walked over to where the dispatcher sat, knowing she had overheard him talking to the deputy. "My name is Mitchell Simmons. I would like to ask you a few questions about Lanny Simpson, if you don't mind."

The woman, about forty, looked at him, but did not introduce herself. "Is this an official investigation?" she asked in an unfriendly voice while staring at his uniform. Her manners were rude; her eyes cold and unfriendly.

Simmons decided he could be as cold to her as she was to him so he replied that it was not an official investigation, only a preliminary one for the Army, but he could make it official if need be. This was not true; he was only in the Army and could not make it official, although he did not tell her this. She looked at the deputy, knowing he would be a witness to what was said and scowled at Simmons, mocking him by saying,

"And my name is Abraham Lincoln. Could I ask you a few questions about John Wilkes Booth?" she glared at him, her voice cold and filled with distaste. He did not know why, but he knew this woman had something to hide.

"I'll see you in court," he said, thinking that if he did find out the truth about Lanny, she would be involved in some way.

"Only if you have a subpoena," she sneered at him.

On his way out Simmons told the deputy that he appreciated his help. The deputy turned his head away so the dispatcher could not see and lifted his eyebrows, cocking his head slightly, as if to say, "She's a bitch."

Simmons drove to Manny's. When the valet came over, Simmons asked about Scott McTune. The attendant looked at him and asked in English, but with a heavy Spanish accent, if he was Ms. Penny's friend. Simmons nodded his head. The attendant said he thought he recognized him and thanked him for belting that jerk, Bradley.

"Scott be here in about an hour; you welcome to wait. You come inside or wait there," he said, pointing to a parking space.

"Yes, that will be fine. Will you tell me when Scott arrives?"

Scott arrived about thirty minutes later. Simmons got out of his truck and stood where Scott could see him. Scott parked his car and walked over.

"Hey solider, I'm kinda glad you busted Bradley. Sometimes he's a pain. I'm Scott McTune. What can I do for you?" he asked and offered his hand, satisfied that Simmons was waiting to see him.

"Scott, my name is Mitchell Simmons, and I'll get right to the point. Lanny Simpson saved my life in Afghanistan, and I came here to visit him, not knowing he was dead. From what I have learned, there are a lot of things about his death which seem suspicious. I understand that there was no autopsy and little press. Ms. Sanderson said you were a detective, and I knew you were military, so I would appreciate your take on what happened to Lanny."

McTune stared at Simmons for a long time before he said, "It did seem strange that his death got so little press, especially when the war was getting so much attention. He was a war hero, and most everyone knew he was engaged to the granddaughter of Amos Gilmore, the most successful and well-liked man in Tyler, probably in all the state of Texas. Anyway, Ms. Sanderson did confront me about Lanny, and I remember her saying she did not believe Lanny killed himself—that there was a big cover up. I told her this was not in my district, and I had no authority there, but I offered to help any way I could. I did wonder at the time why there was no autopsy."

"So it is unusual?"

"Very. In fact, state law says an autopsy must be performed in cases like his."

"Did you know Lanny?"

"I knew him, but we were not close friends. He and Ms. Sanderson came in a lot, and sometimes he came to our rifle range. A few times a bunch of us got together and went for a beer. I could tell he had been in the service, but the only time I recall him mentioning it was the time I commented on how well he could shoot. He said he and his buddy were snipers in the Army, so I guess that was you. I know he could dot an "i" at a thousand yards. I liked him, but as I said, we were not close friends."

"Scott, Lanny and I would be called in when a squad of men were pinned down by sniper fire. Lots of times we crawled over dead soldiers to get to a position where we could be effective. Lanny hated the dead. That is one reason I don't believe he killed himself; he loved life too much and from I gather, he was happy and seemed to have a lot to live for."

"Yes, it surprised me when I heard the news. I never saw him when he seemed depressed, but he lived in Longview and Sheriff Otis Green ran that county like a dictator. The rumor is that not even the governor would question Green's judgment. So when the sheriff said Lanny killed himself, I guess no one would dare question him." He waited several seconds before continuing.

"I am a detective here in Tyler County and do security here for Manny, but it's like I told Ms. Sanderson, I have no jurisdiction up there. So, even though I knew him, I don't see how I can help you."

"Scott, I know you've heard the saying 'If you get enough people asking enough questions, the guilty will make a mistake.' Right now all I want is for a lot of people to begin asking questions. Maybe you can help me with that."

"Yeah, Mitchell, sometimes that does work."

"Scott, most people call me Simmons, and thanks, I'll take all the help I can get."

"Okay, Simmons, I'll ask some questions and let you know if I find out anything you should know. And Simmons, I hear there are some powerful people up there. Be careful."

"Second time I've heard that."

Simmons drove to Cracker Barrel and found Elaine and Penny waiting for him. They ordered lunch and discussed what they had discovered. Penny said her grandparents would

Investigation

help and would talk to Judge Caldwell to see if Joe Evans would help. Elaine reported on her meeting with Johnny Bates, who told her a good place to start would be to find out why there was no autopsy. He said they may have to get a lawyer to file before the case could be reopened. He also thought the new sheriff seemed a little lazy and did not know if he would work with them, but he would drop some hints that the case is being investigated.

Simmons told of his meeting with Tyler's Deputy Scott McTune and that he promised he would ask around. He also asked the women if they knew the dispatcher at the sheriff's office in Longview and told of her strong hostility towards him. "I think she's hiding something. Why else would she not answer a few simple questions? I think we need to put some pressure on her. I got the impression that the deputy did not think too much of her, so he might be some help. If nothing else, he might keep us informed of her actions. Do either of you know him?"

Penny nodded, handed Simmons a cell phone, and said most of the numbers he would need were in the phone. She also discussed using the company attorney, who was on retainer, or retaining Cunningham, Mayer & Collins, a big investigating firm in Houston. After some discussion, they agreed on using the company attorney to try to get Lanny's case reopened.

"I will meet with him tomorrow. I will tell him that if we find anything important, we will pursue it until the end, so other attorneys could be involved."

Their lunches arrived and while they ate, they continued to discuss ways to proceed with their investigation. Simmons reminded them to explore every possibility they could think of.

They finished their lunch, and Simmons said he wanted to meet with the commanding officer of the National Guard to see if he knew Lanny and maybe get him to ask a few questions.

"Maybe someone there will have some info. After all, Lanny was one of them, and if I can make them believe that Lanny did not kill himself, maybe someone will offer to help. At the very least, they would be discussing it and word gets around."

Elaine and Penny decided they would talk to the sheriff's dispatcher while Simmons was at the National Guard, just to see if she was as rude to them as she was towards Simmons. They would meet later at Penny's house.

Simmons drove up to the National Guard gate and saw a soldier who looked familiar. Simmons introduced himself, and the man said, "I remember you from somewhere. You're a sniper, I remember that."

Simmons looked at his name tag–Weathers–and remembered where they had met.

"It was in San Diego. We had a few beers with Lanny Simpson before you shipped out. I remembered you and Lanny had been hometown friends, and that you had orders to Iraq while Lanny and I were going to Afghanistan."

They talked at length about both places, sharing stories about Iraq and Afghanistan until their conversations eventually got around to what had happened to Lanny. Simmons told him of his belief that Lanny would never kill himself him because, for one thing, he hated dead bodies.

"I think he hated them so much he would not want someone to have to take care of his body, as we had to do so many times for our fallen buddies. If he were going to kill himself, he would do it where his body would never be found." Simmons paused and added, "I'd bet my life on that."

Weathers said it was hard to believe because he had known Lanny since childhood. He had not seemed depressed when he came home, but was in good spirits even after the death of his mother.

Investigation

"All he wanted to talk about was Penny Sanderson. She is quite a girl—and rich, too. Maybe you should talk to her?" Weathers said.

"I already have, and yes, I think she is both."

"Okay!" Weathers said, looking at him admiringly.

"You were the one who set old Bradley down. Good for you! Nobody around here likes him or that fancy lawyer, Roy T. Grades, he hangs out with."

"What can you tell me about Grades?"

"Well, my parents live in Tyler, and most of what I know is what they have told me. Bradley runs the Tyler Bottling Company and Grades is the company lawyer. My dad says Grades thinks he's a pretty boy, who is always trying to get his picture in the papers by telling everyone what he has done for the city of Tyler." He waited for Simmons to respond and when Simmons did not, he continued. "I hear him and Bradley always seem to be together, no matter where they go. He does not have an office in Tyler, and I think the bottling company is his only client. He hangs around Judge Caldwell's courtroom here in Longview a lot, even though, as far as I know, he does not have any cases here. That seems kind of strange to me."

Simmons made a mental note to go see Grades. After all, if Grades and Bradley were big buddies, they would definitely sue him. He was sure they knew they could not get much from him, but they could try and embarrass him.

Let them try. I don't embarrass easily.

Weathers invited him inside to meet Captain Sizemore, the company commander. The three of them talked at length about Lanny and the fact that Simmons did not believe he had killed himself and was trying to find out what really happened. Sizemore admitted he had not known Lanny until he was assigned to this guard unit.

"He came in here, did not seem to be under any stress, nor did it appear that he was on drugs. He already knew a lot of the guys and quickly became friends with the rest. I am sure most would be glad to help in any way they can, as will I."

Simmons said for now, if they could just ask questions, someone might get nervous and give them a lead. He thanked them and left.

Penny and Elaine were in the pool when he arrived at her house. He was awestruck at the beauty of the two in bikinis. He knew it had been a long time since he had seen someone in a bikini, and both women were gorgeous, but it was Elaine whom he could not take his eyes off of, even when the maid came to ask if he would like something to drink. He slowly became aware that Penny was watching him and heard her say, "Elaine, you better snap your fingers before he turns into a statue."

"I'm sorry; I was thinking about Lanny." He looked at Penny and saw a knowing smile on her face. Elaine was now looking at him, though not really pleased. His knees became weak, and he could think of nothing to say. Finally, he managed to ask, "Did you talk to the dispatcher?"

The two women came out of the pool and dried off. "The dispatcher seemed very nice and offered to help any way she could, but she also said that Sheriff Green had handled that case personally, so she knew little about it. She did not seem rude to us. The deputy's name is Tyler Conwell, and he's a good guy. He is going to med school in Dallas and is a part-time deputy, working summer months and the desk on weekends. When we left, he followed us outside and said that after you left, she made a phone call and had a heated conversation with someone. He could not hear what was said and did not know whom she called. He did say it seemed whoever she called had given her instructions not to be so belligerent. She later told him she was sorry for acting the way she had toward the soldier."

Simmons told of his meeting with the Guard and thought they would help, at least in getting the word out now that there was new interest in Lanny's case.

Investigation

"What do you know about Roy T. Grades?" Simmons asked them.

Both Penny and Elaine looked surprised. Elaine asked where he had heard that name, and he told them what Weathers had said about him and Bradley—how they always hung around together and that Grades was in Judge Caldwell's courtroom quite often.

"Grades has been hounding me about selling my parents' farm. First he wanted it for the timber, then for a cattle farm, and now he wants to make it into a resort or something like that. He has offered a lot of money for it. . . So much, in fact, I talked to my uncle. He suggested I talk to Penny's grandfather about this because he knows about land. I did, and Mr. Gilmore thinks Grade's offer is a lot more than the land is worth and wondered why he would offer so much. He also said he did not trust him and wondered if there might be oil on the land. Mr. Gilmore is going to have Gilsan check their surveys. He also advised me that unless I had to sell, I should hang on to it for a while." Elaine looked from Simmons to Penny and added, "I don't like him, and I trust him even less. Just something I cannot put my finger on, I guess."

Penny also expressed concern about Bradley and Grades hanging around together. She knew of Grades' involvement in the Tyler plant and that Bradley had him on retainer, but as far as she knew, he had no other clients, nor had he handled any of Tyler's litigation. She was shocked to hear he hung around Judge Caldwell's courtroom so much.

"I will discuss this in our meeting on Monday, along with what to do about Bradley. For the past year I have had the feeling that something was not right at the Tyler plant. It has shown a profit, yet distribution is down and morale is low. But to find out that they hang around Judge Caldwell makes me wonder why. I am not sure if Mother or my grandparents know about this."

Extending Shadows

Penny's cell phone rang and Simmons heard her relate the story of Bradley and Grades hanging around Judge Caldwell's courtroom. When she hung up she said, "That was my grandfather. He wants us to meet him at Manny's at eight. He said he knew about Grades and Bradley being together a lot, but would like to know more about Grades hanging around Judge Caldwell's courtroom. Also, he would like to have an update on what we have found thus far. Of course, I said we would be there. It is hard to say no to him, so I hope that is all right with you two." Elaine and Simmons agreed with the arrangements.

CHAPTER TWELVE

PUMP SOME OIL
Nineteen Eighty

Amos, Everett, and Robert stayed up late devising plans on how to proceed with purchasing leases and testing for oil, as well as discussing drilling plans and forming a corporation. The ladies conversed on many topics, stopping occasionally to listen to the men. There were a million things that had to be done, but the most pressing was the obtaining lease agreements. Amos was tied up with the bottling company and Robert was going back to college. That left only Everett, and he needed help. Amos said he had two people at the Tyler plant whom he thought could help and could be trusted.

Amos and Everett discussed the cost of obtaining leases and came up with a plan. Amos would supply the capital they needed and would have his attorney draw up contracts, with Amos serving as president and Everett as CEO. Initially, all of them would have equal shares. After ten years Robert and Anna would be awarded fifty-one percent of the business, and both would be entitled to a third of the profits accumulated thus far, the same as Amos, Marie, Everett, and Judy.

If there are any profits... Amos thought, but did not say so.

Marie looked at Amos and suggested it was about bedtime. She turned and addressed Judy, "You should find everything you need in the guest cottage. If not, let me know." Then she turned to face Anna, "You and Robert can sleep in your old room."

She watched as a look of shock registered on the faces of Everett and Judy. They stood, eyes riveted on both Robert and Anna, before turning their attention to Marie, and then to Amos, who was chuckling.

Marie related the story of the time they had a layover in Houston, how they had gone to where Anna was living in their summer home in Galveston and found Robert there. She told how Anna had come up with the story about him studying late and staying over, but there were bathing suits scattered all the way up the stairs. She also told them about the conversation with Amos and how furious he was at first until she had reminded him it was not anything the two of them had not done before they were married. After all, they had been dating for over a year. She related the story of the first time Anna and Robert had spent the night at the house and the way they had reacted when she gave them a choice of sleeping in the guest room or in Anna's old bedroom.

Everett and Judy smiled knowingly and looked at Robert and Anna. Amos, still chuckling, added, "Marie told me what she was going to do, but I doubted she would."

Anna turned to her mother and said teasingly, "Mother, this is so much like you! I may never forgive you for embarrassing us in front of Robert's parents, but Robert and I will be in my room, though I don't know about sleeping," she said with a strong emphasis on the word *sleeping*.

Everyone laughed, knowing that the families of Gilmore and Sanderson were now firmly united. Amos arose and said he hoped the Sandersons could see fit to go to church with them tomorrow, leaving little doubt that he expected them to agree. He added that Kaysa would have breakfast ready at eight and would be offended if someone failed to show. Amos then said goodnight and left.

Marie showed Everett and Judy to the guest cottage and commented on the look on Robert and Anna's faces. They had a big laugh, and both Everett and Judy gave her a hug, said goodnight, and went to bed feeling on top of the world.

After church, Amos asked if any of them disliked Italian food. When no one objected, he called Gincarla's and reserved a table for six in a private dining room. During lunch nothing was said about oil.

Once they returned home, Robert and Anna left to go riding, and Amos and Marie drove their guests around town. The two men talked about oil, and the ladies talked a little about flowers, before focusing their conversation on a wedding. When everyone was back at the Gilmore house, they discussed what they should do next. It was agreed that Everett would stay in the guest cottage and work on the oil leases. He had called his work yesterday and asked for some extra time off, which was granted. Judy could not get an extended leave, but was given a week off. After that, she would return to Odessa and make arrangements to return if the oil leases seemed promising.

Once inside the guest house, Everett and Judy realized what an important and life-changing decision they were making. They were both jeopardizing good jobs on the promise of oil that may or may not be there. They had known disappointments before when Everett and his father thought they were about to hit the gusher, only to find nothing but sand. Judy reminded him they were happy in Odessa; they had modest savings, and both had good jobs with good retirement benefits. She hated to lose all that and wondered if they would be as happy with the wealth a big well would bring. But she also knew that finding oil had been an obsession with Everett and his father and now with Robert, too. She wondered what would happen to him if he did not take this chance and later found that someone else had hit it big. And yet, she did not want to wager everything on this one promise. They knew this was a monumental decision, one that must be thoroughly discussed.

Everett understood what she was saying, but reminded her that their investment would be small compared to what Amos would incur and that he was doing this only on his and Robert's word. He might have reservations about what his future son-in-law would think of him if he did not support him in this venture, and it turned into something big, really big.

They were still discussing the pros and cons when Robert and Anna knocked on the door and asked if they could come in to discuss what effect this would have on each of them. Robert had reservations about the oil and wanted assurances that they were not doing this just because of him.

"This will probably mean drastic changes in all our lives, and I think we should discuss it in more depth with Mr. and Mrs. Gilmore. Lay everything—and I do mean everything—on the table, the good and the bad, the chances of success or failure, and how we will handle each. We are both proud families. . . granted Anna's family is wealthier and the impact of a bust would not be as severe to her family as to ours. . . but hit or miss, we cannot let this drive a wedge between us." He paused, looked at his dad, and continued.

"I know I got too excited when I saw the potential for oil. I feel as if I have put the Gilmores in an uncomfortable position. Maybe we need to slow down and make sure this is what all of us want. . . not just you and me, Dad. After all, the oil, if there is any, has been down there for millions of years, so we need to dot every 'i' and cross every 't' before we proceed. We have to make sure that this is the desire of everyone. If anyone has doubts, not that of finding oil, but of a negative impact it might have on us, our families, or the people we do business with, we need to stop and reevaluate our options." Robert looked at each of them and knew he had made his point clear.

Anna slipped her arm around him and said, "Robert, I am proud of you. Here you stand with the chance to make a fortune, but you are more concerned about our families. Now how about we go to bed, and we'll go see Mom and Dad in the morning. You can tell them what you have just told us."

"But tomorrow is Monday. We have afternoon classes back in Houston, and I think we will have to leave early in the morning," Robert protested.

Anna, knowing Robert believed he had pushed everyone into this, stated that she had only two classes and he only had one. Surely they could miss them this one time. This was important, she insisted.

Robert spent a restless night worrying about what he had gotten them into. What if he were wrong? Would Anna's parents ever trust him again? What about his parents? They were gambling their savings, their jobs, their retirement, and their livelihood, all because of him.

The next morning they were on the patio, sipping their coffee, when Anna explained to them what Robert had said and that they should discuss it more. Everyone should ask questions and offer their opinions.

"It's like Robert said, 'Don't hold anything back. Lay it all on the table, and once a decision is made, we live or die with it,'" she suggested.

Amos admitted he was against the idea at first, but was now convinced they should proceed, if for no other reason then a lot of people around here needed the income the oil would generate. Each of them admitted they had reservations from time to time, but now believed they should continue. They agreed they should return to the spring and take some water samples for Robert to take to the University to be analyzed.

To their surprise, it was almost noon when they returned with the samples. Mrs. Gilmore explained this was Kaysa's day off, and she had planned on going to Cracker Barrel for breakfast. "However, Kaysa lives in the cottage just below the guest house, and if need be, she would be more than happy to prepare dinner."

Amos suggested they go to Manny's if that was satisfactory with everyone.

After lunch they drove to the Gilmore Bottling Company and met with the company attorney. During the meeting, Amos instructed the attorney to prepare documents for oil leases, preferably by that evening. Later, he was to draw up the papers to incorporate an oil company, which would be named Gilmore-Sanderson, or Gilsan Oil Incorporated, a subsidiary of Gilmore Bottling Company, a name they had previously agreed to. Amos also instructed the attorney to draw up contracts, in agreement with the aforementioned discussions of the families involved. He expressed his appreciation to the attorney, but reminded him that these documents should be finalized and filed as quickly as possible. He instructed him not to file the incorporation papers until they had acquired at least half of the drilling rights available in a twenty-mile radius of the spring.

Amos gave his secretary the name of two company employees and asked her to have them come to his office. He introduced them and explained about the oil. He asked if they would help contact the landowners and reminded them that this was not to be discussed with anyone outside the room. As they left Mr. Gilmore's office, one of the men suggested that when contacting a landowner, they should mention Amos Gilmore.

"He is well-known and highly respected," the employee said. They all agreed that was a great idea.

They left Amos in his office and drove to the courthouse to begin scouring land deeds, securing aerial survey maps, listing the amount of acres of each farm, writing down names of landowners, and noting the larger ones whom they would call on first. Once they had a list of the landowners, Marie wanted Judy to join her and one of the bottling company employees to visit farms in one area. She suggested that Everett should join the other employee since he was not familiar with the territory. She reminded them to use the maps to cover one area at a time so as not to duplicate a visit; they had to act fast before news of the oil lease purchases became common gossip. Marie suggested that as soon as they had the lease papers the attorney was drawing up, possibly by tomorrow morning, they would get started. All this time she had been jotting down notes on a legal pad, so when no one had anything to add, she concluded, "Let's pump some oil." This was later to be the rallying cry when something needed to be accomplished.

Robert and Anna were excited and wished they could stay and help, but knew they had to finish school. However, a master's degree now seemed less important to both of them. They theorized they could make the three hour drive to Tyler or maybe catch a flight to help on the weekends and get their master's later.

Thus, the first notes of the first pages of what was to become the largest and most successful oil company in the state of Texas were written.

The next few months passed in a flash. They acquired the drilling rights to a large number of farms and ranches. They drilled wells and found oil, lots of oil. Almost every well was a gusher, making the Gilmores and the Sandersons wealthy. Everett and Judy moved from Odessa to Tyler. Robert and Anna graduated college and were married in a lavish ceremony at the church Amos and Marie attended.

Ten years later Robert and Anna assumed fifty-one percent of Gilsan Oil, and Robert replaced his dad as CEO. Gilsan Oil was now a household name with worldwide distribution.

All were wealthy beyond belief, Everett and Judy, Robert and Anna buying large ranches and building huge houses. They traveled the world and for nineteen years they lived lives most people only dream about. They were three wealthy and happy families.

This changed in 1999. Judy died of a brain tumor, and three months later Robert was killed in a plane crash. The deaths of Robert and Judy devastated the enthusiasm they once had.

Extending Shadows

Gilsan Oil was now run by a board of directors and still generated huge profits, but without Robert and Judy, huge profits were just huge profits and did not excite any of them. Profits were not nearly as important to the Gilmores or the Sandersons as it was before. In fact, they seemed to have lost all desire to do anything. Amos and Marie had helped when Penny was a problem, but now, did not socialize very much. Everett was even worse. He shut himself up in his big house and seldom left it. His daughter Susan came to take care of him and tried to get him to go out, but he would not. Day after day, he sat and watched TV and day after day seemed to sink farther down in despair.

After the death of Robert, the problem with Penny, and her divorce from Bradley, Anna only occasionally went out. Sometimes she met with the Ladies Club, but most of the time she stayed home, spending her time in her flower gardens.

Lanny and Penny announced they were getting married which brought joy into Anna's life. Now she had a purpose, and she began planning for their wedding—a huge wedding. Even Everett agreed to attend the event. The families were just beginning to socialize again, mostly because of Lanny and Penny. Then, just like Robert and Judy, Lanny was gone.

CHAPTER THIRTEEN

AMOS & MARIE
Twenty Ten

Simmons, Elaine, and Penny met her grandparents at Manny's. Mr. and Mrs. Gilmore listened intently as Penny filled them in on everything that had happened with Bradley and about their investigation into Lanny's death. They agreed they would meet later to discuss their options concerning Bradley. Mr. Gilmore said he felt the same as Penny about the Tyler plant, and that Bradley had seemed indifferent to him lately. He also agreed that morale at the plant seemed low, yet he reminded Penny that the plant was showing a profit and Bradley's buyout was two hundred thousand, should they decide to replace him. This was the agreement Anna and Bradley had signed when they were married, even though her attorney had advised against it.

"We will discuss this more tomorrow," Mr. Gilmore said.

Marie said they could address this in more detail when Anna came home, but now, what interested her the most, was the investigation concerning Lanny's death. Both she and Amos had thought it strange there were no coroner's report, no autopsy, and hardly any investigation. Both had known this was unusual, but it seemed no one at the time would question Otis Green's authority. He ran Hardin County with an iron fist, so they had let it slide, even though Penny had strongly insisted that Lanny had not killed himself.

"I regret that now. I think we owed it to her to at least listen, but we did not."

Mr. Gilmore mentioned that no one had ever explained, or given any reason why Otis had gone to Fort Smith the day he was killed in an automobile accident. The Arkansas State Police found his badly mangled and burned car where it had gone over a cliff up in the Ozarks, north of Hot Springs. The authorities did not find any evidence of foul play and ruled it an accident, even though there was a short skid mark from only the right front tire just before the car left the road. This was reason enough for some people to speculate it was not an accident, but the investigation was quickly swept under the table. Amos had never considered there might be a conspiracy, but now it seemed strange the case was closed so quickly, especially in light of Lanny's case being handled in a similar fashion. Now he began to have deep suspicions about these events and couldn't help but wonder if Simmons might be right. Maybe Lanny did not kill himself. Maybe Otis Green did not have an accident. Was there something going on up there in Longview? He remembered a lot of people believed there was, and he made a mental note to call Judge Caldwell tomorrow, or maybe drop by for a visit. However, when he thought of Grades hanging around Judge Caldwell's courtroom for no apparent reason, he decided to wait until he learned more on the matter.

Penny and Mr. Gilmore agreed when Anna came in that night, they would set up a meeting tomorrow morning with Bradley. Afterwards, Amos and Marie left for Tyler. As Simmons, Elaine, and Penny drove to her house, they discussed what they had learned thus far, which was almost nothing. Simmons reminded them that they should not expect too much this early in their investigation and mentioned he would like to talk to the dispatcher again. He felt that at this moment, she was the only person their questions had upset. It would be interesting to see if she had changed her attitude toward him after the conversation she had with the person Deputy Evans had told Penny and Elaine about.

Simmons also wanted to chat with Chief of Police Johnny Bates. He was curious to know if anyone believed Bradley's hatred of him had anything to do with Lanny, or was it just hatred of the military. He also wanted to meet with Sheriff Joe Evans, but would wait until Mr. Gilmore decided what to do about contacting Judge Caldwell.

As they approached Anna's house, Simmons noticed a helicopter circle the house and set down on the helipad in the back yard. He was wondering what was going on until he heard Penny say, "That's Mother. I guess the chopper picked her up Houston." A few minutes later the chopper was airborne again.

Simmons was impressed. The only people he had seen traveling by chopper were Army high brass, and none of them in a Sarkozy S-76C. He had read about this aircraft. It seated up to twelve, or eight in its luxury configuration and had a cruise speed of one hundred and sixty knots. *I grew up in an orphanage, and I hardly ever rode in a car, much less a helicopter until I was in the Army, and the choppers there were not Sarkozy's. I am way out of my league here.*

Simmons and Elaine sat on the patio while Penny went inside, returned shortly with her mother and introduced her to Simmons. She was pleased to meet him, she said, but from the way she reacted, he knew this was just a formality. Simmons could see she was a little tense and not accustomed to being involved in something she knew nothing about. Marie had called and informed her about the incident with Bradley, but had said little else. Uncertainty was evident in her actions as she stared at Penny and waited for an explanation.

Penny filled her in on who Simmons was, how they had met, and why he was here, but did not mention what had happened at Manny's. Simmons watched her as she listened intently to Penny, nodding her head in agreement, never interrupting. She was a strikingly beautiful woman, trim and shapely, with large brown eyes, long eyelashes, shoulder length black hair, and diamond-studded crosses which dangled from her ears. She was dressed in what Simmons knew were probably expensive designer slacks and a rose-colored silk blouse.

Once Penny finished filling her in on what was happening, Simmons noticed she relaxed, and her attitude towards him now was warm and friendly. She smiled at him with a smile that could melt an iceberg, and her eyes twinkled. She offered him her hand, and he could tell she was genuinely pleased as she welcomed him to her house.

She is probably in her late forties, but I have never seen a woman, no matter what her age, as attractive, he thought and remembered Penny had called Bradley her ex father-in-law. So how did a jerk like Bradley ever appeal to a woman like this? He could not envision this woman with Bradley. *Wait until I tell the guys in my outfit about these three women, the house, and the Sarkozy S-76C*, he told himself.

Simmons was taken somewhat by surprise when Anna slipped her arm around his waist, squeezed slightly, and said, "Oh, if I were only twenty years younger, aaahhhhh ."

Simmons blushed and could think of nothing interesting to say. He was awestruck, but finally managed to reply, "I have never been this close to three beautiful women in my life. Please don't wake me up from this wonderful dream." Anna smiled and wrinkled her nose at him.

Simmons looked at Elaine and Penny and, seeing they were amused, decided to play along. He continued, "And never in my life have I wished I were twenty years older. Aaaaahhhhh, how nice that would be!"

"That was cute." Anna smiled a beautiful, sensuous smile. "Now let me get out of these clothes into something more comfortable. On second thought, maybe I should get out of these clothes and go swimming with Mr. Simmons," she teased.

Penny and Elaine were enjoying this and teased Anna that she did not have the nerve to do it. They dared her; they double-dog-dared her. They taunted her, but there was a look of shock on their faces when Anna promptly slipped off her shoes, unbuttoned her blouse and laid it on the patio table, slid out of her slacks and panties, and dove into the water.

"Now, what about you Mr. Simmons? I dare you," she challenged, as she swam to the edge of the pool directly in front on Simmons.

His mind was racing as he listened to Penny and Elaine daring him.

Why not? he thought, and stripped off his shirt and pants, turned away from them, dropped his Army issue underwear, and dove in.

Both Elaine and Penny were applauding. "Penny, get your camera," Elaine yelled.

Anna held up her hand and asked them to wait a minute. She unfastened her bra and threw it upon the side of the pool. "Now get the camera," she suggested.

"Wait until I tell those old women at the Ladies Club about this! A picture will be icing on the cake." Penny was shocked and stared at her mother, shaking her head. Finally she asked, "Mother, what has gotten into you? Are you on a high or something?"

"Nooooo, your story was so depressing, and you didn't even tell me about Mr. Simmons knocking old Bradley on his rear I was so disappointed I did not get to see it, I had to let off a little steam and lighten things up."

"How did you know?"

"Well, honey, I have friends at Manny's, and my phone did not stop ringing until after midnight."

She swam to the steps of the pool and walked out. She turned and looked at Simmons, "Well, handsome, you sure are a lot of fun. Here you are in the pool with a naked woman, and you swim to the other side." She picked up her clothing, threw a towel around her shoulders, and walked to the bathhouse.

Penny and Elaine stood and stared. Simmons, who was clinging to the other side of the pool, was unable to utter a word. Finally, he came out of the pool, holding a hand over his privates until he found a towel and wrapped it around his waist. He sat down at a table and said, "Unbelievable!"

When Anna came out of the shower, Simmons picked up his clothes, walked into the shower, and later joined them at the table. The housekeeper, Reina, brought a bottle of wine and four glasses. They toasted their glasses, but no one said a word as they sipped their wine. The festive mood was now serious as Penny filled her mother in on what they were planning to do. Anna listened intently before asking, "Have you found anything?"

"We have some unanswered questions, but nothing solid. Look, why don't we all go swimming, but this time with our swimsuits on?" Penny asked.

Anna said she needed to unpack and that they should go ahead and swim. She suggested that when they got out, they could go to Manny's. Turning to Penny, Anna commented, "I'm sure your grandfather would like to meet us there. I'll call him, and he can have the chopper pick them up and take them to Manny's."

"In that case, maybe we should go and swim later," Penny said, They arrived at Manny's just as the Sarkozy was circling to land.

After dinner, they held an informal meeting about what to do with Bradley. As they talked, Simmons asked Elaine if she would like to dance. They danced to a couple of hot tango tunes. The next one was a slow waltz, and Simmons realized this was the first time he had touched her since they stood together at Lanny's house. She was a good dancer, but he felt like he was all feet. He could feel her body against him, and it was electrifying. She was not quite as tall as he was, but their bodies seemed to fit like pieces of a puzzle. As they danced, the light fragrance of the perfume he had noticed in her car seem to captivate him, though now it seemed like eons ago. The touch of her hair against his cheeks sparked sensations throughout his body, and he realized he had never touched someone who made him feel like this. As they danced, he silently wished the song would never end. She looked at him, and of all the words he wanted to say, all he could manage was, "Wow. . ."

They stood on the dance floor after the song ended and waited for another one. They were unaware of the Gilmores and Anna watching. Mr. Gilmore looked at Penny, who winked and said, "He's hooked." They smiled.

The next song was also a slow waltz and as they danced, Simmons whispered in her ear. "Lanny was right; you are special." She looked at him and saw how serious his eyes were, with that proverbial look of a dying calf in a hail storm on his face.

A million thoughts ran through her head, but the biggest one was, *What am I letting myself get into? I am happy. I love my job. I love to coach the kids. I love my apartment. I love living by myself, and I don't need another person in my life.* She stared at him. *So what, for Heaven's sake, am I doing? This is crazy. I don't need this, and I don't need him.* And suddenly, she walked off the dance floor, leaving Simmons standing alone.

He followed her to their table and without looking at him, she said, "My knee hurts."

The Gilmores looked at her and at each other. Everyone seemed concerned, except Penny who had a sly smile on her face as she looked at Elaine. *Custer's last stand. Elaine won this battle, but I bet she is going to lose the war.* Elaine barely said a word the rest of the night, and neither did Simmons.

After they said good night to Mr. and Mrs. Gilmore, they were ready to leave. As they drove, Anna and Penny made small talk which did not include him. He finally got the courage to ask Elaine if her knee still hurt. She pretended not to hear him, so he gave up and said nothing else.

When they reached Anna's house, Elaine said she had some papers to prepare and must be going. Penny made her promise she would call tomorrow afternoon. She said goodnight to Anna, thanked her for dinner, got into her car, and drove off, never giving Simmons even the slightest wave as she pulled away.

Well, that was interesting. First, I got a cold shoulder from Penny and now Elaine. Turning to face Mrs. Sanderson, he said, "I guess it will be your turn next." He tried hard to hide his disappointment as he looked at the huge house, the heated pool, the Mercedes, and thought of the S-76. These people are wealthy, and Elaine might be, also. She could have inherited a lot of money from her parents, received large insurance settlements, or maybe alimony from a previous marriage. He could not remember Lanny ever complaining of having no money.

"I am way out of my league. I think I should go," he said softly.

"Nonsense, it is just a girl thing. Elaine is a girl who has never been involved with a man before, and she does not know how to handle it. I saw you two on the dance floor, how you looked at each other. . . that is, before she got scared and ran off," Penny said, and added, "Believe me, Mitch, when I knew I was beginning to get seriously involved with Lanny, it scared me. I had never known that kind of feeling before, and neither has Elaine. Give her a couple of hours and call her to make sure she got home safely. Her number is in your phone. Just act concerned, but don't push her. She'll be all right as soon as she realizes what is happening. Now, I will show you to the guest house. I would offer to let you sleep in the big house again, but the way Mother was acting this afternoon, I am afraid she might try to seduce you."

If Anna heard Penny's comments, she gave no indication. She only said, "Mr. Simmons, Penny's right about Elaine. Her emotions are running wild, but she will settle down. She is a very practical girl. Even though I know little about you, I am a pretty good judge of character."

"A pretty good judge of character, hah! What about Bradley?" Penny jabbed.

"He was a weasel, not a man. And my judgment was impaired because of what I went through with you," she shot back, a tinge of anger in her voice.

Penny knew she had touched a nerve and tried to smooth things over. "Mother, will you come with me to show Mitchell to the guest cottage?" Anna smiled, knowing she had won this round as they walked toward the cottage.

Suddenly, Simmons stopped and said, "My duffel bag is in Elaine's car, and I have worn this uniform for two days. Maybe I could use your laundry room?"

"I have a cute little sundress you can wear; I think you would look lovely in that," Anna teased.

"I thought he looked pretty good with nothing on. If I had not seen how he looked at Elaine, I might try and seduce him myself," Penny said.

They walked to the cottage. Anna asked him to slip off his clothes and she would have Riena laundry them. They waited at the cottage door until Simmons pulled off his uniform and opened the door, only slightly, to hand Anna his clothes.

"I will bring them to you in the morning," Anna said and added, "After what you said a little bit ago, I think this is one way to keep you from running away. I think you will find everything you need inside. Goodnight, Mr. Simmons."

Simmons watched through the half-closed door as they walked hand in hand towards the big house. *Two wonderful women*, he thought, still wondering if this was all a dream. He had known Penny a little over forty-eight hours and Anna only three or four, but already he felt an attraction towards them. It worried him that he knew so little about them; in fact, he knew nothing about them. He was aware that even though they were probably extremely wealthy, it seemed they were not really happy, as if there were a lot of empty holes in their lives. He did not know what had happened to Lanny and recalled Elaine's words about not getting involved in something he knew nothing about. That was true, but Lanny would not have run off and left him, so he vowed to stay until he knew what had happened. Then he would go back to a life he knew . . . Army life.

He closed the door and stared at the cottage. Actually, it was not a cottage but a large three-bedroom house, and it was lavish. At the end of the foyer was a huge den, complete with a wet bar, a big screen TV, a pool table, two leather recliners, a leather couch with mahogany end tables, and a coffee table. On one side of the room was a huge painting of a man in buckskin clothes, wearing an old beat-up black hat with a long musket standing by his side.

Beyond the den was a dining room and kitchen. He walked down a long hallway and peered into the master bedroom, seeing a king-sized bed, a desk and chair, and a big screen TV. He stepped inside a few feet and saw a huge bathroom with a marble tiled shower, a Jacuzzi, and two marble vanities. On the other side of the hallway were two smaller bedrooms, each with a queen-sized bed, a desk with a desktop computer, a chair, a TV, and a bathroom.

Simmons chose the last bedroom, showered, and found a terry cloth robe. He lay down on a very comfortable bed, still wanting to pinch himself to see if this was real. If the cottage, as they called it, was this big and this plush, he wondered about the big house. He had only seen the breakfast nook and one lavish bedroom, so he could only imagine what the rest of the house might look like. Suddenly, like a slap in the face, all this hit him again. *What am I doing here? I'm only a kid from an orphanage, and the Army is my only family.*

He lay on the bed, eyes closed, but could see Lanny screaming at him, saying, "Don't touch him." He thought of all this luxury compared to all the hardships they had endured in Afghanistan and knew Lanny well enough to know he would not have married Penny solely for her wealth. The thought of Lanny being a part of all this was all the more reason to believe he did not kill himself. No more sand fleas, no more flies, and no more dead bodies, their flesh rotting in the sun. Lanny would have had all this. . . a life of luxury.

But what had happened to him? Why had it happened? he asked himself over and over. It seemed to him that Lanny could have filled one of the big holes in this family's life. Lanny would have brought joy to a family that needed it. Now it seems they were a family that was just surviving this day while waiting for the next, maybe with nothing to look forward too.

He closed his eyes and thought of Elaine. He remembered how he felt when she walked off the dance floor. Now he wondered if he would see her again, or if she would help him find out what had happened to her brother? While he contemplated all this, he discovered there was a big hole inside himself as well. Right now, he did not know if it could be filled without Elaine.

He took the cell phone out of his pocket, looked at it, and realized he did not know how to find her number. Maybe it's just as well. It was plain to see that she really did not want to talk to him. Calling her would probably make matters worse. "I think I'll just leave tomorrow. Go back to a life I know, to a family I know," he convinced himself.

As he lay staring at the ceiling, there were millions of questions shooting through his head, none of which he had answers for. He felt like a little rubber life raft being tossed up and down on a raging sea that was covering him with salt water. He was dying of thirst, but had nothing to drink.

Sometime before morning he had drifted into a restless sleep and was awakened by a knock on the cottage door. He slipped on the robe and answered it. It was Reina, bringing him his uniform, starched and neatly pressed. He asked about Penny and Anna and was told Penny had left, but Ms. Anna was there. He looked at his watch: nine twenty. He showered and dressed quickly and walked to the house. He found Anna sitting on the patio, drinking coffee.

It was almost ten now, and he apologized for sleeping so late. "In the Army we are up at six, so I don't know why I slept so late."

"I was a little concerned when you were not here for breakfast, but it seemed you had a lot on your mind. I thought you probably did not get to sleep until late."

"That's true, but still no excuse for sleeping so late."

Anna sipped her coffee and said Elaine had called back and apologized for her actions last night, but sadly had not asked about him. "And I apologize for my little episode at the pool. I hope I did not offend you. I got the feeling everyone was so low, I just tried to cheer us up."

"No, ma'am, I didn't get offended. In fact I enjoyed it very much, and yes, I was a little depressed. I did a lot of thinking last night, and I think it is best for me to leave. I have brought back a lot of bad memories to you, to Penny, and to Elaine. I was the cause of the concern your family had over the episode at Manny's, and then I upset Elaine. It seems as if I have been nothing but a downer since I got here." He paused, "I thank all of you for the wonderful food, the hospitality, and most of all for the sincere friendship I felt, but I will be. . ."

"Mitchell," Anna interrupted, and studied him for a long time before she spoke. He realized it was the first time she had called him anything but Mr. Simmons. "What about Lanny?" she asked. Her voice was very soft.

He sat for a long time, holding his coffee cup, but not drinking. Finally he said, "Ma'am, I don't know, but I think it would be best if I go. Elaine warned me about getting involved in something I know nothing about, and that nothing I do will bring Lanny back."

"Mitchell, please call me Anna. Now come inside, and Reina will make you some breakfast."

Without another word, she got up and walked into the kitchen. He sat staring at the door, uncertain about what to do next. He heard her talking to Reina, who came to the door and asked, "Ham, bacon, or sausage? And how do you like your eggs or would you like something else?" Simmons protested saying he did not want anything and that he was leaving.

"Ms. Anna gave you your orders, Sergeant, and I think you had better follow them or you will face a court-martial." Her eyes were warm, almost pleading with him to come inside.

Anna came to the door. "Mitchell, please come inside." Her voice was sincere, and her big brown eyes seemed to be begging him. Still he could not move and sat staring into the distance, seeing nothing. "Mitchell, please," she pleaded.

"Ham and eggs over medium," he told Reina as he walked inside and sat down.

"Thank you," Anna said, and Simmons could see she was sincere. She did not say anything for a long time, but watched Reina as she made breakfast. "Mitchell, I hope you will forgive me for saying this because you know very little about our family, but we are a proud family. We have everything we want, materially, but we would give it all up for what we don't have. We don't have my husband Robert, Penny's father; we don't have Robert's mother, Judy; and we don't have Lanny. They left a void in our lives that we cannot seem to fill. The same is true with Elaine. She lost her father, mother, and brother, but I think she has adopted the school kids, so to speak, and has managed to get on with her life because she has a goal—to teach and coach the kids. However, our family just goes through the motions of living; we have no goals, no ambitions. We exist, but we do not live." She paused, waiting for Reina to refill their coffee cups.

"Mitchell, enjoy you breakfast. I would love for you to join me on the patio when you finish." She picked up her coffee cup and walked outside.

Simmons thought about what she had said as he ate his breakfast. It was about what he had thought last night. He finished his breakfast, thanked Reina, and walked outside. He saw Anna leaning against one of the rock columns and staring out into the distance. She saw Simmons and motioned for him to sit down.

"Mitchell, I want to finish telling you about our family, and if you still want to leave, we have a company plane that will take you wherever you want to go." She waited for him to sit down. "Robert and I met in college and we lived together until I graduated. After that, we were married and were extremely happy. Two years later we had a son that was stillborn. That was a great hurt, but a year later Penny was born and she replaced that bad memory. We were happy again, and we had some wonderful years together. Our bottling company made us a nice living, and Robert found oil on my father's ranch. Robert's father, Everett, and my father formed Gilsan Oil and it made us quite wealthy. They passed the companies on to Robert and me and to his sister. We were on top of the world. We were happy, well-respected, and we wanted for nothing. We traveled the world and did all the things wealthy people do." She paused and sipped her coffee. Simmons could see the hurt in her eyes.

"All that changed when Robert's mother died and then he was killed in a plane crash. Penny was sixteen and could not cope with life without her father. She was suspended from school, was on drugs, and God only knows what else. Her life hit rock bottom; she was out of control, and we could do nothing with her. Finally, before she killed herself, we sent her to a home for wayward girls. She was there for six months, and I was very depressed, almost to the point of taking my own life. I guess the one thing that kept me from doing it was to make sure my daughter survived." She stopped and looked off into the distance.

"Daria, Penny's roommate at the school, probably saved Penny's life and maybe mine, too, because, if something had happened to Penny, I don't think I would have gone on. Daria helped Penny to get on with her life, so before Penny came home, we made arrangements for Daria to come and live with us. Penny graduated high school and waited a year for Daria to finish. They went off to college, and I was alone, alone in this big ole house with nothing to do. I became so depressed, there would be days when I would not leave this house. I had no friends, no goals, and no ambitions. Deep down inside, I knew I was making a mistake when I married Bradley, but I needed someone. I needed a challenge, and I thought I could make it work, but I was wrong. Our marriage was a disaster." She shook her head as if trying to get the memory out of her mind.

"After that, I devoted my time and energy to building a bottling plant in Texarkana as a graduation present for Penny. Two years later she met Lanny, and he was the spark our family needed. He brought life and desire back to us. We all began envisioning ways to include him into our lives. Penny persuaded him to come and live with us. They moved into the cottage, and we began making plans for a wedding—a big wedding. We had purpose in our lives once again, but then, like the others, in an instant Lanny was gone. We were devastated, and once again lost our desire to go forward until you came." She looked at him and smiled.

"Mother called me in Houston Saturday morning and told me what you wanted to do. I was skeptical until I met you, but both my mother and father were excited, because, unlike Robert and Judy, there were unanswered question about Lanny. We did not want to believe it, but I guess we did because we did nothing, even though Penny insisted that Lanny had not killed himself. I guess we thought it was because Penny was so deeply in love with him that she just assumed it. We just pushed it all out of our minds and crawled back into our shells, so to speak."

She walked over and sat across from him. "Then, you came and made us believe that Lanny did not kill himself. Much the same way Lanny did, you gave us a purpose in life. We had to prove Lanny did not kill himself. If you stay, we will have the aspiration to find the truth. We are excited to have a challenge, an inspiration, a desire, but Mitchell, if you leave, I am afraid you will take all that with you."

Simmons sat at the table, his head down, and said nothing for a very long time; neither did Anna. Finally Simmons spoke, "They lived in the last bedroom. I could feel his presence last night." Anna gasped, but said nothing and neither did Simmons. Both were mesmerized by memories.

Reina came in with more coffee. He thanked her and sipped it in silence. Anna picked up her coffee cup, walked over, and stared at the guest house, remembering she and Robert had also shared the guesthouse. They, too, had lived in the last bedroom, while the big house was being built. She could hardly hold back the tears until she felt Robert's reassuring touch on her shoulder. She looked skyward and said, "Thank you, God, for letting him touch me."

She stood on the patio, looking at the things they had built together. Her heart was breaking as she remembered how deeply they had loved one another, how devoted each had been to the other. God might forgive her, and Robert might also, but she could never forgive herself for marrying Bradley. Why had she been so weak? No, she would never forgive herself. She felt ashamed and dirty as she stood there, staring into the distance and seeing nothing until Simmons came up and stood beside her.

"What do you know about the lady dispatcher at the sheriff's office?" he asked softly.

Anna looked at him, at his deeply tanned and slightly wrinkled face. She looked into eyes that were soft and understanding. She saw a man who cared immensely for his friends and for those close to him. "Thank you, Mitchell." She took his hand, and they stood in awkward silence, each deep in their own thoughts about what they should do next. "Let's go for a ride. I'll get Luca to saddle us a horse."

"I never rode a horse in my life."

Anna smiled, thinking of someone else in her life that had never ridden before. That alone awoke some beautiful memories. "I taught Robert how to ride and would love to teach you."

They walked slowly to the barn. Above the tack room door was a picture of a beautiful palomino horse. "That was Dusty," Anna explained.

CHAPTER FOURTEEN

LEAVING HOME
Seventeen seventy-four

Shortly before sun up Gee climbed down from the loft and rekindled the fire. He opened the window shutter and looked out. It was still snowing, and the wind was blowing the snow so hard he could barely see the barn. The snow was at least two feet deep with some drifts almost head high. His mother and Mina came to the window and looked at the snow as Mr. Stewart climbed down and joined them.

"I sure am glad I listened to you last night. It's a blizzard outside. When you get ready to tend to the animals, I will help."

"While you two are at the barn, I will thaw some water. We will have breakfast if you can get into the smokehouse for some meat. I would say that the temperature is around zero since the water was frozen inside, so you probably won't be able to get it open, but you can try," Mrs. Gilmore said.

Gee looked at Mr. Stewart and said they would need snow shoes in snow this deep. Since Gee had only one pair, he would tend to the animals. Mrs. Gilmore reminded Gee again to check the smokehouse and watched as Mina added more wood to the fire.

Gee was unable to open the smokehouse door, so they ate flapjacks and milk gravy for breakfast. When finished, they sat around the fire and told stories of friends and families. They learned that both Mr. Stewart's father and mother died when he was young, and an aunt had raised him. He was fifteen when she passed away and bequeathed the farm to him. He was on his own, and, except for a few animals, all he had was the roof over his head.

He was working in Mooresville in exchange for food and supplies when he met his wife. She was among some Shawnees who came to Grayson's store to trade for lead and powder. He told how the girl was very pretty, with soft brown eyes, light brown skin, and long black hair flowing loosely over her shoulders. When the girl's father saw them looking at each other, he asked, "You like?"

Mr. Stewart said he did not know what to say, but nodded his head when the girl's father asked again. The girl nodded when her father asked if "she like." "You trade?" the girl's father asked him.

Mr. Stewart said he was shocked, but had heard that this was a custom with the Shawnee when a young girl became a woman. He said he looked at the girl's father and then at the girl, who was smiling at him with the most beautiful smile he had ever seen. "I could not speak, but when I finally found my voice, I said, 'Yes, that is, if it is all right with her,'" Stewart told them.

"You trade horse, cow, calf, and three pigs?" the girl's father asked.

Mr. Stewart laughed and said, "I think at that time I would have traded every animal I had. That was the kind of hold she had on me. Anyway, Mr. Grayson let me leave work and go to my place. After the Shawnee took the animals and left, she came and stood by me. I was sixteen and she was fourteen, but back then couples married young. Also, marriages between the settlers and Indians were quite common because far more boys came from the old countries to the new settlements than did girls. Her name was *Shayna*, which means "beautiful" in Shawnee. We were young and strangers to each other and to each other's way of life. We could hardly communicate, but we made it work. We were happy and learned to truly love each other. We were doing quite well until a group of settlers massacred a Shawnee village and took their land. The Shawnee retaliated by killing some settlers, and this escalated into a war between the two. The hatred grew, and soon Shayna and I were easy targets for the settlers' revenge." His voice trailed off as the thoughts of her came alive in his head. He sat with his head lowered, staring at the fire.

Mina had been listening intently. She had been with them only three months, but she had learned English fairly well and understood what he had said.

Mrs. Gilmore had been a teacher back in Pennsylvania and had brought a small chalkboard and a block of chalk with her. She had taught Gee to read and write and now Mina, who was fascinated with writing and would practice for hours at a time. In a short time, she had learned to read, to write and to do her numbers. She said her people called them "talking leaves" and now, she too, could make the leaves talk.

As she listened to the stories, she wondered if she should tell them about her parents, about her village, and about her brother and sister. She had not spoken of them since she came here, but it seemed as if now was a good time to tell them her story.

After a brief silence she spoke of her father, mother, a little brother, and sister. She told of the day they were gathering acorns, and her little brother wanted to go to the chestnut tree, which was a long way from their village. Her sister also begged to go, and she agreed. They were picking up chestnuts, singing and playing a game of tossing the nuts into one of the buckskin bags and did not hear the rider until he was almost on top of them. She screamed for her brother and sister to run, but made a mistake when she tried to pick up a bag of the chestnuts. The rider rode his horse up beside her, and he kicked her to the ground, his spurs cutting her shoulder. He jumped on top of her and hit her on the head. The next thing she remembered she was in the saddle in front of the man, her hands were tied to the saddle horn, and a rag stuffed into her mouth. She tried to get off the horse, but he hit her again as they rode at a fast gallop through the trees. They rode the rest of the day and into the night before they stopped.

"He then tie my hands to tree and get on top of me. He hurt me." She sat with her head down, tears streaming from her eyes.

"Early in morning he hurt me more; it make me sick. I could no move and start throw up. He cut me loose, and we ride till sun overhead. He hurt me again, so I throw up more. I do that when Gee come. It my fault. If I no go to chestnut tree, he no catch me," she said, looking down in shame.

Mrs. Gilmore put her arm around her and told her it was not her fault. Gee came and lifted her off the bench, hugged her, and wiped the tears from her eyes. Mr. Stewart also came over, patting her gently on the back as he embraced her saying, "It is not your fault. No man should do what he did." No one said anything for a long time. All felt her pain, and Mrs. Gilmore changed the conversation.

They talked of the snow and began to compare Shawnee words with Cherokee words. Mina seemed to enjoy this, but Gee could tell that a lot of it made her uncomfortable as she continued to have memories of her family. He changed the subject again by wondering out loud about his trap lines. Had the wolves found his traps? He was sure they had; the wolves were intelligent animals. If they had not found them, the bears surely would have. His traps were baited with deer meat, and they could smell a deer miles away, even one buried under the snow. To his surprise Mr. Stewart also began talking of trapping, and Gee could tell right away that Mr. Stewart knew as much or more about trapping as Gee did.

They were discussing the bears when Gee saw his mother and Mr. Stewart make eye contact more than once. He saw his mother smile at him and him smile at her. Gee did not know if he approved of this or not. He had not trusted Mr. Stewart at first, but now Gee found him to be easy spoken and fun to talk to. Gee did not know for sure if he liked him, but he did not dislike him either. Maybe he did not know him well enough. He thought about this as Mr. Stewart began to include Mrs. Gilmore and Mina in conversations that eventually came back to the weather.

By noon it had stopped snowing. The temperature was rising, but the snow had not melted very much. Mrs. Gilmore asked Gee if he could try once more to get the smokehouse open. If he could, she would make venison steaks for super.

Gee and Mr. Stewart did manage to open the smokehouse door and came back with a back strap of venison. Mrs. Gilmore cut the tenderloin into one inch slices, put them on sticks and cooked them over the open flame, continually adding lard, salt, pepper and spices.

When they finished the meal, Mr. Stewart commented that it was the best steak he had ever eaten. Gee could see that his mother was pleased as she smiled at him again. "Thank you, Mr. Stewart. I am glad you liked it, and I hope you will come and join us again sometime."

Gee thought it was good to see his mother smile. He could not remember her smiling before Mina came. Now she was smiling once more.

"I will do that, Ms. Gilmore, but please call me Sam."

"And you can call me Audie," his mother said confidently.

Gee looked at them and at Mina, who was smiling and wrinkled her nose at him.

The next day the snow was almost gone. Gee and Mr. Stewart went to the barn, saddled their horses, and led them back to the house. Mr. Stewart mounted, took off his hat, and addressed Mrs. Gilmore.

"I thank you so much for your hospitality, and I would like to ask if I could come calling."

"I would like that, Sam. Do be careful going home," Gee's mother said, giving him a big smile.

Sam put on his hat and tipped it to Mrs. Gilmore. He looked at Gee and back at Mrs. Gilmore and added, "I do want you all to be careful. I am still afraid of what that vigilante mob might do. If I hear of any plot against you, I will come to warn you, night or day."

Gee and Mr. Stewart rode their horses through the timbers and onto the wagon trail leading to the trading post. A little ways later they reached the place where Gee was to leave the trail and ride to Crawley's Ridge to check his trap lines. Before parting, Mr. Stewart asked Gee if he had any objections if he came calling on his mother. Gee said he was welcome to visit any time and thanked him for telling them about the vigilante.

"One other thing, Gee. I want to ask if you will stay close and be watchful; you never know what the vigilantes might do. I would hate for something to happen to you all." The way he said it, Gee knew he was sincere.

They said their goodbyes, and Gee turned left toward the foothills of the Appalachians while Mr. Stewart continued toward the trading post. Gee checked a few of his traps and found none had been disturbed. He decided the snow had been too deep for the game to move. Gee really did not have his mind on the trap lines, though. It seemed all he could think about was what Mr. Stewart had said about him staying close. This was nagging at him so he turned his horse toward home and arrived about noon.

His mother greeted him at the door and inquired about his traps. He explained that the game had not moved, probably because of the deep snow. He came home early because it was time for Mina to learn to shoot.

For the next two hours they practiced. Gee began by getting her acquainted with his musket, explaining how each part worked. He taught her how to hold it, how to place her feet apart, how to line up the sights, and how to lean into the muzzle recoil when she squeezed the trigger. Gee had her fire the musket several times with only powder in the priming pan. After she became comfortable with the flash that the priming pan made, he loaded it with a musket ball. Mina, knowing he had loaded it with a musket ball, jerked the trigger even before she brought the sights on target. Gee could not tell where the ball hit, only that it had come nowhere near the rock he had set up as a target. He reminded her to slowly squeeze the trigger until the musket fired.

"Let it be a surprise to you when it does fire; that way you will not be jerking the trigger," he explained. After the third shot, Mina was no longer jerking the trigger, but was squeezing it and leaning into the recoil.

On her fourth shot she shattered the rock. Next, he taught her to shoot his dad's old musket loaded with nails. She really enjoyed seeing the nails kicking up dirt in a large circle around the target.

"Me like," she said as they walked over to see where the nails had hit the ground.

Later they tended to the animals and cut firewood which Mina helped carry to the wood shed. It was still February, but the day was warm enough to be early spring. The snow was almost gone, the sky clear, and the full moon seemed close enough to touch. They ate beans, fried cornbread, and leftover venison for supper and went to bed at dark.

Sometime after Gee had gone to sleep, he was awakened by his mother's screams that the barn was on fire! Gee grabbed his overalls, climbed down the ladder, and ran barefoot towards the barn. He saw his mother running towards the spring with a bucket in her hand. Gee had made only a few strides when he saw the muzzle flash of a flintlock. He lunged head first behind the woodpile, feeling the hot air as the musket ball whizzed past his head. He hit the ground hard, almost knocking the breath out of him. As he struggled to get his breath, he could hear his mother screaming for Mina to get back into the house.

In the light of the burning barn he could see three riders about a hundred yards away and began cursing himself for not getting his musket. Somehow, he had to get to the barn and release the animals or they would soon burn to death. Saying a short prayer, he made a run for the barn, zigzagging as he ran. He felt the slap of a fifty-caliber musket ball as it tore through his shirt, just missing his chest. He sprawled head first behind a log they had intended to cut up for firewood, heard the blast of another musket, and felt the musket ball impact the log. He lay close to the log, knowing that the first rider to fire would be reloaded by now. He was lying close to the log, trying to decide what to do. Raising his head, he peeked over the log. He saw his mother racing towards the barn and heard another loud boom. This time it came from the direction of the house. He heard a man scream and yell that he was hit. "Let's get out of here! We'll take care of him later," another rider said.

Gee raced to the barn and helped his mother get the animals out. Mina ran up holding his father's musket and his pistol. He took the pistol and motioned to the wagon. They managed to throw collars, harnesses, and his saddle into the wagon and push it out of the barn before one wall collapsed and the loft fell in. In a matter of seconds the hay caught fire; only a moment later, the entire barn was engulfed in flames. Soon another wall collapsed, and the roof fell in. All they could do was back away from the intense heat and watch it burn.

Gee stood thinking about all the corn and hay they had worked so hard for—all that was now gone. He was also mentally kicking himself for not taking Mr. Stewart's warning more seriously and for failing to get his musket before he left the house. If he had, he could have gotten at least one of the riders. Slowly he became aware of Mina on one side of him and his mother on the other. They were holding onto him very tightly, and his mother said, "We can rebuild the barn. I am just thankful that we all are safe and that we got the animals out." However, Gee knew they were in trouble. They had no corn or hay to feed the animals for the rest of the winter. He put his arm around Mina and said proudly, "You hit one of them. If only I had not been so stupid, we might have gotten them all."

She managed a small smile, but knew this was happening because of her. If Gee had left her in the woods, they would still have a barn. She decided she would leave in the morning so they would have no more trouble because of her.

They stood a while longer watching as the fire slowly died down, the smoke hanging low over their head as they turned and walked to the house. Gee picked up the scattergun where Mina had dropped it and went inside. He reloaded the scattergun with an extra heavy load of powder and nails and told them to get some sleep. He was going to stand guard the rest of the night. He did not think they would return tonight, but if they did, he would be ready.

He sat by the woodpile until daybreak, trying to decide what they should do and how to protect themselves against another attack. He came up with a plan to encircle the house with a wire about a couple of hundred yards out and waist high. He would make a holster for the pistol, attach it to a fence post, and tie the wire to its trigger. He could set it up at night and take it down in the morning. It would not hit anyone, but would give them a warning if someone came with the intent on burning their house. He would go to the trading post and get a roll of wire.

It was then that he saw Mina slip from the house and began walking towards the woods. He rushed to her and asked, "Mina, what are you doing?" She was crying. He took her hands and asked again, "Why were you crying?"

"Me go. Me why they burn barn."

Gee wiped the tears from her eyes and held her tightly for a long time. He saw his mother in the doorway, motioning for them to come. Inside the house Gee and his mother talked with Mina, assuring her she was welcome and should not blame herself for the barn. "You are part of our family, and there is no way we will let you leave," they assured her.

"Me stay. Me happe."

After breakfast Gee left for the trading post and arrived about mid-morning. Mr. Randolph listened intently as Gee told of the three men burning their barn and trying to kill him. He asked Mr. Randolph if the man he had kicked in the face and his buddy had been there.

"They were here yesterday, and there was another man with them. He was a little runt of a man with cold, beady eyes. They called him 'Snag.' They wanted to know if I had seen Cain Johnston, and when I said 'no,' they said they were going to his cabin to see if he was there. I think that was a lie because as far as I know, Johnston doesn't have a cabin around here."

Gee asked Mr. Randolph if he had a spool of wire and explained what he intended to do.

"Yes, I have the wire. Gee, I've also got an old rusty pistol back there that's in such bad condition, I'm afraid to shoot it so I'll give it to you. You might need your good pistol."

Gee thought about this and said, "Okay, if you are sure about giving it away."

That afternoon Gee, his mother, and Mina worked hard putting up the wire and mounting the pistol in a big gourd strapped to a pole. Gee loaded the old pistol with a little powder and tied the wire to the trigger. He walked to the wire and pressed against it. The old pistol fired. He came back to the post and reloaded the pistol, this time with a lot of powder. He did not care if the old gun exploded when it fired; it was only meant to be a warning. Even though the pistol was in the dry, Gee knew he would have to change the powder every few days or moisture would wet the powder, and it would fail to fire.

The next day, they dug through the smoldering embers of the corn crib and found some of the corn which had not burned. The fire had been so hot and burned so fast, it only burned the top layer of the corn. Gee figured there was enough corn here to last two or three weeks, more if they rationed it. First they had to get it dry. They did this by loading the corn in a basket and carrying it into the woodshed. Gee hoped he could trap enough game to trade for more corn to last them the remainder of the winter.

After finishing moving the corn, Gee was working on a lean-to to keep the animals dry when he saw movement just inside the wood line. Seeing three Indians emerge from the timber, he grabbed his musket and aimed it at the lead Indian. He did not fire, however, as the Indian was holding a white flag. Gee turned to look at his mother and saw her step in front of Mina.

"They are not taking her unless she wants to go," he uttered under his breath.

Mina ran to him, yelling, "They my people, no shoot. You no shoot," she said excitedly.

She waved her arms, ducked under the wire, and began running toward them. Gee held his musket ready and watched as his mother walked toward the wire. Halfway between the wire and where the Indians were, Mina stopped and motioned for Gee to come. He hesitated before walking slowly up to her, keeping his musket ready. Mina told him her people would come to them and for him to lower the musket. Sure enough, after a little hesitation, they walked their horses slowly towards Mina. At about twenty feet they stopped, and Mina told them they were welcome at their house.

One dismounted and walked towards Mina, holding up his right hand as a greeting and nodding his head to Gee and his mother. He spoke to Mina, asking where her village was and why was she here. Mina answered in rapid-fire Cherokee, telling him about her parents, their village, what had happened to her, and that these people had taken her in when she had no place to go.

"They be good to me. They buy me shoes," she said, holding up a foot so they could see her shoes.

The leader turned to the other two riders and asked if they knew her. They shook their heads. One of the Indians spoke, and Gee understood he was asking Mina if she wanted to go with them. If she did, they would find her village.

Mina thought about this, and Gee's held his breath. What if she says she will go? What will I do without her? These and many other questions raced through his mind. He exhaled only after she shook her head and said she did not want to leave.

"They good to me, still good to me, even me why barn burn."

The Indians listed intently as she told of the men who burned the barn and tried to kill Gee, pointing at him.

One of the Indians asked if she had been told to say those words, if these people were the ones who had taken her and now would not let her leave. He insisted that if she wanted to leave, she should step over to where he was standing. Mina shook her head and backed towards Gee and Mrs. Gilmore.

"Me stay," she said confidently, and the leader nodded his head slowly.

"You are welcome at my house because you are Mina's people. Would you like to water your horses or come inside for something to eat or a glass of milk?" Mrs. Gilmore spoke to them in Cherokee. They looked surprised that Mrs. Gilmore spoke their language. The leader looked at the other two who were nodding their heads.

"*i i,*" they said and got off their horses.

The leader said his name was Ashwin, and the other two were Sahin and Balik. Gee introduced himself, Mrs. Gilmore, and Mina. Each of the Indians nodded in agreement and followed Gee to the wire where they listened carefully as he explained what it was used for.

Gee untied the wire, and they led their horses to the spring. When the horses finished drinking, Mrs. Gilmore and Mina met them at the woodpile with three glasses of milk. Gee selected a stick of wood to sit on, and each of the Indians did the same as they drank the milk.

Leaving Home

Gee noticed they kept looking at the house, and he wondered if they suspected that someone else was there. "There is no one else inside," he said and made a joke that while he could not show them the barn, they could come see the house. They nodded.

They walked inside and looked around. Gee could not decide if this was the first time they had been inside a white man's house or if they expected more. Mina whispered to Gee that it was a custom with her people to give the guests a gift. Gee went to a wire hanging across a corner of the house and selected one of his father's shirts and gave it to the leader, Ashwin, who, in turn, gave Gee a bag of tobacco.

The four men sat at the table, and shortly, Gee and the Indians were at ease and talking freely. Mrs. Gilmore cooked some beans and cornbread and invited them to eat.

Later, Gee asked them how they knew how to find their place. Ashwin said they sometimes traded with Mr. Randolph and had watched from the trees when Gee kicked the man. He said they were curious about the girl, knowing she was a Cherokee, and followed the wagon tracks to here. When they returned to their village and told their chief, the chief said for them to come and see if she was a slave. If she was, they were to bring her back.

It was almost dark when Gee went outside to tend to the animals. Sahin and Balik went to help, but Ashwin stayed behind, talking to Mina and Mrs. Gilmore. When they came back inside, Mrs. Gilmore suggested she would make them some pallets to sleep on. Ashwin said they had been traveling for four days, making camp each day, and they would camp in the trees tonight and leave in the morning.

Gee did not go to the loft to sleep, but moved his bed so he could be near to the door, just in case someone came to burn the house. Sometime later, Gee was aware of Mina lying on the pallet beside him. It felt good having her here. He was afraid to move for fear she would get up and move back to her bed. Later, he drifted off into a peaceful sleep that was interrupted by the sound of someone screaming.

"Gee, help! Gee, the Indians got me! Help!" Gee ran to the door and yelled to Ashwin that Mr. Stewart was a friend.

"Mr. Stewart, they are friendly. Ashwin, show him where the wire is, and y'all come to the house." He was relieved that it was not the vigilantes, but still amused.

Mrs. Gilmore lit the lamp and was sitting at the table with Mina when the men came in. Mr. Stewart looked a bit shaken. "I sure thought I was a goner when they pulled me from my horse," he said, pointing at the Indians. Everyone laughed, and he continued, "I was just riding along, letting my horse lead the way. I was thinking about what that group of vigilantes might do, and I was so glad to finally see you cabin. The next thing I knew, I was lying on my back with a knife at my throat. I sure am glad that they," he looked at the Indians, "that you are friendly." He paused and turned to look at Gee. "Anyway, Gee, the reason I came is that the vigilantes are planning to burn your house and string you up so I came to warn you. A friend of mine said he heard one of them telling a man they found Cain Johnston's saddle and what was left of him after the wolves and buzzards had their fill. They told anyone who would listen that you had killed him, took the Indian girl, and his horse.

"What is the matter with people? Don't they know if I stole his horse, I would have taken his saddle, too?" he asked in disgust.

Remembering how bad *So qui li* had looked, and that he had once worn a saddle, Gee looked at Mina and asked if she thought the horse she found was the one the red-haired man had ridden. Mina shook her head and said she did not know. Gee hoped it was. Either way, Johnson had paid for what he had done to her with his life, and he hoped he had left her his horse.

"Are you sure about the vigilantes? When do you think they will come?" Mrs. Gilmore asked, fear and concern in her voice.

"I think they would have come tonight, but were waiting for two more men. That would make five of them, maybe more, so you must leave early in the morning or they will kill all of you."

There was silence in the room. Gee doubted they could hold off five men—or possibly more.

"We can't leave. Where would we go?" he asked aloud to no one in particular. "We will stay and defend out property. I'd rather die than run. I'm not leaving. I'm gonna stay and fight."

"Gee, you cannot fight them all by yourself. They will kill you all."

There was silence in the room until Ashwin spoke and said they would stay and fight. After all, they were protecting one of their people. After some thought, Mr. Stewart said he would stay also. Then he added soberly, "But someone will probably get killed. Even if we do survive, there will be more of them later. They will keep coming until you are dead." He turned and looked at Mrs. Gilmore, "I really think you should go."

"You can go if you like, but I'm not leaving," Gee said firmly. Mr. Stewart shrugged his shoulders because he knew how Gee felt. He had been in those shoes himself. Maybe if they survived the first assault, the vigilantes would leave them alone. Unlikely, but it was something to wish for. In the meantime, they should make plans on how best to defend themselves.

After quick discussions, it was agreed that Sahin would stand watch until daylight. At daybreak Balik would stand guard down the trail until they could set up an ambush. They discussed how best to defend their place and agreed that one man should be on top of the house, one on top of the smokehouse, one by the woodpile, and one by the spring. They would make another woodpile for someone else across from where the barn had stood. All locations were selected in order that they might catch the vigilantes in a cross-fire.

Mr. Stewart said they would probably wait on the edge of the woods until after dark before lighting their torches, then race in to set the house on fire. If there were only five of them, three would probably stop to cover the front door, shooting anyone who came out, while the others would throw their torches on top of the house.

"I think we should make a ladder to climb up on the roof and fill every container with water to put out the fire, just in case they manage to set the house ablaze." He also suggested they take down the wire because it wouldn't be wise to alarm the vigilantes. "We should not fire until they stop, and then shoot the one closest to you. It looks like it will be clear tonight with a full moon so we will have no trouble seeing them. Mrs. Gilmore, I think you and Mina should find a place down by the creek to hide. They would like nothing better than to get Mina; just make sure you stay there until we come get you," Stewart instructed.

Just before dark, everyone took their positions and waited. It was almost midnight when Gee, who was hiding behind the woodpile next to where the barn once stood, heard the sound of horses moving on the trail and saw riders emerge from the timbers into the moonlight. Gee could make out six riders. After a few moments he saw two of them strike matches and light the torches. Five riders came toward the house at full gallop. Two of them tossed their torches upon the roof while the other three stopped at the front of the house. They aimed their muskets at the front door and yelled, "Gilmore, send the squaw girl out, and we'll let ya live. If ya don't, we gonna kill ya all."

The words had no more than left his mouth when five muskets fired, and two men were knocked from their horses immediately. Another man slumped in the saddle but fell seconds later. The two men who had thrown the torches raced from the yard only to have Balik swing his lance and knock one from his saddle. He drove the lance deep into the man's chest just as another shot rang out. The other man's horse stumbled and fell, his right front leg broken by the musket ball, throwing the rider from horse. The horse was struggling to get to his feet, and the rider was crawling around, frantically trying to find his pistol when Sahin reached him. In one swift motion Sahin slit the man's throat. The man's hands went to his throat, trying to stop the blood; he gurgled and coughed, his hands still clawing at his throat before he collapsed and fell face first on to the ground. A few seconds later, Gee raced to the ladder and saw Mr. Stewart passing buckets of water to Ashwin who was on top of the house, pouring water on the fire, which was quickly extinguished.

Seeing the fire was out, they picked up the vigilantes' weapons and dragged their bodies away from the house. They caught two of the horses that had run a short way and stopped. Gee reloaded his pistol, walked toward the creek, and called to his mother.

"Is everyone all right?" she asked.

"Everyone except the vigilantes," Gee reported proudly.

Gee went inside and came back with a lamp and looked at the bodies. Gee did not know three of them, but one was the man with a broken jaw and the other was the runt of a man with his beady eyes still open, staring at nothing. The man Gee had encountered at the trading post was not one of them. Gee walked to where the horse with the broken leg was still struggling to get to his feet.

"I was aiming at the man, not the horse. I guess I need to practice with the pistol. Now I have got to put him out of his misery." He shot the horse between the eyes.

"One of them got away. There were six of them, but one stayed behind," Gee explained as he reloaded his pistol.

"Are you sure?" Mr. Stewart asked.

"Yeah, he stayed at the edge of the timbers and left when the shooting started."

"This is not good," Mr. Stewart noted, taking off his hat and scratching his head. "Mrs. Gilmore, I had hoped this would not happen. This is just like what happened to me; I tried to fight them and lost."

Extending Shadows

Looking at Gee, Mr. Stewart continued, "Gee, you will lose too. The only way for you to live is to leave. The one that got away will make up a tale about how you and the Indians slaughtered them for no reason. He will gather a bunch of people, and the next time they come, there could be twenty or more. They will burn your house, and if you are here, they will kill you, your mother, and Mina. There is no way you can fight twenty men and survive. You have got to leave—and leave in the morning, too. You should not stop until you get as far as Ryan Station. Mr. Ryan is a friend of mine so tell him I will pay for your keep when I bring you the money for your farm. Tell him why you left here, but ask him not to tell anyone. He is a good man, and you will be safe there. I will stop by Mr. Randolph's and tell him what has happened. If anyone asks him about you, I'll tell him to say you have left to live with the Indians. The man that got away will know the Indians helped you tonight, and if they think you are living with the Indians, maybe they will not pursue you. I will ride to Mooresville at first light and meet you at Ryan's Station as soon as I can."

Gee protested strongly, saying he had rather die than run.

"Gee, you have a responsibility to take care of your mother and Mina. You cannot do that if you are dead. Not only will you die, but believe me, so will they. They will kill you all."

"You be welcome at our village. There you can start new. The Cherokee will give land to farm and help build house. Our village will protect you and make sure you have food until spring. We will do this because of what you did for one of our people." Gee saw the other Indians nodding their heads as Ashwin spoke.

Gee looked at his mother, at Mr. Stewart, and at Mina.

"You are right." His shoulders slumped, and his eyes watered. He swallowed hard, but knew if he saved his mother and Mina, he was doing exactly what he had to do.

At first light they began loading the wagon. Mr. Stewart said they should load the farm equipment on the wagon first. "The road will be soft from the recent snow, and you should load only the things you cannot do without, like clothes, blankets, kitchenware, meal, flour, salt, and meat from the smokehouse—just enough to live on until I bring the money for your farm."

They loaded the wagon as quickly as they could, managed to catch a rooster and five hens, which they put in a wooden cage and tied to the side of the wagon. Gee slaughtered one of the hogs and opened the hog lot gate. He had no choice but to turn the other two loose; there was no more room on the wagon.

Two cows, a calf, and the two vigilante horses were tied with ropes behind the wagon. They left two hours after daylight, stopping only briefly at the edge of the woods to look back and wave to Mr. Stewart as he left. Mrs. Gilmore was crying softly. Mina put her arms around her and said, "You be happy with my people. They be good to you like you be good to me."

Gee slapped the horses with the lines and yelled, "Giddy up, aahah!"

The wagon began to move, with Gee, Mrs. Gilmore, and Mina sitting on the seat, Ashwin and Sahin walking their horses in front of the wagon, and Balik behind, making sure the horses and cows followed. Gee did not look back—he wanted to, but knew he would cry if he did. He looked straight ahead, thinking there would be no one left to take care of the graves. He kept trying to tell himself that someday they would come back, but deep down inside, he knew they would not. He put his arm around Mina, smiled at her and at his mother, and said, "We'll be okay." His words were anything but reassuring.

CHAPTER FIFTEEN

CHIEF BATES
Twenty Ten

Anna saddled the horses, and in a short while Simmons learned to relax and enjoy the ride as they walked their horses. As they rode, he was surprised at how easy Anna was to talk to. She listened intently and was genuinely interested in what he said. He talked freely about his childhood, the orphanage, and how proud Lanny was of Elaine. He admitted he was attracted to her, even though he had known her for only three days. He felt like he had known her for ages, maybe only because of Lanny, he admitted shyly.

Anna also talked freely about her family; he was mesmerized by the things she said. She told of a family that went back to the late 1700s, of Gaither Gilmore and his Cherokee wife. How their family fortunes mostly began with him when they found gold on their property. She also spoke of the hardships and the joys each generation had enjoyed. She spoke of Robert and told the story of the swimsuit on the stairway in Galveston. He could feel her hurt as she talked.

As they rode, Simmons was aware of several oil wells and could only wonder about the wealth of this family, and yet how fragile and unhappy they were. He thought of the truth of the old saying, *Money doesn't buy happiness.*

As they rode, they discussed ways to investigate Lanny's death. They were almost back to the barn when Anna's cell phone rang. Simmons did not want her to think he was eavesdropping, so he prodded his horse ahead as she pulled her horse to a stop, a look of disbelief on her face. Shortly, she reined her horse close to Simmons.

"That was Penny. They found Bradley's boat in Lake Palestine, which is between here and Tyler, about ten this morning. He was not in it, nor did he come to the office this morning. It seems some fishermen remembered seeing him and a soldier launch his boat early Sunday morning. This morning, when they noticed his truck and boat trailer had not been moved off the parking lot, they called the sheriff. She said Johnny Bates called her and said Roy Grades was in the courthouse a little while ago saying Mr. Bradley had told him he was upset about losing his cool Friday night and wanted to apologize to the soldier. He said Mr. Bradley told him he had called that soldier Saturday afternoon to apologize, and just to show him there were no hard feelings, they made plans to go fishing on Sunday. Johnny also said the rumor was that Sheriff Evans was sending a deputy to bring you in for questioning."

"Ms. Anna, Bradley did not call me, and if he had, I would not have gone fishing with him. I have never been fishing in my life." She nodded her head in agreement.

As they neared the barn, Simmons saw a patrol car stop at the big house. Even at this distance he could see it was Gregg Davis. Anna called to him and said they would be there as soon as they cared for the horses. Gregg met them at the barn.

"Mr. Simmons, the sheriff asked if you would come downtown. He would like to ask you some questions," he said very professionally, though not unfriendly.

Before Simmons could answer, Anna said, "Gregg, Penny called and told us what had happened, but Mr. Simmons was here all day Sunday."

"Mrs. Sanderson, I am only doing what I am told."

Anna turned and faced Simmons. "Mitchell, it has been my experience that it's best to have an attorney present before you answer any questions, no matter what they are." She paused, deciding what to do next. She turned to face Gregg, "Gregg, I will bring Mitchell down, and we will have our attorney meet us at the sheriff's office."

"Mrs. Sanderson, I was told to bring him in."

"Gregg, you tell Joe what I said. I will bring him in, or if you like, you can say you could not find him. Either way, he is not going down there without an attorney," she said persuasively.

"Ms. Anna, he is not going to like it, but I will tell him what you said." He turned and faced Simmons, "You know, when I saw you at Lanny's place, I told you Lanny and I had been friends. Weathers, over at the National Guard, told me what you said about him hating dead bodies. That got me to thinking, and I tend to agree with you. I can't really put my finger on it, but there seems to be something going on in this town that is not right. There are too many circumstances, too many unanswered questions. First it was Lanny, then Otis, then Gentry at the jewelry store, and now it's probably Bradley. Simmons, I am on your side, like right now. I could arrest you if you refuse to come with me, but I won't." He tipped his hat and walked slowly back to the patrol car as Simmons and Anna stared after him.

Anna called Penny, who was in a meeting with her grandfather and Phil Garrison, the lead attorney for Gilson Oil. They had been waiting to meet with Bradley. Anna explained to Penny what the deputy had said, and that the sheriff wanted to see Mitchell, but that she had advised him not to meet with the sheriff without an attorney. Penny asked her to hold on a second, and the phone was silent. When Penny came back, she explained that Amos and Phil would take the chopper and be in Longview in twenty minutes. Amos would familiarize Phil with the case on the way, and he wanted Anna to wait if she got there before he did so he could go in with her.

"Under the circumstances, I think I should stay here and maybe meet you all later. Keep me informed," Penny said after she finished outlining the plans to Anna.

Anna relayed to Simmons what Penny had said, and that an attorney and her father would meet them at the sheriff's office. She then dialed the sheriff's office, "This is Anna Sanderson. Tell Joe we will be there in twenty minutes," she told the dispatcher, leaving no doubt that she expected the sheriff to be there when they arrived. Twenty minutes later, Anna and Simmons met the chopper as it set down on the back lot of the sheriff's office building.

As they walked into the sheriff's department, one of the first things Simmons noticed was the absence of the lady dispatcher. He had hoped she would be there because he wanted to tell her he was still investigating.

The desk sergeant said the sheriff was expecting them. "Down the hall, first door on the right." He grinned and nodded his head toward the hallway. The way he said it made Simmons wonder if he was not a little amused.

Joe Evans was about five feet eight and may have weighed 150 pounds at the most. He wore a white Stetson and a khaki uniform; but for the Stetson, he reminded Simmons of Barney Fife from the old Andy Griffith Show. He was about thirty, with wrinkled white skin and a hawk-like nose. His ears were a little large, and he stared at Anna with small, beady, brown eyes that were not very friendly. Simmons could see the sheriff was thoroughly enjoying himself. He did not introduce himself nor acknowledge any of them, but turned his attention to Anna.

"Gregg told me what you said, and I want you to know that I am sheriff of this county," he said in a hostile voice, staring belligerently at Anna.

The words had no more than left his mouth, when Anna shot back, "Until the election," she said with authority. Her voice was stern and demanding.

The expression on the sheriff's face changed quickly as he realized this was neither a woman nor a family to cross. What she said could be true, and she could make it happen.

"I am sorry; I really did not mean it that way."

Anna glared at him. Simmons could see the sheriff wilting under her stare. She asserted, "Mr. Evans, I treat people with respect, and I expect to be treated likewise." She continued, her voice ice cold. Simmons shot a quick glance at Mr. Gilmore, who had not said a word and was smiling, knowing he did not have to say anything. Anna could handle this, and he was proud of her.

"This is Mitchell Simmons, attorney Phillip Garrison, and, of course, you know Mr. Gilmore," Anna said coldly.

Evans arose and offered his hand to each of them. "I am Joe Evans, and again I am sorry. I have been under a lot of pressure lately." His voice was no longer hostile nor did he speak with authority.

Anna did not let him off the hook so easily and stated bluntly, "Seems like a good sheriff would be able to handle pressure," she said, still annoyed.

Simmons watched Evans and was amazed at how his attitude had changed. This woman was dressing him down like a drill sergeant takes down a new recruit. This woman was not to be messed with. He could only imagine the pressure Amos Gilmore could inflict!

"Yes, ma'am!" Evans was now anxious to change the subject and asked them to be seated. He turned to face Simmons. "Mr. Simmons, I asked you to come in because the man you had an altercation with Friday night is missing. A witness saw him and a solider launch his boat yesterday morning, and no one has seen him since." He paused, "This is only a preliminary investigation, but I need to know where you were Sunday morning."

Before Simmons could answer, the attorney asked, "Mr. Evans, you have a sworn statement from this witness, I presume?"

"Ah, no. Not at this time," Evans squirmed.

"Mr. Evans, then what you have is hearsay. Is that correct?" Evans dropped his head and did not answer. The attorney continued, "As to where my client was, we may speculate that a person can be many places on a Sunday morning at many different times. You will need a specific time before you can ask that question."

Evans looked at Simmons and at the others; he was now meek as a lamb, completely frustrated and uncertain how to continue. Simmons could see he was out of his comfort zone and now regretted this whole episode; at this point, he wanted out of it as quickly as possible. From the cocky sheriff he was when they arrived, he was now the lowest of the low. . . and it showed.

Simmons wondered what he might have been subjected to had Anna not insisted on coming with him and bringing an attorney. He imagined that the sheriff had intended to grill him and make a big impression, maybe even bring in the press. Mr. Gilmore still had not said a word, but Simmons could tell that he disliked the way Evans had acted and still might verbally tear him to pieces.

Simmons could see Sheriff Evans would rather be on the street selling newspapers, or maybe going door to door selling Bibles, anywhere but here in his office, amending his question to Simmons so as not to antagonize Amos Gilmore or his attorney.

"Yes, between the hours of five and six," Evans continued.

"A.M. or P.M.?" the attorney asked rather sternly, though quietly amused. "A.M.," he admitted softly.

"You may answer, Mr. Simmons," Garrison said. "I was in the guest cottage at Mrs. . ."

"You have someone who can vouch for that?" Evans asked, trying hard to feel a little more important.

"We have security cameras that cover the cottage and the gate. If he left, they would show it, unless you think he sprouted wings and flew," Anna shot at him.

Wow, she's still cutting him to pieces, Simmons thought. *I am glad this woman is in my corner.*

Evans looked from Simmons to Anna and said, "Ok, Mrs. Sanderson. I believe you, and I appreciate your help. Thank you all for coming in." He was clearly pleased that this was over and wanted them out of his office as quickly as possible.

They walked outside. Anna thanked the attorney and turned to Simmons just as his phone rang. At first not realizing it was his phone, he finally took it out of his pocket and turned it over and over. "I'm sorry, I don't how to answer it. I've never had a cell phone." He handed it to Anna, who looked surprised, but answered it. She listened and nodded her head.

"That was Penny. Scott McTune told her he wants to talk to you, but not on the phone. He asked if you could meet him at Manny's."

Simmons stood confused; things were moving too fast for him. All of a sudden his mind would not focus. *What am I going to do?* Suddenly, he was on a mountaintop in Afghanistan, he and Lanny, and they needed time to find out why the squad was pinned down by small arms fire. They needed time to plan their next mission. *I've got to take out the enemy. They are picking my men off one by one, and I have to do something quick or my men will be dead. Dead. . . seems like everywhere I turn there are the dead. Lanny is dead, my men are dead. . .*

In his mind he was frantically searching for someone alive, running from one body to the next. *More of the Taliban were coming. He was a sniper, but did not have time to aim—he was firing wildly. More were coming. More and more! They covered the mountains. He was shaking, still firing as fast as he could.* All the while, he could hear someone calling his name.

"Mitchell, Mitchell," he heard, but no one called him Mitchell. They called him Simmons.

Again he heard someone call. This time someone took hold of his shoulders. He looked at them, confused, and it finally dawned on him that it was Amos calling to him. He heard him ask if he were all right.

"Can you go with us to Manny's? Penny will meet us there." Simmons tried to focus, tried to understand what the man had said, but an instant later he was back on that mountain, running from the Taliban, dragging dead soldiers into shallow graves, frantically trying to bury them, pulling their dog-tags off.

He screamed at Lanny, "Lanny, what is Manny's? Who is Scott McTune? Who is Penny? Where are they, Lanny?" Lanny did not answer. Lanny was dead. Everyone was dead. He had to keep firing, had to protect his men. They were dying. His head was exploding. "Lanny, Lanny," he tried to scream, but nothing came out. He was wet with sweat, as his head was exploding. He realized he was walking, but the Taliban was following. He looked at the chopper. That's not a Medevac. What am I doing here? I have got to get them out of here. I've got to get my men off that mountain. They are dying up there.

"Lanny!" he said aloud and turned to look into the eyes of a older man, whose face was filled with deep concern. He saw a man who took him by the shoulders and gently shook him.

"Mr. Simmons, are you alright? You are white as a ghost and wet with perspiration. Can I get you something?" He stood staring at the man. Slowly, his head began to clear, and Simmons could see it was Mr. Gilmore. He looked at him for a long moment as the realization of where he was slowly came back to him.

"I'm sorry, Mr. Gilmore. I don't know what happened. It seemed like my head just exploded. Things were moving so fast, I could not think. I was in Afghanistan and everybody was dead." As his head cleared a little, he knew it was true. He was in something he knew nothing about, with people he barely knew. Lanny was dead, and nothing would bring him back and I may be losing my mind.

"And I don't even know how to answer the phone," he said to no one.

"Mitchell, the mind does funny things when a person is under stress. A lot has happened to you since last Friday. It might be wise for you to let you mind rest before you meet with Mr.

McTune." Simmons considered this. Maybe Mr. Gilmore was right, but his mind seemed to be functioning once again. . . at least he was not on the mountain.

"Mr. Gilmore, I consider Scott a friend. I will go ahead and meet with him. I think I am alright now." And yet, deep inside, he wondered if that were true.

They dropped Anna off at her house and soon the S76 sat down at Manny's.

"Mr. Simmons, will you get some rest when you are finished here? Penny will be here shortly, and I will call her to make sure you do. Rome was not built in a day, you know."

Simmons walked the hundred yards from where they landed to the front entrance as the S76 turbines began to whine.

"Mr. McTune is waiting on you. If you will follow me, please," the doorman said as he led Simmons to a small office just off the main lobby. Scott arose from behind a desk, and they shook hands.

"Thanks for stopping by. Mrs. Sanderson called and told me about the little episode with Joe Evans. She also mentioned the episode a few minutes ago and said you seem to be under a lot of stress. Simmons, we have all experienced stress at one time or another." He looked at Simmons, wondering if he should continue.

"Penny will be here shortly. I think what I have to say concerns her also. So, could I get you a beer or something to drink until she gets here?'

Simmons thought about a beer, but decided he needed a strong cup of coffee. Scott called a waiter, who brought two cups of coffee. Both he and Scott were sipping coffee when Penny and Mr. Gilmore came in.

"I caught him just before he lifted off and wanted him to be here, if that's all right with you," Scott nodded his head.

"Let's go into the conference room. It will be more comfortable in there."

Inside the conference room Scott asked them to be seated and summoned a waiter to bring more coffee. He looked at each of them, as if wondering where he should start. Finally he said, "Look, I don't know if this has anything to do with any of you, but I thought it strange, especially since Bradley is missing. Simmons, when you threw him out of the dining room, the curtains were torn down. I am told that when our maintenance man came to re-hang the curtain, he found a small black bag containing what he thought were glass crystals in those curtains. He gave it to housekeeping, and they cataloged over one hundred chips of glass. This seemed so unusual, the housekeeper showed them to several other employees. A couple of them made comments that the glass chips looked like uncut diamonds. Anyway, they were dropped in the safe, which is our procedure when an employee finds articles belonging to our guests. The safe has a drop box where all money, checks, receipts, and other properties are deposited until Monday. It is electrically timed and cannot be opened till then." He paused and looked at each of them.

"I know you are wondering where this is leading, but let me finish. About seven on Saturday morning, Bradley came here looking for a black bag that contained rare coins, according to him. He said he lost it in his encounter with the soldier. He was told a bag with glass chips had been found, but none with coins. He insisted he had glass chips with the coins, but the coins were the most important. He ranted and raved for the safe to be opened. He was furious; he said he had to have that bag and threatened to burn the place if they did not give it to him. They tried to convince him the safe could not be opened until Monday morning, but Bradley became very belligerent—so much so, the police were called, though he left before they arrived. All day yesterday, all the employees could talk about was diamonds in the bag. You know how something like that can spread. Even the local news made reference to a black bag of diamonds found at Manny's.

This morning the safe was opened, and it appeared the bag did contain diamonds. Bradley had claimed there were rare coins along with glass crystals, but as there were no coins; the police were called. The bag was carried to a jeweler who confirmed they were diamonds, probably worth somewhere around ten grand, according to how they were cut. I was called to investigate because he is a resident of this county. I'm wondering if the diamonds might have something to do with Bradley being missing.

"I understand that attorney Roy Grades had implied that the soldier at the boat ramp was Simmons." McTune stopped and seemed to be thinking about something serious. "We found Bradley's boat a couple of hours ago. Inside was an envelope with Lanny Simpson's name on it, and inside the envelope was what appeared to be a diamond, according to the officer on the scene." He turned and faced Penny. "I know you and Lanny were to be married, but why would Bradley have what appears to be a diamond with Lanny Simpson's name on it? Since Bradley is missing and is employed by you, I would like to have your thoughts on this."

They stared at him and no one said a word. There were many questions in their minds, but no answers. He was waiting for someone to answer, when his cell phone rang. He listened intently, nodding his head occasionally, and said, "Yes, but is it our jurisdiction or Barney Fife's?" He looked around, slightly embarrassed, and corrected himself, "I mean Joe Evans. The county line runs through the middle of the lake, you know." He paused, nodded his head, and said, "I will be there ASAP." He flipped the phone closed and turned to look at the others.

"Divers found Bradley's body in some shallow water not far from where his boat was found. It is our side of the county line, so I have to go. Think about what I said, and if you think of anything that might be relevant, please let me know." He stared at Simmons.

"Simmons, the accusations Grades made against you were the reason I wanted to talk to you. I'm afraid the media will now have a field day with this, so I will tell them you have been questioned and told not to leave the state. That's the best I can do." He left and all they could do was stare.

"What's going on here?" Amos asked, and called Anna. "The authorities found Bradley's body, and we need to go the Tyler plant. I'll pick you up in twenty minutes and will fill you in on the way."

They lifted off. Before the chopper set down to pick up Anna, Simmons said to Mr. Gilmore, "Look, I know I would not be any help in a company meeting since I know as much about business as I do about a cell phone." He smiled and watched Mr. Gilmore for some reaction and saw concern on his face. He continued, "I would like to get off at Mrs. Sanderson's and go meet with Chief Bates. I would love to hear his take on all of this. Would that be all right with you?" Somewhat reluctantly Mr. Gilmore agreed, but advised him to get some rest. Simmons got off the chopper when Anna came aboard.

Amos filled her in on Bradley's death and the diamonds as they flew. Even though Scott had not said how Bradley had died, they assumed he was murdered, and the diamonds were the reason why. They wondered about the envelope with Lanny's name on it and about the diamonds found at Manny's. Where had the diamonds come from? Why did Bradley have them and what had he intended to do with them? It seemed like the questions were numerous and the answers few, but at least one of their problems was solved, they no longer had to contend with Bradley. Still, this unnerved them. They could have dealt with him, but to have someone kill him. . . Yes, they were a little more than unnerved. Anna began taking notes on a yellow legal pad.

Simmons drove to the police station and asked the desk sergeant if he could see Chief Bates. The sergeant looked at a man who was walking toward the door. "Chief, someone would like to see you."

Simmons introduced himself. Bates looked amused and studied him intently before he spoke, "For a man who just got into town on Friday, you sure have been making some big waves. I'm Johnny Bates. What can I do for you?"

Bates was in his early fifties, tall and well-built. His slightly wrinkled face was well-tanned. His black hair was graying at his temples and was a little long, hanging almost over his right eye. He had a pleasant smile and a soothing voice and seemed like a likable guy.

"Chief Bates, Elaine told me she had filled you in on what we were doing and that you had offered to help." Simmons hesitated, wondering what he should say next and decided to get right to the point. "I am convinced that Lanny did not take his own life, and I would love to have your take on him and also on Arnold Bradley. I am sure you have heard about the diamonds, and that Bradley's body was found in the lake."

The chief watched Simmons closely for a few seconds, though Simmons could not tell what he was thinking. The chief continued to stare at him before looking down at his watch, "Simmons I have to pick up my grandson for a Pee Wee football game. Why don't you come along and we can talk on the way? I will drop you back here later." Simmons hesitated, but decided he would go.

As they drove, Bates asked him why he thought Lanny had not killed himself. Simmons related the story of how Lanny hated dead bodies and would not want anyone to be troubled with his. If Lanny wanted to kill himself, he would have done it in a way where his body would never be found. Simmons could see that Bates was contemplating this and asked Simmons how long he had known Lanny. Simmons replied they had been together constantly for almost four years in Afghanistan. They rode in silence for a couple of blocks before Simmons asked the chief if he had known Lanny.

"Yes, I coached both Lanny and Elaine in Little League." He paused, concentrating on the road, as if deciding whether to continue. "Lanny's dad, Carl, and I married sisters. We were devastated when we heard Carl was dead and about a month later it was Lacey, Lanny's mother. Then it was Lanny."

Bates turned right onto another street and said nothing more until Simmons asked about Lanny's father. Bates waited, and Simmons began to wonder if he had asked a question he should not have asked.

"He let a tree fall on him." From the way he said it, Simmons decided this was something he did not want to talk about, though he did not know why. The chief made another turn, and Simmons was aware of the neighborhood they were in. It was not a slum area, though it was close. The houses were small, close together, and most of them looked identical. Simmons saw some black people in a few houses and Mexicans in others. Young kids played in the yards, and older boys just loitered around, sitting on cars with broken windows and windshields, some sitting on blocks with no wheels. As they drove, Simmons realized he had not seen a white family and had decided they were just passing through a rough neighborhood until the chief stopped at a house almost hidden with overgrown hedges, knee-high grass, and no car in the driveway. The chief told Simmons he would be right back.

He knocked on the door and waited until a skinny kid came out, holding a helmet and wearing a Titans uniform. He looked to be about six years old with hair that almost covered his dark brown eyes. He hugged the chief, but looked puzzled when he saw Simmons. They walked to the car and the chief said, "This is Simmons. He was a friend of Uncle Lanny's. Simmons, this is Miguel, the best running back since Hershel Walker."

"It is nice to meet you, Mr. Miguel. Maybe I can have your autograph? I never had a chance to get Hershel's, but I would much rather have yours, anyway." The boy smiled politely.

Bates and Miguel talked football as they drove to the football field. Bates took a couple of lawn chairs from the trunk and walked toward the other side of the field. The chief was greeted by the fathers and mothers of several teams and stopped and chatted briefly with each. Simmons continued walking and stopped at the forty-yard line. The game had already started when Bates came over and offered Simmons a chair. He sat down and simply said, "Politics."

They watched the game until it was obvious his grandson was not going to play, at least not when the score was close. As if in answer to the question Simmons was thinking, but would never have dared to ask, Chief Bates said, "My daughter married right out of high school and had Miguel before she was nineteen. We tried to talk her out of marrying at that time and encouraged her to go on to college, but sometimes kids don't do what you want. Now she hardly ever comes out of the house. We have tried to get her to move in with us, but I guess as long as we support her. . ." He looked at the field and said nothing else. Simmons could feel this man's anguish.

They watched as the Titans fell behind twelve to nothing. Miguel still was not in the game, and Simmons could see that Bates was beginning to lose interest. Simmons wanted to ask the chief about Bradley, but did not know where to begin, although it seemed like Bates was waiting for him to ask.

"Chief Bates, I would love to hear what you think about Bradley—I mean about the diamonds he lost at Manny's and why he was so upset with me." Bates stared at the field and looked around, probably to make sure no one was listening, Simmons thought.

"He lived in Tyler. I met him a couple of times, but I mostly know only what Lanny and Penny said about him, which was very little. Frankly, I can say that I was not overly impressed with him and was shocked when Anna married him. The diamonds... I have been thinking about those." He paused, contemplating what he should say next. There were questions in his eyes as he stared at Simmons, as if trying to decide if he could trust this man. He waited, looked at the scoreboard, and at his grandson.

"Did you know that Lanny took an uncut diamond to Gentry's Jewelry to have a ring made for Penny? No one knew where Lanny got the diamond or what Gentry did with it. There were some diamonds in the safe that did not burn when the store burned. Anyway, Lanny's diamond was not there. Gentry lived in the back of the store and died in the fire. The fire department did an investigation and found no cause to believe it was anything but an accident. However, they could not determine the cause of the fire. The police department did a little investigating, but not very thorough, I'm afraid."

He looked at the group of kids sitting on the bench, maybe to see if his grandson was in the game, and saw he was still sitting. Bates stared at Simmons and said, "Now, Simmons, this is just between me and you, but I talked to the D.A. this morning. We are considering reopening the case on Gentry, because of the possibility of criminal intent in light of the diamonds. Of all the accidents we have had in the last year and a half, his was the only one in our jurisdiction. We've had a lot of things happen with no clear-cut explanations. For instance, Lanny's father cut a tree that fell on him, but no saw was ever found. And why would he go to the back side of his property to cut a tree that he apparently had no use for? When Lanny committed suicide, Sheriff Green said there was a note, but no one saw it and no gun was found. Sheriff Green ran off the side of a mountain with only one wheel leaving a skid mark. Gavin Gentry died in a house fire and now Bradley? I am curious to know if it will be an accident, or maybe someone will try to blame someone else for his death." He looked at Simmons, leaving no doubt as to whom he was referring.

He continued, "For a county that may go a year with only a few fatal accidents, and maybe one homicide every two or three years—and that is usually an open and shut case involving jealously or infidelity—well, all this makes me wonder."

Simmons mind was spinning, and he remembered what Elaine had said about this town being almost ready to explode. "Wow!" *Was that all he could say?*

After the game they dropped Miguel off. On the way back to the station, Simmons asked, "Chief Bates, do you mind if I call Penny and tell her what you said about the diamonds? I will not mention the part about the D.A., of course. They are in a meeting in Tyler, and I promised I would call after I talked to you."

The chief looked at him and contemplated his answer before he spoke, "I guess that would be okay. I have always been friends with the Sandersons, just don't mention the D.A."

Simmons took the phone out of his pocket and looked at it. Embarrassed, he handed it to the chief and asked him if would show him how to find her number. "They don't have these things in Afghanistan. Penny gave it to me, but I guess she did not know I knew nothing about cell phones. I was too embarrassed to tell her. Maybe I should have because I've wanted to call Elaine all day."

Bates took the phone and showed Simmons how to find the contacts. "Once you find the contact you want, just touch it, and it will dial the number," he told him. Bates then dialed Penny's number and handed the phone back to Simmons, who briefly relayed what Bates had said. There was a long silence, and Simmons could visualize Penny running all this information through her head. She asked if she could speak to Chief Bates. Simmons handed the phone to the chief and said, "She would like to talk to you."

Bates listened carefully, nodded his head a couple of times, looked at his watch again, and said he would check with his wife and call her back. He handed the phone back to Simmons. "She wants us, including you, to come to Manny's for dinner. She said to be sure to tell Carrie... she's my wife... that Anna, Amos, and Marie will also be there. I will drop you at the station, and if my wife hasn't made other plans, we will meet you there."

Simmons left the station, his mind preoccupied with what Bates had told him. He thought he was driving on the road to Manny's until he realized he was heading west instead of south. He turned around and tried to backtrack, but knew he was lost when he saw the airport. He almost panicked until he realized there was a GPS in the truck. He was familiar with GPS—they had them in the Army—but this one was entirely different. He pulled to the side of the road, and after a little experimenting, found how to work it and typed in "Manny's." He did not stop at the entrance, but drove to the parking lot and looked to see if Scott's car was there. It was not.

Inside he greeted everyone and made the mistake of calling Anna, "Mrs. Sanderson." He saw her frown, and her eyes flashed displeasure at him, so he made a mental note not to do that again. Penny and Anna began asking questions about what Bates had said. Amos cleared his throat, reminding them to let Bates tell his story himself. "After all, it is never a good idea to conduct business on an empty stomach," he remarked, leaving no doubt as to who was in charge. He ordered a bottle of wine on ice and seven glasses, but waited until Bates and Carrie came in before opening it.

To Simmons, it was obvious all the others knew each other, especially the ladies, who were chatting non-stop. Simmons was an outsider here, and he felt like it. He sipped his wine and listened. During dinner the waiter gave Penny a note. She read it and dialed a number. She listened intently, thanked the caller, and hung up. "That was Scott McTune. He gave me some of the details

Chief Bates

about Bradley's death. He died of blunt force trauma to the head, and it did not appear to be self-inflected. There were some other things he was not at liberty to discuss, but one of the things he told me earlier was that an envelope with Lanny Simpson's name on it was found. Inside the envelope was what they presumed was a rather large, uncut diamond. Now McTune thinks perhaps the envelope was planted there in an effort to make it look like Bradley was responsible for the diamonds found at Manny's. He does not know what the envelope meant except maybe to make it appear that Lanny had taken the envelope form Gentry's safe." Penny paused and looked at Chief Bates, waiting for him to offer his insight and to relate to them what he had told Simmons.

Bates got to his feet slowly and walked to the head of the table. "Look, there are a lot of unanswered questions here, and in light of what we have learned, it makes me wonder. Everyone assumed Lanny's father's death was an accident; thus, there was no investigation. I am not sure why there was no coroner's report. Then there was Lacey, who you probably know was Lanny's mother and my sister-in-law. Did she really have a heart attack? She never had any symptoms of heart trouble, and I think her death was also rushed through the system with no coroner's report. Lanny's death was not an accident, but made to look like it was suicide. Then there was the accidental death of Gentry. All the cases, except Gentry's, were handled by Sheriff Otis Green, who also died in an accident. I don't believe his death was investigated very thoroughly, either. Lots of people thought Sheriff Green had too much power, and I think a lot of the higher ups were glad he was out of office." Bates hesitated and took a large drink of wine.

"Now we have another death. It will be interesting to see if Bradley's death is an accident or possibly made to look like one. The presence of the diamond seems to link Bradley's death with Lanny's. I don't know if any of you are aware that both Carl and Lanny carried quite a few uncut diamonds to Gentry's before his death. Where did they get the diamond? I recall Carl once said he needed Lanny here to help him with a project. I did not think much of it at the time, but now I wonder. There are a lot of things that seem to be tied together—maybe too much to be just a coincidence."

Everyone sat and stared, not knowing what to say or what to do, and unaware that Anna was writing down everything that was said.

CHAPTER SIXTEEN

THE CHEROKEE
Seventeen ninety-four

Gee made his way along the old wagon trail that wound its way along the foothills. When they passed the Grimes place, he did not see anyone nor did he expect to. The road was indeed soft from the recent snow, and the traveling was slow, yet they kept moving, stopping only at a ford to let the horses drink or to free the wagon if it mired in the mud. When that happened, they cut small saplings to use as pry poles to lift the wagon and cut small tree limbs to place under the wheels. The only time he knew the Indians were still with them was when they came to help with the wagon. A few times he had seen movement off to the side, as they moved parallel to the wagon so as not to draw attention to Gee and his family, even though they had not seen a single soul.

About thirty minutes before dark, they pulled off the trail and made camp. Ashwin suggested they not build a fire because there was a small settlement a half day's ride off, and someone might see the fire. He did not know if they had heard about Gee and his family taking in an Indian, but if they had, they might not be friendly.

They ate cornbread and a pot of beans Mrs. Gilmore had cooked before they left. They fed and hobbled the horses, then milked and tied the cows to a wagon wheel, knowing the calf would not stray far from its mother. Ashwin said he, Sahin, and Balik would share the guard duty then leave at first light. There was little talk as they prepared for bed. The Indians cut small cedar branches and lay them on the ground. They put a deerskin over the branches and covered themselves with another one. Mrs. Gilmore removed her mattress and laid it on the cedars Gee had placed underneath the wagon. She and Mina lay down and covered themselves with a quilt. Gee unrolled his pallet, laid it on some cedars not far from the wagon, and covered it with a quilt. He lay with his musket by his side and the pistol next to his head so he could reach it quickly, if necessary.

Later in the night, Gee awoke to find Mina lying next to him with her arm around him. He looked at her, and in the light of an almost full moon, he could see her smiling at him. He put his arm around her and pulled her close to him. She snuggled close, and he put his finger on his lips and touched her lips. She raised her head to face him. He had never kissed a girl before and did not know why he did so now, but he kissed her lightly and quickly turned his head away. He heard her giggle and thought, *What was so funny? This was the first time I ever kissed a girl and she giggles.* He did not understand and did not know if he has done it right or not, but he knew that nothing he had ever done before had felt so good.

As they snuggled close, she squeezed him and said, "Me *na s qi ya i*."

"I like you too," Gee whispered.

He awoke to the sound of the Indians hooking the horses to the wagon. Gee feared what they might think of him lying with Mina until he realized she was not beside him. What would they have done if she had been? What would they have thought? He could not imagine what his mother would have said, and he wondered if he should tell her. He decided to wait until he could talk to Ashwin and ask him what he should do. He only knew there was no way he was going to tell Mina not to lay with him.

There was some cornbread left from yesterday, so they had milk and cornbread for breakfast, then quickly broke camp. Shortly after daybreak, they were moving again.

The Cherokee

Ashwin said it was about three days to Ryan's Station, but after that, the going would be better because they could travel on the great wagon road. Gee had never been this far from home, but he had heard stories of how the settlers used the great wagon road to travel south and west, looking for more and better land.

They stopped about noon and made a small fire. Mrs. Gilmore fried pork tenderloin and cornbread. Ashwin and the other Indians came to eat and talked of riding along with the wagon, but decided it best to keep to the timber, at least until they reached the station, though they had not met anyone on the trail.

Gee wondered if he would have a chance to talk with Ashwin tonight about Mina. Right now he could hardly wait in hopes she would come and lay with him again. She had been on his mind all morning; even though he had never even been close to a girl before, he knew he wanted Mina for his wife. He was unsure how to ask or what to do, but he vowed to himself he would also talk to his mother tonight.

Later that afternoon, Balik rode to the wagon to say two riders were coming. He suggested that Mina hide in the wagon until they pass by, just in case they were unfriendly. He quickly faded into the woods, and soon Gee saw the two men approaching. Gee could see they were farmers; one of them was leading two of the strangest looking horses he had ever seen. They were not as tall as a horse, but had strong muscles and big ears. Their disposition was slow and gentle.

Gee could tell the two men were a little nervous about the wagon, but seemed to relax a little when they saw that Gee was young and with an older lady. They stopped at the wagon and said good evening to Gee and tipped their hats to Mrs. Gilmore. They seemed friendly enough and asked Gee where they were headed. Gee did not want to tell them that they were going to live with the Cherokee, so he said that they were just headed anywhere they could find better land they what they had left in Virginia.

The man with the strange horses said, "People say there is a lot of land in South Carolina and Georgia, but I have been told that it's at least a two-week trip. Another man said he had been over the mountains, and there were great tracks of land there, but I don't think you can get over the mountains this time of year—too cold and too much snow."

Gee could not contain his curiosity any longer and asked the man about the strange looking horses. The man laughed and said they were not horses but mules. "They are a cross between a mare and a donkey, and they are supposed to be stronger, eat less, and gentle as a lamb." Gee was impressed and inquired as to where he had gotten them.

"I got them in Wilmington from a man who lives in New York. He breeds a donkey with a horse and raises them until they are old enough to sell. If they work as well as people say they do, I am going to buy a donkey and raise some myself." He looked at the sun and said, "Well, I guess we'd better be going. We want to cover as much distance as we can while it is still light. It was nice meeting you; I hope you find some good land. But y'all be careful. The road gets pretty rough with some deep gullies before you get to Ryan's Station. Just make sure you don't slide off into one of them. Good day." He tipped his hat to Mrs. Gilmore, but before he left, Gee asked how far it was to the station. The man replied that they might be able to make it there in two days, providing they stayed out of the gullies. He rode away, leading the mules.

It was almost sundown before Gee found a suitable campsite. This time they built a fire, and Mrs. Gilmore made supper. They sat around the campfire, most of their conversation revolving around the mules.

Later, Gee walked over to where Ashwin was making his bed and asked if he could talk to him about Mina. Ashwin did not seem surprised when Gee told of Mina coming to his bed. Gee said he had only kissed her and wanted to know if he could take her for his wife, that is, if Mina would agree. Ashwin asked him

The Cherokee

what his mother had said. When Gee told him he had not talked to her, Ashwin suggested Gee should discuss it with her first.

"If she has no objections, then neither do I. It is Cherokee custom, however, to have our chief appoint a grandmother to decide since Mina has no parents. I think that would be best."

Gee was helping his mother get her mattress from the wagon when he asked, "Did you know that Mina came to my bed last night? I kissed her, but I swear that is all. We were lying close together when I went to sleep, but when I awoke she was not there. Momma, she is everything I have ever dreamed of, and I want her for my wife. I think she wants me, too, but Ashwin said I should ask you. He also said I would have to wait for their chief to appoint a grandmother to decide if Mina can marry since Mina has no folks." He paused to catch his breath.

"If you say 'yes' and the grandmother says 'no,' what will I do?

"My child, I think the wishes of Mina would be enough, so you should ask her. If she says 'yes,' then I would love for you to marry her. Yes, I would absolutely love it," his mother answered softly.

Later, Gee saw Mina standing by the campfire and walked towards her. She watched him until he got close, then turned and walked away without saying a word. Gee thought that was strange, but remembered she had not said a word to him all day. *What have I done? Is she mad because I kissed her? I think she kissed me back, so what is wrong? Is she mad that I told about her coming to my bed? That must be it.* He called out to her, but she did not answer, just lay down on the mattress and covered her head. Gee stood looking at the mattress and at his mother, seeing that his mother did not know what was wrong either.

Gee went to bed, hoping Mina would come to his bed again tonight, but she did not. He spent a sleepless night and was determined to find out what was wrong as soon as it was light.

They were on the move again early the next morning, and Mina would not look at him nor ride on the seat between him and his mother, opting instead to sit on top of a mattress in the back of the wagon. When they stopped to eat lunch, he tried to talk to her, but she turned and walked away. Gee did not know what to do. He made his way to where Ashwin, Sahin, and Balik sat and asked them if they saw the way Mina was acting.

"We see," Ashwin said, and added, "It is a custom of the Cherokee, if young brave wants to marry girl, he kills deer and lays it at her door. If she accepts the deer, cooks meat, and gives some of it to him, that means 'yes.' I think she has made it clear she would cook and give you meat, but since you did not kill a deer or even go hunting for one, she thinks you do not want her. I think it wise you kill deer."

"But how can I kill a deer? We are always on the move," Gee asked. "You go now. I see plenty deer sign. You catch wagon down the road."

Gee hurried to the wagon, got his musket, saddled one of the vigilantes' horses, and left without eating. He walked the horse slowly and later saw a deer feeding under a white oak tree. He raised his musket, but saw the deer had two small fawns with her. Even though he wanted very badly to kill a deer for Mina, he could not bring himself to shoot. He hunted for two more hours and saw nothing. He knew it was more important to get Mina and his mother to Ryan's Station so he gave up and headed back to the trail. When he saw the wagon tracks, he followed them until he caught up to the wagon. *Maybe when we reach the trading post, I can go hunting while we wait for Mr. Stewart*, Gee thought. In the meantime, he hoped Mina would understand that he was trying to take a deer.

After they made camp, Gee saw Ashwin talking to Mina. As Ashwin spoke, he saw Mina nod her head and look at him. She smiled at him, and his heart melted. That night she came to his bed; they lay close, and she was still beside him when morning came.

Ashwin awoke them at first light to a sky that was blood red with clouds billowing in the northwest. The temperature, which had been mild, was now dropping, and the wind was blowing hard. Ashwin urged them to hurry because a big storm was heading their way. They broke camp in record time and started towards Ryan's Station at a fast pace. By noon, the temperature was close to freezing and the wind strong, whipping the wagon tarpaulin so hard that Gee feared it would rip to pieces.

They prodded the horses to go faster and were making good headway until they reached the gullies; there the going became treacherous. The wagon became stuck several times, once almost turning over when it slid into a deep gully. Most of the wagon's contents had to be unloaded, and it took the better part of the morning to get it loaded again and back on the road. A short time later, they were on flat ground, and the going was smoother until it began to snow. Though only light at first, it was snowing hard by mid-afternoon, and the road was quickly covered.
An hour later the snow was a foot deep, and the horses were stumbling and sliding, having great difficultly pulling the wagon. Ashwin discussed their options. They had two choices: they could stop and wait out the storm, though admittedly they did not know how long it would last or how much snow would fall. If the snow got really deep, they would be stuck here, unable to move. The other choice was to leave the wagon and ride the horses to Ryan's Station. They had to be close to the station so they decided that would be the right decision; they could make better time on the horses. Even if they did not make it to the station before dark, the horses could find their way along the road if the snow did not get too deep. If it did, they were in trouble.

They quickly unhitched the horses, and Gee and Mina rode one horse while Mrs. Gilmore rode the other. They led the other two horses, but the cow and calf could not keep pace, so they had no choice but to leave them. Maybe they would make their way along after them; if not; they might be able to find them when they came back for the wagon, providing the snow was not too deep. If it were, the animals would probably freeze to death. Gee hated the thought of losing the cows, but he had no other choice. They had to keep moving at a fast pace.

The wind was now fierce, and it was snowing so hard Gee could not see where they were. The only choice was to let the horses find the road and, hopefully, stay on it. They plodded along as fast as they could but were slowed by the deep snow, now nearly two feet deep. Even the horses were beginning to have trouble walking. Gee could tell the light was fading, which presented them with another decision: should they stop and build a lean-to for shelter or should they push on? It was agreed that they had no other choice but to keep going. It would be almost impossible to build a lean-to in this storm. Surely the station could not be far, but they had no way of knowing.

It was almost dark when Gee heard dogs barking. At first he did not know if the sound was wolves or coyotes, or maybe he was so cold he was imagining things, but soon he could tell it was dogs. Hopefully, it was not wild dogs, but the dogs at Ryan's Station.

At the station, Mr. Ryan went to the window to see what the dogs were barking at. He could barely make out the forms of the five riders. As they came closer, he could see that three of them were Indians. One was a white man, and the other was a woman. When they stopped in front of the trading post, he saw an Indian girl was riding behind the white man. He was cautious, but decided anyone out in this weather could not be a threat. He walked out on the porch and yelled for them to come inside. Gee and Mina dismounted and helped Mrs. Gilmore. Mr. Ryan suggested the women come inside while the men put their horses in the barn.

Mr. Ryan was still a little uneasy about them until Mrs. Gilmore told him of their ordeal and that Mr. Stewart had advised them to leave. They would buy more land when Mr. Stewart paid them for the land they had left. When the storm hit, they had to leave the wagon because the horses could not pull it. They were lucky to have made it to Ryan's Station before the snow got too deep.

"Mr. Stewart said you would let us stay until he brings the money for our farm," Mrs. Gilmore explained. "Yes, you are welcome here," Mr. Ryan assured her.

After taking care of the horses, the men came in, and Mr. Ryan added more wood to the fire, took their overcoats, and draped them over chairs to dry. He shook hands with the Indians, and Ashwin introduced Gee.

"Warm yourselves and I'll get some tea," Ryan replied in a welcoming tone.

Later Mr. Ryan came back with the tea and assured Ashwin that if it stopped snowing by morning, they could take another pair of horses and go back for the wagon. He said they would use the horses to make a two set of tracks about the width of the wagon wheels and hook both teams to the wagon. Surely, both teams could pull the wagon; if not, they would pack whatever they could onto the horses. He said this time of year, the snow melted fast and would probably be gone by tomorrow afternoon. He did not think anyone would be traveling in this kind of weather, so the wagon should be safe.

"The only concern I would have is the bears and wolves. They will have everything torn apart if we don't get to it soon." He paused and looked at Mrs. Gilmore. "You must be worn out. I will make you and Mina a pallet here in the store." He walked behind a rack of clothing and returned with wool blankets for each of the men.

"There is a lot of hay in the barn so you should be able to keep warm. In the morning I will have my wife, Nisha, make you some breakfast.

He went to the back of the store and returned with two rolls of cotton padding and more blankets. He laid them on the floor for Mrs. Gilmore and Mina and said he would add more wood to the fire later in the night. Mrs. Gilmore and the others thanked him and said goodnight.

Gee and the Indians made their way to the barn. Though it was not snowing as hard, the wind was still howling. Gee climbed up into the loft and found a place in the hay. He rolled up in the blankets and pulled hay over him. In a few minutes he was warm and lay thinking of how lucky they had been. If they had been a few hours later, they probably would not have made it to the trading post. If they had been unable to build a lean-to, their only choice would have been to kill and skin a couple of the horses and lay the carcasses close to the wagon, using them to break the wind. They would have had to lay close together under the wagon, covering themselves with the skins. Their only other covering was in the wagon and would have been soaking wet and useless. Even still they might not have survived in weather like this; any exposed skin would have frozen in a matter of minutes.

As he lay there, Gee worried about Mr. Stewart, who was probably on his way to Ryan's Station. He said a silent prayer that Stewart had found shelter, but decided if he did not show up within a week, they would have no other choice but to move on without him. If that happened, he worried that they would have no money and nothing to trade. If they could not get back to the wagon soon, they would not have their cows or their household goods.

He closed his eyes tightly, trying to rid his mind of these thoughts. *All because we took in Mina...* Gee was immediately mad at himself for even thinking such a thing. Even had he known what was going to happen to them, he knew he would not have left her. He drifted off to sleep knowing that whatever became of them, he would never regret helping Mina. She was, and would be, a part of his life for as long as they lived, whether it turned out

The Cherokee

to be a long life or a short one. He contented himself with that thought.

Gee was awakened by a rooster crowing and heard Ashwin and the two Indians feeding the horses. They were discussing the weather and nodded to him as he climbed down the ladder. He could see that it had stopped snowing, and the temperature was beginning to rise. The sky was bright blue, and the snow was melting off the trees, even though it was just beginning to break day. Gee was grateful for the weather and hoped they could soon leave to get the wagon.

Gee saw Mr. Ryan waving and motioning for them to come inside. They walked into the store to the smell of bacon frying. It was a welcoming aroma; after all, none of them had eaten since the previous morning. Mr. Ryan showed them the washbasin on the porch. Oddly, the water was not frozen, so maybe it had not been as cold as he had thought.

"When you wash up, come into the kitchen," Mr. Ryan said.

Gee and the three Indians took turns washing their faces and hands before returning to the kitchen. The store at Ryan's Station was bigger the Mr. Randolph's, and it was well stocked with most of the things people in the area would likely need. A room and a kitchen had been added to the side of the store where Mrs. Ryan was cooking bacon with biscuits and gravy on a cast iron wood stove, the first one Gee had ever seen. But what surprised Gee the most was Mrs. Ryan herself. She was a Cherokee, with long black hair and big brown eyes. She was tall and strong and was about his mother's age, Gee decided. The three ladies were talking nonstop in Cherokee when a little boy, about five years old, came in and clung to his mother's apron, watching suspiciously as the men gathered around the table.

Mr. Ryan said grace, and after breakfast the men saddled their horses, put collars and harnesses on the other horses, and made their way toward the wagon, thankful it was warmer and the snow was melting fast. They moved along at a fast pace, and about halfway back to the wagon, Gee saw two cows standing in the middle of the road. One of them had an udder so full of milk that she could hardly walk. Not far from where she stood, the calf was curled up in the snow. To Gee's surprise, it was still alive. Gee dismounted and milked the cow just enough to give her some relief before he hobbled her, knowing the other cow and calf would not leave. They would pick them up on the way back.

Gee and the Indians reached the wagon just as a black bear scampered away. "Just in time! That bear would have torn everything in the wagon apart if we had been a little later." They found the contents of the wagon were just as they had left it, only soaked with snow. They hitched both pairs of horses and began the muddy ride back to the trading post.

They waited seven days on Mr. Stewart and made plans to leave the following morning. Stewart had either died in the snowstorm or decided not to buy their farm. Gee confronted his mother with the thought that Stewart could have decided not to pay for the farm. After all, why pay when he could just take it, knowing they had left without a plan to return?

"He will come if he is able," Mrs. Gilmore said sternly, though she had a look of anxiety on her face.

Late in the afternoon, Gee heard Mr. Ryan's dogs barking and saw a rider leading two horses and a donkey. As they got closer, Gee was relieved to see that it was Mr. Stewart. Gee could see the weariness on his face and told him to go in and warm himself and that he would tend to the horses. Mr. Stewart said he was obliged and slowly dismounted. Gee led the horses to the barn, took off their harness, and fed them. While the donkey was eating, he looked at him more closely, remembering what the man had said about breeding a mare with a donkey. He was particularly proud to see that the donkey was indeed a stud and the two horses were mares. He would try and breed them if Mr. Stewart did not object.

The Cherokee

When Gee entered the store, Mr. Stewart was relating how his house, barn, and all his out buildings were burned to the ground when he reached home. Three of his horses had perished in the barn. His cows were gone, and his hogs had been shot. Two horses and the donkey had been stabled in a shed and had probably broken loose before they burned. The only reason he could think that someone would do such a thing was that they had seen him at Gee's house or, at least, had noticed him going there.

"I did manage to get my savings from the bank, but everything else is gone. I stopped by Mr. Randolph's and waited out the storm. He said that the day before I got there, about a dozen men had ridden past the store, but did not stop. On the way here I passed your place, and all the buildings was burned to the ground; only the chimney was still standing."

No one said a word for a long while. "If y'all don't mind, I would like to come along with you," Stewart said, leaving no doubt that he had nowhere else to go.

Gee did not think it was his place to answer, so he looked at the Indians and Ashwin, who nodded his head and said, "You welcome at our village."

"I sure do appreciate it. I don't believe the vigilantes would come this far, but I think we need to leave as soon as possible. I would hate to put Mr. Ryan and his family in jeopardy."

Shortly before sunrise the wagon was packed. Mr. Stewart paid for feed and hay, but Mr. Ryan would accept no pay for food or shelter. As they prepared to leave, Mr. Ryan said, "You all are welcome here anytime, and I do mean all of you." He looked at Sam and added, "Sam, I am sorry about your place, but it seems like the Gilmores are mighty fine folks. I know the Cherokee are. They will take care of you until you get back on your feet." He reached down and picked up his son, put his arm around Nisha, and waved goodbye.

They drove the wagon onto the great wagon road and headed south, traveling along the foothills of the Appalachian

Mountains. Three days later they were in the rolling hills west of Salem. They had not seen any other settlers, probably because most people knew not to travel this time of year. They left the great wagon road south of Salem and turned west onto what was, at best, a rough wagon trail. Several Indians eyed them suspiciously as they passed through a large village and some smaller ones. Ashwin stopped in each village and told them why they were passing through and where they were headed.

After two day of travel, they were welcomed heartily by the village where Ashwin lived. The entire village came out to greet them. Apparently, someone had informed the village prior to their arrival. The village was on the banks of a large creek and contained about twenty families, each living in round houses with floors dug down into the ground about three feet deep. The walls were made of small saplings woven together and layered with mud and straw. The roof was dome shaped with a hole in the top that allowed smoke to exit. These were the winter houses. Close by was also a summer house. The summer house stood about six feet high and was rectangular shaped. It was made by standing three poles upright for the corners. There was a wall along the back and also one on the side with a roof made from small saplings lying from wall to back, making a triangle shelter covered with straw and mud.

The village had a council house large enough for most, if not all, of the inhabitants to attend meetings and social gatherings. It was a circular building that sat on a mound of dirt in the center of the village. It was in this building that Mr. Stewart, Gee, Ashwin, Sahin, and Balik met with Chief Prajeet. Ashwin explained everything that had happened, including why Mina was at the Gilmores and how the Gilmores would not give her to the vigilantes. He added that it was the reason their houses were burned. Now the Gilmores and Mr. Stewart were there asking for a place to live and for help until spring. The chief listened intently and said that the matter would have to be discussed with the elders of the village, but if they agreed, the group would be welcome in the village. The chief said this was the law they followed, but he knew no one would object. He thanked them for protecting one of his people.

"Tomorrow we build house for you," Chief Prajeet told them.

Later, Gee reminded Ashwin about his wish to marry Mina. Ashwin said that according to Cherokee custom, Gee must first kill a deer. Gee could hardly wait until tomorrow so he could go hunting. He did not know that the next few days would be spent building houses.

At daybreak, everyone in the village, as well as some men from neighboring villages, helped as Mr. Stewart showed them how to build a log cabin. The Indians had axes but were fascinated by the cross-cut saw which Gee had thoughtfully brought along. All of the village men helped to saw logs, cut down trees, saw them into lengths, and drag them into the village. Mr. Stewart showed other men how to cut notches and hew the log so each log would lie on top of the log beneath it. The women and children carried mud from the stream, mixed it with straw, and packed it between spaces where the logs did not fit snugly. By mid afternoon, they were cutting poles for the rafters and laying smaller poles across them for a roof. All that was left was to cover the roof. They did this before sundown, and the Indians helped Gee move their belongings from the wagon into the cabin. It was small, but they were grateful to have shelter without having to worry about it being burned down.

Seeing how quickly they had built the cabin, Mr. Stewart asked Chief Prajeet if they could build a log house for him At first the chief shook his head, but with the insistence of some of the village men and with the assurance from Mr. Stewart that he would build a log house even bigger than the one they had just finished, he proudly agreed.

That night the chief invited everyone to gather in the council house for a feast with singing and dancing. A huge bonfire was started and torches lit. The chief thanked everyone for helping to build a cabin, to welcome the visitors, and to thank them for taking care of one of their own.

Suddenly, Gee remembered that it was a custom of the Cherokee to give a gift. He rushed outside, grabbed a torch, lit it from the bonfire in the center of the village, and rushed to their cabin. He found one of his father's denim shirts and hurried back to the council house. The chief was still speaking, so Gee eyed Ashwin, holding up the shirt and nodding toward the chief. Ashwin came over and said, "When Chief stop talk, give him shirt." Gee did this, and the chief was pleased. He held up the shirt for all to see and took a necklace of beads, bone, and teeth. These he placed around Gee's neck.

"Thank you for the gift. I have been told that you want to marry our Mina." He looked at Gee, who was frantically nodding his head, even before the chief finished speaking. The chief nodded his head and was about to speak, when someone in the crowd yelled loudly,

"Him no one of us. He no kill deer. He must go."

Every eye in the council house looked at the man who spoke. He was tall, his head shaved except for a lock of long black hair which hung from the top of his head past broad shoulders to slightly below his waist. He was around twenty-five and very muscular with dark bronze skin. His eyes were cold, and his thin lips parted as he snarled at the chief, "I want her for wife."

"You have already chosen wife."

"She not here when I choose. I want her. I kill him; take her," he said, pointing first at Gee, then at Mina.

Gee watched the chief and saw his anger build. He was not sure what was going to happen next, but he knew he would die before he would let the man have Mina.

The Cherokee

The chief waved for the young man to come forward and said, "My son, you know what Cherokee law says. If young man kills a deer, lays it at her door, she cook it and gives him meat, then they can be married as you have done with your wife. You cannot kill a man or take a woman for your own pleasure. You must obey the law. If you do not, you will be banished from this tribe and must find another tribe to take you in. This is what I speak. If they do what is custom, they can be married. You will not harm or be unfriendly to them. They are now part of our tribe. I have spoken."

The man snarled at the chief, whirled, and left the council house. Soon the council house was once again alive with dancing and singing. Gee looked for Mina and was happy when she came to him. She took his hand, and they danced to the rhythm of water drums, cane flutes, and clinking seashells. Later they slipped outside and walked hand in hand in the moonlight. They sat on a log, and Gee told her he would go hunting for a deer as soon as they could build a house for the chief.

"Chief give me grandmother; she take me and say it okay we marry. Now Chief say we can." She smiled at him with a smile that left him numb from head to foot.

"I love you," he whispered

"Me know; me love you, too." She put her arms around his neck, pulled his head down, kissed him, and ran back into the council house.

The next day Mr. Stewart and Gee helped the Indians build a large cabin close to the council house for Chief Prajeet. A day and half later the work was finished, and Gee took his musket and left to go deer hunting. A little way into the woods, Gee became aware of someone following him. He feared it was the man who had threatened him. He ran a few hundred yards and hid. Soon two boys came slipping along, and Gee could see they were tracking him. He waited until they were only ten feet away before he stepped from behind a tree, pointing the musket at them. The boys immediately threw their hands out as if trying to shield their bodies from a musket ball. Staring at the muzzle of the musket, one said, "No shoot, we come to help with deer." The boy never took his eyes off the musket.

"I am Shakunt; he Ratri. We you brothers now."

Gee looked at the two. They were about nine or ten, wearing deerskin pants and rabbit hide coats woven together by strips of rawhide. One boy was slightly taller than the other, but both had big brown eyes, black hair, and admiration in their eyes. They could be brothers. Gee asked, "Do your father and mother know where you are?"

The taller boy shook his head. "It okay. We come here plenty times. We help bring deer to pretty girl. We no like Dhiren. He bad spirit. He name mean strong."

"Thank you for wanting to help, but who is Dhiren?" Gee asked.

"He son of chief. We no like. Him bad man."

"Shakunt, I know your name means blue jay, but what is the meaning of yours?" Gee asked, looking at the taller boy.

"Me name mean 'night'; I no sleep night when little."

"I am pleased to meet you, Shakunt and Ratri. Thank you for telling me about Dhiren, but please stay back until I shoot a deer. Then you can come and help."

Both smiled and nodded their heads.

About thirty minutes later Gee shot a nice doe. The two boys came running and helped drag the deer back to the village. They left it in front of Mina's adopted grandmother's door. Soon several women helped skin and cut the meat so Mina could cook it.

Later that night she gave Gee some meat. Not only was the venison good to eat, but it was the most satisfying meal he had ever eaten. Now he could take Mina for his wife. They sat in the moonlight and talked about getting married as soon as possible. As they watched a falling star, Gee knew it was a good omen.

The Cherokee

"We marry soon. Everything good," Mina said. Gee walked Mina to her grandmother's house since under Cherokee customs, she could not stay in the cabin with Gee until after they were married. Mr. Stewart observed the same custom though, according to Ashwin, he could sleep in the cabin because neither he nor Mrs. Gilmore were Cherokee. Still, Mr. Stewart made his bed in the wagon instead of in the cabin, not wanting to offend anyone.

Gee suspected Mr. Stewart and his mother might be making plans to marry. He had seen them talking to each other in low whispers and saw how they looked at each other. Once they held hands as they walked to the river to wash clothes. Gee liked the idea and knew Mr. Stewart would be good to her. Since his mother had loved his father so much, he had doubted she would ever remarry. Now he was hoping she would; they would be a family and no one could hurt them anymore. Little did he know that the same racial hatred they had left behind would continue to follow them, only this time it would not be from his own kind. Rather, it would be from the Indians. Soon, they would be forced to move again.

CHAPTER SEVENTEEN

DIAMONDS
Twenty-Ten

Anna looked at her notes and said, "Robert and I made notes of everything we knew and everything we needed answers to when we were forming Gilsan Oil. We were surprised at how helpful it was, and I guess it is just habit for me to do this. I thought it might be useful if I did the same here."

Everyone looked at her and nodded their heads. "Seems like there is little we know and a lot we don't know, but I agree with you. If you don't keep a record, over time things seem to run together and you tend to forget. I guess that is one of the reasons we keep records at the police station," Chief Bates said and asked Anna, "What do you have that we do know or need to know?"

Anna looked at her notes, studied them carefully, and replied, "We know we have Lanny, his father and mother, Otis Green, and Gavin Gentry—all who died rather mysteriously and with hardly any investigations. We know both Lanny and his father sold diamonds to Gentry. Now we have Bradley, dead. We have Susie Carter, the dispatcher who was very rude to Simmons, and Joe Evans who seemed overly anxious to question him. We have Roy Grades, a pal of Bradley's, almost directly accusing Simmons of being involved in Bradley's death and that he hung around Judge Caldwell's courtroom. And, we have the diamonds Bradley lost at Manny's and the one found on his boat with 'Lanny Simpson' written on an envelope. Anyone want to add to this list?" They shook their heads.

Chief Bates arose and stood a long time before he spoke. "I will talk to the D.A. tomorrow. Maybe I can get him to reopen the Gentry case. If he does, we might be able to find out about the diamonds Carl and Lanny brought to him and what became of them. The only death not in his district was Bradley's, so I might be able to convince him to investigate the others. Anna, since you live in his district, it might help if you called him and suggested he have the grand jury reopen some, if now all, the cases which Otis Green marked as closed. Mr. Gilmore, I'm sure you have a lot of friends in the capitol. One of them might be able to persuade the Arkansas State Police to give us a copy of their files on Otis Green." He looked around and saw everyone nodding their heads.

"I have a gut feeling the diamonds will be the key to our case. If the ones Bradley had were that valuable, I would be interested in knowing how much the one Lanny had was worth. If there are other diamonds that we don't know about, we could be talking about something that would generate large sums of money. . . enough to involve a lot of people. . . maybe people who are powerful enough to arrange some, if not all the deaths. I think we have to find out where the diamonds came from. If we can do that, maybe we can trace them."

He paused when Penny's cell phone rang and nodded for her to answer it. "That was Scott McTune," she told them. "He would like to join us, if we don't mind."

"Of course, if that is okay with you all. I was finished anyway," Bates said. Everyone nodded in agreement.

Scott came in and greeted everyone, calling each by name, and said, "I am sorry to crash your party, but if you don't already know, I have been assigned to investigate Arnold Bradley's death. I know you are interested in this, so I will share all the details I can without jeopardizing our investigation. Bradley was killed by blunt force trauma to the head. There were no signs of a struggle in his boat, but there was an envelope with what appears to be a large uncut diamond inside and the name 'Lanny Simpson' written on it, as I've already told Penny. We found some receipts that Bradley had signed here at the club and several tax forms Gentry had signed at the courthouse. A handwriting expert confirmed that it was neither Bradley nor Gentry's handwriting on the envelope. We appraised the diamond that was found on Bradley's boat, and it is not worth very much. We are satisfied it is not the diamond Lanny carried to Gentry. Chief, I understand that you found a receipt in Gentry's safe showing he had insured this diamond for fifty grand. Is that correct?" Bates nodded his head.

Scott turned and faced Amos and Marie. "We found a wall safe when we searched Bradley's house. Inside the safe we found a key to a lockbox at Guaranty Bank. Judge Stone signed a warrant granting us permission to open the box. Inside we found an iPad and some documents. We had our computer geeks open it up. I am not at liberty to discuss some of the information on it, but one of the things caught our attention, which is the reason I wanted to meet with you. The iPad had copies of lease papers on most of the equipment at the Tyler Bottling Company. Other papers confirmed the original equipment was sold to a Carrier Leasing Company and leased back to the bottling company with payment due in November. A photocopy of a document revealed the plant was to be sold, pending transfer of 3.3 million dollars to a Swiss bank account. Unfortunately, we have no way to verify the Swiss account, nor do we know how the sale was to be handled. We could not find any record of a Carrier Leasing Company, either. I cannot give you the documents themselves, but I can make copies. Were you planning on selling the Tyler plant?"

He paused and looked at Amos, Marie, and Penny; he saw all three were petrified. They stared at each other, not believing or having any answers to explain what was going on. There was silence in the room as Scott waited for their response.

Simmons did not understand all that Scott had said, but judging from the look on their faces, he knew it was serious.

What surprised him most was how calm Anna was. She stood and walked the length of the dining room, holding the scratch pad, lightly tapping a pencil against her forehead to the beat of the band playing in the main dining room. She stopped pacing, looked at Amos and Marie, and said, "Daddy, call Phil and have him get word to all the media networks that due to the death of Arnold Bradley, the Tyler plant will be closed until further notice. All salaries and bonuses will be honored.

"And Mother, call Cunningham, Mayer & Collins and have them stop all transactions—and I mean absolutely *all*—concerning Tyler Bottling Company. Not so much as a 't' can be crossed.

"Penny, increase the production of both Longview and Texarkana to cover the loss of Tyler. The commitments of Tyler must be fulfilled. Do whatever it takes to make this happen. I will call State Auditor's office to see what the hell is going on. There has to be another set of books other than the ones Bradley presented to them. How in the hell can he sell something he doesn't own!"

She turned to Scott. "Scott, I would hope that your report on this matter will not be leaked to the media." She turned and faced Simmons. "Mitchell, I am afraid that for the time being, you will be the only one working on our. . . what shall we call it? Our diamond investigation." She stopped pacing and stared at Penny. "How could I have let this happen? I am afraid it is my fault. I was too lax on the Tyler plant. I was the one who signed an agreement, against attorney advice, giving Bradley control of the plant." She paused, looked at Penny, and then at the scratch pad. "I guess I will have to make another list. How could Bradley think he could pull this off? Taking control of a business in one thing, but taking ownership is another. There have to be other people involved."

"Ms. Sanderson, when you mentioned the diamond investigation, it started me to thinking. Maybe I should be the one making a list. Look, just because we found a key to a lock box in Bradley's house doesn't necessarily mean that it belonged to Bradley." McTune hesitated, "I think I may have jumped to a conclusion too quickly. Listen, we do not know if the information we found in the lock box is correct. The key, lock box, iPad, and documents could have been planted as a diversion, maybe to embarrass us or to sidetrack our investigation of the diamonds. I would be interested to know when and who obtained the lock box and who last opened it. As I said, there was other information on the laptop, mostly personal, but the info about the plant was in a hidden file. This, too, may have been a way to confuse us.

Everyone watched Anna pace up and down the side of the table. After much thought she looked at Scott and said, "Scott, you could be right. I, too, may have jumped to a conclusion. Maybe we should back off and let you finish your investigation. If the documents are correct, we have probably already lost the Tyler plant, at least for the time being. If they are false, we look like fools and have wasted a lot of time and energy, not to mention the embarrassment of shutting down the Tyler plant."

"Dad, Mom, Penny, what do you think?"

Amos had been listening closely. The years of being certain of what you were doing before acting were clearly evident in his body language and in his voice as he spoke. "Yes, Anna, I think we may be putting the horse before the cart. I suggest we do nothing until we learn more about what is happening. When we do know, then we will deal with it." He arose and continued, "Scott, we are grateful for your concern. I will fund any additional investigation, both money and manpower, that you might need which the county might not agree to. Now, will you please join us for dinner?"

"Thank you, but I am working tonight. Maybe some other time."

He was almost to the door when Simmons called to him. "Scott, one thing I had forgotten. Maybe Chief Bates knows more about this than I do, but I remember Elaine saying Roy Grades was hounding her about selling her father's farm, even to the point of offering her much more than the land was probably worth. So much more, she confided in Chief Bates and Mr. Gilmore about it. In light of the fact that he and Bradley hung around together, and both Bradley and Lanny were in possession of diamonds, I wonder if there could there be a connection?"

McTune paused at the doorway, turned, walked back to the table, and sat down. He looked at Chief Bates, who said, "Yes, she did ask me what I thought about the offer, and I suggested she talk to Mr. Gilmore. I told her he has more experience with land acquisitions and would be honest with her. She later told me that Mr. Gilmore advised her not to sell."

McTune turned and looked at Mr. Gilmore, who commented, "Yes, that is true. I had forgotten about that. You may be on to something here. I think we need to look into this."

"Carl once said he needed Lanny to come home, that he had a project he needed help with. Within a year he, Lacy, and Lanny were dead. Could be the project he needed help with concerned diamonds," Bates said. He stared at Scott and continued, "Lanny and Carl gave Gentry diamonds, and Bradley had diamonds. We don't know about Otis Green, but there could be a connection here. As I said before, I can ask the district attorney for help, but I think asking the sheriff would be useless. However, I am sure Gregg Davis would be more than willing to help us find where the diamonds came from. Also, I understand you know a fine private detective firm in Dallas which you might want to consider."

He looked at Anna, but it was Marie who spoke for the first time. "We would be more than happy to enlist the services of Morgan and Morgan; I think this is the firm you were referring to. We could use their services for this as well as for the Tyler plant. They are licensed by the state and would not be restricted by county lines."

"That is an excellent idea, Marie. I will call Danny first thing tomorrow morning." Amos said.

"Mr. Gilmore," Simmons interjected, "I was wondering if we could get current aerial maps of the Simpson property and compare it with older ones that might be available elsewhere. We did this a lot in Afghanistan; you would be surprised at what you can learn. Maybe I am assuming that the diamonds came from this property, but we need to know since Grades was so interested in it."

"Mitchell, I think that can be arranged, but maybe we should use different planes to do the filming, possibly different days as well. If something is not right, we do not want someone to think we are suspicious." Simmons realized it was the first time Mr. Gilmore had not called him Mr. Simmons. This made him feel a little more comfortable. . . more a part of the discussion.

Mr. Gilmore continued, "Yes, you could be right about this. I will have our pilot make the arrangements to film it, and we can compare it to the topographical and oil survey maps we have at Gilsan Oil. There are several maps available on the Internet, too." He waited, looked around the table, and asked, "Would anyone care to add anything else to Anna's list?"

Everyone laughed and Marie asked, "When do we eat? I'm starved." The others nodded their heads and agreed with Marie.

"Okay, but we need to meet at the Tyler plant tomorrow, say at nine. Anna, I will send the chopper for you and Penny. Johnny, you and Scott will keep us informed, will you not? Mitchell, I would like for you to go with our pilot when he films, if that is possible." Simmons nodded his head.

"I'll let you know when," Mr. Gilmore said and looked at McTune. "It is getting late so why don't you join us? We promise no more business talk while we eat." After McTune had agreed to stay, the group placed an order and opened the curtain to enjoy the band while waiting for their food.

Later, at the guest house, Simmons looked at his watch: 8:45. He could not get Elaine off his mind. What if there were diamonds on her farm? What if that is the reason her family is dead? He looked at his phone; yes her address and phone number were listed. He dialed her number. When she answered, he said, "Elaine, I will be at your house in an hour. Please open the door for me. If you don't, I will sleep in your doorway and stay there until I can talk to you." Not giving her time to say no, he hung up the phone.

Simmons climbed in the pick-up and typed Elaine's address into the GPS—fifty minutes to her house. He called Penny as he drove and told her what he was doing and that he would check with her later.

Forty-eight minutes later he was knocking on Elaine's door. She opened it, stepped back, hands on her hips, and glared at him. He did not care; he stepped inside and closed the door.

"What are you doing here?' she demanded.

"Have you talked to Penny?" Simmons asked.

"Yes, she said to let you in. So I did. Now. . . say what you came to say and leave. I have a class to teach tomorrow, in case you didn't know."

"Elaine, did Penny tell you about our meeting tonight?"

"No, she said to let you in and you would explain. So, I let you in. Now what?"

"The diamond Lanny had and the ones Bradley had, could have come from your parents' farm. This may be the reason they are not alive today. If something happens to you, who gets the farm? Do you have a will? Any close relatives other than your Aunt Lacey? Has anyone else besides Grades tried to buy your farm either from you or your parents at any time that you are aware of?"

She held up her hands, and Simmons could see the concern in her eyes, her beautiful sea-green eyes. He ached to take her in his arms and hold her, to protect her. To tell her everything

Diamonds

would be all right. He could not understand how quickly and how deeply he had come to care for her, but he knew without a doubt that he did. And that he could not help it.

"Mitchell! Wait, wait a minute. Stop it. One question at a time," she said harshly.

She walked over to the couch and pointed to a recliner. He walked to the recliner, but did not sit down. "Would you like a glass of wine?"

"Elaine, did you know that Bradley was dead?"

"Mitchell, would you like a glass of wine?" she demanded.

"Yes! No! I don't know. Elaine, I'm worried about you. I think you could be in great danger."

"Mitchell, do you or do you not want a glass of wine?" Her eyes were flashing at him as he nodded his head. She pointed to the chair. "Sit down, and I'll get us a glass of wine."

"Elaine, I'm serious; you could be in danger." He followed her into the kitchen.

She put her hands firmly on her hips, stomped her foot, and almost screamed at him. "Mitchell! Sit down. Now," she commanded, pointing to a barstool.

She poured two glasses of wine, set one in front of Simmons, and walked to the kitchen table. She sat down and pointed a finger at him, "Stay!"

He looked at her, saw how determined she was, and barked obediently, "Woof! woof!" He saw the flash of anger only for a second. When it disappeared, she smiled and said, "Good doggie." They laughed and stared at each other.

"I am sorry I embarrassed you Sunday night." Her beautiful sea-green eyes searched his face.

"I guess I deserved it. I did not mean to come on so strong; it's just that I. . ."

"Mitchell, please stop!" she interrupted. He shrugged his shoulders.

"Do you want me to roll over?" He knew he had said the wrong thing when her face exploded with anger.

"Would you please leave? And close the door behind you!" She walked away from the table and emptied her wine into the sink. She turned and faced him, pointed toward the front door, walked into her bedroom, and slammed the door. He heard the click of the lock.

Simmons stood and stared. He wanted to make her realize he was concerned about her safety, but decided nothing he could say would make any difference, especially not right now. It would probably make things worse. He walked to the door, opened it, turned the lock, and closed it behind him.

He sat down on the steps for a long time, trying to decide what to do. "I might as well go back to Longview. I guess coming here was a mistake," he muttered.

He drove south on US 59 and made the turn onto Texas 155, reliving the events of last Friday, a Friday which now seemed like eons ago. When he arrived at the gate to Anna's house, it was closed; he did not know the combination. Pulling to the side of the driveway, he shut off the engine and lay over in the seat. It was not the most comfortable bed he had ever slept in, but it was a lot better than the fox holes in Afghanistan.

He was awakened by the sound of a horn. He rose up and saw someone walking toward him through the fog.

It was Anna. She stopped and stared at him, "Mitchell, what in Sam's hill are you doing here? Are you sober?" "I'm sorry; I didn't know the combination." Anna was annoyed, he could tell.

"Do you not know how to use the phone, for heaven's sake? You slept in the truck! I can't believe it."

"Anna, I am going to Lanny. . . I mean Elaine's farm to look around. I was going to ask her last night if it was okay, but she threw me out. So I am going whether she approves or not."

"You went to Texarkana last night?"

"Yes, ma'am."

Diamonds

"Don't call me *ma'am*," she said angrily, and added, "Mitchell, I am on your side, too. Will you please remember that?" She stared at him for a long time.

"The chopper was grounded because of low visibility so I am driving to Tyler. If you go to Lanny's place, please be careful. We can talk more when I return." She turned and walked back to a long, black limousine. A man in a chauffeur's uniform opened the rear passenger door for her. He nodded to Simmons and drove away.

Simmons sat trying to decide what to do. He had not thought of going to Lanny's place until seconds ago, and it puzzled him why he had said he was going there. *Am I cracking up?* he asked himself. He started the truck and drove to the Waffle House, drank coffee, and ate ham and eggs over medium. He stared out the window at the traffic... some cars going this way, some going that way. *So what am I doing just sitting here? Better yet, why am I here in the first place? I don't know what I am doing, and I'm probably going to get someone killed... maybe even me.* But he was thinking of Elaine. He paid his check and drove through the traffic. Sure enough... some cars were going this way and some going that way, but now he knew where he was going. *I'm going this way.* He rolled his window down and let the cool fog blow onto his face.

He found the two silos, but did not turn into Lanny's drive. About a half mile later he found an old Jeep trail and drove until it could not be seen from the road. He removed the keys and locked the truck. In this fog it would be easy to lose your direction so he made a mental note of the sounds of the highway.

He walked straight ahead until he could barely hear the sounds of the highway and turned left, walking parallel to the road. About a half mile, he found an old trail and decided this led from Lanny's barn probably to the back side of the farm, maybe to where Lanny's father had let a tree fall on him. As he walked along the trail, he became aware that the trail showed signs of recent use. This puzzled him so he stopped every twenty to thirty feet to look and listen, as he had done many times in Afghanistan.

About three hundred yards later, he heard the unmistakable click of the safety on a rifle. He dove to his right and felt the whiff of a bullet and heard the muzzle blast of a large caliber rifle. A small tree beside him exploded, wood and bark flying in all directions. He hunched over and ran a zigzag course away from the shooter as another shot rang out, but this one was not close enough for him to hear the bullet. He continued to run until he came to a wire fence running beside a stream. He looked at the stream and saw it was relatively shallow with banks almost head high. He quickly slid under the fence and jumped into the muddy water, stopping to listen for someone running after him. He did not hear anything and decided it would be safer and easier to follow the stream bed than fight the tangle of underbrush like that he had just plowed through.

He slipped slowly down the stream towards the sound of traffic. As soon as he saw the highway, he crawled out of the stream, staying just inside the woods, and walked maybe a thousand yards back towards Longview. He came to another stream with a culvert big enough to crawl through. It was a perfect hiding place. From there he could watch his back tracks and set up an ambush, if necessary. He considered trying to flag down a car, but knew no one would stop for a wet and muddy stranger. After about fifteen minutes, he was satisfied no one was following him. Simmons took out the cell phone and thumbed through the contacts to find Gregg Davis.

When Gregg answered, he said, "Gregg, this is Simmons. I need some help. Someone took a couple of shots at me. I am hiding on the side of the highway next to a creek about a half mile west of Lanny Simpson's place."

There was a second or two of silence, and he began to wonder if Gregg had heard him. Then Gregg replied, "Are you all right?"

"I am fine. Just stop on top of the hill before you get to the creek. I will come to you. I had rather no one knows I called you."

"Why?"

"I will explain later."

Simmons made his way slowly just over the top of the hill and hid in a place where he could see down the highway. About ten minutes later he saw the patrol car approaching with lights flashing, but no siren. He waited until the car was about a quarter mile away before he walked up the shoulder and stood beside the highway.

"What are you doing?" Gregg asked when he sat down.

"It's a long story. Turn around and go back to town. I'm afraid they are watching my truck, and I need a weapon before we go back."

"Okay, but don't make me have to pull your teeth. Spill it."

"Gregg, where do you think Lanny would have gotten an uncut diamond large enough for a jeweler to insure it for fifty grand?"

"Where did you hear that?"

"Chief Bates said the papers were in Gentry's safe, but the diamond was not."

"Okay, okay. So you were in the woods looking for diamonds without hunter's orange. Don't you know it is deer season?"

"Gregg, whoever shot at me knew I was not a deer. The only thing that saved my life was that he did not click off the safety until I stopped. I've heard enough of those clicks; I knew to duck and run."

"Where were you when you were shot at?"

"Maybe a quarter mile in back of Lanny's house. Gregg, you know better than I do the circumstances of Lanny's father's death, and Chief Bates said his mother never had any symptoms of heart problems. Lanny would never kill himself. Gentry and

Bradley had ties to diamonds, and they are dead. Otis Green is the only one not tied to diamonds as far as I know."

Simmons could see the wheels turning in Gregg's head as he thought about this, and Simmons waited for him to respond. When he did not, Simmons asked, "Did you know Otis Green well? I mean, like, were you friends? I've heard he ran the county like a dictator. Is this true?"

He waited, but Gregg said nothing. "And don't make me pull your teeth. Where do you think Lanny got a diamond worth fifty g's?"

"Man, you are full of question."

"Dammit, Gregg, don't play games with me. You've got a lot of people in this county dead, and tonight someone tried to add me to the list. You sit over there and won't answer my questions. Makes me wonder if you were really a friend of Lanny's and where you stand. Answer my questions, or let me outta the car."

Gregg did not say a word, nor did he stop the car. Finally he replied, "Simmons, remember I told you something was simmering in this town. Well, there are some powerful people here with very long memories. I try and do my job and not make waves."

"Stop the car, or I'm going to jump. You'll have a helluva time telling the media why I jumped, cause that would make a lot of waves, wouldn't it? I really thought you were a standup guy, but I was wrong. Now stop the damn car."

Gregg stopped the car. Simmons got out and slammed the door so hard the passenger side door glass shattered. The car shook, and the blue lights on top rattled so hard Simmons expected them to break or fall off. He did not care.

Gregg heard the glass break, but never turned to look. His eyes were fixed straight ahead as he drove off. Simmons ran the three miles to the Sanderson house. After all, he was used to running with a fifty-pound back pack, so this was a piece of cake.

Diamonds

One car slowed as he ran, and he wondered if he was going to get shot, but right now, he was so angry he really did not care. He was fed up with this town. He was going back to Afghanistan. Real people with real guts lived there.

He reached the gate of the Sanderson ranch. It was closed, and he still did not know the combination. *I think I will just go into town and catch a bus outa this place*, Simmons said to himself, but the memory of Lanny would not let him leave. *If I leave it will be feet first.* He also remembered that his duffel bag was in the trunk of Elaine's car.

He looked at the gate and found the intercom button. He pushed it and looked directly into the camera.

"Mitchell, why are you on foot?" Penny asked as the gate opened.

"It's a long story." He ran double time up the drive.

CHAPTER EIGHTEEN

TALL GRASS
Seventeen seventy-four

Two days later the chief's cabin was finished. Ashwin, Gee, and Mr. Stewart were sitting on a log admiring the rather large cabin and watching as the chief approached, leading two horses. He gave one to Gee and the other too Mr. Stewart.

"It gift to you for teaching my people how to make house. Now all chiefs want house like mine," he laughed. Both Gee and Mr. Stewart protested the gifts of the horses until Ashwin said they should accept the gift. It is the custom of the Cherokee to repay for something that is important to them, he insisted.

They thanked the chief, and noticing that both of the horses were mares. Gee told Mr. Stewart about the mules the farmers had and asked if he would be willing to try to breed one of them to his donkey. If they were as good as the farmers said, maybe they could use them to work the crops.

"Maybe we should breed two of them so we can have a pair," Mr. Stewart suggested, not really sure if Gee was serious. As they continued to discuss the matter, Gee became aware that Dhiren was watching them and immediately noticed the hate in his eyes. This worried him not only for Mina's sake, but also because Dhiren was the chief's son.

He asked Ashwin if there was something he could do to make friends with Dhiren. Ashwin shook his head and said, "Someday you must fight to death. He no stop hating because he want Mina."

"What do I have to do to marry her?'

"You must find a spot for ceremony, and it must be blessed for seven days by the tribal priest. You gather wood to build big fire on the day of wedding. You and Mina will stand by fire, each covered with blue-stained deer skins. You stand while village priests bless both of you, and village sing songs. The blue skins will be removed, and both will be covered with white one. You give Mina meat, and she give you corn. The meat is symbol that you will provide for her, and the corn a symbol she be good wife. She then be wife."

Mr. Stewart listened intently and asked Ashwin if he and Mrs. Gilmore could be married with a Cherokee wedding. Ashwin did not know, but said he would ask the chief.

Chief Prajeet agreed that they could be married the same as Gee and Mina. They decided on a spot down by the river and began to carry wood for a bonfire. The tribal priest initiated the daily ritual of blessing the site.

The next day as Gee and Mina were carrying wood Dhiren stepped in front of them. He glared at Gee and said, "When I kill you, she be mine."

Gee stopped, not knowing what to say, but Mina stared at Dhiren, "I no cook meat for you. I no be yours."

"When I am chief, you no have to cook. I take you."

"Never. I kill myself before I be your wife."

"Then both will die." He laughed and walked away.

Gee watched him and wondered what he should do. *If I do not kill him, he will kill Mina and me, but what will the chief do if I kill his son?* Deep inside he knew he had no other choice, no matter what the consequences, but he would talk to Ashwin. Maybe if he told the chief, they could avoid a confrontation.

Gee told Ashwin what Dhiren had said, and Ashwin met with the chief, who called them to his cabin. Ashwin ask Gee to tell the chief what Dhiren had said and to ask him what he must do.

"My son hard-headed; he no listen. If he try hurt you, you must defend yourself. He know if he breaks law, he be sent away. No more I can do."

"Chief, if we can stay until planting time, then we will buy land and leave. I don't want to hurt your son because you have been good to us."

"I will meet with Cherokee council and tell them how you help and want land. If you find land you like and no village claim land, I will ask Council Elders to let you live on it. You cannot buy land. The Cherokee not own land like the white people; land belong to Great Spirit. If they give you land, it belong to your tribe, and they no take back."

"Thank you. I will not hurt your son unless he tries to hurt Mina or me, and I will try to stay away from him."

"I know good land. No other village claim," Ashwin said.

Gee could hardly wait to tell Mr. Stewart what Chief Prajeet had said, and that Ashwin knew of land that no village had claimed.

They left early the next day, and by late afternoon, Ashwin had led them up a game trail to the top of a large plateau. From there they could see a huge valley of grassland with rolling hills and two rather large streams which merged together at a flat plateau before disappearing through a gap in the cliffs at the other end of the valley. Since there was very little undergrowth, clearing the land for farming would be relatively easy. Both Gee and Mr. Stewart knew this was the place they would like to live, that is, if another tribe did not claim it. The only problem was discovering a way to get down into the valley and finding trees to build a cabin and barn. They decided to make camp and explore the valley in the morning.

A little after daybreak, they rode the rim of the valley until they found a steep trail where they were able to make their way down into the valley. They rode around the inside edge, noticing a lot of deer and elk sign. As they rode, they looked for a desirable site on which to build a cabin once they found trees and gained permission to move there.

Close to the northern end of the valley they came upon a waterfall that fell from the face of a cliff about fifty feet high into a deep blue pool surrounded by rocks. A short distance away, they could see a cave entrance about six feet in diameter in the face of the cliff. Dismounting, they walked into the cave for about twenty feet where it opened into a wide chamber with a tall ceiling. This far inside the cave, it was hard to see, and Mr. Stewart warned that they should go no farther without ropes and torches. In the darkness they could easily slip from a ledge or fall through a crack in the rocks. Gee wished he could keep going since he could hear the sound of falling water from somewhere deep in the cave.

They came out of the cave, mounted, and rode up a deep draw. They were excited to see a large stand of timber in a valley that ran back towards the base of the mountain. It was not far from the first stream, which was deep and wide with lots of mink and otter sign.

"There be plenty fish here. This place called Tall Grass. I see it from up there one time," Ashwin said, pointing to the top of the hills. "But I never come down. Now I like plenty much. It day ride from my village; next village is far. White settlement is day ride on great wagon road and have trading post. I trade," he said, pointing to the east.

They climbed back to the rim of the valley. From this vantage point all they could see was the grassland; the timber was hidden behind the cliffs. Maybe this was why no one had settled here. They tried to ride around the rim, but huge boulders made riding impossible.

Back at the village Gee and Mr. Stewart discussed the possibility of trading or buying the land with Mrs. Gilmore and Mina. Mr. Stewart said he had a little gold from his savings back in Virginia. Gee reminded Mr. Stewart that Ashwin said he would like to bring his wife and come with them to this land.

"I think he would be of great help to us. We will ask him to meet with the chief tomorrow about the possibility of buying the land," Mr. Stewart remarked.

Gee remembered what the chief had said about the Cherokee not owning land, but he said nothing.

The next day they met with Chief Prajeet, who said as far as he knew, no tribe had claims on the land, and he would tell the tribal council of their interest when they met before planting time. He did not think the Cherokee would sell tribal land, but did not foresee a problem with them living there, especially since Ashwin also expressed a desire to go. All were excited and could hardly wait until spring.

The next day Gee, Shakunt, and Ratri were walking their horses, looking for game, when Dhiren stepped from behind a tree and loosed an arrow at Gee. Gee saw him just in time to heave himself to the side, but felt the arrow as it struck his left shoulder next to his collar bone, knocking him from his horse. The impact of hitting the ground temporarily knocked the wind out of him, but gasping for air, Gee saw Dhiren running toward him with a knife in his hand. Still struggling to catch his breath, Gee managed to pull the flintlock pistol from his belt and fire point blank into Dhiren's chest. The impact of the fifty caliber lead ball stood him up straight before his legs collapsed and he fell to his knees, then onto his side. He rolled over onto his back, moaned and tried to speak, but the words never came out. With glazed eyes, Dhiren gulped his last breath.

It seemed a long time before Gee could get his breath, the intense pain from his wounded shoulder causing him to gasp even more. He tried to rise, but realized his left arm would not move. He collapsed back onto the ground and was aware of Shakunt and Ratri trying to help him. He thought he heard one of them call for someone to go get help, while the other packed dirt around the arrow shaft to stop the bleeding. Gee tried to say something, but could not since the trees around him were beginning to spin.

He pulled at the arrow shaft, but a hand caught his, as the trees seemed to draw in on him. Drifting out of consciousness, he thought of Mina. He vaguely remembered someone helping him onto his horse, the look of horror on his mother's face, and Mina holding his hand. Someone was holding him down, breaking the arrow shaft and pushing it on through his shoulder. He screamed and slipped back into unconsciousness.

It was dark when Gee regained consciousness enough to see Mina, Mr. Stewart, Ashwin, his mother, and Chief Parjeet standing in the candlelight. He looked at the chief and barely managed to whisper, "I did not want to kill him." The chief nodded his head slowly and left.

The medicine man came and placed leaves and herbs over his wound and gave him some bitter liquid to drink. It was a long night as he drifted in and out of consciousness. Delirious and burning up with fever, Gee raved at the men in flaming body armor who held him over burning torches. They were prodding his shoulder with red-hot irons, Gee moaned. At times he would scream for his father to make them stop; other times he would cling to Mina and his mother, begging them to put out the fire or to get the animals out of the barn.

For three days Mina and his mother never left his side, keeping him cool with wet cloths when his fever spiked and drying the perspiration when it fell, giving him bean soup and milk whenever they could get him to eat, all the while keeping a close look outside at the snow which had been falling steadily for the last two days and was now over three feet deep. The temperature hovered around zero, and everyone in the village struggled to keep warm. Several were huddled in the council house when the roof collapsed, killing two of the villagers. Later, one of the houses burned, taking the life of a small baby. The cold was so extreme, several young calves and pigs froze to death.

Gee began improving on the fourth day and was aware that he had little use of his left arm. The next day the snow stopped, the weather warmed, and the snow began to melt. Gee had regained some strength in his arm and could lift it off the bed.

The next day he was able to go outside and saw the Indians burying Dhiren and the others who had died. They were weeping and moaning, but when Gee started towards the graves, Ashwin stopped him and asked him not to go. As Gee looked at the Indians, he noticed they were not friendly. He asked Ashwin if it was because he had killed the chief's son. Ashwin only stared at him and said, "We talk later."

Gee stood and looked at them and could see the Indians did not approve of him witnessing their burial rituals. Ashwin asked him to go inside. Later, Gee asked Mr. Stewart why the Indians' attitude toward him had changed.

'They think you are a bad spirit. I saw this when I was with the Shawnee," he explained. He looked at Mrs. Gilmore before he continued, "We should make plans to leave as soon as possible. I think the only place we can go is to the cave. At this point, we may have no other choice."

A little later Ashwin came in to talk to them. He said the village thought Gee was the cause of their troubles. He was an evil spirit, and by now, most of the other villages would know their feelings towards Gee so none of them would take him in. He agreed with Mr. Stewart that the cave would be the only place they could go. They should leave as soon the snow was gone, he advised. They could make it to Tall Grass in a day, and he would go with them. They could live in the cave until they could build shelter.

The next day, as they loaded the wagon, Mr. Stewart saw Chief Parjeet watching them. He went to the chief and asked about the possibility of buying the land at Tall Grass, but the chief only pointed in that direction.

"Go," he said before he turned and walked away.

They finished loading the wagon, and Gee noticed that neither Sahin or Balik nor anyone in the village offered to help—

no one except Ashwin. Gee asked Ashwin if this meant he and Mina could not get married. Ashwin nodded his head and said, "You take Mina as white man's wife. She stay in cabin while you hurt; she no longer can be Cherokee wife." He paused and looked at each of them. "You no longer welcome in village, and me no, too, because I help. I go with you, but wife no go. I find another wife, one who give me son."

Gee could not help but wonder if this was not one of the reasons Ashwin wanted to go with them. Either way, he was extremely pleased he had chosen to come with them. They surely would need his help, and maybe if he were with them, the other Indians would not harm them. They left the village, but no one came out to say good-bye. Gee was sad because he had enjoyed being with them and regretted that he was the reason they had to leave.

It was almost dark when they reached the rim of the valley. They made camp and agreed they would search for a way to get the wagon down the steep slopes in the morning.

The next day, Mr. Stewart and Gee searched in one direction and Ashwin the other. It was almost noon when they met back at the wagon. Ashwin said he had found a gentle slope where they could go down—not a straight descent, but at an angle. Later that afternoon, they maneuvered the wagon around several huge boulders to the place Ashwin had found. They rode to the slope and decided if they locked the rear wheels, it should not be a problem to move the wagon down. It was almost sundown when they finally reached the cave. They spent the night in the cave, where they would live until a cabin could be built. They hobbled the horses and cows and built a fire to keep wild animals away. Ashwin and Mr. Stewart decided to sleep outside, one standing watch until midnight and the other until morning.

The weather was warm for the next few days and it was not long before they had built a small cabin. Mr. Stewart suggested if they were permitted to stay, they would use it as a smokehouse when a bigger house could be built. Though Gee still did not have full use of his left arm, he was improving every day. Plans were made to build another cabin for Gee and Mina when they were married and one for Ashwin. At first, Ashwin strongly objected, but when Mrs. Gilmore said he would need one when he found a wife, he relented.

The weather was good for the next two weeks, and they constructed another cabin, a lean-to for the cows, plus another lean-to for the eight horses and Mr. Stewart's donkey, which they planned to breed as soon as a mare came into heat. Mr. Stewart said they would build Ashwin a cabin the next day, to which Ashwin replied, "I sleep in cave till get wife." They tried hard to convince him, but he shook his head. "Me like cave, hear water. It put me sleep."

Gee and Mr. Stewart were living in one of the cabins while Mina and Mrs. Gilmore lived in the other. They were not sure about living together before they were married and went to Ashwin for advice. He thought about this and said, "Me only Cherokee man here. I be the village priest and marry you."

They readily agreed and picked a spot next to the cave and gathered firewood for the fire. Soon they had wood stacked waist-high. "It make big fire," Ashwin said as he blessed it.

Seven days later Gee and Mina stood in front of the fire, each covered with blankets that were somewhat blue, originally having been white blankets that were stained with bluish clay taken from the river bank. Gee gave Mina meat and she gave him corn. Mr. Stewart and Mrs. Gilmore sang as Ashwin removed the blue blankets and covered both with a white one.

"You are now man and wife," Ashwin announced proudly.

The same ceremony was repeated for Mr. Stewart and Mrs. Gilmore, after which everyone at the small gathering danced, sang, and told stories until it was almost dark.

Gee led Mina into their cabin and stood looking at her, thinking of the day he had found her, and he thanked God he had not left her to die. She was the most beautiful thing he had ever seen as she stared up at him with those big, beautiful, brown eyes. She slipped her arm around him and said, "Me happe to marry."

He held her close for a long time, feeling the vibes of love pass through them. He gently untied the strings to her dress and let it fall to the floor. She stood naked and unashamed before him as he slipped out of his buckskins, laid her on the cotton mattress, and covered them both with deerskins. They lay close, kissing and touching, exploring each other's body before they made love. Both knew that nothing in the world could be better than this.

Afterwards, they lay exhausted, but continued to caress each other, soon drifting off to a peaceful sleep, still holding each other very tightly.

The next morning, it was after sunup when they came outside to find Mr. Stewart and Gee's mother sitting together next to the waterfall. Gee and Mina came over to them, said good morning, and walked on to the waterfall to get a drink.

Gee stuck his head under the water, shook it like a dog, and splashed water on Mina, who squealed and, in turn, splashed the almost ice cold water on him. They embraced and stood swaying back and forth, gazing into each other's eyes, unaware they were not the only people in the world who were happy.

Finally Gee looked around and asked about Ashwin. "He left early to go hunting. . . maybe hunting for a wife," Mr. Stewart said.

"That would be nice," Gee's mother said.

There was a brief silence as each of them contemplated what their village might look like in years to come.

"Mr. Stewart, what are we going to do today? Do you think we need to burn the grass so we can get ready to plant our corn and tobacco, or maybe clear land for a garden?" Gee asked.

Mr. Stewart looked at him and at Gee's mother and said, "Gee, I was hoping that since I am now part of the family, I might persuade you to call me 'Sam.'" He stopped and stared off into the distance before he continued, "I will not try to replace your father,

Gee, but I do love your mother very much. I will do everything I can to take care of her and make her happy." He waited and Gee nodded his head. He added, "I do believe we can be happy here. This is a beautiful valley, and we will soon try to make sure we can stay. When the Cherokee council meets, we will see if Ashwin will let it be known that we would love to stay here. I believe since Chief Parjeet thinks we brought bad luck to his village, he and the other Cherokees will want us here instead of in their village and they will speak on our behalf."

Gee looked at his mother and saw her smiling at Mr. Stewart... Sam. At that moment he knew she loved Sam, and that they, too, were happy. "Maybe if Ashwin finds a wife, he, too, will be happy," Gee said.

"Audie, we have worked very hard for the past two weeks. Today is a beautiful day. I think we should saddle our horses and explore this land. What do you think?" She nodded her head.

They rode for most of the day, seeing rolling hills of grass and fertile hollows mixed with a few trees. They rode down one of the streams until they found a place to cross and rode to the other stream, which ran along the foothills of the valley. They followed it down it to where the stream cut its way through steep rock cliffs. They could go no farther and turned back to the south, finding another place to cross the first stream, and made their way back to the cabins.

They dismounted, led their horses to the waterfall, and let them drink from the pool made by the falling water. Sam cupped his hands and let the falling water fill them and offered the water to Audie. She drank from his hands, but spilled most of it. Both of them giggled like two young kids.

"I wish we had a gourd to drink out of," Sam said. He looked at the waterfall and walked hand in hand with Audie to the cabin they had built beside the cave, close against the cliff. Gee and Mina's cabin was on the other side of the cave.

Sam and Audie's cabin was a single room about ten feet square with a dirt floor. It had a deerskin door, but there were no windows, chimney, or fireplace, only an opening covered with deerskins. They would build a fireplace before winter. On the other side of the room, a cotton mattress lay on a crude bed made from cane poles and two wooden, straight back chairs, brought from Audie's home in Virginia. A barrel for flour and another barrel for meal were used as tables. A stack of five stoneware plates, three wooden bowls, and a few forks and spoons sat on top. Cast iron cooking pots and pans hung on wooden pegs driven between the logs. The few clothes they had hung on the limbs of a cedar sapling standing in a corner. Quilts and deerskins lay across a wooden pole wedged into the other corner.

The only thing different in Gee and Mina's cabin was a cotton mattress lying on deerskins spread on the ground and a box of hand tools they used for a seat. All of their other supplies, mostly farm equipment, were still in the wagon.

"When Ashwin returns, we will build his cabin and start on a barn. After that, I will ask Ashwin to take me to the trading post to buy some other things we need," Sam said.

"Sam, if you will build the fire, Gee can go milk, and Mina and I will get supper started. I think I will cook some beans with fatback, fry some cornbread, and stew some venison. We have enough sugar and flour for a cake. I will make one to celebrate our new home. How does that sound?"

"And it's the first day we have not worked from daylight to dark since we left Virginia." He walked to the ring of rocks stacked almost two feet high with two metal rods across the top, laid some small kindling into the middle of the ring, and started a fire.

After supper, they sat around the fire on log seats, both Sam and Gee complimenting Audie and Mina on the wonderful meal they had prepared, especially the cake, which was the first cake Gee could remember eating. They watched the sun slide behind the cliffs knowing it would be at least another hour before it got dark at the cabin because the high cliffs blocked the sunlight. They listened to the falling water, and each said a silent prayer of thanksgiving for where they were and what they had. *God has taken care of us,* Audie thought.

The silence was broken when Sam, looking at Gee, said, "Gee, I have been thinking about what you said about the... uh... the animals." He searched for words. "What did you call them?"

"Mules!"

"Ahh... yes. Mules. This valley is a perfect place to raise horses or mules. The land between the cliffs and the stream with its steep banks would make an excellent pasture and would keep the animals in, except for the place where we came down with the wagon and where we forded the first stream. We could put a fence in those places and use the land on this side of the stream to raise horses. We could build a bridge and farm the land between the first and second streams. I think there is some rich topsoil there, washed down from the mountains centuries ago." Sam watched as the others nodded their heads in agreement.

"This valley is pretty much hidden unless you happen to be at the rim, which is where we were when we first saw it. I suspect few Indians and no settlers have ever seen it. If you think about it, unless you travel by canoe, the way we came is the only way in. The only place you can see the valley is at the very edge of the cliff, but it is strewn with huge boulders, making riding a horse very difficult. I think we were very lucky that Ashwin found the one spot where he could see the valley and that he showed us where it was."

He paused and looked at the cliff. "We can plant a garden in the cut-out of the cliff between the waterfall and the barn. A short fence between the sides of the cliffs would keep the animals out, and we would have the barnyard fertilizer and water close by."

"We need to explore the cave and find out how big it is and how far it is to the water we heard falling. I would like to know where that water is going since it is not coming out this way," Gee said.

"Gee, I think we should wait for Ashwin. It is very dangerous to explore it without being harnessed together with ropes. You never know when you will step on a place that might give way underfoot, and you could fall hundreds of feet. That happened to a man not far from where I lived. They never found his body."

No one spoke for several minutes. Gee turned to face Sam and asked, "How big do you think this valley is?" Sam thought about this for a long time before he answered. "It's hard to say. We did not ride up the long draw where we crossed the first stream and did not ride to the end of the second one, but it looked like many acres of grassland. There appeared to be a draw of big trees to the right of where we came down with the wagon, but there's no way of knowing how big that area is until we ride it out. South of where the stream cuts through the cliffs, there was another draw; I could see more grass and and timber."

Sam looked around the valley, reached down, picked up a stick, and began to draw on the ground as he spoke. "Look, we came in here, on the northwest side, crossed this draw to the cave which is on the north side of this other draw. The first stream starts here on the north side and runs to here," he explained, pointing with the stick to the lines he had sketched. "The two streams run together at this point and flow out through the cliff on the east side. This hollow here at the south side is the one with the grassland. On the west side is where we saw the timber." He paused and studied the marks on the ground and saw he had drawn a crude five-pointed star. The others saw it, too, and stood to stare at it.

'It's the shape of a star! This is the star I saw falling the night I found Mina! I knew she would bring us good luck," Gee said excitedly.

Tall Grass

Sam and Audie looked at each other, remembering what they had lost because of Mina, but as they looked at each other and at Gee and Mina, they realized that maybe what they had found was worth more than what they had lost. Audie had not thought about it, but she knew she would not want to go back if it meant not having Sam. Maybe Mina had brought them good luck after all.

CHAPTER NINETEEN

BOOBY TRAP
Twenty-Ten

When Penny met Simmons at the door, she saw he was very angry. "Mitchell, what is going on? Is it Elaine again?"

"No, it's not Elaine," he said angrily, as he opened the refrigerator door and took out a beer. "Did you know Gregg Davis is on the take? The sorry SOB so much as told me so. All that crap about him being Lanny's friend... If it weren't for the yellow streak up his back, I might think he had killed Lanny, but he's a jerk who doesn't have the guts. He said 'Don't make waves—that a lot of powerful people around here have long memories.' Well, he's going to find out I can make monstrous waves."

Penny interrupted, grabbed his arm, and led him to a chair on the patio. "Mitchell! Mitchell, please calm down," she implored. Speaking louder this time she asked, "Would you please tell me where have you been and why you were walking?"

Simmons sat down hard in a patio chair, took a long gulp of beer, and leaned back, resting his head against the back of the chair. Slowly he began to feel some of his anger subside.

"I was at Lanny's house, and someone took a couple of shots at me. I called Davis to pick me up, and he basically told me to mind my own business. 'Powerful people with long memories so don't make waves,' he said."

He downed the rest of the beer, stopped and looked at Penny, and began to feel the anger rising once more. Getting up, he walked over to a refrigerator and took out another bottle.

He drank half of this bottle in one swig, walked to the edge of the patio, and looked out at the rolling hills. In his mind he saw Lanny screaming at him not to touch the body. He finished the beer in another gulp and was aware of Penny standing beside him.

He tried hard to relax, to control the anger. Had he not been trained that angry men make poor decisions and poor decisions get you killed? Had he not seen enough of this in Afghanistan? Had he not seen many of his men make poor decisions, and later, had he not picked up their body parts?

He walked down the patio steps and stood by the pool, trying to get his mind to focus. . . maybe seeing Anna naked in the pool. . . or Penny teasing him with the boots. . . or feeling Elaine's body against his on the dance floor. He tried, but the only thing in his mind was Lanny screaming at him, *Don't touch him, don't touch him.*

Again Penny came over, stood beside him, and shook his shoulder. "Mitchell, is the truck at Lanny's house?" He nodded. "Well, let's go get it," she insisted.

"Penny, someone out there has a high-powered rifle. They tried to kill me, and I ran like a scared dog. I was going to get Davis to take me back when I got a weapon. It's a good thing, too. He could have shot me in the back. When I get a weapon, I'll get the truck myself and I hope to fu. . .," he stopped. *Can I not talk without using language like that?*

"I hope they try to shoot me again. They are going to find that I can take care of myself." He looked at the pasture and saw the horses grazing peacefully. Some of the tension began to leave him. Finally, he added, "I won't let you go; you might get hurt."

"Mitchell, when the day comes that I am afraid to go where I please, I might as well be dead. I am going with you," Penny insisted.

"Neither of us are going, not until I get a weapon. I survived eight years of being shot at, and some creep out there will not make me run when I have a weapon."

Penny watched him for a long time, trying to decide whether to tell him about the weapons in the safe. After several seconds she convinced herself he was determined to find a weapon and would find one somewhere else if she did not give him one.

"Mitchell, my father gave me a Remington 243 when I was twelve years old, and I know how to shoot. He has an arsenal of guns in a safe inside the house. You pick the ones you want. I'll take my 243, and we'll go get the truck. If you don't let me go, I'll leave your ass here, take one of the hired hands, and go by myself." Simmons stared at her and he knew she meant it.

"Okay."

Penny opened the safe, took out her 243 and a box of ammo. Simmons chose a Winchester 270 semi-automatic and put a 357 Smith & Wesson revolver in his belt. He stuck ammunition for both weapons into his pockets. They walked to Penny's Ferrari, and Simmons laid the two rifles between the seats.

Turning to Penny, he told her in a deliberate tone, "Let's go, but when we get there, I am going in alone. You understand?"

Penny pulled out of the driveway, but did not reply. She only looked at him and said, "Elaine called this morning and said to get your bag out of her car. What happened between you two?"

Simmons shrugged his shoulders and looked out the windshield.

"Like everything else since you took my boots... Everything is all." He stopped and shrugged his shoulders.

Penny stared at him and said nothing as she drove towards Lanny's house.

"The truck is about a half mile past Lanny's on an old Jeep trail. Drive to the top of the hill just beyond there and let me out. I will slip back to where the truck is to make sure no one is around it. You drive at least a couple of miles up the road and turn around. Come back and stop on top of the hill where you let me out. Then get out of your car and find a spot where you can cover both your car and the Jeep trail. When you see me come out with the truck, I will drive to where you are, and we'll unload the weapons. I wouldn't want Davis making waves by arresting us for having loaded weapons in our vehicles.'

"I'm going in with you."

"No, you are not. One person makes enough noise, let alone two."

She knew he was not going to give in so when she reached the top of the hill, she pulled to the side of the road. He picked up the Winchester, got out, and closed the door softly. He took the 357 out of his belt, loaded it and the rifle, and eased off the shoulder of the road.

Penny drove about three miles before finding a place to turn around, then drove back to the hill, stopped the car, and got out. She walked around to the passenger side, picked up the 243, loaded it, and found a place behind some huckleberry bushes. She sat down and placed the rifle muzzle in the forks of the bush, pointing it towards the old logging road. She sat and waited, going over in her mind what she should do if she had to shoot. It was then a wave of panic swept over her. She had shot deer, coyotes, and gophers, but could she shoot a man, a human being? A cold chill ran over her as she thought about it. She decided she could, if they were trying to shoot Mitchell.

A couple of cars passed by, slowed and looked at her car, but did not stop. About five minutes later, she saw Simmons walk to the edge of the highway and motion for her to come.

She drove to where he stood. He opened the door and sat down, standing the Winchester between his knees. She looked at him, saw the concern on his face, and could tell he was in deep thought.

"What's wrong?"

"I think there is a bomb under the truck. I could see where someone had laid in the grass besides the driver's door." He waited, looking off into the distance, then took a piece of paper from his shirt pocket and handed it to Penny.

She read aloud, "I miss my buddy Lanny so much. I can't live without him." Penny gasped and looked at Simmons for further explanations.

"It was lying on the ground about thirty feet in front of the truck. I would not have seen it had I not walked around the truck to make sure it was not booby-trapped." He sat looking at her, trying to decide what to do. He opened the door and got out.

"Turn around and drive east a few miles and call the state police. Don't use 911. I don't trust the sheriff's department and don't want Davis around until the state police gets here. I am going back to guard the truck to make sure no one removes the bomb. If they saw us here and know the bomb did not go off, they will probably try to remove it. Also, call Chief Bates and ask him to contact the FBI; the building of a bomb is a federal offense."

"But Mitchell, what about you? They will kill you if they can."

"Penny, please do what I say and don't come back this way until I call you. I'll be all right. Like I said, people have been trying to kill me for the last eight years." He walked a few steps, placed a finger on the safety of the Winchester, and slipped into the woods.

She turned the car around and drove a couple of miles before pulling to the shoulder. She logged onto the Internet, found the number for the state police and dialed. She told them what had happened and where to find Simmons and the truck. She reminded them a second time about the bomb in the truck. She called Chief Bates and retold the story to him, including Simmons' instructions that he call the FBI and not let the sheriff's department know what was happening. She thought of calling Elaine, but decided against it. Simmons might need to call, and she did not want her phone to have a busy signal. She pulled back onto the highway and a half-mile later found a side road, pulled into it, and turned around, facing the highway. Several minutes later she heard a siren and saw a state trooper's car speed by.

After getting out of Penny's car, Simmons slipped into the wood close enough to see the truck, found a hiding place with good cover, and waited. About five minutes later he saw movement in the woods in front of the truck. He wished for a pair of binoculars like the ones he'd had in Afghanistan, but the riflescope would have to do. He used thumb and finger to click off the safety so it made no noise, and he slowly slid the rifle to his shoulder. Looking through the scope he saw two men, three hundred and twenty yards away. Simmons was a sniper, and it was imperative that he know distance. He could be off a couple of yards, but no more than that. Both men were armed and were scanning the truck and its surroundings with binoculars. He was formulating a plan to capture at least one of them alive when he heard the distant sound of a siren. The two men also heard it because they turned around and faded into the woods.

Simmons thought of pursuing them, but decided it could wait. He would let the state police handle this. He slipped back to the highway, unloaded his weapons, and was laying them on the ground when the trooper stopped and got out of his car. Simmons held his hands far away from his sides and in plain view. The trooper had his hand on his weapon, but relaxed a little when he saw Simmons was in an Army uniform.

Simmons introduced himself and gave a brief description of what has happened, including the two armed men he had seen. The trooper, whose name tag said "Travis Dalton" was about thirty, dark-skinned with brown eyes and black hair. His physique told of many hours in a gym. He eyed the weapons Simmons had laid on the ground.

"Those yours?" he asked.

"They are not registered to me, but yes, I brought them here."

Booby Trap

Dalton walked over and picked up the weapons, checked to make sure they were unloaded, and put them into the cruiser.

"The young lady who called you is somewhere up the highway. She is worried about me. Can I call her and tell her I am okay? She's driving a red convertible. Did you see her?"

The trooper shook his head. "You can call her, but tell her to stay put until I know what's going on here." Simmons called Penny and related to her what the trooper had said.

"I am coming there."

"Unload the 243 and put it in the trunk before you come." Simmons knew it was useless to argue with her and asked her to hold on. "She is Amos Gilmore's granddaughter. She doesn't mind very well," he told the trooper.

"Tell her to stop in front of my patrol car and stay in her car. That's an order."

"You heard what he said." Simmons heard Penny hang up.

"You sure there was a bomb?" The trooper had no more gotten the words out of his mouth when a huge explosion sent flying glass, smoke, and fragments of metal into the air.

Both men fell to the ground, Dalton drawing his revolver and pointing it in the direction of the blast. "Damn," he said and stared as the smoke began drifting towards the highway. He got off the ground, hurried to his cruiser, radioed for backup, and instructed them to call the fire department. He picked up the Smith & Wesson and walked to where Simmons stood.

"You have ammo for this?" Simmons nodded. "Load it and let's have a look."

They slipped slowly into the wood to where they could see the truck. All the windows were blown out, and the top of the truck was rounded upwards. The cab was ablaze inside, and the paint was beginning to melt on the doors.

"I think we should get back. The gas tank will blow before long," Dalton said, and they walked back to his cruiser just as Penny slid to a stop. She got out of the car and ran over to where

285

Simmons and Dalton were standing, asking if they were all right and what had happened.

"Yep, you follow orders really good," Dalton said. As somewhat of an afterthought, he added, "And you turned out to be a fine young lady." Simmons did not know what he meant and did not have time to ask. Penny was still showering them with questions.

"They blew up your truck," Simmons said.

She stood looking in the direction of the truck for a few second, reached inside her jacket pocket, and handed Dalton the note. "He found this." She stared at the trooper for a long moment. "I remember you. You helped me after I wrecked my car." She took hold of his arm and said, "Thank you. I am sorry I was so rude and immature. You did not have to do that. I am sorry. I was going to tell you later, but I was so stoned, I didn't remember your name."

"You are welcome. In a way, I guess I did. It's a long story, but I am glad you got your life straightened out. I heard about your fiancé, and I am sorry. This was his place, wasn't it?" Penny nodded.

Dalton read the note, turned to Simmons, "Where did you find this?"

"About thirty feet in front of the truck. I would not have seen it, but in Afghanistan we learned to look for IEDs."

"Seems like someone wanted people to think you committed suicide."

"Seems to be a pattern here. They said that about Lanny, but I was with him for four years, and I know better."

They heard more sirens approaching from both directions, and Dalton asked Simmons if he could have the S & W back. He unloaded it and put it back into his car as a fire truck and two state police cars arrived at about the same time.

"Put the fire out, but disturb as little as you can," Dalton told the fire chief. More sirens could be heard in the distance—

Booby Trap

one was Chief Bates and a little later, two deputy sheriffs' cars arrived. Gregg Davis was in one of them.

Cars begin stopping and other rubberneckers slowed, inquiring as to what had happened. Gregg began directing traffic, never once coming close to Penny or Simmons.

A Channel 7 news crew arrived, trying to interview anyone who would talk. One of them approached Simmons, who referred all questions to Trooper Dalton. They tried to interview Penny, but she turned away from the camera and said, "No comment."

Chief Bates came over and asked if they were okay. Trooper Dalton took statements from Simmons and Penny, and as soon as the fire was out, another trooper took photos of the truck, the note, and the serial numbers of the two weapons Simmons had put on the ground. "You can pick them up later if everything checks out," the trooper told him.

A tow truck arrived and was told to take the vehicle to the state police evidence lot. One of the troopers would escort him, making sure no evidence was tampered with. Dalton's cell phone rang. He answered, nodded his head, and looked at Simmons and Penny. "My dispatcher said the FBI would be here shortly, and they asked you not to leave."

Chief Bates came over and said there was nothing he could do here and that he was leaving. "But if you need me, just call," he assured them.

Ten minutes later, the FBI arrived to photograph the scene, take statements, and remind Dalton that since the use of explosives was a federal offense, they would take over the investigation. They asked Simmons, Penny, and Dalton if they would come to the state police headquarters and meet with the director. Simmons knew this was not a request, but an order, so naturally the Army soldier promptly agreed.

A little later Simmons saw Davis talking on the radio of his patrol car. When he finished his conversation, Davis came over to where Simmons was standing and told him, "The sheriff asked if you would drop by."

Simmons said nothing, just turned and walked away.

Upon arrival at the state police office in Longview, Simmons, Penny, and Dalton were met by FBI investigator Alan Chippernal. He read their statements and had a sketch artist meet with Simmons to get a composite of the two armed men. The note and the truck would be sent to a FBI lab for analysis since an explosive device was used.

Simmons told Chippernal the sheriff's department asked him to come in and he wanted to know if he was required to comply with the request. "I don't trust them," he said and wondered why Chippernal did not seem surprised.

"This is a federal case, so you do not have to meet with them or answer any of their questions. If they try to bring you in for questioning, remind them the FBI has jurisdiction in this case and call me at this number." He gave Simmons one of his cards. "We will be in touch. Thank you and the young lady for your cooperation."

Simmons and Penny got up to leave. Halfway to the door, Simmons stopped and looked at Chippernal. "Mr. Chippernal, would it be possible for me to get a license to carry a firearm?"

Chippernal studied Simmons, looked at his watch, and waited a few moments before he spoke. "Mr. Simmons, after Chief Bates called and I learned who you were, I read the service records of both you and Mr. Simpson. You have my thanks for what you have done." He paused, and Simmons could see he was contemplating what to say. "Mr. Simmons, since there have been two attempts on your life, I will see if I can clear it through proper channels to make you a deputy investigator for the FBI. It is just a title, but it will give you permission to have a legal weapon on your person. I will be in touch."

Simmons expressed his gratitude and turned to leave.

"Mr. Simmons, it would please us if you and Ms. Sanderson would let the FBI investigate this matter. Good day." By the way he smiled and the way he said it, Simmons knew Chippernal would welcome their help.

Penny and Simmons walked through the lobby and saw Anna talking to a female officer. She fell in step beside them. "Never a dull moment around you, handsome." Turning to Penny she said, "Daddy wants us to meet him Hangar C in thirty minutes. How about we get a sub to go on our way?" She left no impression other than that she expected them to go.

Amos was waiting for them inside the hangar next to a Real Life Sky Jumpers Cessna King Air with the words, "If it can't kill you, it ain't fun" painted on the fuselage. Two men were loading camera equipment into the plane. When the last one was loaded, one of the men nodded to Mr. Gilmore and said, "We can set up the mapping equipment once we are airborne. Who's coming with us?"

"Mitchell and I will be coming." He turned to Marie, "While we are gone, lease a chopper with a cargo door for that equipment over there," he said, pointing to several boxes stacked in the corner of the hangar. "When we return from this trip, Simmons will go with the Henry and film the Simpson place from another angle. I don't want to draw attention to what we are doing so we will use two different aircraft. Marie, you and Penny wait for me; when I am finished here, we'll go to Manny's. I will have them drop Mitchell off at Manny's when they are finished."

He turned and spoke to a man standing just behind him. "Henry, there is a helipad at Manny's, which I'm sure you are aware of, so when you are finished with the second flight, all of you join us for dinner." Mr. Gilmore looked at his Rolex. "Say around six. Three hours should give us plenty of time to survey the farm. We can discuss what we have seen, and by tomorrow the survey maps and video should be ready to compare to the ones we have at Gilsan." Henry nodded his head.

The King Air made a high altitude northbound pass over the Simpson farm. Ten minutes later it circled and made a low level southbound pass and returned to the airport.

Simmons and Henry boarded a Bell 206 Jet Ranger which had the passenger door removed. The camera and other equipment were already mounted into place. They made a low level eastbound pass and a few minutes later climbed to a thousand feet and made the westbound pass, continuing on to Manny's.

During dinner they discussed what they had seen. No one reported seeing anything unusual, except the chopper pilot said the road that turned off Farmers Market 26 on the north side appeared to be more traveled than would be expected for just a dirt-logging road. They made a note to explore this more once they had the maps.

Early the next day, Anna dropped Simmons off at Longview Bottling Company. He met Amos and Henry in the conference room to view a video presentation that one of Mr. Gilmore's assistants had set up. They compared the videos they shot yesterday with aerial maps of Digital Globe, TerraServer, Bing, and Google, along with the survey maps from Gilsan Oil. The only anomaly they could detect was the dirt road the chopper pilot had mentioned.

Another image had caught Simmon's attention. It could have been a camouflaged area at the base of a hill maybe a quarter mile from where the shots had been fired at him. This area appeared to be somewhat different in color from the rest; it could be trees or different light images, but the color was apparent even when filmed from different angles. He was aware of this from the many reconnaissance photos he had seen in Afghanistan. It was enough to arouse his curiosity, but he also realized that it could be very dangerous to explore this area. After Gregg Davis, he was wary of whom he could trust, so he did not mention this in the meeting.

Booby Trap

After the meeting broke, Amos and Simmons boarded the S-76, and he instructed the pilot to make one more pass over the area in question before proceeding towards the Sanderson Ranch. Simmons made a mental note of what appeared to be a well-camouflaged area. He would get a GPS fix on it from a topo map.

On the way to the Sanderson's, Amos's cell phone rang. He listened intently and nodded his head. He called Anna and told her to meet the chopper because they needed to be in Tyler by 4:00 p.m. for a meeting with the board of directors to discuss Bradley's replacement.

The chopper set down at the Sanderson's ranch. Before Anna boarded, Simmons asked if it was necessary for him to come along. He was relieved to be told he could stay behind at the Sanderson's.

Simmons walked to the refrigerator, opened a bottle of beer, and sat down on the patio steps thinking about the different colored area. He was almost certain his instincts were right about the area so he sat thinking of how he could examine it without getting himself killed. He was deep in thought when Reina came out carrying a huge plate of food. He thanked her, ate it all, and walked down to the guest house. He was almost to the steps when he saw it—his duffle bag with the boots sitting on top. A deep hurt and a sick feeling began building inside of him as he stared at the boots.

He walked to the duffle bag, picked up the boots, and slung them as far as he could toward the barn. The boots kicked up dust as they tumbled and finally skidded to a stop. He kicked the bag off the steps, stepped upon the porch, and slumped into a chair.

"Damn you, Lanny," Simmons said aloud, knowing he did not mean it. He sat staring at the horses grazing on the fading green grass. They did not have a care in the world, but knew someone would feed them when the grass was gone. Someone always had. *What about me? Yeah. . . what about me?* He fought the urge to feel sorry for himself.

"What am I going to do?" he said again and continued to stare at the horses for a long time before finally getting up and walked into the house.

At the fridge he opened a beer and stood at the window, looking at the horses again, trying to decide. Sometime later he was aware of someone knocking on his door. He opened it and saw Penny standing on the porch, looking at the spot where the boots had landed.

"Mitchell, may I come in?"

He stepped aside and asked, "You want a beer?"

She nodded. He went to the kitchen and came back with two bottles of beer, opened them, and handed one to her. He took a long drink and shrugged his shoulders. "I tried to call Elaine last night and again today when I was in Texarkana. I left a message, but she did not return my call," she said softly and sipped her beer. "I see she has been here. Did you to talk to her?"

He shook his head, walked outside, and set his duffel bag back onto the porch, then walked over, picked the boots up and set them on top of the duffel bag. He turned and stood staring at the horses.

"Maybe, I'll call and thank her for bringing my bag home," he said mockingly.

"I don't think that would be a very good idea. If Elaine won't return my calls, she is really upset. . . or maybe I should say really confused. She's a very bright girl, though; she'll figure it out."

"That won't concern me. I'm leaving." "No, you are not leaving."

"Yeah, I'm fed up with all this."

Penny sat looking as him, seeing he was really upset. She did not know what to say to him. "Okay, run. I tried that one time and ran straight into a reform school," she said, with a mixture of anger and sadness. She continued to stare at him. "Yeah, run. That might be something you're good at." Almost flinging the words at him, she turned and left. He watched her go down the steps and walk towards the big house.

Simmons walked into the house and got another beer, then another, then another, gulping them down as fast as he could. He opened another one and set it on the coffee table. The last thing he remembered was lying down on the couch.

Cold water hit his face.

"Damn!" he yelled. When his eyes focused, he saw Anna standing over him with an empty water glass in her hand and anger in her eyes. "Get up and come to the house for dinner. We will take you wherever you want to go in the morning." She walked outside and headed for the big house.

It was obvious she had talked to Penny. He washed his face, looked in the mirror to brush his hair and saw two red, swollen eyes looking at him.

He stripped off his clothes, stepped into the shower and turned the cold water wide open. *If I am leaving, they can wait.* After a long shower, he walked dripping wet to the linen closet, found a towel, dried off and threw the towel on the floor. As he was shaving, he heard a car door slam up at the big house. *Probably Penny,* he thought. He took his time and brushed his teeth. He went outside and brought in the duffel bag, dumping most of its contents on the bed. He found clean underwear, desert camo pants, a white tee shirt, and a camo hoodie. As he dressed, he looked at the pasture and saw the horses coming to the barn.

They have more sense than I do, he thought.

He made his way slowly up to the big house where Anna, Penny, and Elaine sat on the patio. He stopped, looked at Anna and Penny, then stared at Elaine, but said nothing.

"They say you are leaving," Elaine said. He nodded his head.

"Why? Because of me?" He shrugged, walked to the fridge, and took out a beer.

"Maybe you have had enough of those. I saw eight empty bottles sitting on the coffee table," Anna said.

Defiantly he opened the bottle and took a long drink. *I don't owe these people anything except the price of eight, no nine, beers,* he thought as he stood looking at the three women.

"Dinner is ready. Do you want me to serve you out here?" Reina asked.

"No, we will come inside. It is little cool out here," Anna replied, looking at Simmons.

"I'm not eating. I'm leaving." He killed the rest of the bottle and set it hard on the table. "I'll send you a check for the beer."

He turned around and took a step towards the patio steps, but stopped when he heard Penny say, "Lanny would be proud of you."

He whirled and glared at her. "You've been throwing that in my face since the day I got here. You had two damned years to do something, but you didn't. Maybe Lanny would be proud of you, too. Go to hell." He walked to the guest house, stuffed his clothing into his duffel bag, slung it over his shoulders, and threw the boots into the yard, again. When he returned to the patio, he pitched the phone on the table where Penny was sitting and continued walking down the drive just as the shadows began to fade.

CHAPTER TWENTY

MULES

Seventeen seventy-five

Gee and Sam were working on the other lean-to when they say Ashwin approaching, leading two horses. On one of the horses was an Indian woman.

"This new wife. Her name Kali. Her man die two snows ago," he said, dismounting and helping her off the horse. Everyone introduced themselves. Kali bowed slightly to each of them as Ashwin introduced them and did her best to repeat each name. Audie nodded, walked to where Kali stood, and offered her hand.

"Welcome to our village. It is not much, but we will be happy. Next, we will build a house for you and Ashwin," she said in Cherokee.

Kali had a wide smile, big brown eyes, and a soft voice. She was almost as tall as Ashwin, big boned, strong, and well-built—and a lot younger than Ashwin. As they shook hands, Audie could see they were hands that had worked hard, as would be expected for someone who had to support herself. Audie looked at the other horse and saw a small pack tied to each side. *She has about as many personal items as we do. I think she will fit in just fine.*

Mina bowed, took Kali hands, and held them in front of her. "They be good people. You will like. Are you hungry?" Kali nodded her head slowly, but said she could wait until the rest ate. Sam and Gee stopped working on the lean-to and asked where

Ashwin would like his house. He looked at Kali, who was looking at the waterfall. She pointed to it and said to Ashwin, "If you like, I like hear water." After dinner they began to cut logs and notch them; before supper that evening, they had built the walls about three-feet high.

Two days later, they finished a cabin identical to Sam and Gee's except Ashwin did not want a roof with shingles. His roof was made with poles and reeds, leaving a hole in the center for smoke to exit. He cut reeds and laid them on the inside of two split logs to make a bed. He laid deerskins over the reeds for the mattress and cut a log into two-foot lengths, setting them upright to make a table. Kali carried grass and laid it on the ground for a floor. Audie and Mina saw this and later did the same to their cabins, while the men worked on the roof.

When the roof was finished, they went hunting. There was plenty of game so they had no trouble taking deer for meat. Later, they sat up their trap lines, securing enough furs to take to the trading post within a week. Audie used the chalk and the small blackboard she had brought with her to make a list of things they needed: meal, flour, salt, lard, and, if it were possible, some chicken wire and a few more chickens.

"One of our chickens is missing, and I'm afraid something will get the rest of them without chicken wire. If we could get some pigs to raise for our lard, that would be nice, too," Audie said.

The men needed ropes to explore the cave, as well as more powder and lead for the muskets. "Some tea would be nice," Sam added.

Two days later, the sky was blue, the sun warm. At first light they loaded about fifty pelts of mink and otter, harnessed four horses, and hitched two to the wagon. The other two horses would be used to pull the wagon up the draw and out of the valley. Once on top they would hobble the two horses and take them back down the draw on the way home. They arrived at the trading post a little after mid-day. It was owned by a broad-shouldered, blue-eyed German named Altus Ludvig. He was a little wary seeing a strange wagon this early in the year—especially one with two white men and an Indian—until he recognized Ashwin.

Ashwin introduced him to Sam and Gee, giving a brief description of what had happened in Virginia, all because they took in an Indian girl. He told him about living with the Cherokee and about having to leave because the village thought Gee was a bad spirit. They had moved to a valley a half day's ride west of there, one that Chief Parjeet of the Dinkar tribe said they could live on. He said the supreme council would probably let them live on the land as long as they wanted.

Sam told Ludvig what supplies they needed and loaded the wire, ropes, and a crate with two pigs. Eight chickens with their legs tied together were placed into the wagon. Sam also bought dresses and bonnets for Audie, Mina, and Kali, along with some cloth and sewing thread. This was less than the furs were worth, so Altus offered to pay the difference with Continental currency or he could put it on the books for later. Sam said they would have to come back to get seeds for planting, and to put it on the book.

They left for home, arriving as the last rays of light faded. The women were excited to have new dresses and bonnets. Mina began jumping up and down and squealing. She grabbed Sam around the neck and hugged him hard, saying, "Thank you, thank you. I so proud! I so happe!"

Audie and Kali also expressed their gratitude. "Sam, you shouldn't have done that for me, but I am happy you did. I will repay you," Audie said, smiling and wiggling her hips.

The next day Ashwin said one of Sam's mares was in heat and asked if they still wanted to breed her to the donkey. Of course, that was what Gee wanted, but Sam had reservations. What if it did not work? They could lose the colt she would have. Looking at Gee, however, Sam saw how badly he wanted to try for a mule, so he relented. They soon learned that the donkey was too short to mount the mare. The only alternative was to build a ramp and let the donkey stand on the ramp as they backed the mare against it. They cut logs and packed dirt on top of them. This effort was unsuccessful since the donkey kept falling off the side of it. They decided to build a second ramp a small distance from the first one, thus enabling the mare to stand between the two. A little bit before dark they managed to get the mare bred.

"If I had known it would be a day's work, I would never have agreed," Sam muttered to himself. "If we do get a mule, what good is having just one? There is no telling when another mare will come into heat. We only have ten horses, and four of them are studs. Oh well, that is done now, and we can breed the next mare without having to build a ramp. We have enough horses already, and I guess I would like to know what a mule looks like." He took the sweetgum twig he had been chewing and tossed it away.

The next few weeks everyone worked from sun-up until sundown. The three women worked the same as the men, clearing a place for a garden and burning grassland to prepare for planting tobacco and corn. During this time they also bred another mare to the donkey.

The time to plant was soon to arrive, so Gee loaded his furs into the wagon and all of them went to the trading post. Ashwin introduced Kali, Audie, and Mina to Mr. Ludvig, who held out a big hand and shook hands with each. As he shook hands with Mina, he looked at Gee. "Don't rightly say I blame you for taking her in. She sure is a fine-looking young lady. You, too, Ms. Audie and Ms. Kali." Both Ashwin and Kali had learned to speak enough English to understand most of what he said.

"Do you have a wife, Mr. Lugvig?" Audie asked.

"I do," and he walked to the rear of the store and called, "Oneka, someone here would like to meet you."

A short time later, a lady came out of a back room followed by two small boys, around the ages of two and four years old. It appeared the woman was expecting another. She smiled and bowed slightly, "I am Oneka." She was not as tall as Audie, and her skin was not much darker. She had dark blue eyes, light brown hair, and wore a simple white dress.

"I am Audie... my husband, Sam, Ashwin and his wife, Kali, and my son, Gee, and his wife, Mina." She pointed to each as she spoke and added, "Oneka, it is very nice to meet you. You have two fine-looking boys."

Oneka nodded and patted her stomach. "I hope this is a girl," she said with a warm and tender smile. She pulled the boys in front of her. "This is Gabe and Fredrick," laying her hand on each boy's head as she called their names.

"Oneka is half Seneca. I know Seneca and Cherokee were not fond of each other, but that was a long time ago. I hope you all can be friends," Mr. Ludvig added.

"What our elders did, we did not. We be friends," Kala said.

"Fine, fine. Oneka, please take the ladies back and fix 'em some tea. Oh, and would you bring us men some, too?"

Sam purchased corn seed, but decided he would buy tobacco seed later. Mr. Ludvig advised that he should buy now if they wanted tobacco seed. It was getting scarce because all the new settlers were planting tobacco.

"The price of seed has gone through the roof. Last year a fifty-pound bag sold for three Continental dollars; this year they are selling for eight. People around here think I am trying to cheat them, but I have to pay six dollars for a bag. I've heard people say they will go to ten or twelve by planting time, if you can even get them."

Oneka and the other ladies came out and brought four cups of tea. It was the first time Sam had ever tasted tea, and he wondered why there was such a fuss over it up in Boston. *Ain't no wonder they threw it in the harbor,* Sam thought.

Before they left the trading post, they had decided to buy a bag of tobacco seed and extra corn seed.

Three weeks later, Gee asked Ashwin if he would ride with him to the trading post. The killing of the chief's son had bothered Gee, and he did not want to be confronted by any of the Indians. Not that he was afraid, but he wanted to avoid trouble, if possible. Gee told Sam they were going to the post, and Sam said he would come along. He wanted to find out when the Supreme Council would meet so he would know their decision about permitting him to buy the land they were living on, the land they now called Star Valley.

At the trading post they learned the council was to meet near Salem in three weeks. Sam told Mr. Ludvig that if they could buy Star Valley, or if the council would let them live there, they would plant cotton next year.

Three weeks later Ashwin and Gee went to the Supreme Council meeting, Sam deciding it would be best if he did not go. After all, he had no claim to the land, as did Ashwin, who was a member of one of the tribes, and Gee, because he was married to a Cherokee woman.

When they arrived at the council, Ashwin hinted that if they were not allowed to live on Tall Grass, the others would move with him back to his village. The council met and when it came time for Chief Parjeet to speak, he told of Ashwin and Gee and what had happened at his village, something most of the Indians knew already. He said Gee was a bad spirit, and he had befriended a Cherokee girl. Because of this, the whites had burned his home. Gee was married to a Cherokee, and by Cherokee law, he was entitled to live in a Cherokee village. He said Ashwin and Gee wanted to live in Tall Grass, unless another village would make a home for them.

Gee saw that most of the tribal chiefs were staring at him, but he could not decide if it was fear or hate he saw in their eyes. He hoped it was just fear.

Chief Parjeet asked if Ashwin could speak to the Council. He was granted permission, so Ashwin began by telling of the falling star he had seen which led him to the valley where he now lived. "The valley is in shape of star, and I know Great Spirit want me live there. Him see same star," he added, pointing to Gee. "Great Spirit want him there, too. Great Spirit give me wife; I take there. No village want Tall Grass, but we want."

Gee looked around and saw most of the chiefs were now smiling and nodding their heads. The chief of the Supreme Council also saw the heads nodding. He stood and said, "Supreme Council will meet. We make decision."

Ashwin nodded his head slowly, thanked them, and walked outside with Gee.

"They give us Tall Grass, or as you say, Star Valley, I think." They stood waiting for the council to decide. Gee noticed that none of the Indians came close to where he stood. Ashwin saw this, too, and said, "You bad spirit; you kill chief's son. They afraid of bad spirit."

A few minute later Chief Parjeet came to them and said, "Supreme Council say you live Tall Grass, not come to my village."

"Chief, I am sorry about your son, but I had no choice. It was either him or me."

The Chief looked at Gee with a mixture of fear and regret in his eyes. He said nothing, just turned and walked away.

"We go," said Ashwin. "Ashwin, what now?"

"Tall Grass your village now. Supreme Council rule and no go back."

"No, not my village, our village. You, Sam, Mother, Kala, Mina, and me. We will file papers in Salem, and we will be equal owners."

"Gee, Cherokee no own land. It belong to Great Spirit," Ashwin insisted.

Extending Shadows

As they rode Gee explained to him that the white man claimed land, and if the Indians didn't, someone else would file claim to it. "Ashwin, there will be more settlers this spring and more the next one after that. If the Cherokee don't file for their lands, they will be pushed farther back into the mountains. I know it is not right, but it will happen. Their land will be taken from them. Talk with Sam; he will tell you this is true."

They reached Star Valley late the next day, and Gee broke the news to a joyous Sam and the women. Each was anxious to hear the details. Gee held his hands high and yelled, "I told you the falling star was good luck, and so is Mina!" Gee said, putting his arm around Mina and squeezing her to him.

"We will celebrate by killing one of the chickens and making chicken dumplings," Audie said proudly. The next two weeks they continued to burn and clear the land until they had cleared twenty acres. They cleared so much land, they needed to make another trip to the trading post to buy a sack of cotton seed, plus seed for the garden and harnesses for the two vigilante horses. The day after they returned home, they began using the turning plow to break ground for planting. All were excited to see the fertile black soil with very few rocks. They envisioned a bumper crop of cotton, corn, and tobacco.

A few days later, the ground was plowed and dragged. Sam used a double shovel to lay off the rows while Ashwin, Gee, and the ladies dropped the seed and covered it with their feet. They prepared the garden by spreading horse manure over the land and plowing it under with the middle buster, making seed beds for the garden seeds. The next day the garden was planted.

Ashwin discovered two more of the mares were in season, and they were bred to the donkey without trouble. Gee said by this time next year they would have four mules. Sam nodded, but still had his doubts.

During the summer months the cotton and corn grew and so did the weeds and grass. Controlling them was a never-ending chore, both in the fields as well as in the garden. They spent many long hours with a hoe in their hands. It was agreed that the next piece of farm equipment they would purchase would be a cultivator... and maybe a planter. Once they had these, they would clear more land to farm. "We will do that after harvest," Sam had said.

The first harvest was more than they could have ever dreamed. They had plenty of vegetables with enough dried peas and beans to last through the winter. They had corn to feed the animals and tobacco to sell or trade for more horses, mostly mares. They spent the fall clearing land, erecting a building in which to store the tobacco, and a barn for the animals.

They had a feast on Thanksgiving and gave thanks for what they had accomplished. Mina had indeed brought them good luck.

Or so they thought.

CHAPTER TWENTY-ONE

FBI

Twenty Ten

He was almost to the gates when a car pulled up beside him.

"Mitchell, please wait," Elaine said as she got out of the car and came over. She took him by the arm, pulled him close, and laid her head against his chest. He felt her tears soaking the front of his tee shirt.

"I'm sorry, Mitchell," she said softly. "I don't want you to go." She handed him the phone. "Mitchell, come to Texarkana with me. Let's forget all about this. Nothing we do will bring Lanny back."

She looked up at him, tears streaming down her face, and waited a long time before she continued. "I am sorry, but I lost my parents and then I lost Lanny. He was my rock; he was always there for me. I was afraid to get involved, to let myself care, I was afraid you might get killed, and I really did not think I could go through another death." She continued to sob. "I try to pretend that I am strong, and I try not to let myself get close to anyone, not even to my students. I am really very emotional. Penny has been here for me, and I've been here for her. We lean on each other." She laid her head onto his chest again and continued to cry.

He let his duffel bag slide off his shoulder to the ground. He looked at the gates, then back towards the big house and saw Penny's Ferrari pull in behind Elaine's car. She got out and stood next to it, holding the cowboys boots. "Mitchell, I am sorry. I had no right to say what I said. Please forgive me."

Simmons looked at her and back to Elaine. He stood for several long seconds, staring at the boots. "Those were for Lanny." Both Penny and Elaine gasped, but it was Penny who collapsed and slumped to the ground. Her head thumped the pavement hard, and she did not move. Simmons saw a trickle of blood seep down the side of her face. Both Simmons and Elaine rushed to where Penny was laying. Simmons yelled at Elaine not to touch her.

"She might have broken something. Call 911 and then Anna."

He secured her head with one hand and gently rolled her onto her back, taking great care not to let her head move. He lifted her slightly and eased an arm from underneath her head, again making sure her head did not move. One of her legs was bent in an awkward position. He slowly moved it, feeling the hip, knee, and ankle. Nothing was broken. Simmons had been trained to take care of the injured as well as to shoot.

He was aware of Elaine telling the 911 dispatcher where they were, and also of her talking to Anna. All the while, he held Penny's head with one hand and ripped off his tee shirt with the other. He dabbed softly at the big knot just above her right eye, wiping away the blood. A few seconds later, Anna and Reina rushed up.

"What happened?" Anna asked, bending down to lift Penny up.

"Don't move her!" Realizing that his tone was a little harsh, he gently added, "I think she fainted and hit her head when she fell, but don't move her until we know about her neck and back." He looked at Anna and saw horror in her eyes. "I think she will be all right, but she'll have a big shiner. She can tell everyone that her mother did it," he kidded, trying to make the situation a little less tense.

Anna relaxed a little, especially when Penny began to move. "Penny... Penny, this is Simmons. You are all right, but please don't try to move until we know for sure. Just lay still and try to breathe normally."

Penny blinked her eyes and tried to nod her head, but Simmons was holding it firm. She tried to move her hands to where Simmons was holding her.

"Elaine, take hold of her feet. Anna, you and Reina hold her hands. We have got to keep her immobile, just in case there is some spinal cord damage."

"Let me up," Penny moaned.

"Penny, you are not getting up. You fainted and fell. You have a big knot on you head, and if you have any spinal cord damage and move, you might be paralyzed for the rest of your life. Now lie still; the paramedics will be here shortly. Penny, listen to me. Do not move. You hear me? Do not move!" Simmons demanded, loudly. Penny relaxed somewhat.

The ambulance arrived, and the paramedics examined her thoroughly, carefully sliding a board beneath her and strapping her to it. They loaded her into the ambulance and beckoned Anna to ride with them. Simmons and Elaine followed in Elaine's car.

Ten minutes later Amos and Marie joined them in the waiting room just as a doctor came in to tell them Penny was fine.

"Nothing broken but her pride, I think. She has a small laceration and a big contusion on her forehead. She will have a black eye, but she should be fine. In the event she should complain of headaches, get her back here. I have explained this to her, but like I said, I think it's mostly her pride that is hurt."

About five minutes later a nurse led Penny into the waiting room, and she apologized for causing so much trouble. "That is the dumbest thing I've ever done. Well almost. On the way here all I could think was, *I hope the same nurses are not on duty as when Daddy died.* I remember cussing and spitting on them, so if they were here, I knew I was in for a bad time.

"The paramedics told me what you did was the right thing to do. Thanks, but Mitchell, if you try to leave again, I will have you arrested for assault and battery."

"I think we all should go to Manny's. I bet none of you have eaten, and the meal Reina had prepared before handsome, over there, decided to leave is cold by now." Anna turned to Elaine and said, "I know you have to be in Texarkana for school tomorrow, so we will have the chopper drop you there after dinner. I will have Hector bring your car before you leave for school, if this is okay with you."

Elaine looked at Anna and at Simmons, who was avoiding making eye contact with her. "I can get someone to cover my classes tomorrow. No need for all that trouble."

Simmons sat with his head down and finally said, "I don't think I should go to Manny's. I think I should be going. I'll take a cab out and get my bag and. . ."

"Mitchell!" Penny, Elaine, and Anna interrupted and yelled almost in unison.

He ignored them and continued, "Look, from the day Elaine picked me up, I've done nothing but cause you trouble. . . Bradley, Elaine, the truck, and now Penny. If I get on the chopper, it'll probably crash."

Amos spoke, his voice echoing authority throughout the room. "We are all in this together. If one goes down, we all go down. Mitchell, I think you need to stay, not only for us, but also for yourself. I think you would regret leaving. We have a lot of work that needs to be done and that means all of us."

That is the second time he has called me Mitchell, Simmons thought and noticed that everyone was nodding their head. *I cannot stay*, he asserted to himself. *I'll get these people killed.*

He shook his head, arose, and walked to the door, but could not open it. He did not fully understand why, so he stood staring at the door until he heard Elaine say, "Mitchell, please," and her voice choked. Finally, he turned to face her as his phone rang. Fumbling around, he found the phone.

He answered and nodded his head. "I'll be there," and he snapped the phone closed.

"Okay, it seems like every time I try to leave, something happens. So I am going to stay. I'm staying until we see this thing through. I may get somebody killed, but I lost a lot of my men in Afghanistan. I did not like it because each one of them took a part of me with them, but I learned to go on, just as you all did when you lost Robert and his mother. Just like Elaine when she lost her entire family. I don't like it, but we go on." There was a long silence, a very long silence, and it was Anna who broke it.

"Elaine, if you want, you can leave your keys at the desk and Hector will pick up your car and drive it back to the house. That way, we will all be on the chopper when it crashes with Mitchell."

The chopper did not crash. During dinner Penny told what Agent Chippernal of the FBI had said about making Simmons a deputy investigator, which would give him the authority to carry a weapon. Simmons could see that they were impressed, especially Amos, who said, "Alan is a good man. Known him all of his life."

"That was Chippernal who called earlier. I got the impression that he was aware of the situation in Longview. But why would the FBI be working on a case that should be handled by the sheriff's department unless there is more to it than we know? I am meeting with him tomorrow, and I'll see if he will fill me in on this," Simmons said.

After they ate, Elaine called and got someone to cover her class the next day, freeing her to go to Tyler with Simmons to meet Agent Chippernal. When they arrived at the FBI office, Simmons introduced Elaine, but Chippernal had recognized her immediately. "The basketball queen! I got a lot of enjoyment watching you play and also seeing how you handled yourself with the media. You were a winner at both. It is a pleasure to meet you."

He continued, "I understand Lanny Simpson was your brother. Ms. Simpson, do you think he took his own life?"

Elaine looked at him and said with determination, "No, we were very close and he would have told me if something was bothering him."

"He was engaged to Ms. Sanderson, is that correct?" Elaine nodded her head. He looked at Simmons and asked, "You were with him in Afghanistan; what do you think?"

"Lanny hated dead bodies, both ours and the Taliban's. We picked up a lot of them. If Lanny were to kill himself, he would have done it where his body would never be found. I would bet my life on that."

"You almost did yesterday. Do you think the bomb was somehow related to Lanny's death?"

"Not only to Lanny's death, but I believe to the death of Elaine's parents, Otis Green, Calvin Gentry, and Arnold Bradley."

"Very interesting," Chippernal said.

"Why do I get the feeling you know about this?" Simmons asked.

Chippernal just smiled. "How about the young lady. . . uhh. . . Ms. Sanderson? You were with her yesterday," he said, leaving no doubt there could be no secrets here. Chippernal continued, "I understand she took a nasty fall last night. Is she going to be okay?"

"Yes, sir, she is going to be fine. I think it hurt her pride more than anything else."

"Okay, Mr. Simmons. You came here wanting to be allowed to carry a weapon. Agent Taggart will get you processed, if you two will step over there." He pointed to a room across the hall.

Simmons and Elaine tapped on his door and heard him say, "Come in." He looked up and saw Simmons and Elaine.

There was a wide smile on his face as he introduced himself to Elaine.

"Ms. Elaine, I am Wayne Taggart. I was a senior when you were a freshman. You probably don't remember, but I asked you out a couple of times. I had a mile high crush on you, as did almost every boy in school. After high school I made many trips from UT to Tyler—even went to Pine Bluff a couple to times to watch you play. I was devastated when you got hurt. I was looking forward to seeing someone from our school play professional basketball."

He looked at her, and Simmons could see the admiration in his eyes. It was apparent to Simmons that he really was serious.

"It is so nice to see you again, but I wish it could have been under happier circumstances. I am sorry about your parents and about Lanny. Maybe we can find out what really happened." He picked up a manila folder, did not look at it, and turned to Simmons.

"You were with a Ms. Sanderson when you were here. Could I ask what your involvement with her is?"

Wow, here we go again. They want to make sure Elaine knows I was with Penny.

"No offense, Mr. Taggart, but I'm sure it is in the record. However, to answer the question you did not ask, yes, Penny... uh... Ms. Sanderson and I are friends. Penny and I are only interested in what happened to Lanny, as they were engaged to be married. Penny and Elaine are best friends, but Elaine is the only one that I have a two-mile-high crush on."

Elaine blushed, and Wayne Taggart smiled. "I didn't think it was a good idea to start our partnership without full disclosure." He looked at Elaine and winked. "Mr. Simmons, might I call you Mitchell or Mitch?"

"Either, but my Army buddies just call me Simmons."

"Okay Simmons, let's get you all fixed up—a briefing, a photo, credentials, and a badge so you can be a deputy FBI agent—everything you need except a weapon. We don't actually provide that, but one will be available should you so desire. After yesterday, I think that might be wise."

He picked up the folder again, looked at both Simmons and Elaine, and paused as if searching for the right words to say. "We, the Agency, have been interested in the. . . let's say. . . the events in Longview, except they were in the jurisdiction of the sheriff's department and we had little evidence with which to intercede. Now with the bombing of Ms. Sanderson's truck, we are free to investigate any irregularities that might be linked to this case."

Taggart paused, waiting for Simmons to comment. When he did not, he continued, "I have been assigned to this case, so you and I will be working together, so to speak. It is highly unusual for us to include a civilian in our investigations, so you will be working undercover. . . well, sort of undercover. . . because I understand that the Gilmores know of this. Still, Agent Chippernal is sticking his neck out, but it is believed that you would continue to investigate this on you own. It might be that we could help each other. We will furnish you with a laptop, and you will be assigned a number which will give you access to most, but not all, of our database. This laptop is encrypted and is the way you are to contact me. No phone calls. Just type in the number we give you and follow directions. The PC might be helpful if you needed to run a check on something or someone." He paused and looked around.

"Since you are undercover, and I am your only contact, should you say or do something to embarrass the FBI, your cred pack will be a phony and you will be prosecuted for impersonated an FBI officer. Otherwise, you will have our full cooperation. Am I clear on that?"

Simmons nodded.

"Now Simmons, go down the hall to the second door on the left where you will be processed while I entertain Ms.

Simpson. I think this will be the most pleasant duty I've had in a long time." He smiled.

"Elaine, remember my crush is a mile higher than his," Simmons kidded.

An hour later Simmons had been briefed, photographed, issued credentials, a badge, and a laptop. He was then instructed to go to Taggart's office, which was empty except for a paper bag sitting on his desk. A sheet of paper was stapled to the bag with "Mitchell Simmons" written in big, black letters. He looked inside the bag and saw a 9mm Glock with a shoulder holster and two clips loaded with 9mm hollow points. He was inspecting the weapon when an agent walked in, pulled the sheet of paper off the bag, ran it through the shredder, turned and left, never saying a word.

Simmons folded the top of the bag, pocketed the clips, and walked out into the hallway looking for Elaine. He saw Elaine talking to a female agent; both women were laughing. *It was good to hear her laugh,* Simmons thought. He looked, but did not see Agent Taggart.

They left the agency and drove to Cracker Barrel for lunch. On the way Simmons asked about Taggart.

"He got a call just after you left."

"That's good. At least he didn't have time to hit on my girl."

"I don't think he was trying to. . . as you say. . . hit on me. We attended the same school. I do remember him asking me out, and I was tempted to say 'yes.' He was very popular in school and really good-looking, but he was a senior, and, well, I was just a freshman. Lanny was very protective of me. . . I took Lanny's advice and said 'no' the next time he asked."

She looked at him for a few seconds, smiled, and said, "Uhh. . . as far as me being your girl. . . Well, that is debatable." But there was a twinkle in those beautiful, sea-green eyes.

"At least you did not say you were *not* my girl."

While eating lunch, they discussed everything that had happened while she was in Texarkana. Simmons told her of his belief that there might be diamonds on her place.

"Diamonds. Okay, there are diamonds on my dad's place. So?"

"Elaine, listen. There were once diamonds in Prescott, Arkansas, and that is not too far from here. Lanny had a diamond large enough for Gentry's Jewelry to insure it for fifty grand. Bradley had diamonds. Where did the diamonds come from, and why are Lanny, Gentry, and Bradley dead? I don't know why Sheriff Green is dead, but I get a feeling he was somehow involved."

He took a long drink of iced tea and continued, "Did you know that Amos and I filmed your place and made maps? We compared them with other maps and found an old logging road, which appears to be well used, on the back side of your property. Also, the underbrush at the foot of a hill about a quarter mile from where I was shot at appears to be discolored. I saw things like this in Afghanistan when someone wanted to conceal something. I did not mention this to anyone because, right now, I don't know who I can trust, but I want to check this out."

"Mitchell, they tried to kill you once. They will try again if you go back out there. I don't want you to go."

"Elaine, someone out there probably killed Lanny—maybe even your mom and dad. There may be diamonds on your property worth a lot of money."

"They are not worth getting killed over," Elaine pleaded.

"Elaine, not only are they stealing from you, they are killing people who get in their way. Who knows who might be next. . . Maybe an innocent person who just happened to come near. There have got to be diamonds or something on your property worth a lot of money. Why else would they kill so many people? If there are, it could make you rich."

"It has never been a goal of mine to be rich. I am happy just the way I am."

"Yeah, I know, but I've always dreamed of marrying a rich woman." "Then marry Penny."

"Elaine, don't be sarcastic. You know what I mean."

"But you don't listen. I am happy just the way I am. I'll say it again, and maybe you can understand. I a-m h-a-p-p-y." She spelled out the words and insisted, "Can't you see that?"

"No, I can't see that. Lanny is dead, maybe your mom and dad were killed, and you are happy the way you are. Bullshit, you are using that as an excuse. You've pulled back into your little shell and don't seem to care about anything else."

She stood up, glared at him, and walked away. He thought she was going to the ladies' room and sat staring after her. Finally, he shook his head and walked towards the ladies' room just in time to see her car leaving the parking lot.

Simmons went back to his table and sat for a few minutes, hoping she would come back. He dialed her number, and when it went to voice mail, he hung up and dialed again. Same thing.

"Damn it." Then he remembered the bag with the Glock was still in her car; so was the FBI laptop.

He called Penny, who answered on the first ring. "Penny, Elaine won't answer her phone when I call her, so I need you to call her and tell her the pistol and laptop the FBI gave me are in her car. Ask her if she will drop them by your mother's house. Will you do that for me?"

There was a long silence. Finally, Penny said, "Yes, I will call, but don't hang up. I want to talk to you."

Simmons slipped the phone in his shirt pocket, but did not close it. He paid his bill, walked outside, and sat down in a wooden rocker, waiting for Penny to get on him again for upsetting Elaine. "Mitchell, where are you?" Came a voice from his shirt pocket.

"Sitting in a rocking chair at the Cracker Barrel in Tyler. Did you talk to Elaine?"

There was a long pause and for a moment Simmons thought she might hang up.

"Yes. Just keep rocking. I will be there in ten minutes."

Fifteen minutes later, the red Ferrari pulled up to his rocking chair and she motioned for him to get in. "Maybe they could make a sequel to *The Runaway Bride* and call it *The Runaway Girl Friend*," Penny said as she maneuvered her way out of the parking lot.

"She doesn't want to be a girlfriend; she doesn't want anything but to crawl into her shell and tell the world, 'I A-M H-A-P-P-Y j-u-s-t t-h-e w-a-y I a-m.'" He spelled out the words.

"Mitchell, maybe she is. . ."

"No, she's all alone and. . . and. . ." His mind was racing.

"Penny, Elaine is scared to death. She knows her mother and father may have been killed, same as Lanny, maybe because of the diamonds on her parents' farm. Now it is in her name. How could I have been so dumb? They may be stalking her now, waiting for an opportunity to make her death look like an accident. Penny, call her and tell her not to leave your house. Make up any story you have to, but don't let her leave. *Order* her not to leave. I am calling Chief Bates and will have him put out an APB on her. Maybe he can pick her up as she goes through Longview."

Simmons wondered what he should do next, but was thrown against the door. He looked at the speedometer. She was going ninety in a thirty-five zone while dialing the phone.

"Penny, what are you doing? You are going to get us killed!" She did not answer.

"Elaine, go to Mother's house and don't answer the door for anyone." A pause. "Look, do what I say, and I'll explain later. Elaine, do what I say! Just don't leave the house, you hear me? Elaine, do you hear me? Elaine? Elaine!" She looked a Simmons. "She hung up on me."

Now the speedometer showed one hundred twenty. *At least we are in a car made for speed and on a highway, so thank goodness for that*, Simmons thought. He dialed Chief Bates and got his answering machine.

"Chief Bates, this is Mitchell Simmons. Look, Elaine is on her way from Tyler to Longview, and I think she might be in danger. Will you pick her up and keep her until we get there? If you don't see her, we think she is headed to Anna Sanderson's house. Under no circumstances should she be allowed to leave. Please call me back when you get this message."

Simmons reached down and made sure his seatbelt was securely fastened as Penny weaved through the traffic at speeds sometimes exceeding one hundred forty mph.

"Where were you when I called?" he asked Penny, trying to keep his mind off the speed at which they were traveling.

"I was in a meeting with Mother, my grandparents, and a half dozen lawyers on the Bradley mess. He had liquidated all the Tyler assets and was ready to sell the company. Somehow, he managed to transfer the company into his name, at least on paper. Like I said it is a mess."

"Look, if you have to go back, I'm sure Elaine will stay at your mom's house."

"No, I believe you when you say she is in danger, and she is more important than the bottling plant. And really, I don't have to have be there; they can fill me in later."

They arrived at Penny's house and were relieved to see Elaine's Honda. She was sitting on the patio and did not look very happy as she glared at both Penny, and especially at Simmons.

"If this is some trick to keep me from going to Texarkana, it's not going to work. Get your stuff. . . and would you please stop leaving things in my car? I am leaving." She stood and glared at Penny.

"Penny, I can't believe you let him talk you into this."

"Elaine, if something should happen to you, who gets the farm?" Simmons asked.

She looked from Simmons to Penny and back to Simmons, and he knew she had thought about this. She turned her back on him and did not answer.

"Your Aunt Carrie and who else?" Simmons asked. Still she did not answer.

Penny walked over and put her arms around her and squeezed her tight. "You helped me, now let me help you. I am sorry. I did not know you might be in danger until Mitchell mentioned it."

"And like a dummy, it took me forever to realize it. I was so caught up in trying to find out about Lanny, I could have let something happen to you," Simmons said, and waited for Elaine to answer. She said nothing, and he asked again.

"Elaine, who gets the farm?" he asked rather loudly. "Elaine, who gets the farm?" This time his voice was very soft as he walked to her and took her hand.

"Elaine?" he asked again and saw tears flowing down her cheeks.

Her voice was unsteady as she leaned against him and answered, "My father had two brothers. I never met them and I don't know where they are, but I think one of them once lived in Tyler." She paused and brushed a tear from her cheek.

"But Aunt Carrie would get the farm, I guess."

"Do you have a will?" She did not answer his question, but added, "I knew I should not have carried you by there. I was warned to stay away."

"What?" Simmons and Penny shouted at the same time. Elaine jumped.

"You were warned to stay away? When? How?" Simmons asked and looked from Elaine to Penny, who was standing with her hands over her mouth.

"Oh my God!" she gasped, and Simmons wondered if she was going to faint again. She managed to sit down and repeated, "Oh my God! Elaine, why did you not tell me. . . tell someone?"

"Penny, a lot of people have been killed, maybe because of Dad's farm. I did not want anyone else to die."

"When did they tell you to stay away. . . and how?" Simmons asked.

"Maybe a couple of months after Lanny died. They put a note on my car."

"Where was your car when they did this? At you apartment?"

Elaine nodded

So they know where she lives. Of course, they know where she lives. Simmons, are you brain dead? They were watching or had some kind of surveillance camera at Lanny's house. That is how they knew who I was when they shot at me and when they tried to blow me up. Maybe the only reason Elaine and I are not dead is because Penny and Gregg Davis showed up when they did. Simmons, you have to use your head. These people are not playing.

He looked at Elaine. "What did the note say?"

"Stay away from the farm, or you'll be next," she whispered.

"Do you still have the note? We need to compare it to the note I found at the truck." She nodded.

Simmons sat down, looked at both Elaine and Penny. "Look, I am reminded of what Anna said about writing down what you know and what you need to know. Penny, can you get us a piece of paper?"

Penny returned with a notebook, and they began to write what they knew or what they suspected. They listed Lanny, Gentry, Sheriff Green, Bradley, and the diamonds. Elaine's father had diamonds; Lanny had them; Gentry had them and he died in the fire, and Bradley had diamonds. Bradley and Grades were big buddies and hung around Judge Caldwell's court room. Bradley had also managed to take control of the plant in Tyler, taking the profit from the sale of equipment and planning to sell the building for $3.3 million. Were they connected?

If there were diamonds on Elaine's farm, and Simmons would now bet they were, then someone was stealing them. Since Elaine would not sell, she was ordered to stay away or be killed.

As long as she stayed away, she was in no danger, but since she carried me by her place and I began snooping around and asking questions, they planned to get rid of me. That would be a warning to her—that if she did not stay away, she would be next. If they killed her, then Carrie or her dad's two brothers would inherit the farm, and they would probably sell it as fast as they could.

The more Simmons thought about this the more convinced he was that they had also killed Elaine's mother and father. "I think we can add Elaine's mother and father to that list, also," Simmons said and looked at Elaine who was crying softly. "Elaine, I am sorry, but that is even more reason to find out who is responsible."

"I knew about the diamonds, but I just did not want to get anyone else killed," she said barely above a whisper.

Simmons and Penny were shocked and waited for her to continue. Finally, Simmons said, "I am worried more about you more than anyone else. You know you cannot go back to Texarkana, don't you?"

"I have to go; I have a job," she said, but not with much enthusiasm.

"Elaine, call them and explain why you have to have a leave of absence. I am sure they will understand. If they don't, I will pull some strings," Penny said.

"But I don't have any clothes—no personal items or anything."

Penny's phone rang. She answered and said, "Okay." She turned and looked at Simmons. "That was the Ford dealer. He has your truck ready. We can go down there now, and if you like, you can take Elaine to Texarkana to get her clothes, just in case they are watching her car."

"It's not my truck."

"Mitchell, it is registered and insured in your name. My present to you for what you have done."

"What I have done is put everyone in danger of being killed. I won't have it."

"Well, it will sit on the lot until the tires rot off, and I will take Elaine to Texarkana."

"Penny!" he shouted, clearly irritated at her, but beginning to realize that what she said made a lot of sense.

"Okay, I will use it until I leave. Then it can sit in the shed until the tires rot off," mocking her choice of words.

"Nobody is taking me anywhere. I am taking my own car and I'm going home."

Simmons kicked a patio chair, and it skidded to a stop just before going into the pool. He stared at Elaine, then at Penny, and pointed his finger at Elaine.

"Elaine, when and if you go, I am going with you. I am not going to let you get yourself killed.

"What are you going to do? Kick another chair?"

"Damn it, Elaine. Have a little sense, will you?"

"You are pretty good with the words, damn it. Too bad you are not good for anything else."

He stood staring at her, still pointing his finger and trying to think of what to do next when he heard the whip-whip-whip of rotor blades and saw the S-76 descending to the helipad. A few seconds later, it was making so much noise that no one could say a word. When the door opened and the steps were down, Penny yelled, "We'll take her in the chopper." She ran up the steps and into the chopper.

"Mother, we are taking Elaine to Texarkana to get some of her clothes. We think she is in great danger and cannot go home. She will stay with us."

"What happened?" Anna asked and peeked outside at Simmons, who was standing with his finger still pointed at Elaine. Penny quickly related the recent events. "I have some calls to make on the Bradley mess. You take her, and I'll stay here."

"Elaine, you have to go with her, at least for now. When we get back I will check with Taggart. I think if they believe someone is transporting diamonds across the state line or dealing with someone outside this country, then it is a federal offense. If so, the FBI will protect you." He looked at her, his eyes pleading, and added, "I know you once told me to go back to the Army, that I was getting into something I knew nothing about, and you were right. But right now the most important thing is to keep you safe, and we cannot do that if you are in Texarkana alone. Elaine, please."

Elaine stared at him. "Damn it," she said and walked to the chopper.

Aboard the chopper Penny called the Superintendent of Education for Texarkana City Schools and explained to him in detail what was happening and her belief that Elaine was in danger. He agreed to give her two weeks leave, but insisted she drop by his office as soon as possible to make a formal written request. Penny hung up. "Bull."

Penny dialed her secretary, but got her voice mail. She called her plant superintendent and told him to have her secretary or someone meet them at the Carson Air hangar in twenty minutes.

The S-76 set down in front of the hangar, and Simmons saw a trim and well-dressed woman of about thirty-five, standing beside a black SUV. Penny introduced the woman as Janis as she drove to Elaine's apartment.

When they arrived at Elaine's, Penny and Janis said they would go inside to help her pack.

They got out of the SUV and for some reason Simmons thought of the booby-trapped truck. He yelled for them to wait and asked Elaine if she had a back door key.

She looked at him, nodded, and asked why.

"You all stay here; remember the truck."

Simmons walked to the rear of the complex and found Elaine's apartment number. He looked at the rear window and saw it had been pried open. He walked back to where they were standing and asked Penny to call the police.

"Tell them someone has broken into your apartment, and there might be a bomb inside. I don't want to take any chances," Simmons cautioned.

A few minutes later a squad car arrived, and Simmons told the officer what had happened to his truck while it was on Elaine's farm. "I want to make sure there is no bomb here since the window was pried open," he explained. The officer looked at him suspiciously and asked for his ID. Simmons showed him the FBI badge. *To hell with being undercover. This was Elaine.*

The officer radioed for back-up and also for the bomb squad, and soon two officers from the bomb squad arrived. After learning what the situation was and not wanting to take any chances, they decided to vacate the building, which had three apartments at ground level and three above.

After the building was vacated, one of the bomb squad officers broke the glass on the rear window and, using a mirror attached to a flexible cable, inspected the inside of the window, window frame, and blinds. Once he knew it was safe to open the window, he raised it and immediately smelled gas. He came back to the bomb truck and told a uniformed officer to call the fire department. He went to the bomb squad truck, put on a gas mask, walked to the rear of Elaine's apartment, and went inside.

About five minutes later he came back and spoke briefly with his partner and called for more back-up. More police cars and a fire truck arrived, and the apartment building was roped off to keep away the onlookers. Simmons saw an officer talking to Elaine. Janis was instructed to move her SUV away from the house.

A police lieutenant, who had been talking to one to the bomb squad officers, came over to where Simmons was standing. "You FBI?" Simmons nodded.

"There appears to be a bomb inside the front door, so I want everyone except the bomb squad to move away. We are clearing this block, just in case something goes wrong."

"I saw a lot of IEDs in Afghanistan. How is it triggered?"

"A package of C-4 explosives and a battery placed under a recliner moved close to the door. A button was taped to the arm of the chair so when the door opened, it would strike the button. That would detonate the C-4 and the gas. It would not have been pretty."

"How much C-4?"

"With the gas it would probably be enough to destroy the three apartments on this end, if not more. Definitely enough to kill the person opening the door."

Simmons walked back towards the end of the street, which was now surrounded by newspaper reporters and a WTRV news crew. Putting his hands over his face, he kept walking to where the SUV was parked, opened the door, and sat beside Elaine, who was, understandably, very shaken. He slid his arms around her and pulled her gently to him.

"They told you what it was, right?"

"Yes," she whispered.

He held her close and said nothing "What now?" she asked.

"Once they disarm the bomb, we will get your personal items and go back to Anna's. I'm afraid that your clothing is ruined by the gas. We will get you more clothes, but in the meantime, the most important thing is to keep you safe."

Later, the police escorted them to the airport. Penny thanked Janis as they boarded the chopper and lifted off. Simmons asked the pilot to avoid the Simpson place. "I am sure whoever is there knows this chopper and might try and bring us down."

On the way Penny called Anna, and they decided go to Manny's.

When they landed to pick up Anna, Simmons picked up the FBI laptop and the Glock. He logged in and typed the number Taggart had given him. He was instructed to hit the encryption key and leave a message. He typed a short message about the bomb at Elaine's apartment and said they were going to Manny's.

"Walk outside at 1800," came a reply, and the screen went blank.

As Penny and Elaine discussed clothing and what personal items she would need, Simmons was thinking of how he could check the off-colored patch of woods on Elaine's place. He would need a metal detector, thermal binoculars, night vision goggles, and a night vision weapon's sight, just in case. All of these things he had access to while he was in Afghanistan, but not here. He knew the National Guard would have them, but it would take an act of Congress to get them. Then he thought of the FBI; they would have them or they could get them. He would ask Taggart about this tonight.

They picked up Amos and Marie, and Simmons called McTune to see if he would meet them at Manny's. McTune did not answer, and Simmons did not leave a message.

He wanted to talk to McTune. He felt he could trust him, but just in case, he would not mention his involvement with the FBI. As they walked from the chopper to Manny's, Simmons whispered to Elaine, asking her not to mention his role with the FBI to Scott McTune, should he show up. When he saw Amos looking at them, he said, "I asked her not to run off and leave me tonight." They laughed.

CHAPTER TWENTY-TWO

AMBUSH
Twenty Ten

No one said much as Penny related to Amos and Marie what had happened in Texarkana. Both were shocked and said they had seen the news report. Simmons studied Amos and saw despair on his face. He was not accustomed to not being in control and it showed.

"Is there anything can we do?" He looked at Simmons and added, "We have two men from Harold and Hartwell investigating Bradley's attempted takeover of the Tyler plant. Do you think we could use two more men to help us with this? If you do, I will make it happen."

Simmons contemplated this and figured that Harold & Hartwell must be a well-known investigating firm. But did they need more men on this? That would mean more men that he did not know if he could trust.

"I'm not sure. As you all know, the FBI is investigating the bombing of Penny's truck. I believe they will find that the truck, the bomb at Elaine's apartment, the diamonds, and the deaths are related. The bombing of the truck and the bomb at Elaine's are federal offenses, thus making all of this under their jurisdiction. They have the manpower and the resources to find who is responsible."

Simmons looked at his watch. It was 1750. "If you will excuse me, I think I need to go the men's room. If I see Scott

McTune, I want to talk to him. If I am not back before you order, order a burger and fries for me."

As he made his way towards the front entrance, he saw McTune and quickly turned into a hallway and waited for him to go to his office, hoping McTune had not seen him. He peeked out and saw Scott talking to the doorman. *I don't want to talk to him until after I meet with Taggart*, Simmons thought, and waited for the conversation to break up.
1755, and he wondered if there was an exit door at the end of the hall. He walked down to look: there was not, so he made his way back to where he could see the doorman.

"1800. I hope Taggart is a patient man." Five minutes later he walked past the doorman, careful not to look at him, and stepped outside. He saw a flicker of light inside a car and walked to it. As he neared the car, a man got out of the passenger side, opened the rear door, and sat down.

Simmons sat in the front.

"It's past 1800. This is Agent Crofts."

"Yeah, but I did not want Scott McTune to know I was meeting you. I am not sure whom I can trust. Nice to meet you Crofts." The agent just grunted.

"We need to check the laptop," Taggart said, taking it from Simmons and handing it Crofts.

"What can you tell me about the bomb in Texarkana? They will fax us a report as soon as they gather all the facts," Taggart said.

"Somebody wanted her dead. C-4 and a house full of natural gas. Trigger was a button taped to a chair and wired to a small battery. When the door opened, it would strike the button."

"You were there?"

"Yeah, it hit me that Elaine was scared. Penny and I had convinced her to stay at the Sandersons' until we find out what is going on. She agreed, but insisted on going to get her clothes so I went with her and Penny to Texarkana. I almost let them walk into the house before I realized someone had tried to kill me when I was at the Simpson place, and they might have her targeted as well. The front door had no sign of forced entry, but the rear window had been pried open."

"You said you did not want McTune to know we were meeting. You don't trust him?"

"It's not that I don't trust him; it's just I don't know who I can trust. Like one of the sheriff's deputies told me, 'there are some powerful people here with long memories. Something big is going on up there.'"

"Such as?"

"Diamonds, I think. Lanny had a large diamond. Gentry, the jeweler, insured it for fifty grand. Bradley had diamonds. They are all dead, along with Elaine's parents and Sheriff Green. I think someone is stealing diamonds from the Simpson place. We flew over it; the old logging road on the back side of the property appears to be well used, and there was something else I did not mention to anyone. There is something off colored at the foot of a hill. I saw a lot of this in Afghanistan when the Taliban was trying to conceal something."

"So you want to check this out?"

"Yes, but I will need some specialized equipment."

Taggart considered this a long time before he spoke. "Place a list of what you need on the laptop. You will also need backup, and I will go through command to see if I can get satellite thermal surveillance. I will meet you tomorrow at the Sanderson house, say at 13:00. This would not draw suspicion since they would expect us to interview Ms. Simpson. We will formulate a plan when I learn regarding what kind of help we can get. Is this okay with you?"

Simmons nodded and asked about protection for Elaine.

"I will try. By the way, our investigations don't reveal anything to warrant that McTune should not be trusted. I'm sure he will want to talk to you."

Simmons walked back into the dining room as the waiter set his burger and fries on the table and noticed the others were finishing their meal.

"I took the liberty to order you a glass of wine. I guess I am partial to wine; it seems to calm one's nerves and maybe it makes a person think a little better," Amos said.

"I hope you are right." He toasted his wine and saw Scott McTune approaching.

"I saw it on the news, and I'm sorry," he said to Elaine and acknowledged the others at the table. He turned and faced Simmons, "When you finish your burger, I would like to talk to you."

"Maybe you should speak with all of us," Amos objected, a little annoyed.

"Mr. Gilmore, with all due respect, I need to get a statement from Mr. Simmons. After that, I will be happy to meet with you all."

Once inside McTune's office, Simmons asked, "What was that all about? I mean, you don't think anyone in there is involved in this?"

"Simmons, I learned a long time ago: the fewer the people who know what is going on, the fewer people you don't have to trust. You get my drift?" He paused and gazed intently at Simmons. "Just like you. . . Why were you avoiding me before you went outside? I watched you on the security camera and whoever you met knew the places the cameras did not cover." He paused, stared at Simmons, and sat back waiting for an answer.

"Scott, I don't know who I can trust, but I believe Mr. Gilmore is one."

"You didn't answer my question."

"Scott, there are some things a person cannot discuss. You know this."

Scott shrugged and waited a long time before he said, "Let's go meet with Mr. Gilmore."

During the meeting Scott filled them in on some details of the Bradley investigation, including traces of heroin found in his boat. "This has been sent to the crime lab in Austin for further analysis. Most heroin has a signature which sometimes reveals its origin. We have been unable to find Roy Grades, but we know he met with Susie Carter, the dispatcher for the sheriff's office, in Longview. She is also the sister of Judge Caldwell's first wife, which might explain why Grades hung around the judge's courtroom."

He looked at each of them, waited for someone to comment, and continued. "We found an Army uniform at Bradley's that was purchased from a military surplus store in Lufkin. Turns out that Ms. Carter was the one who bought it. She told the clerk it was for her husband to wear as a Halloween costume. We have requested that the sheriff interview Ms. Carter or grant us permission to talk to her about Bradley since we have no jurisdiction up there, but, so far, we have not heard from him. I am sorry I have to tell you, but most of the people I am interested in are in Longview. Like I said, we have no authority up there. It may be that Bradley's killer did not know where the county line was, and this is the only reason we are involved."

He looked around the table, and his gaze stopped on Simmons. "Does anyone have questions or something they want to add?"

"Scott, Elaine's father had two brothers, one of whom may have lived in Tyler. Do you know about this?" Simmons asked.

"I was not aware of it, but I will look into it." He looked at Elaine and asked, "Do you know his name?"

"I think it would be Jarred, and his other brother was Arlie. It was a long time ago, and I remember very little about them. Aunt Carrie could probably tell you more."

"If you don't mind, don't say anything to your aunt or uncle about this," McTune added.

"What! You are not implying they have something to do with this? That is ridiculous." Elaine glared at him, her eyes blazing.

"Ms. Simpson, to be a good investigator, you can never rule out anyone, and the less people know the better. Please understand this. We could be talking about a lot of money here, and a lot of money makes people do unusual things."

He looked around the table and his gaze stopped on Simmons. As if an afterthought, he changed the subject and said to Mr. Gilmore, "If any of you find something that might be helpful, I think we can get more accomplished if we work together. I will certainly keep you informed of what I find." Saying goodnight to all, he left.

The warning not to say anything to Elaine's aunt and uncle was very interesting. Now Simmons wondered why Chief Bates had not put out an APB on Elaine when he had asked him to, and why he had not returned his call. Why had he not called to check on her? He must have heard about the attempted bombing because the news listed her name and address. He tried to recall what they had talked about and wondered if he had missed something. Scott must know something. He was right about everyone being a suspect. Now Bates had a good reason to be involved: his wife would get the farm or at least a third of it—or all of it, if Mr. Simpson's brothers were not alive or could not be found. Yes, that is interesting.

"Elaine, what Scott says makes a lot of sense. Now look. . . before you jump down my throat, think about this. How well do you know Chief Bates?" Simmons asked

"Mitchell, that's insane. I refuse to listen to this."

"Elaine, please hear me out."

"Mitchell, please shut up and go back to Afghanistan."

They stared at each other, Simmons with concern on his face and Elaine with red-hot anger on hers.

Ambush

Anna stood and spoke to both Simmons and Elaine with a voice Simmons had heard the day she took down the sheriff. "Will you two please stop it?"

There was a long, long silence as Simmons and Elaine continued to glare at each other. "Go ahead, Mitchell. You can tell the others this crap, but I don't have to listen to it." She got up and left the room, leaving all except Simmons to stare after her. He did not stare because he was following her.

"One more for the Runaway Girl Friend," Penny added.

Simmons followed her into the lobby. She saw him and went into the ladies' room. Simmons leaned against the wall opposite the door and waited. It was a good five minutes later when she opened the door and saw him standing there. She quickly closed the door and locked it.

"Mitchell, go away," she shouted from inside.

"Elaine," Simmons said in a low whisper. "I am not letting you get yourself killed. Where you go, I go. I'm either with you or following you, so please come out and talk to me."

There was a long silence. Finally, he heard the lock click. The door opened, and she stood in the doorway, visibly shaken. Simmons took her in his arms and held her as she continued to shake. He ran his hand through her hair, then cupped her face in his hands and kissed her. She kissed him back, wrapping her arms around his neck for just an instant, but then turned her head away, still continuing to hold onto him.

"Mitchell, I'm scared."

"Elaine, you have a lot of people in there that will do everything possible to keep you safe. Come back with me." She hesitated, but nodded her head.

As they walked back to the dining room, Simmons was a little surprised when she slipped her arm around his waist. "I am sorry for the way I acted. I didn't want to admit it, but I am scared. I don't want to get anyone killed, which is what would have happened to Penny and Janis if I had opened that door.

Even right now, I am putting all of you in danger, just by being here. I should not be here. I should never have left Texarkana, and I should never have gone to the farm," she said to no one in particular.

Amos arose and took her hand. He spoke softly but with determination.

"Elaine, that is your farm. You have every right to go there, and we will get to the bottom of this. Remember when I said we are all in this together. We will watch over each other, and we will find who killed Lanny and why."

There was silence interrupted by Simmons' phone. He answered and heard only, "You should not go anywhere without the laptop," said a voice-generated call, and the line went dead.

"What?" His first thought was that Taggart was trying to get in touch with him, but why a voice-generated call? Maybe something big had come up? He might need the laptop, but it was in the chopper. If the laptop had a message on it, he should go get it.

"I'm sorry. I have got to get the laptop out of the chopper. Is the pilot there?"

"Yes. In light of all that's happened, I thought it best for him to stay with the aircraft."

Simmons started toward the front door, but an uneasy feeling caused him to stop. *I don't recall giving Taggart my cell number. I guess he could have gotten it off the papers I filed, but why a voice-generated call? Why not a text message?* That uneasy feeling was getting stronger. *Who else knows my number besides Penny, Anna, Elaine, and Chief Bates?*

He could not think of anyone else, but someone at the phone store could have given it out. As he contemplated this, he continued to think of Chief Bates. It was Bates who worried him the most. He looked at my phone the day he showed me how to use it and could have gotten my number. He had seemed like an upright guy, but the thought of Carrie inheriting Elaine's farm made him wonder. *This is no time for me to start trusting people.*

"Something doesn't seem right," he convinced himself. He turned and made his way to the rear entrance, drew the Glock, and checked to make sure a bullet was in the chamber, removing the clip to make sure the clip was loaded. Why had he not fired the weapon? What if the ammo was no good or what if the weapon did not fire? He ejected the live round from the chamber, put the bullet between his teeth, and pulled it from the brass. It was filled with powder. He pushed the bullet back inside the case and slipped it into his pocket. He took another round from the clip, removed the one from his pocket, and compared them. The weight seemed to be the same, and, as far as he could tell, both were identical. He snapped the clip into the weapon and racked a shell into the chamber, still kicking himself for not having fired the weapon. *I have to start using my head, or someone will blow it off. But why am I so suspicious? Am I overreacting?* Still, the voice-generated call worried him.

He opened the door, stepped outside, slipped off his shoes, and waited for his eyes to adjust to the dim light.

Why am I taking off my shoes? Am I paranoid? he asked himself again and decided it made him feel better to know he could slip around without making any noise. For some reason, his gut feeling was telling him to be careful. He eased up the side of the building, staying close to it and in the shadows whenever possible. He paused before reaching the front and waited. A hundred yards off to his right he saw a head rise above the top of a car, appearing to be looking at the front door. Simmons studied the scene and saw that the man was standing between two parked cars. Simmons could see something lying on top of one, but could not make it out clearly. The man appeared to waiting on someone. Simmons looked for a way to get closer and noticed the man's vision would be limited in his direction. Just as he had done many times in Afghanistan, he formulated a plan on how to get closer. Halfway back the way he had come, he remembered a dark spot not illuminated by the lights of the parking lot. This dark spot extended fifty yards in roughly a 45-degree direction towards the man. If he could make this, he would be a little behind the man and could slip to within thirty yards of him—well within the range of the Glock, that is, if it fired. If it did not, he still had a chance to make it to the darkened tennis courts and the dressing rooms inside. He could set up an ambush there. He had been taught to always have a backup plan. He watched the man as he ducked his head down and saw the flicker of a light. He was lighting a cigarette, and the light would temporarily impair his vision. Simmons moved quickly to the black spot and made his way along his planned route until he was within fifty yards to the right of the man.

Simmons was a sniper and had no problem with this range, but he wanted the man alive. If he could get closer, he would have a better chance to do that. He saw the glow of the cigarette and heard the man's foot as he snuffed it out on the asphalt. Now Simmons could see that the object lying on top of the car was a hunting rifle. The man picked up the rifle and looked through the scope at the doorway. Simmons moved, holding the Glock in firing position as he did. He slipped from car to car, always watchful of the shooter, whose attention was concentrated on the door of Manny's. One more car and he would be looking down the rows of cars, thirty yards from the man. He made it to the car and stepped around it, crouching low in shooting position, the Glock aimed at the man's chest.

"Drop the rifle," he said coldly, but loud enough for the man to hear.

The man whirled to face him and fired a wild shot that ricocheted off metal somewhere behind Simmons. Simmons fired two shots, so quickly it sounded like one. The man's body slammed into the car next to him. He groaned a low groan and slid to the ground, his weapon falling beside him.

Simmons ducked behind another car and waited, fully expecting more trouble. He waited several seconds, listened, and saw nothing except Scott and another man running from the doorway, weapons drawn, taking cover behind a column.

"Scott, it's me... Simmons. Over here," Simmons yelled, and watched as they made their way towards him, darting from one parked car to another. McTune yelled something to him, but all Simmons heard was the sound of squealing tires as a black SUV roared from between two building and sped down the driveway.

He saw McTune looking in the direction of the SUV. After several second, McTune and the other man began making their way towards him, keeping at least one car between them. Simmons slipped two cars to the right. When he saw McTune, he stepped into the light and faced him, holding the Glock with both hands in front of his face, his legs spread in firing position. He saw Scott point his weapon at him, and he immediately wondered if they would shoot each other.

"Lay the gun down, Simmons."

"You lay yours down. Someone just tried to kill me, and I am not laying my gun down." He waited for him to make a move. When he did not, Simmons added, "Scott, I hope I can trust you. If I can't and you shoot, I can still put a bullet in your head. I am a sniper, you remember, so put it down—and him too," pointing at the security guard.

McTune stood for a couple of seconds before he lowered his weapon and said, "Put it down, Earl." The man did as he was told, and Simmons lowered his weapon.

"What happened?" McTune asked.

"We had a shooter over there. See if you can get someone on a black SUV that just left."

McTune holstered his weapon and began dialing his phone. About four seconds later, he was telling someone to have everyone be on the alert for a black SUV which had left Manny's seconds ago. He walked to where he could see the body and dialed another number. Simmons heard him say a man was down at Manny's and to send the crime lab guys and the coroner's office.

"Simmons, please put the weapon away."

"How did you know you would need the coroner?"

"You're a sniper, aren't you?"

He turned and said to Earl, "Inform the guests and make sure no one leaves the building until we clean this mess up." He eyed Simmons and added, "You want to get me up to speed on this? We will make a formal statement later."

Simmons gave him a sketchy account of what had happened, including the message for him to get his laptop and how he had that gut feeling something was not right.

"Why did you not seek my help?"

"Yeah, me and you walk out the front door, and I'm dead. Maybe you, too."

McTune listened intently and asked, "Who you working with? You undercover for the FBI, DEA, Homeland Security, or what? You've got a Glock, an encrypted laptop, and no telling what else. It's got government fingerprints all over it."

Simmons just stared at him and said, "I need that laptop from the chopper. I will be right back."

"Simmons, I trusted you a little bit ago. Don't make me regret it."

"I'll be back," he said over his shoulder. Reaching the chopper, Simmons told the pilot he needed the laptop that was on the third seat on the right side of the cabin. He also asked if the pilot would call Amos for him.

"Tell him someone tried to ambush me. I will be tied up with the authorities for a while so if they want to go home, I will have Scott give them permission to leave. Also, tell them maybe they should think about some extra security. No telling who might get hurt if they try to get at Elaine again."

Ambush

Simmons typed in the numbers and Taggart answered, "We have a dead suspect at Manny's. I think you better come." Taggart was there in ten minutes.

Simmons gave him a detailed description—how he had ordered the man to drop the rifle, but he had turned and fired. "I had to take him out before he could fire again."

Simmons had a lot of questions, but decided to wait until he could talk to Scott. The way things were now, he felt he could trust Scott, but did not know if he could trust Taggart. After all, someone knew his cell number and that he did not have the laptop with him. Taggart would know, but why send a voice-generated call when a text would have been easier? Except maybe a text would be easier to trace. He admitted he didn't know.

Another thing bothered Simmons. Why were they trying so hard to kill him? All I have done is ask a few questions and make a few waves. Then it hit him. *They think I saw something when I was at Lanny's place. That has to be it, but what is out there to see?. It has be diamonds. I've got to find out.*

"Did you get a list of the equipment I need?" Simmons asked Taggart.

"Yes. We will discuss this tomorrow, maybe at ten.

"Taggart, do you have my cell number?"

"No. We use the laptop. It is secure."

"Someone has it. They sent me a voice-generated call to remind me to keep the laptop with me." Taggart ran his hands through his hair, adjusted the shoulder holster, and added, "You're saying they were watching you and knew the laptop was our method of contact. Who knew about the laptop besides Ms. Simpson?"

"You mean who knows about it besides the FBI?" He stared at Taggart, trying to get some kind of read.

Taggart stared back at him, and Simmons said, "The Gilmores and the Sandersons. I trust them."

Taggart studied him for a bit and nodded his head, adding, "Simmons, we think Bradley was using the bottling company for the distribution of drugs. From what we learned, the Gilmores were a little lax on the operations of the Tyler plant, and Bradley had managed to transfer stocks into his name. We believe he was trying to sell because he wanted out. We did not tie the diamonds to all this until he lost them at Manny's. Now, we believe they were using the diamonds to purchase drugs. That would explain why we never found a money trail or any transfer of funds."

He looked at Simmons. "I'll take the laptop and tomorrow we will get you an encrypted phone. "

"Taggart, someone told these people about the laptop, so they knew I was working with the FBI. And it may be one of you. Someone knew I did not have the laptop with me. You could have gotten my cell number from the papers I filled out. Right now I don't trust anyone." He glared at Taggart. "But Taggart, listen to me. I have survived eight years of someone trying to kill me, and if it is you, I will see that you die a slow and painful death. Remember that. Remember that well. Now, how about we go and see if McTune has an ID on the dead man, unless you already know." Taggart said nothing, just turned and walked toward McTune.

They talked to McTune and found the dead man had no ID, which did not surprise them. McTune said the lab guys would get prints, DNA, trace the clothes, the rifle, and other stuff.

Simmons cell rang. It was Anna, wanting to know if they should wait to take him with them. He looked at McTune and said, "I'll be there in a second," and made his way to the dining room to explain that his phone may be bugged.

"I am not going with you because I don't want to put you all in danger. Right now, I don't think they will try to harm Elaine or any of you. I believe they think I saw something at her parents' house which is why they tried to take me out. Now they probably think I have disclosed that information so I believe their efforts will be to try and cover up whatever they think I saw. I will call you tomorrow, but you should still be careful."

Amos protested, but Simmons said it might be hours before they were through there. He walked with them to the chopper and watched as they lifted off, then turned to see Taggart motioning for him.

"McTune said you could wait until tomorrow to give an official statement. How about I give you a lift to a motel? We can meet there tomorrow, say at ten."

"Yeah, you pick one, as long as it is reasonable."

Taggart left him at a Days Inn. Simmons went inside and sat down in the lobby. As soon as he was sure Taggart had left, he called a cab and asked the driver to take him to a Best Western he had seen out near the airport.

Once inside his room Simmons shaved, showered, and laid down on the bed. He went over in his mind who might have known he had the FBI laptop and if it were possible that someone had tampered with it when he did not have it with him. The only time he remembered after he left the FBI Headquarters was when he had left it in Elaine's car while they went into the Cracker Barrel. Or maybe the pilot of the chopper had the opportunity. Possibly the agent with Taggart had switched laptops.

He had been in the back seat, and I would not have noticed. Or maybe it was bugged even before I got it. There were so many questions he did not have the answer too. Simmons laid the Glock beside his head and finally drifted off to sleep, but a girl with beautiful sea-green eyes and wet hair kept motioning for him to help her.

At 0800, he rode a cab to the Days Inn, but instructed the driver to drop him two blocks behind it. Unless Taggart was a mole, he felt he was no longer a target because whoever was trying to kill him would know he would have informed the FBI about what he had found. Still, he was not taking any chances so just to be on the safe side, he took the Glock from his shoulder holster, checked to make sure a shell was in the chamber, and put it in his left hand pocket. By now, everyone knew he was right-handed and would not expect him to fire his weapon with his left hand.

He slowly made his way to the motel and flashed his badge. He informed the desk clerk he was waiting on another agent and made his way to a seat in the lobby with a good view but protected from any attack from the street and close to the men's room. He picked up a morning paper and glanced at the headlines about a man killed at Manny's. The police and the FBI were withholding all information. So the newspaper knew the FBI was there, and now McTune knew he was with them also. He did not read any more, though he pretended to, as he watched the door.

He saw Taggart and Chippernal approaching and stepped out of sight inside the men's room, leaving the door slightly ajar as he watched. They entered, went to the desk clerk, flashed their credentials, and looked to where the clerk said Simmons was waiting. They stared at an empty table, but walked towards it. Simmons stepped out of the men's room with his left hand in his pocket.

"Why don't we take a drive?" Chippernal asked.

"I think this will do just fine." He nodded for them to lead the way.

They sat, and Simmons moved a chair so that Taggart was between him and an outside window. He sat down, laid his right hand on the table, and kept his left under the table and on the safety of the Glock.

"I understand your caution. Was there any time you did not have the laptop with you except when you left it on the chopper?" Chippernal asked.

"Yes, I left it at Taggart's office while I was being processed." He watched Taggart for some kind of reaction, but there was none. "After that, I left it in Elaine's car while we had lunch. The only other time I can think of, besides the chopper pilot, is when I met you and Agent Groff at Manny's."

"Do you know if Elaine... er... Ms. Simpson had locked her car?"

"I believe she did."

"But you are not sure."

"Look, any amateur can jimmy a door in seconds. What difference does it make?"

"Cracker Barrel seems the most likely place for it to have been tampered with. If it was, we can get access to their security tapes and find out who it was or maybe find an eye witness." He paused as a waiter came to take orders.

"Three coffees." Chippernal continued after the waiter left. "I know you have doubts about whom you can trust, but please cooperate with us. If we have a leak, we will find it, and we will find out what is going on up here. Just try and be patient."

"Did you get the equipment I asked for?" Simmons changed the subject.

Chippernal and Taggart looked at each other and stared at Simmons as the coffee arrived. When the waiter left, Chippernal said they were in the trunk of his car, all except the rifle with a thermal scope. They could not get it on such a short notice. "We believe you plan to use this equipment to go to the Simpson place, but we will have to be included in your plans before we can let you have them," Chippernal told him.

"So, if you are the bad guys, I go in, but never come out. No thanks."

"Simmons, if we wanted to take you out, we could have done that last night when you changed motels. Simple... one of us would have been the cab driver you called, and when you stepped out of the cab at the Best Western, you would have been killed. We would have a witness come forward and say it looked like a transit worker, and, of course, our cab driver would agree and give a vivid description of the imaginary assailant." He waited to let Simmons think about this before he continued. "Simmons, you had men to cover your back in Afghanistan, and you are going to need the same here. You try and go in alone, you won't make it. This is probably a powerful, well-organized group with far-reaching clients. Who knows what kind of surveillance they have.

Simmons looked at Taggart, shrugged his shoulders, took a long drink of coffee, and summoned the waiter for more.

"You can come, but I'm going in alone. If I have to shoot someone, I don't want it to be the man behind me."

"At 2300 we will have a satellite overhead with thermal imagery so we will be able to monitor your progress and keep you informed. You will be wired and dropped off east of the old logging road. Our command post will be two minutes away, in case you need help. Otherwise, you will be on your own."

Simmons thought about this and sipped his coffee for several long seconds as he contemplated what to say. "Do you have satellite data on the Simpson place?"

"Like I said, we were a little slow in tying the diamonds to the Simpson place, but we have data from two different satellites—not enough to detect any anomalies other than the well-used logging road, but we will have more this afternoon." He paused and looked to make sure the waiter was not listening.

"Our investigation reveals that you and Amos Gilmore did some surveillance, so we assume you have a target area in mind."

Simmons was a little surprised. He watched each of them intently, still trying to decide if he trusted them.

"How many people know of this?"

"At the local level, only the two of us, but of course, we had to go through the chain of command to get the equipment, so we really don't know. We only hope if we have a compromised agent, then it's only a leak, not a mole. We have turned this over to Internal Affairs, but that will take time and, like I said before, we want to act before they cover up and regroup."

Ambush

"Okay, let's do it," Simmons said, but with some reservation. "Okay, shall we take a ride and formulate a plan?"

"You make your side of the plans, and I'll make mine. We can compare them later."

"We will need your cooperation."

"And I need to stay alive. Be at the Best Western at 1800. I'll find you."

"Can we give you a ride somewhere?" Taggart asked.

"I can manage. See you at 1800."

CHAPTER TWENTY-THREE

EARS

Seventeen seventy-nine

After harvest they split and hewed logs for a floor in each cabin and added a kitchen to Sam and Audie's cabin. All the cooking was done here after Sam came home with a cast iron cooking stove he ordered from a traveling salesman. They had plenty to eat and, even though the winter was mild, the trapping was good. They traded furs to Mr. Ludvig for many of the things they needed, including cloth, needles, and thread the women used to make clothes, sew quilts, and make a new cotton mattress for each cabin.

As the days of winter drew on, Gee noticed that Kali was with child and that one of the mares was also showing signs of having a colt.

In January Kali had a beautiful baby girl. They named her *Bandhura*, which means "pretty" in Cherokee. If Ashwin was disappointed by her not being a boy, he did not show it. Many nights they stayed up until way past dark, playing with the baby.

In early February, the rains came and flooded all of their farmland between first and second creek. Sam had a feeling this was a yearly occurrence. When they first arrived last year, the land looked as if it had been recently flooded. If this were the case, it was the reason the soil was fertile; sediments settled on it each year.

Early one morning, Ashwin awoke Gee. "You have moole. Him got big ears," he said, holding his hands at least two feet apart.

Gee was horrified and ran to the barn. Ears two feet long! He would be the laughing stock of Barnes Crossing, the name given to the community where the trading post was. He opened the stall door and saw the little creature coiled in the corner, its mother licking those long ears. He stood and stared at it in disbelief. Even a donkey did not have ears that big, yet he was pleased to see they were not two feet long.

He was unaware of Ashwin and Sam standing behind him until Sam said, "Yeah, he's sure got long ears, no doubt about that."

Gee turned and saw Sam smiling at him. "I really did not think she would have a colt of any kind. Don't seem natural for a donkey to breed a mare, but it did work. Yep, it happened, and I'm proud of you. I guess we will call him 'Ears,' huh, cause that is the biggest thing about him."

Three weeks later another mule colt was born; it, too, had big ears, though maybe not as large as the first one. Or was it they had gotten used to the big ears? At least, they now had a pair of mules.

Just before planting time, the other two mares gave birth. Most of the mares they had traded cotton for were bred and should have their colts beginning in late fall. In two years they could start selling mules, providing they could break them.

As Gee thought about this, he knew he would have to prove to the people that the mule was superior to the horse for farming. The mule would have to be gentle, trained to work with another mule to pull the plow or the wagon, and he must be able to obey commands. At the Trading Post he heard that the mules were not able to reproduce, that both the mule and the hinny were infertile. The conversation he had with the traveling salesman seemed to back up that claim, but he would try one of his hinnies as soon as she came into estrus. The male mule, which the salesman said was called a john, could not reproduce and would have to be castrated. If he was not, he would not be gentle, according to the salesman.

The next January, Ashwin and Kali had a boy they named *Noksi*, which means "star" after the place where he was born. Gee and Mina were still childless. They dearly wanted a child of their own, but took great joy in Ashwin and Kali's two youngsters.

They had lived in Star Valley for four years now, and each year Ashwin and Gee would go to the Supreme Council and plead with the elders to file claims for their land. If they did this, then they could file for Star Valley. Sam worried that Star Valley would be taken away from them. After all, they had no official claim to it. One settler had already moved onto the land just beyond the place where the large stream cut through the cliff, and more settlers were arriving every day. Since the Indians had no claim to the land, every year new settlers pushed the Indians farther back into the mountains. Also, the colonies were fighting a war with Great Britain, and some of the Indians were siding with them. This made the settlers more determined to take the land away from them.

Thus far, Star Valley had not been affected by the Revolution. What little information they got came from the Trading Post. However, it was rumored that the thirteen colonies would soon gain their independence from Great Britain and would form individual states that would govern themselves. It was rumored that North Carolina would be the first to vote for independence.

Sam and Ashwin talked about this and agreed to go to the next council. Even if they could not get them to file for their lands, they should file a claim to the land in Star Valley.

This time Sam went with Gee and Ashwin to attend the council meeting. Each of them tried hard to make the Indians understand that even though they lived on the land, they had no legal claim to it, and that their way of life was changing. The white men already outnumbered the Indians, and they must file claim for their lands or lose them.

Ashwin informed the council elders that if they did not want to file for their tribe's land, he wanted to file on Tall Grass, where he now lived. The council agreed and made a big joke of making their mark on the paper Sam had prepared for them to sign.

They left the council meeting and traveled to New Bern, the capitol of the North Carolina colony. They filed a claim, and a day later they had a property deed to over four square miles of land, heretofore to be known as Star Valley, listing the owners as Sam and Audie Stewart, Gee and Mina Gilmore, and Ashwin and Kali Tall Grass. The deed required the signees to have a last name so Ashwin chose Tall Grass.

With a deed to their land, they knew this was to be their home. They bought more cows, hogs, and chickens. Once all those animals began to reproduce, it seemed like they had been flooded with animals almost overnight. They build another barn to hold the extra corn that was needed to feed fifty or so horses, mules, and other animals.

Ashwin and Gee became skillful at breaking the mules and teaching them to work together as a team. The hardest part was teaching them to obey commands. They did this by loading a ground slide with the rocks which they planned on using to build chimneys and fireplaces in each of the cabins. They would use the plow line, slap the mule's hips, and say "giddy up", or they would pull the plow line to the right and say "gee." If they pulled it to the left, they would say "haw" and by pulling back on both lines with a "whoa," they trained the mule to stop. It did not take the weary mule long to learn these basic commands so soon the mules were pulling the wagon.

Early one spring day, they harnessed Ears and another mule, hitched them to the wagon, and went to the Trading Post. It seemed like everyone in Barnes Crossing wanted to know more about the horse with the big ears. Gee was happy to demonstrate how quickly the mules obeyed commands, how well they worked, how gentle they were, and, most importantly, how much stronger they were than most horses. He did this by hooking Ears to a ground slide loaded with feed, which Ears pulled with ease. Gee then asked if anyone wanted to see if their horse could pull the slide. Two settlers volunteered their horses, but neither horse could pull the slide more than a few feet before they started bucking and trying to get out of their harnesses.

Gee explained to them how easy it was to train a mule, but if someone was interested, he could buy a pair that was already trained. One settler agreed to buy a pair as soon as they were trained. Gee explained that the mules could do light work at two years of age, but they should wait until they were three years old before subjecting them to extremely hard work.

"These two are three years old. You can work them from daylight to dark, and they will still be ready for more. They don't eat as much as horses, either," Gee said proudly.

It wasn't long before they were flooded with requests for mules. When a pair became available, they were sold or traded for mares. Their herd of mules grew and so did the profits. To a lot of settlers, they were known as "those well-to-do mule traders who lived in Star Valley."

One day Gee and Ashwin were riding the southwest corner of the valley looking for game. In the five years they had lived here, they had yet to explore this part of the valley. As they topped a small hill, there at the edge of the cliffs was a small lake. The water was crystal clear so it must be spring fed. Gee saw water bubbling up at the base of the cliff. He looked around and back towards his cabin. It was almost a straight line from there to the cave.

They had explored the cave a few years back and found a waterfall inside. It was not large, but it fell on three different layers of rock before flowing into a hole about the size of a wagon wheel and falling several more feet. When they tossed stones down the shaft, it took maybe two seconds for it to splash to the bottom. They did not know where the water went from there. Now Gee wondered if that water might be flowing into this lake.

They continued to ride around the south rim of the valley until they came to the cut in the wall of the cliff. On this side of the valley, the stream ran against the cliff wall. On the other side of the stream, Gee noticed that it did not flow against the wall. He told Ashwin he would like to explore the other side if they could find a place to cross.

They rode up the creek bank until they found a narrow spot with a tree lying across it. They dismounted and crossed on the log and walked down to the cliff wall. There was a distance of at least fifty feet from the creek bank to the base of the cliff. They walked another hundred yards and the cliff ended. In front of them was a flat meadow and about a quarter mile away, they saw a house. Gee and Ashwin decided that it must be the Johnson place. Someone at the trading post had said Johnson lived near the cut.

After walking back to where they had left their horses, Gee drew a sketch on the ground of the cut in the cliff and the stream. He marked the place where they had crossed and how the stream did not flow close to this side before telling Ashwin what he was thinking.

"It is fifteen miles from our house to the Trading Post because the only way to get out of the valley is on the northwest side. Then we must make our way around the west and south rims before we can head east towards the Trading Post. Also, we cannot load our wagons full, and we have to use more horses since we have to climb the steep slope out of the valley." He continued to draw on the ground.

"We could build a bridge along here because the second stream follows the cliff until it runs into the first stream here. Then they flow away from the other side of the cliff, leaving room for a wagon trail." Gee stood looking at the cut.

"Me see what you say. It be good to go to Post that way," Ashwin said, pointing to the cut in the cliff. "We make road to Mr. Johnson's, we be to Post and back in half day."

"And we could load the wagon full since we don't have to climb the valley wall," Gee continued. "Sure would be a lot easier and quicker this way. Let's go tell Sam and see what he thinks."

They rode to the barn, and Gee heard Mina screaming as she came running to him with arms outstretched. At first he was alarmed that something might be wrong, but saw she was squealing with delight. She ran and jumped into his arms. "Momma Audie say we gonna have baby!" She was kissing him on the cheek, ears, and neck, and continued to squeal with delight.

This was a shock. It took Gee a few second to grasp what she meant. He laughed and turned her around and around, looking at her and caressing her stomach and kissing her. At this moment they were the only people in the world.
"I knew you were the luckiest star to ever fall from the sky—and that you fell down to me," Gee told her, smiling with happiness.

He forgot all about telling Sam about the cut. All he could think of was that they were going to have a baby. He was going to be a daddy.

"I'm gonna be a daddy!" he shouted.

They celebrated that night with Audie and Kali making chicken and dumpling and fried apple pies. It wasn't until the next day that Gee told Sam about his plan to build a bridge. Sam said that Ashwin had mentioned it, but had decided to wait until Gee came down to earth before going to look.

After dinner, they rode down to the cut. They rode up and down the stream bank below where First Creek and Second Creek ran together, a point Audie had named Double Creek.

About two hundred yards above where the log lay across the creek, they found a sloping side of the creek bank. They rode down into the stream and followed it upstream a hundred yards to a place where they could climb out on the other side. They were able to get the horses across the stream by getting them down into the stream on this side, walking them upstream and climbing out on the other side. Once on the other side, they rode back down the creek towards the cut in the cliff. They passed through some big timber that could be used to build a bridge and out into a rocky meadow with spindly corn stalks from last year's harvest. *Mr. Johnson did not make much corn off this*, Sam thought. From there they rode to Mr. Johnson's house.

"Mr. Johnson, this is Sam Stewart. Are you home?"

"Whatcha want?" came a voice through a slightly-opened door with the muzzle of a musket in plain sight.

"Uh. . . we live in the valley behind the cliff and would like to talk to you."

"I'm listening."

"Mr. Johnson, when we take our cotton to the post we have to go around the rim of the valley. That is a fifteen mile trip."

"So?" interrupted the voice from within.

"Well, we found that there is room for a wagon road between the creek and the face of the cliff down there.

We were wondering if we built a bridge, would you mind if we made a new road to join your road to the post?

We would cut the road through the timber and not go through your corn patch.

"Don't want no road, but I'll sell it to ya." "Um . . . the road?"

"No, the farm." There was silence.

"Since my boy died, we have been a -thinkin' of going over the mountain to Tennessee. They say thar's some mighty fine land over thar. If'n we could sell this place, me and the missus would move."

"I'm sorry about your son. I. . . we did not know." "Nobody came. Dug the grave myself," he said, pointing to a grave covered with rocks as he stepped outside.

"The boy came down with fever, and it n'er broke" He leaned the musket against some firewood stacked on the end of a creaky porch. "You interested?" he asked.

"Oh. I don't know. How much land do you have?"

"Quarter section. It starts o'er yonder in back of the house and follows the cliff around to thar," he said, pointing to a hill on the south side of the house. "Then back up that thar ridge to the ditch and the ditch back to the cliff. It ain't much for growing corn, as you kin see, but they say it would grow good tobacco. I don't have the money to buy those seed, and if'n I did have, I wouldn't pay what old man Ludvig gets for 'em. Too damn high, if'n you ask me."

"Well, I might be interested if the price is right. Do you mind if we ride around and take a look?" Sam asked. "The price will be right. We ain't had a good crop since we moved here. The man I bought it from just show'd me the land down at the end of that hollow. He said the rest was just like it. Should'a rode over it myself or stayed in Pennsylvania. We didn't have much land thar, but it was good land." He paused and continued, "Yeh, go ahead and take a look see fer yer self."

Sam, Gee, and Ashwin rode back to where the creek came through the cut and then south to the hollow below the hill. There were a few acres of good fertile soil here, but when they turned up the creek, the ground became rockier as they neared the cliff. They followed the creek, which was little more than a ditch with shallow banks and little water.

"I don't think even tobacco would grow here. Do you?" asked Sam as they rode back to the small, mostly run down house without a barn or other buildings of any kind, only an outhouse.

"If'n ya buy it, I'll tell you about the cut at the upper end of that hollow."

Sam was interested in this place only because it would save them ten miles each way when they hauled their cotton to the Post.

"How far is it to Barnes Crossing?" Gee asked
"About four miles, but good road. . . stays hard year round."
"How much do you want for it?" Sam asked.

Mr. Johnson looked around and gazed at the skimpy corn stalks. He rubbed his uncut beard and replied, "Give me two of them there mules I heard you sell, with bridles and harnesses, a cow, and two twenty-dollar gold pieces, and she's all your'n. Won't take nothing less, but I'll throw in what I know about the cut for free."

"You mind if we water our horses?" Sam asked, pointing to a watering trough out by a lean-to with two of the poorest horses he had seen since Mina had found So Qui Li. "Yea, but ain't much water. We gotta tote it from the creek."

Sam nodded his head and looked around for a well. Not seeing one, he wondered if they used the creek water for their drinking water. If they did, it was no wonder the boy died with the fever; probably came from dirty water.

They walked to a watering trough made from a hollow tree, split open. The ends were closed by another log jammed into each and caulked with cotton. Sam asked both Gee and Ashwin what they thought about this place.

"Be short way to trading post; not good for much more," Ashwin replied.

"Yeah, but I wonder what he means about telling us about the cut." Gee looked at Sam and added, "I think we could let go of the mules and a cow. I don't have any gold, but we might trade him a hog and some chickens. I don't see any here," he whispered.

"We can try," Sam said

The horses would not drink the water. Gee looked at the water and saw it was brackish and soured. It had been in there a long time. No wonder the horses wouldn't drink it.

They walked the horses to where Mr. Johnson stood. Sam said he had no gold, but could trade some hogs and chickens to make up the difference.

"Well, I guess we will need them when we get to Tennessee." He looked around, scratched his beard again, and thought about what Sam had said. "Well, let me see what the missus says." He went inside and came out shortly.

"So bring two mules, a cow, three hogs, and a dozen chickens over here and ya got a deal. Ain't nee'r see'd no gold, anyway. Jist thought it might be purty." He laughed.

"Two pigs. . . a boar and a sow. . . and the chickens," Sam countered. Mr. Johnson nodded his head. "Mr. Johnson, you have a deed to this land, don't you?" Johnson nodded.

"I'll sign her over to ya when you fetch the animals, and then I'll tell ya about the cut."

"When do you want to leave? We can bring the mules and stuff over tomorrow or the next day, or if you want to come over and pick out the animals you want, you can come any time. You can have any of them except one old cow and an old sow. They're kinda like family pets. Our women folk would be right mad at us if we trade them." Sam looked at Mr. Johnson, who nodded his head again.

"Be over thar tomorrow and take a look see."

"It's a deal, then." Sam reached up, and they shook hands.

Mr. Johnson came early, but he did not come down the northeast wagon road. When Gee saw him, he was coming up from the south with the bony horses pulling the wagon. *How did he get there?* Gee wondered and went to find Sam. They discussed this as Mr. Johnson drew near.

It was the first question they asked after they had greeted him.

"Well, you see that crack in the cliff down yonder?" He was pointing back towards the south end of the valley.

"Well, it looks like just a crack from here cause the crack cuts back into the cliff, but thar's a big hole in the cliff big enough to drive a wagon through. I found it about a year ago when I wus following a deer trail. I thought of telling ya when I see'd ya, but was afeared ya would tell somebody about how bad my land wus. The missus and I had decided to move to Tennessee and wus going to try and sell it, and if'n ye told, well, that is tha reason I didn't want you on my land. I woulda told ya when I sold the land, cause I knowed you had to go around the top of the cliff to get to the post."

"We understand." Gee could see Sam was a little angry as he walked with Mr. Johnson to the barn.

Mr. Johnson picked out the mules and a cow. They helped him catch the pigs and put them into a crate made of small poles tied together with ropes. The caught a rooster and hens and put them in the same wire coops they had used when they left Virginia. All these they loaded into the wagon.

"Mr. Johnson, pick you out a bull for telling us about the hole. You will need one when you get to Tennessee." At that, Gee knew Sam had gotten over his anger.

"Yer a fair man," Johnson nodded and scratched at his beard.

He picked out a young bull and tied the mules, bull, and cow behind the wagon. Gee, Ashwin, and Sam followed him to the hole in the cliff and watched as he drove the wagon though.

"We can be at the post in two or three hours this way with a full load," Sam said.

They rode to Mr. Johnson's place and helped him load his few possessions into the wagon. He signed the deed, handed it to Sam, and asked. "Would you sorta keep an eye on my son's grave? The missus be proud if ya did."

"We will, Mr. Johnson, and good luck to you."

Gee sat on his horse and watched as they left, not knowing that he, too, would also be leaving one day.

CHAPTER TWENTY-FOUR

DAVIS
Twenty Ten

Simmons watched Chippernal and Taggart drive away. He waited fifteen minutes and asked the desk clerk to call him a cab.

"Where too?" the cab driver asked. "The Ford dealership."

"Which one?"

"How about we start with the closest one?"

At Hardin County Ford, Simmons picked up a black and silver F150 Ford Lariat, complete with matching bed cover. He left the dealership and stopped by Walgreens to purchase a throw away phone. Then he called Penny.

"Thanks for the truck," he said when she answered.

"I didn't know the number, and I almost did not answer. Where are you and when are you coming here?"

"I'll be there in ten minutes."

"Someone is waiting to see you."

He smiled and thought of Elaine waiting for him, but as he drove up the driveway, all he saw was the Sarkozy sitting on the helipad and a deputy sheriff's car in the drive. He stopped the truck and called Penny.

"What's Davis doing here?"

"It's okay; we will protect you."

"Yeah, right." He hung up the phone and slipped the Glock out of the shoulder holster and into his left front pocket. He pulled up to the back of the house and saw Anna, Penny,

Elaine, and Gregg Davis standing beside the chopper. He sat for a short time before getting out of the truck and walked to where they were standing.

Seeing that Simmons was displeased, Anna asked, "Mitchell, why don't you two sit on the patio and have some coffee? Penny and I have to go to Tyler. The Bradley mess, you know. Elaine, you can come with us if you like."

"I think I need to stay here. These two heroes might try and kill one another."

Simmons watched as they boarded the chopper and lifted off. No one spoke until Rinia brought coffee and left. It was Davis who broke the silence.

"Simmons, I would like to help you find out what is going on here."

"Why? So you can tell your thugs how to kill me? Or maybe you think you can do it yourself."

"Simmons, I was a Navy Seal. If I had wanted you dead, we would be standing here holding flowers. What I said about powerful people, I was trying to warn you what you were up against. I admit that I did not do all that I could have at first, so get that chip off your shoulder, shut up, and listen." He glared at Simmons.

Simmons was well aware of the challenge in Davis's voice, and he was prepared to answer, knowing this was the moment of truth. He stared at Davis for a long while, trying to decide. Maybe what Davis had said was meant to be a warning. Finally, he asked, "How long were you in the Navy?"

"Twenty-one years."

No one said anything for quite some time. Simmons responded, "Okay, I am giving you the benefit of the doubt. I hope you don't make me regret it."

"Fair enough." Davis paused and continued, "We need to take a walk. Elaine, will you excuse us?"

"Elaine can hear what you have to say."

"Okay, but some of the things I want you to hear are classified, so we will talk about them later. A lot of what I am about to say is my thoughts only, but most of it could be true. When I first came here, Gentry and I coached Little League baseball and became pretty good friends. He told me he had been buying diamonds from Lanny's father before Lanny came home. Gentry asked me where I thought the diamonds came from, and I said Lanny might be sending them from Afghanistan. Gentry said he was concerned that something might be illegal and would ask Sheriff Green. I think he did, and I believe the sheriff told Susie Carter, the dispatcher. Once I overheard them talking about diamonds. Another time I heard Susie tell him Roy Grades knows someone that can make it happen, but I didn't know what she was referring to."

He looked at Elaine and said, "I'm sorry, but when your father died in a freak accident and your mother died of what I thought were mysterious circumstances, I became suspicious and began asking questions, especially since no autopsy or coroner's report was filed. I guess someone told the sheriff because he called me in and said this was not my case. He basically told me what I told you—that some powerful people had long memories—and he warned me to concentrate my efforts on writing tickets."

"Numerous times I saw the sheriff and Susie discussing something. They were always in hush-hush conversations, and she spent a lot of time with Grades and Bradley. About three months after Lanny came home, he gave Gentry some diamonds and wanted him to make rings for Elaine and Debra."

He looked at Elaine, "Did you know this?"

"Lanny gave me a ring, but I didn't know about the other one. I don't know why he would give her one; I never thought they were really that close."

"Did you ever wonder where Lanny would get the money for a ten-thousand dollar ring?"

"I never cared much for jewelry so I had no idea it was that expensive." She looked at Davis and at Simmons. "What about the one for Debra?" Simmons asked.

"About the same, according to Gentry."

No one said anything for several long moments. Davis went on with his story, "What I am about to tell you is what Gentry told me, and I have no reason to believe it's not the truth. A few weeks after Gentry made the rings for you and Debra, Lanny brought him a huge, uncut diamond and wanted it cut and mounted for an engagement ring for Penny. It was so large Gentry was afraid he could not cut it properly, so he insured it for fifty grand and FedExed it to Antwerp Diamonds in Belgium. They said it was indeed rare and extremely valuable, and that the price for cutting it would be fifteen grand. US. Gentry said two days later Lanny came in with the money so he wired it to Antwerp.

"About six weeks later, Gentry called me and said the diamond was back. It was perfect, and he raved that he had never seen one like it. He said he was going to set it in platinum, and Penny was going to be shocked when she saw it. He said I should come by and look at it, and I promised him I would be there the next day. But that very night he burned to death in his store, and the diamond was not found. The next day we got a call that Lanny had killed himself. The sheriff would not tell me who called it in and made no record of the call.

"After the deaths of Lanny and Gentry, it seemed Sheriff Green, Susie, Grades, and Bradley were very nervous. Just why, I can only theorize, but I think they were stealing diamonds from Lanny and maybe Gentry was buying the diamonds from them. It could be they were afraid Gentry had told someone so they killed him and possibly took the huge diamond.

"Two days later the Sheriff died in a questionable car accident. After his death Joe Evans was appointed to serve out the remainder of Sheriff Green's term. Everything seemed too settled down after that, that is, until you started asking questions and Bradley lost the diamonds at Manny's. Then Bradley was killed, and someone tried to kill the two of you. Why would someone not be afraid to start killing people unless they felt they had protection? Whoever they are, they could be responsible for the deaths of a lot of people, so a few more would not be a problem for them." He paused and waited again before continuing, "And one other thing, no one has seen Susie Carter or Grades since Sunday afternoon, and I get the feeling that Sheriff Evans is scared to death." He paused again and looked at Elaine.

"Elaine, I really need to talk to Simmons in private. It is best, for your own safety, that you don't know what I have to say." Simmons objected, but Elaine got up and went into the house.

"Simmons, I want you to know why I am here. And just so you know that you can trust me. . ." He showed Simmons a DEA agents badge and credentials.

"For several years the DEA believed an unusual amount of drugs were flowing into this part of the state, maybe through the Tyler Bottling Company. We had been working on this for about two years and were getting nowhere. We could not discover how they were being imported or how they were paid for. Most of the time there is a money trail in drug dealings, but we had been unable to find one." He paused, "The DEA director in Austin asked me if I would go undercover. I jumped at the opportunity, and someone pulled some strings to get me hired as a deputy. When you started asking questions about Lanny, and Bradley was killed, we feared it would hinder our investigation. Thus, I tried to scare you off by telling you about some powerful people. However, we soon realized that maybe you could be of help, especially since Bradley lost the diamonds. We now believe the diamonds, the drugs, and some of the murders are tied together, but we don't know who the players are. Whoever they are, they are well organized and very dangerous."

All the time Davis was talking, Simmons was wondering if Davis was working for the other side. *If he were, he would be doing just what he is doing right now—trying to convince me that he is on my side and pick me for information. Anyone can get a badge and phony papers,* Simmons thought.

"When Chippernal came up with the plan to make you a deputy agent, I was skeptical at first. However, we do need to know if there are diamonds out there before we can determine if our theory is correct."

"So, Chippernal and Taggart answer to you."

"No, technically Chippernal is FBI and director of the Tyler office. Since there are drugs involved, I am the agent in charge of this investigation. All procedures were my responsibilities until the bombings. That gave the FBI equal jurisdiction to get involved so now we are both investigating this case and sharing our information."

"So you know about tonight and what I am going to do?"

"What *we* are going to do."

"The hell you are. I am going by myself, or I'm not going. Chippernal so much as admitted they had a leak, maybe a mole, and I'm not getting shot in the back. For all I know, the whole Tyler office is on the take—maybe even a DEA agent."

"Simmons, I was trained for espionage just as you were trained to be a sniper. Like you, I am good. I eliminated targets and. . . I repeat. . . I eliminated targets before they know what hit them. If you had been on my hit list, well, you would be dead. I would not have stood in a parking lot, sending you a call saying 'come out' so I could shoot you." He stared at Simmons thoughtfully, "Also, there is something else. I hoped I would not have to bring this up, but when you signed the papers to be a part of the FBI, it meant you had to follow orders. So wise up and help me find out what's going on here."

Simmons stared at him, trying to decide what he should do. "Tell me about Chief Bates and his family."

"We ran them through our database and found nothing, but a man in his position would know how to cover his tracks. We do wonder how he can afford some of the things he owns on a police chief's salary so we are checking on that."

"What about the Gilmores and the Sandersons and even Elaine? I am sure you have profiled them."

"As far as we can tell, the Gilmores and Sandersons are clean. They were a little lax in overseeing the Tyler plant, especially since Bradley had questionable associations with a drug cartel in San Antonio even when he worked at the Security and Exchange Commission. The Longview and Texarkana plants and Gilsan Oil seem okay. We did not run a check on Ms. Simpson."

"Why not? After all, the diamonds are probably coming from her place."

"That may have been an oversight, but we did not think she was involved." "Anyone I don't know about?"

"In light of the fact that Bradley and Grades were close, we think Grades was probably involved with the diamonds, but we don't know for sure. One other thing. . . We wondered why he spent a lot of time in Judge Caldwell's courtroom. The judge's decisions—or lack of decisions—are sometimes questionable. Also, it was Judge Caldwell's influence that Joe Evans was chosen to fill out the remainder of Sheriff Green's term."

"Tell me about Susie Carter."

"The sister of Judge Caldwell first wife. . . and she spends a lot of time with Grades. There were some questionable dealings, but we tend to believe both she and the sheriff were small time players, or else the sheriff would still be alive. We will know when we pull in the big fish—and we will pull him, or them, in sooner or later. This investigation is being watched by the higher ups."

"How about Scott McTune?"

"Good man, good investigator with a spotless record. We think he can be trusted."

"How many people are in the FBI office?"

"Seven, usually, but they now have two more from Internal Affairs looking into operational protocol."

"You said that you and Lanny were friends."

"Yes, when Lanny came home from the service, not long after, I came here. Gentry had gone to school with him and talked him into helping us coach a Little League baseball team. As you know, Lanny was the type of person everyone liked, and I was no exception. I got him to play on our softball team, and afterwards, we played a little golf and spent time at the shooting range until he started seeing Ms. Sanderson a lot. I think he was in love with her, and I was happy for him."

He hesitated, trying to decide what to say next. "Simmons, I want you to know what I said about not doing all I could have done was for the benefit of Ms. Simpson. I busted my can trying to find what was happening. We were getting close to bringing Sheriff Green in for questioning on a number of charges before, well, you know what happened, which may or may not been an accident."

Simmons nodded his head and looked closely at Davis. He was about forty-five, dark, tanned skin, dark brown hair graying slightly at his temples, and brown eyes that were always surveying his surroundings. He was in excellent physical condition and when Simmons first saw him at Lanny's house, he had taken him for an okay guy. All that had changed when he thought Davis was on the take. Now he was inclined to believe Davis was an honest man and that what he said was true. It's hard to imagine that both the FBI and the DEA would be on the take. He decided if Davis were a Seal, it would be nice to have him cover his back—unless he was the mole in the department. Time will tell.

Davis

I just hope I am around to see it, Simmons thought as he looked at the horses grazing peacefully in the pasture. He wondered why people could not be that way.

Davis walked to his car and said he would be in touch. "You don't have my number."

"I saw it on Penny's caller ID. And Simmons, you are the only person outside the Bureau who knows who I am. You are bound by the FBI's code of ethics, so don't blow my cover." He got into his car and drove off.

CHAPTER TWENTY-FIVE

DIAMONDS
Twenty Ten

Simmons walked into the kitchen and saw Elaine sipping a cup of coffee.

"You two didn't kill each other, I see." Simmons could tell she was a little annoyed.

"Elaine, what do you think of him? Do you have any reason not to trust him? I thought he was on the take, but now I'm not sure."

"You are not sure about anything, are you? Except that I can't go to my classroom." Now he knew why she was so annoyed.

"Look, Elaine, after tonight we will know more about what is going on, and then maybe you can go back to your classroom. I am going to find out what happened to Lanny, whether you want me to or not."

"Look, Simmons," she said mocking him. "I don't care what you find out. How many times do I have to tell you that? All I want is for you to get out of my life so things can get back to normal."

He walked over, took the coffee mug from her hand, picked her up out of the chair, and kissed her. For a second she responded to his kiss, but stiffened, got one arm free and slapped him. He wrapped his arms around her, pinning her arm to her side and kissed her again, long and hard. For several seconds, she was stiff as a board, but slowly she relaxed and kissed him back. They held the kiss for a long time and when they broke apart,

Simmons could see tears running down her face. He kissed the tears and held her close, swaying gently back and forth.

"It will be all right," he said

"Mitchell, I keep trying to get you out of my life, but you won't go." She slipped out of his embrace and walked to the window. "I've never had feelings for anyone before. In fact, I have never been with a man before, and it scares me."

He walked to the window and took her in his arms.

"I will never hurt you," he said, running his hand through her hair.

They stood for a long time before becoming aware that Reina was watching them. She, too, had tears streaming down her face. "Love is such a beautiful thing. I just choke up when I see it." She turned and began taking food from the fridge. "I'll make you some lunch."

Elaine looked at him and under her breath muttered, "Love?" She had never thought about being in love and felt a cold chill of uncertainty flood her body. *Was she in love?* She did not know. *What am I thinking? Get real, Elaine. You don't need a man. All you need is to get back to your classroom.* She pulled away from him and walked out onto the patio.

Simmons followed her onto the patio and took her hand. She removed her hand from his, but continued to stand beside him as they looked out at the pasture. Simmons told her what he had thought earlier about the horses.

"I know." After a long moment she asked, "What are you and Gregg planning to do tonight? I heard you say you were going in alone. Where are you going?"

"The FBI believes someone is taking diamonds from your place and using them to buy drugs. They believe the Tyler Bottling Company distributes them or think they did when Bradley was in charge. We want to know if that is true, so we are going in there tonight to see if we can find anything. If we find probable cause, we can get a search warrant and go over every inch of your place."

"Why not just get the search warrant first?"

"For several reasons. First, you have to have probable cause to get a warrant, and second, the FBI does not want anyone to know they are interested in your place because when they move, they want all the facts. Another thing. . . a judge has to sign the warrant, and Davis has reservations about Judge Caldwell. Do you know anything about him?"

She shook her head. "Is Davis with the FBI?"

"No, he is a deputy sheriff that has been working on this for a couple of years. I think Chippernal and Taggart are planning the mission, but Davis and I are involved." He really hated that he could not tell her Davis was with the DEA, but he had no other choice, even though he was certain she would keep his secret.

"When are you going?"

"Sometime tonight, before 2200 I think. They will let me know."

"Please be careful."

"Elaine, what about Chief Bates—in light of Lanny giving Debra a diamond ring? I know you don't want to believe they could be involved, but please give it some thought."

"Mitchell, I hope they are not. It would hurt so much to know they were responsible for. . ."

Her voice trailed off, and she took his hand, led him to a chair beside the pool, and sat down.

She picked up her cell phone and dialed a number. "Yes, could you have Chief Bates call Elaine Simpson at this number?" she said to someone on the other end.

"What are you doing? Better still, what are you planning on doing?' Simmons asked.

"I think it is time that I join the investigating team. I want to meet with Johnny and Aunt Carrie. Will you go with me?"

"Sure, but I need to be back here before 2200."

They sipped the wine and watched the horses as they waited. A couple of minutes later the phone rang. "Johnny, we have some information about Lanny and would like to talk to you. Do you mind if Mitchell and I come by your house this evening?"

She listened and said, "Great, we will see you about six... and Uncle Johnny?

Thanks."

"What do you have in mind?" Simmons asked when she hung up.

"I don't know. I just need to talk with them. Mitchell, they are the only family I have, so will you please let me do things my way for a change?"

"I would not dare infringe on your investigation." He pulled her close to him and kissed her on the forehead, holding her close for a long time.

They were still watching the horses when Elaine asked, "Mitchell, I haven't seen Debra in over a year. Will you go with me? We have plenty of time before we go see Aunt Carrie. She might even want to come with us."

"Okay, it will give me a chance to see how Miguel's football team is doing."

Twenty minutes later, Elaine pulled the Honda into Debra's driveway. Simmons noticed the grass still had not been cut. If he had not known better, he would have said the house was abandoned. There was no car in the drive, and the curtains were drawn tight.

"I had rather go alone, if you don't mind."

Simmons watched her walk to the door and ring the doorbell. She waited a little bit and knocked on the door. Even from where he sat, he could hear her say, "Debra? It's me, Elaine. Can I come in?" She waited. "Debra, please let me come in and talk to you."

Several minutes later, Elaine came back to the car. "She was home. I heard Miguel yell that someone was at the door. I heard her come to the door and saw her peep through the peephole, but she would not open the door."

Diamonds

She backed out of the drive and drove away. Simmons could see that she was clearly upset. He did not know what to say.

"We have some time to kill, so why don't I show you where I went to school and maybe drive down to the lake."

A little before six Elaine pulled into the driveway of a rather large, two-story house in an upscale neighborhood with well-kept lawns and expensive cars in the driveways, including this one. A black Cadillac Escalade sat in the drive, and a BMW was parked in the carport.

Carrie met them at the door, made a fuss over Elaine, and ushered them through a large, formal living room and into a large den. Johnny Bates sat in front of a 70" flat screen TV watching the six o'clock news. He got out of a leather recliner, shook hands with Simmons, and introduced him to Carrie. He hugged Elaine and said, "What a pleasant surprise! It is good to have you drop by. It's been a long time. Your aunt will have supper ready in a bit, so you two sit and make yourselves comfortable. Can I get you a beer, a glass of wine, or something?"

He looked at Simmons and at Elaine. It seemed to Simmons that he looked a little nervous, compared to how he had acted when they ate at Manny's or when they had chatted at the Peewee football game.

"We did not come by to eat, but I cannot resist Aunt Carrie's cooking. I'll go in and see if I can help her. Would you two like for me to bring you something to drink?" She looked at Simmons.

"Maybe a glass of sweet tea, if you have some made."

"Sweet for me, too. We old Texas folks like our sweet tea," the chief said.

Elaine brought the tea, and the two of them watched the news, occasionally commenting about something on the screen.

After a delicious meal of country-fried steak, potato salad, fried corn, butterbeans, and chocolate pie, Bates suggested they sit on the patio while the ladies did the dishes. They walked out onto a large, covered patio with Citronella torches burning, giving the patio a warm, flickering glow that twinkled in the water of the swimming pool and on a Doberman pinscher who did not seem too pleased to see him.

"That's Roger. Named him after my favorite quarterback, Roger Staubach."

They sat down, and Simmons asked about Miguel and the football team.

"He does not get to play much. As much as I hate to admit it, I am afraid he is not very good. Maybe come spring, I can get him on a baseball team. I think he would be better at that. Elaine was the only true sports star in this family. I don't know how that happened, except that from the time she was big enough to hold a basketball, she was either dribbling or shooting at the basket." He laughed and added, "She was good, really good."

"So I am told."

A short time later Elaine and Carrie came out with a bottle of wine and four glasses. They sat at the patio table and talked about Miguel. Everything got really quiet when Elaine said she had stopped by Debra's to visit them before she came here. Elaine decided she did not want to hurt their feeling by telling them Debra would not answer the door, so she said Debra must not have been at home. Chief Bates suggested that she was probably asleep.

"So, what did you find out about Lanny?" he asked, clearly eager to change the subject.

Elaine wondered how she was going to ask him about the ring. When she could not think of a good way to bring up the subject, she asked, "Did you know Lanny gave both Debra and me very expensive diamond rings? Do you know where in the world he could have gotten them?"

Simmons watched closely for some kind of reaction from Bates. He dropped his eyes and did not look at either Simmons or Elaine. This worried Simmons; when you have nothing to hide, you look the person in the eye. Bates had looked him in the eye at the football game, but not today. Why? Simmons had a gut feeling that Bates was hiding something. He was sure of it when he saw Bates glance at Carrie, who had a look of horror on her face.

"When you deal with people as long as I have, you learn that mostly there are two type: the ones who have problems and the ones who want solutions. When you called, I knew something was bothering you." He took a long drink of wine and went on, "Elaine, I know it looks bad, and I should have told you and Simmons about the ring, but I guess I was trying to avoid a subject that hurts Carrie and me very much."

He took another long drink of wine, put his arm around Carrie, and continued, "When Lanny joined the Army, the first time he came home on leave, he brought a friend with him. That night Lanny and his girlfriend came by and asked if Debra could go with them to a movie. The next four nights Debra and this guy went out. Three months later Debra said she was pregnant. She swore that he did not rape her and made us promise not to tell Lanny, or anyone until after she graduated from high school. She did not want to marry this boy and did not want the baby, but as time went on, she changed her mind about the baby. We made up a story that she had run off and gotten married, but when her husband found out she was pregnant, he said the baby was not his and left. I guess we were convincing because I think everyone believed us." He paused and looked at Carrie.

"Lanny came home from the service after Carl died and spent a lot of time with Debra and Miguel. I don't know why she did it, but I think Debra told him the truth. I guess he blamed himself for what had happened and gave her a ring. Unfortunately, Debra never left the house so she gave the ring to Carrie to wear until she felt like getting out. She never has, so we still have the ring."

No one said anything for quite some time. Simmons looked at Elaine and saw tears in her eyes. She hugged Carrie, walked over to Bates, who looked very relieved, and laid her hand on his shoulder.

"I am sorry. Sorry I doubted you, and sorry I have not tried to help Debra. I was so selfish after I finished school and so caught up in my own life that I spent little time with you, with Lanny, or with my parents."

They left the Bates house, and Simmons asked, "Do you believe him?"

"Of course I believe him. Don't you?"

"He would not look me in the eye when he talked, nor would he look directly at you. I think he is hiding something."

"What!" she exclaimed in disbelief. "I think you are so convinced that they did something wrong, you cannot see the truth. Are you so jealous of them that your judgment is impaired?" She hesitated. "I can't believe you are so. . . so. . ." she stopped.

"Go ahead and say it. 'So stupid.'"

"Yes, if that's what you want me to say."

"Okay. Well, let me tell you what stupid thinks. Both Bates and Carrie were so nervous tonight, they would not look me in the eye. Bates knew your father had found diamonds, but did nothing when he was killed. Nor did he question what happened to your mother. And why would Lanny give a ring to Debra, if in fact he did, and why would Debra not wear it? Also, the day you left me in Tyler, I called and left a message for him to stop you. He never called back or asked about you when your apartment had a bomb in it. And another thing, I really don't think he could have a big, fancy house with a swimming pool in an exclusive neighborhood, not counting the Escalade and BMW, on a policeman's salary."

He waited for her to reply. When she didn't, he added, "I know you saw the big ring on Carrie's finger, but did you notice the large diamond necklace and earrings she wore? Plus, Bates said Debra hardly ever leaves the house. That means she does not work, and he supports her—all this on a chief of police salary? I don't think so."

Elaine glared at him, but since she did not say anything, he knew she was thinking about what he said.

His phone rang. It was Chippernal telling him he had failed to get approval from his superiors. The reason? Whatever he might find would not be admissible in court because the search would be illegal since they did not have a warrant.

"If you go, you must surrender your badge and not be associated with the FBI. However, if you still want to go, we will correlate the plan and nothing will change except no one from the FBI will go with you to the target."

Simmons could tell he was very disappointed. "I will meet you at the Waffle House on Third Street," Simmons said.

"What time?"

"Before 2200. Go in and order coffee."

Elaine would not say a word or look at him as they rode to the Sanderson ranch. Elaine stopped in front of the guest house, said nothing, and looked straight ahead with the engine still running.

Simmons got out, slammed the car door, and walked inside without looking back. He heard the car pull away and muttered to himself, "I don't need this. As soon as I find out what happened to Lanny, I'm getting out of here." He took a shower, laid down on the bed, and mentally went over what he might need tonight other than the night vision goggles. What kind of security would they have and how many booby-traps? He lay there thinking if he were the one setting up the security, how would he do it? He decided he would have motion detectors in an outer loop that triggered thermal imaging camera feeds to a video command post. He might have a couple of dogs and probably a photoelectric beam around the inner perimeter, as well as a trip wire that would detonate explosives, thus protecting the command center.

I also would have a couple of men guarding the command center and maybe someone at the old logging road, he thought. *It would be hard to penetrate this type of defensives unnoticed, so the best way would be to have them come to me.* He could handle the guards, but if there were dogs, he would need a lot of cayenne pepper. He was trying to think of what else he might need when the doorbell rang.

It was Elaine; she sat down on the porch swing. Simmons watched her for several seconds, then walked over and stood in front of her. She looked up at him, her eyes searching his.

"Mitchell, I am sorry, but it is hard for me to believe that Johnny and Aunt Carrie are involved. Still, I did a lot of thinking about what you said. And there are also some other things that point a finger at them." She hesitated as if trying to find where to begin.

"I remember when I was in high school, my parents were struggling financially. I know because they did not have the money to buy me a new dress for my Senior Prom. I think that not having any money was probably one reason Lanny joined the Army. I was away at school when Lanny came home on leave, and a few months later, Debra told Johnny and Carrie she was pregnant. She wanted to have an abortion, but they did not have the money for it. Johnny was only a lieutenant, and they lived in the house Debra now lives in. I remember overhearing my parents discussing how Johnny and Carrie were struggling to make their house payments. I later learned Dad and Mom gave them two-thousand dollars, telling them to pay it back whenever they could. You remember Gregg saying Gavin Gentry purchased diamonds from my father. I think it was about that same time. I really never gave it any thought, but now I know that my family had money because my father gave me a car and spending money. He also bought a new truck, and Mom got new furniture for the house."

"Like I said, I was so caught up in my own life, I really did not think anything about it at the time. But soon after my parents died, Johnny and Carrie bought a new house and gave their old one to Debra." When she paused, Simmons sat down on the swing. She laid her head on his shoulder. "Mitchell, they are the only family I have, and it breaks my heart to think they might be involved in something this serious."

She laid her head on the back of the swing. Even in the twilight, Simmons could see tears in those beautiful sea-green eyes. "Look, maybe we are wrong, but if they are guilty, you don't need that kind of family."

They sat on the swing for a long time, both deep in thought, neither saying a word. Finally, Elaine broke the silence. "Penny called and said the Tyler plant was a big mess, and they were spending the night in Austin. I don't want to stay in that big old house. Can I use one of the bedrooms here?"

"Sure, but I will probably be gone most of the night. We could get Hector's wife to stay with you, if you like."

"No, I will be fine. I just did not want to stay in the big house. It's too big and fancy for me." She paused, then asked when he was leaving.

"In about thirty minutes."

CHAPTER TWENTY-SIX

GOLD

Seventeen ninety-three

It had been eighteen happy and prosperous years since Ashwin had married Mina and Gee. Mina had given birth to a boy they named Jones after Gee's father. Two years later she gave birth to a girl they named Audrey, after Gee's mother.

Ashwin and Kali had two more children: a boy, Jivin, who was a year younger than Jones and a girl, Saloni, who was the same age as Audrey.

Planting time would be here in a couple of months, and the men were at the Trading Post, discussing what they should plant this year with Mr. Ludvig.

"Maybe we should plant more cotton. I hear a man up north has a machine that will separate the fiber from the seed ten times faster than people can do it by hand. If that's the case, I think there will be a huge demand for cotton as soon as more people learn about the machine," Gee said.

"I heard about that. I think they call it a cotton gin. Don't know where the name gin came from, though," Ludvig said.

"I think we need machine. Many my people need cotton," Ashwin said.

"Gee, you and Ashwin might be right. How much is cotton seed, Mr. Ludvig?"

"They are a dollar for a hundred pound bag, but the burlap bag is very strong. There are a lot of ways to use those bags."

"Where do you think a person might get one of those machines?" Sam asked.

"I don't know, but I guess you could buy one. There is a traveling salesman who comes through about once a month when the weather is not too bad. I will ask him if he knows."

They told Mr. Ludvig that if there were a way they could get one of those cotton machines, they would come back and buy more cotton seed. It seemed to him, if the cotton machine worked, a lot of the mills that make more cloth would buy their cotton.

"When do you think the salesman might come through? The weather is getting better."

"I really believe he will be here within the month."

"Now, since it doesn't take us as long to get here, we will come back in a couple of weeks. If the salesman comes by, find out as much as you can about the cotton machine. I think we might be really interested in buying one."

It was three weeks before they made it back to the Trading Post, and Mr. Ludvig was anxious to tell them what the salesman had said about the cotton gin.

"It is sold by a company up in Norfolk, and if you buy it from the salesman, it can be shipped to Wilmington. From there, it will be loaded onto a freight wagon and brought to Salem where you can pick it up. This is how I get the supplies I need. The gin should be here in a couple of months—plenty of time before the cotton is ready to harvest. The cost of the gin would be ninety-three Continental dollars or seventy-five dollars in gold. The cotton gin will have to be paid for when it arrives, but if you need, I will put it on the books until harvest time."

"Let us think about this; that's a lot of money," Sam said.

"Sam, I think we have a partnership here in Star Valley. The cost of the cotton gin should be split three ways. Ashwin and I can repay you our part at harvest time or with the furs we trap.

Gold

I think that is the only fair way to do it, so we can buy the gin, if Ashwin agrees." Ashwin nodded his head.

"So, I guess we need three sacks of cotton seed," Sam said.

Before planting time, Ashwin and Gee went to the Cherokee Supreme Council meeting as they had done every year since they had been at Tall Grass. Ashwin was made a member of the council because they considered him the Chief of Tall Grass. Each year Gee would remind the council to make deeds to the land they lived on.

"Make a map of the land the tribe claimed, giving each family a piece of the land," Gee told them. "Then take the maps to New Bern, the capitol of North Carolina and have them make a deed." Gee reminded them that the white man's treaty was not being honored. He also told them if they needed help, he would be happy to go with them. Only a few of the Indians did what he asked, and each year more were pushed off their tribal lands. They could protest to the government, but with no one acting on behalf of the Indians, it was useless.

Every year Sam made a trip to Salem to pay his taxes and to make sure no one had laid claim to Star Valley. Each time he went, he offered to help the Indians with their deeds. They had made a lot of money with the mules and now tobacco was in great demand. He reminded them that all of this was possible because the Indians had given them the land they now owned. He was sad to see the Indians lose tribal land because they did not have a deed.

Numerous times he tried to make the Indians understand that even though the land belonged to the Great Spirit, they should lay claim to it, for no other reason than to protect it from the white man. As before, however, most of the Indians would not listen nor would they go to the trouble to make deeds to their lands.

The cotton gin arrived in time for them to gin the cotton. They ginned the fiber from their cotton, wrapped it in bundles, and carried them to the trading post. The cotton was popular with both the settlers and the Indians. They sold some of the cotton for dollars, but most was traded for either horses or tobacco.

They raised and sold mules, cotton, and tobacco. This was another year they had a bumper crop of cotton, and they were now in the process of building a bigger barn, not only for a place to store tobacco, but cotton, also. They sawed their own logs by making a ramp to roll them up onto a scaffold. They sawed the logs with Gee standing on top and Ashwin, on the other end of the cross cut saw, standing on the ground. They alternated the sawing between themselves and Jones and Jivin, who were now sixteen and seventeen and as strong as the mules. Together they sawed enough boards to build the barn, but they dreamed of a house big enough for all to live in.

In the eighteen years the three families had lived in Star Valley, they never once had a serious disagreement. They only thing that even came close to a problem happened when Sam wanted to use the waterfall to make a sawmill. Everyone was opposed because they loved the waterfall and did not want to see it ruined by building a water wheel in it. Sam tried to convince them that the water would still fall, but they pointed out to him that it would ruin the beauty of the falls and also the walkway they had built along the side. Many a time, they had stood under the water, bathed, or played in the pool made by the falling water. It seemed to them the water was almost always the same temperature, making it cool in summer and warm in winter. Sam did sulk for a few days, but there were no confrontations. From time to time they experienced some petty disagreements, but nothing that was not forgotten the next day.

After much discussion they agreed to build the big house. They would purchase the boards at a sawmill powered by a water wheel four miles north of Barnes Crossing.

Gold

From early fall to late spring they worked on the big house. They hired three men from Barnes Crossing to help and worked from daylight to dark most days when the weather permitted, but did not work on Sundays. The hole in the cliff was put to good use, not only for taking their crops to the trading post, but also for hauling the lumber. Going through the cliff hole saved three hours on their trip to the water mill. However, there was a problem. As they traveled through the Hole, which is what they had named it, the ground became soft and they would get stuck in the mud. Many times they would spend an hour or more, just getting the wagon unstuck.

Before the house was finished, they talked about building a bridge across Second Creek. The ground was firm all the way to the Johnson's old place. The house had fallen down years ago; the only way to tell a house had once stood there were the remaining rock columns used for the foundation and the rocks piled on top of a grave, which Sam and Gee always made sure was free of grass and saplings.

The soft ground at the Hole was the reason Gee was here at Second Creek looking for the place where they had ridden their horses into the creek twenty years earlier. He found a place, though he was not sure if it was the same one, and urged his horse down the steep bank. He continued riding upstream through some stirrup deep water. After this the water became shallow, and in some places, barely over ankle deep. In other places, the water just trickled.

Gee stopped his horse, looking at the far bank and back down the creek. As he did, he saw something shining under a rock his horse's hoof had overturned. He dismounted, walked over, and picked up a shining object a little smaller than an apple seed.

"*s this gold?*" he asked himself. It looked like gold, but he had heard about fool's gold. He was not sure, so he wrapped the small nugget in his bandana and put it in his pocket. *Sam will know*, he thought. He turned over another stone, and there were more specks, one about the size of a pea. He added these to the one in his bandana and turned over another stone. Still more specks and now Gee was sure it was gold. He left these specks and rode hard to the house to find Sam.

His mother and Sam were sitting by the waterfall, a pastime they enjoyed a lot lately. The years of hard work had taken its toll on both. He dismounted, walked over, put an arm around Mina, and led her to where Sam and his mother sat. He took the bandana from his pocket and unfolded it until the specks were visible, then held it in front of Sam. Gee watched as Sam's eyes widened as he raked the specks with his finger. He picked up the larger one and put it between his teeth.

"Gold," he said under his breath, as if not believing what he was looking at. He held the bandana so Audie could see. "This is gold, real gold," he whispered and gazed at it for several seconds before asking, "Where did you find this?"

"Come and let me show you. No, let's find Ashwin, Jones, and Jivin. Then we'll all go. I want them to see this, too. There is more."

Ashwin was sitting in front of his cabin when Gee motioned for him to come over. He showed him the gold and asked him if he wanted to see where Gee had found it. Ashwin nodded, though he did not seem very excited.

Gee asked if he knew where the boys were. Ashwin said they were probably fishing on Clear Pond, though it was muddy in early spring because the creek flooded it each year. It was also where the water they had heard in the cave came out of the ground. After the spring rains, however, the pond became clear. Then Clear Pond was also filled with fish.

Sam was too excited to wait. He went into the house and came back with a shallow pan. He saddled his horse and waited for Ashwin to call his horse. The horse came slowly to the barn,

Gold

and Ashwin gave him a handful of corn. The three of mounted and rode to Second Creek.

Gee showed them the specks he had left in the stream. Sam stared and dismounted his horse, almost in shock. He reached down and scooped up a pan of sand and small rocks. He began to pan the way he had heard an old prospector from Pennsylvania tell how he did it. As San washed some of the sand away, there in the bottom of the pan were many little shining specks. He showed them to Gee and Ashwin, then staggered over to the boulder and sat down.

"Gold," he said, still in disbelief. He took off his hat and rubbed his head. "Maybe lots of it." They began turning over rocks, but soon realized the gold was not under the rocks, but on the side downstream of them covered mostly with a light layer of sand. There was also gold in the stream bed, not only just below the rocks. In less than an hour, they had filled Gee's bandana with gold.

"I think there is enough right here to buy a horse!" After that, they all held hands and danced round and round, kicking over more rocks and splashing water on each other, whooping and hollering.

They were still whooping and hollering when they reached home. Sam showed Audie and Kali the gold. They were all talking at once until Audie reminded them what would happen if people knew there was gold here. She related to them what her parents had said when gold was found in Pennsylvania.

"People went crazy, killing one another, not obeying the authorities or the boundaries of a person's land. It was complete chaos." She paused and looked at Sam, "Look, if you want to destroy this valley, just let it be known there is gold here. If they know there is gold here, an Army could not keep the madmen out. They will ruin our crop—maybe even try and run us off our land. We will have no peace and no privacy. Thank about that."

Extending Shadows

The men looked at her, knowing she was right. They walked their horses to the barn and unsaddled them, each with their own thoughts of what they should do. They walked back to the waterfall. The bandana with the gold was lying on a rock with everyone staring at it.

As Gee walked up, he noticed Jones and Soloni holding hands. This was the first time he had seen them holding hands, but he had seen them making eyes at each other before. *What is Jones doing?* He is just a kid, but then Gee remembered he was only sixteen when he and Mina had started holding hands, and Jones is seventeen. He did not object to them holding hands; in fact, he was glad. Soloni was a good girl and pretty, too. He looked from them to Mina and could tell she knew what he was thinking. She smiled. *She approves, too,* he thought.

But today the topic of discussion was gold. How could they use the gold and not let anyone know where they had gotten it? The gold had to be exchanged for bank notes even though Sam did not fully trust the bank. After the Thirteen Colonies became the United States and adopted a constitution, they began issuing bank notes. Maybe they will be okay, Sam thought, and began discussing ways to exchange the gold for the bank notes.

While they were discussing the gold, Gee happened to look at Audrey. She was flirting with Jivin, and Gee saw he loved every minute of it.

"Audrey, will you please act like a lady?"

She pretended not hear him and continued to giggle and make eyes at Jivin. She puckered her lips in a kiss and wiggled her breasts.

I will not have this; she is only fifteen. Gee got to his feet and called to her rather loudly, "Audrey, go in the house," with a look that said, "I will deal with you later."

Audrey stared at Gee and looked to her mother for help, but Mina's face was expressionless. Gee saw the displeasure on

Gold

her face as she turned to Jivin, smiled defiantly, and very slowly made her way to the house.

Gee watched Audrey go and turned back to Sam and Ashwin, noticing they, too, especially Ashwin, had looks of displeasure on their faces. *Well, she is my child, and I will. . . I will what?* he asked himself and began thinking that maybe this would not be bad. *With Jivin, she would be here, not with some settler's son who was always on the move, looking for better land, and who would take her to God knows where. Like Bandhaura, who had married Altus Ludvig's son and was now living somewhere in Georgia. Still, Audrey is only fifteen. Does Mina know? If so, what does she think about it?*

"I am sorry. She is still my baby, and it shocked me to see her making eyes at a boy. . . any boy," he said and looked at Ashwin, who finally smiled knowingly at Gee.

They were still discussing the gold when Kali called that supper was ready. They sat down to a table with pork chops, potatoes, beans, and tea. Gee noticed Jones had moved from his usual spot at the table to the one next to Soloni. He saw that Ashwin and Kali had also noticed. Gee smiled, and so did Ashwin and Kali. He stole a quick glance at Audrey. She was looking down at her plate, but was not smiling. He looked at Mina, who wrinkled her nose at him, but her eyes said she approved.

As they ate, Gee saw that Audrey was not eating. She was picking at her food with a pouty look on her face and not saying a word. "Audrey, you are excused. Please go to you room." You could hear a pin drop as everyone looked at Gee. Audrey looked surprise, hesitated for a moment, then bolted from the table.

Mina stared at Gee; he could not tell if she was displeased or merely surprised. Audie arose, went to the cooking house, and came back with a cake, complete with egg white frosting, and a jar of honey. Everyone complimented Audie on the cake, but little else was said until Sam asked, "After our chores, why don't we all meet by the waterfall?" He had said *our* chores so everyone knew the entire family was supposed to meet.

After the meal was cleared and all the animals were fed, Sam, Gee, and Ashwin lit a torch and sat by the waterfall. Sam packed tobacco into a corncob pipe and waited for the others to join them. Everyone did except Audrey.

At first Gee was annoyed that Audrey was not there, but remembered she had not been in the room when Sam suggested they meet. Also, he knew it was a longstanding rule that when children was sent to their room, they were not to leave until told to do so.

"Jivin, would you mind going to Audrey and telling her I would like for her to join us at the waterfall?" Jivin smiled and said, "Yes, sir." He soon returned with Audrey. They were not holding hands, but walking side by side, really close. Audrey did not look at her father; rather, she looked intently at her mother as if looking for her approval. Mina saw her staring, but gave no evidence of it.

They sat around the flickering torch discussing a way to use the gold without arousing suspicion. It was Audie who suggested a plan. She did not believe anyone there knew that Sam had sold his farm when he left Virginia. Since he went to Salem every year to pay his taxes, he could also be paying taxes on his farm in Virginia as well. If he were to say that he was now selling his farm, that would account for him having gold.

Sam considered this and said her plan might work. His farm would be worth twice as much, or more, now. If they could make people believe he was going to Virginia to sell his farm as Audie had suggested, this would account for the gold. Everyone mulled it over and began refining the plan.

Sam would begin by dropping hints he was going to sell his farm in Virginia to the man who had been renting it for twenty years. If fact, he could say that this was part of the rental agreement: the man could buy the farm at the going rate and, in fact, had already been applying part of what he paid for rent. This would be subtracted from the purchase price, but would still leave quite a lot of money that could be paid to Sam in gold. All agreed this plan might work. Every time Sam went for more supplies for the big house, he would mention that as soon as the house was built, he had to go to Virginia to close the deal on his farm. No one seemed to doubt this.

The big house, which is what they now called it, was finished in early spring. It was big, but not elaborate, more like a workable farmhouse. It was two stories high, had a large sitting room, a dining room, a bedroom on the first floor, and four bedrooms upstairs. There was a chimney on each side of the house, one for the sitting room and the bedroom directly above it. The other chimney was for the other bedrooms directly above each other. Sam and Audie's old cabin served as a cooking house and a place to keep all their food stuff—canned goods, dried peas and beans, and seeds for next year's planting. The potatoes were sprinkled with lime to keep them from rotting and stored there as well.

Gee and Mina's cabin was where all their meat was smoked and cured, while Ashwin and Kali's cabin became a washhouse, complete with water flowing through a trough from the waterfall into the cabin. Inside was a large kettle hanging in the fireplace with two number two wash tubs sitting on a bench with scrub boards.

The furniture of the big house was sparse, but that would change over the years. They would have enough money to buy whatever they needed because everyone, including Audie, Kali, and the girls, joined the men and the boys in learning to pan for gold. It seemed gold fever had taken hold of each of them, and they panned for it every spare minute they had. Before the spring rains, they had over thirty pounds of gold.

Sam made a crude set of balancing scales and took a five-pound bag of salt, dividing it into five equal parts. He took one part of the salt and found a rock that would balance with the salt. When the gold balanced with the rock, it was a pound of gold. Audie and Kali sewed bags that would each hold one pound of gold. With gold selling at twenty dollars an ounce, they had almost ten thousand dollars in gold. They were rich, very rich.

Gee found a loose stone in the wall of the cave and worked to remove it. Once removed, they chiseled a larger hole about three feet into the cave wall behind the rock, put the gold inside, and slide the rock back into place, making it a perfect hiding place.

Once the spring rains came, the streams were flooded and they could no longer pan for gold. It was decided that it was now time for Sam and Ashwin to make their trip to Virginia. Early the next morning they were at the Trading Post, buying supplies for their trip, but really having no intention of going to Virginia. Instead, they would ride north on the Great Wagon Road, stopping at Mr. Ryan's Trading Post, providing he was still there. They would hang around a day or two, letting people know what they were doing. They would leave heading north, but double back and make their way home, riding parallel to the wagon road.

They loaded a pack horse with the supplies they would need and set out mid-morning. Gee, Audie, and Kali were there to wave good-bye. After all, they had to make this look like the real thing.

They made Ryan's Trading Post on the fourth day, and Mr. Ryan met them at the door. After introductions, he did remember them. "That was a big snow storm! I'm glad it melted off fast so we could get your wagon back here," Mr. Ryan recalled. Sam told him they would like to stay a couple of days to let the pack horse rest.

During the next two days, the men swapped stories and talked of the number of settlers they had met. How are they all going to find land? This was a question that was discussed most often among the locals, as many settlers came through and bought supplies.

On the third day they left Mr. Ryan's and arrived home five days later. They stayed close to home for a week. It was a week that Sam needed; the trip had been a nightmare for him. After all he was not a young man anymore and he felt it now more than usual.

All that was left to do was to exchange the gold for money. These days hardly anyone used gold to buy goods. Gee and Sam discussed this, and Gee suggested Mr. Ludvig might help. Both of them felt that they could trust him, and, as Sam pointed out, Mr. Ludvig would not be overly surprised if Sam told him he had been paid in gold for his farm. They could buy supplies from him, paying with gold, and no one would question it.

The next day Gee and Sam rode to the Trading Post. They told Mr. Ludwig that Sam had been paid in gold for his farm and asked if they could pay for their supplies with gold dust. Mr. Ludwig had no problem with that; in fact, he had another customer who paid with gold. Sam was tempted to ask where this customer lived, but thought better of it. The less discussion about gold, the better.

CHAPTER TWENTY-SEVEN

SEARCH

Twenty Ten

Simmons left the Sanderson's and stopped by the grocery store. He bought three jars of cayenne pepper and drove to the Huddle House. He called Chippernal and said for them to pick him up here. He parked up the street with a good view of the traffic and waited.

Ten minutes later they pulled into the parking lot. Simmons waited a couple of minutes before he drove in to join them.

"You sure are cautious. Do you think all this is necessary?" Chippernal asked.

"I'm still alive, so, yeah I do."

Simmons sat in the back of Chippernal's car and inspected the equipment, making sure it was operating correctly. Chippernal said the plan was for them to drop Simmons off before they reached the Simpson's property. Chippernal and Taggart would drive past the old logging road, turn around, and come almost back to it. There was a place where they could pull off the highway, hide their car, and set up the satellite receivers. Gregg Davis was also taking part in the operation and would be on the hill above the Simpson's drive.

"We will check our communications when we get there. We have been given access to the satellite from 2310 until 0200," Chippernal said.

Extending Shadows

"Let's do it," Simmons said and handed Taggart his badge and ID papers.

When they reached the stream crossing the highway, Simmons got out, slipped down the side of the road, and waited to make sure no one was watching him. He looked at his watch. It was eleven o'clock. He waited for the goggles to power up, slipped to the other side of the road, and cautiously made his way into the woods.

Eleven minutes later, they made radio contact. Simmons adjusted the volume on his ear buds as Chippernal said they had a thermal fix on him. A few seconds later, Chippernal reported that they had a fix on the target area which showed some weak thermal images emitting from the base of a steep hill with stronger thermals moving around in a small area. These may be guard dogs in an enclosure, he suggested, and gave Simmons the GPS coordinates. Simmons compared them to the ones he had taken from the topographical map. He noticed that the coordinates did not match, but knew that after September 11th, the government programmed errors into positioning satellites that transmitted signals to private users. Simmons used the coordinates that Chippernal had given him and programmed them into his GPS. The target was 2400 yards at sixteen degrees.

"You can proceed toward the target as you please. We will monitor you and your surroundings and keep you informed," Chippernal said.

Simmons moved slowly towards the target, on the alert for anything that was not ordinary while keeping an eye on the GPS and sweeping the metal detector back and forth in front of him. At 600 yards, he stopped and waited for a good five minutes. Chippernal noticed he had stopped and asked if something was wrong. He waited a minute before he answered "negative." He was uncomfortable with someone watching his movements and, except for the night vision goggles, he wished he had attempted this on his own.

Search

If they have an outer perimeter, it should be within the next couple hundred yards. He eased forward another twenty-five yards, then another. He looked hard at his surroundings, seeing nothing out of the ordinary. He made two more steps and the flash of a motion detector camera almost blinded him through the goggles. He leaped to his left and knelt low behind a tree, the Glock in his hands, fully expecting to be fired upon. He scanned the direction the flash had come from and finally saw the camouflaged camera about five feet above the ground. Wires led from it towards the target area, and he knew they would be connected to a monitor. *They know I am here.* He walked toward the camera, which flashed twice more. He aimed the Glock and fired a single shot into the camera, just to give them something to think about and to let them know *I am armed and not going away.*

Almost immediately, his ear buds crackled with Chippernal wanting to know what was happening and if he was okay. He smiled, and if not for the thermal satellite, he would not have answered. However, he replied,

"Yeah, they know I am here. Can you cover the old logging road? "We have it secure."

"Okay, Davis, you and your backup cover the Simpson driveway."

It was a few seconds before Davis answered, and Simmons knew he was thinking, *How in the hell did he know he was not by himself?*

"We've got it covered," Davis said.

"We have images of three people. No wait; it is probably a man with two dogs. Simmons, I think you should get outta there now; the dogs will tear you to pieces," Chippernal said.

"Just keep me informed as to their ten-twenty." Simmons paused and looked at the GPS.

"Davis, I am going to lead them to you. I guess I'll find out just how good the Seals are."

Simmons punched in the coordinates of the Simpson house on the GPS and headed toward it. He reached the house and walked the driveway toward the highway.

"Where are they now?" he asked

"Almost to the place you were when you were detected."

"Okay, I hope they are telling me the truth. If not, I will be a sitting duck," he said to himself.

About a hundred yards from the road Simmons sprinkled the cayenne pepper for fifty yards, made a right turn toward the stream, and emptied the other bottle of pepper as he walked. He found the stream and headed towards the target area, emptying the last bottle of pepper as he walked.

"Simmons, what are you doing and where are you going?" Chippernal demanded.

Simmons did not answer and carefully made his way toward the target, seeing only one camera. It did not flash, confirming what he had hoped would happen. The man had turned off the surveillance, fearing he might get into it himself, so they probably had explosives. He only hoped they had disarmed them as well, but still he looked hard for a trip wire or a place where there was fresh earth overturned. He liked his legs and did not want to step on a land mine.

Simmons neared the target and saw a small light emitting from a crack in the rocks somewhere beneath an overhang in the side of the hill. A camouflage net hung over a dog kennel. So this was the off color he had seen from the air. He stood, formulating a plan as to how to proceed, when shots from an automatic rifle rang out, followed by a couple of shotgun blasts. He waited for several minutes and then heard Davis say, "Subject down. One of the two dogs captured."

"Do you need medical?" Chippernal asked. "Just a body bag," he heard a few seconds later.

"Someone may have heard the shots. Call 911 for an ambulance and the sheriff, then handle this just as you normally

Search

would," Chippernal said and then demanded, "Simmons, give us a report."

"Target area does not seem to be occupied. Give me ten minutes."

"Kelso, go and exchange places with Cumming. If any authority shows, other than the Sheriff, tell them this is a sheriff's department operation. Simmons, let me know when target is secured. If you find anything that will give us jurisdiction there, I will send Cumming and Taggart to help," Chippernal barked his orders.

"Subject had a fully automatic assault rifle. That alone is enough for us to move," Davis said. "I am calling THP for help in securing the area," he heard Chippernal say.

Simmons slipped underneath the camo. He saw an animal cage and a faint light coming through a two-foot wide crack in the side of the cliff. He cautiously peered inside and saw a small, partially-opened door erected in the crack. He stuck the Glock in the small opening and flung the door open wide. He removed the goggles and rolled them inside. Nothing. He waited several seconds and dove headfirst into the opening, protecting the Glock as he hit the concrete floor. He rolled onto his back, swinging it in all directions.

The room was nothing more than a chamber in the cave except for the concrete floor. A couch, a chair, a small filing cabinet, and a table sat below a single light hanging from a wire in the roof of the cave. On the table was a Mac that had the picture from the security camera on the screen. Simmons wondered how many more people were seeing it. He took some comfort knowing the night vision goggles covered most of his face.

At the far end of the room he saw a tunnel, which appeared to run farther back into the darkness, but he heard no sounds. He found his goggles, put them on, and was somewhat surprised to see they were not broken. He crawled slowly into the cave for about twenty feet.

    The cave was rather small, of varying heights with a set of steel rails running back as far as he could see. He waited a couple of minutes, still not hearing anything. He moved back into the room and removed his goggles. He found the filing cabinet to be considerably light and moved it closer to the table. He set the Mac on the filing cabinet and carried the table into the cave. If someone was in there and tried to make their way out, they would bump into the table unless they were using a light or turned on lights in the tunnel. In either case, Simmons would be ready.

    As he came out of the cave, he noticed a security safe mounted in a crevice behind the site where the filing cabinet had been positioned. He ran his hand carefully around the safe, searching for a wire that might be a booby-trap, but found none. He looked at the locking mechanism and knew he could not open it. He turned his attention to the filing cabinet and removed a folder from the top drawer. The others drawers were empty.

    He turned to look at the Mac and saw a shadow of movement in the doorway. He knelt in firing position, waiting for a target. He waited. Finally a doberman made two steps into the room, paused, and looked at him. Simmons pointed the Glock at a spot on the dog's chest and waited. The dog sneezed and stared at him, but did not attack.

    He's got a nose full of the cayenne pepper, Simmons thought. Not taking his eyes off the dog's chest, "Sit," he commanded.

    The dog sat, still looking at him. "Lay."

    The dog made a couple of small steps with his front feet and lay down. He eyed Simmons, but showed no signs of aggression. He sneezed again. Simmons wished he could do

Search

something to help him, but knew it would take an hour before the effects of the pepper wore off.

"Stay."

He watched the dog for a few seconds and slowly made his way to him, keeping the Glock pointed at his chest. Simmons knelt down about six feet away from him, with his side facing the dog, and slowly moved his other hand a few inches towards the dog, making sure he did not look him in the eye or do anything that might seem threatening to him.

"Come," he said and waited. After a few long seconds, the dog arose, stepped cautiously towards Simmons, and sniffed his hand. The dog was now completely relaxed, so Simmons slowly scratched the underside of his chin. The doberman held his head upwards, wanting more and wagging his short tail.

Simmons stepped around him, walked outside, and opened the gate to the kennel letting the dog go inside. He then removed a can of dog food from a case beside the gate, opened it, and gave it to the dog before closing the gate.

He went back inside the cave and thumbed through the folder. There were several pages of instruction on how to arm and disarm the security system written in English and about the same number of pages written in what he presumed was Spanish. There was also a topographical map of this area. It showed the locations of the motion cameras and two places that were marked with the letters XP, one on the old logging road and the other on the trail behind the Simpson house.

"Simmons, give me an update." He heard Chippernal's voice in his ear buds.

"The logging road and the trail behind the Simpson house are rigged with explosives. I am coming out, but will have Ms. Simpson pick me up. I will meet you after she picks me up."

"Simmons!" He heard Chippernal shout, but did not answer. He heard his name again and turned off the radio.

He called Elaine. She answered the phone on the first ring. He explained briefly what had happened and asked if she would pick him up on top of the hill before she got to her place.

"Stop on top of the hill with your left turn blinking; that way I'll know it is you."

"I will be right there."

He began making his way towards the highway, hearing several sirens. He turned his radio back on and heard Chippernal calling for him, but still he did not answer. He reached the top of the hill, and Elaine's Honda was there, the left turn blinking.

He was surprised. "That was quick," he said as he sat down in the car.

"I was waiting on you." She reached over and squeezed his arm. "I'm glad you are okay. What now?" she asked.

"Let's go see Chippernal." He keyed his radio.

"Chippernal, we are coming to you. The four ways will be blinking."

"About time." He was clearly displeased.

Down the hill and around a curve, he saw the lights. The whole area was lit like a Christmas tree. Elaine pulled to the side of the road as Chippernal approached. Simmons handed him the folder and told him the location of the explosives were marked with a XP on the topo map. Chippernal slipped the folder inside his jacket just as a WLOT news van pulled up. Simmons nodded toward the van and said, "Good luck. I was not here. I will call later."

"Simmons, you can't leave," Chippernal ordered.

"You have my badge, remember? Let's go, Elaine." She made a U-turn and drove away.

On the way to the Sanderson's ranch, Simmons related the events of the night, including the episode with the dog.

"Where did the dogs come from?" Elaine asked.

Simmons stared at her. "Good question. Matter of fact, that's a great question. If we can find who bought the dogs, it could be the break we have been waiting for."

Search

He called Chippernal and told him Elaine wanted to know who bought the dog. There was a long silence before Chippernal answered, "Wow. I guess I am getting too old. I will put someone on it right now. Tell her I said thanks. . . and call me early, will you?"

He turned to Elaine. "He said thanks, and he will put someone on it. It should not be difficult to find someone who bought two well-trained Dobermans."

They talked about dogs, but did not mention that Chief Bates also had a Doberman. They discussed the cave and the possibility of diamonds being on her place as she drove to the guest house. Elaine shut off the engine and stared at Simmons a long time. "I still don't want to stay in the big house."

"There are three bedrooms here, but I'll let you share mine."

"Mitchell, I was not lying; I have never been with a man. Since I've waited this long, I think I can wait till my wedding." She wondered why she had not thought of her wedding night since her teenage daydreams.

"I would never force you to do something you did not want to do."

"I believe you, but I am afraid I might want to, so I'll take the first bedroom. Maybe we could have a glass of wine?"

"I would like that," Simmons said.

For some reason he did not fully understand, Simmons had a restless night. He awoke thinking his Humvee was being fired upon until he realized it was his cell phone ringing. He picked it up; it was Gregg Davis, and it was 0630.

"We have a search warrant and will begin our search at seven, if you want to be there."

"I'll be there."

He left Elaine a note and slipped out the door.

They searched the cave chamber while an agent opened the safe, finding a hand full of small diamonds. They entered the cave, which extended about 100 yards to a section encased with heavy timbers at the end. Among the small rocks and dirt were two shovels, a pickax, two five-gallon metal containers and a four-wheeled cart sitting on steel rails. There were more timbers stacked on each side of the cave, apparently to use to shore up the tunnel as the cave was dug farther back.

In the beams of their flashlights, they saw some sparkles among the rocks. Simmons used the pickax to loosen some rocks and dirt while Chippernal and Taggart shoveled until the two buckets were full. They sat them into the cart and pushed it to the chamber.

Now what? Simmons wondered, then remembered the muddy stream he had used to escape the day they had shot at him. *Why had it been muddy? I wonder if they used the water to wash dirt from the rocks. I think that is what they do when panning for gold, so maybe it works with diamonds, too.* He had no way of knowing, but it seemed like a good theory.

He told Chippernal his theory and took the buckets towards the stream. When they reached the stream, they heard falling water, somewhere upstream. Fifty yards upstream, the water flowed to the hill making a four-foot waterfall.

A series of four three-foot square boxes sat on top of each other in a rack, each a foot above the one below. The racks could be moved under the waterfall on two short rails. In the top rack was a box with the bottom covered with a screen having a square opening, the box beneath it had a half-inch screen, the next box about a quarter-inch, and the last one was probably a sixteenth-inch. Beneath this rack was a cloth. Scattered around were several rocks of varying sizes. It was clear that this was a small operation, and maybe a primitive one, though none of them knew anything about mining diamonds

Chippernal dumped one of the buckets of rocks and dirt onto the top screen and pushed it under the waterfall. A wooden paddle stood by the boxes, so he stirred the mixture, inspecting the contents of the box as he stirred, although he was

Search

unsure about what he was looking for. He lifted this box off the rack and dumped the rocks into the pile. He did the same with the next box. After the rocks were removed from the third box, they stared at two shinning clumps. Were these diamonds? They inspected the diamonds and decided that they were real, as far as they could tell. The other box yielded three more diamonds of various sizes. In the cloth were some very small crystals. Five diamonds from one bucket—they could not believe it, though neither knew what the diamonds might be worth.

Yes, this might be a small operation, but with diamonds this easy to find, a larger operation was not needed. They stared at each other in disbelief. "Looking at all the rocks scattered around, I'm sure other diamonds have been found. Since no taxes have been paid, I think we have probable cause to continue our investigation," Chippernal said.

"And I believe we can say Lanny did not kill himself," Simmons said. "I agree," Davis said.

"One other thing. . . I believe the diamonds we found belong to Ms. Simpson. If she should sell them and pay the taxes, I bet the IRS would have no objection to you taking these to her. The others will be held as evidence," Chippernal said, reaching into his pockets and handing Simmons three diamonds.

"We will have the lab guys glean this place and the bomb squad disarm the explosives and secure the site. After we finish here, how about meeting us in Tyler this afternoon? We still have a lot of work to do."

"What about the dog? Is he evidence, too?" Simmons asked.

"Yes, but I think we can release him to the care of someone else since Davis has the other one. You interested?" he smiled.

A couple hours later, the evidence cataloged and loaded, Simmons walked to the kennel. The dog was lying peacefully, watching the people, but stood and wagged his tail when he saw

Simmons approaching. Simmons opened the gate, knelt down, and spoke to him in a soft voice. The dog came to him, and Simmons scratched him under his chin. He held his head up and wagged his tail.

Simmons saw the dog did not have a collar, and since he had no leash, he took off his belt and placed it around the dog's neck.

"Okay, Dobie, let's go see Ms. Elaine. I just bet a girl like her will like you."

Why he had called the dog Dobie he did not know, but when he said it, the dog looked at him approvingly and perked his ears. *No way. . . he is just responding to the sound of my voice. Still, he wondered.*

Dobie walked at his side as they made their way to the Simpson house, making a wide circle around the XP spot. *I don't care if they are unarmed. I have seen what IEDs can do.*

Simmons opened the door of his pickup. Dobie jumped in and sat down.

"Good boy," he said and scratched under his chin.

When they arrived at the Sandersons', Simmons opened his door and commanded the dog to "stay." Dobie sat, and Simmons saw he knew what that command was. He wondered if he would obey the "attack" command, also. He had a feeling he would.

Simmons got out of his truck and saw Elaine coming to him.

"I brought you a present." She stopped when she saw the dog. "I don't like dogs."

"You've got to be kidding. All country girls like dogs. His name is Dobie, and he was left on your farm, so he belongs to you—and so do these," he said, holding out the diamonds.

"I don't like dogs. I don't need rocks and don't call me a country girl."

Search

Simmons thought about getting in the pickup and driving away, but knew he could not.

This is how she is. She has not learned to share her life with anyone and is accustomed to being in control. So, I think I will stay unless she runs me off. He thought about this and at the moment was unsure whether she would or not.

"They are not rocks; they are uncut diamonds." He held them out for her to get a closer look. "They came from your place."

She stared at him, not knowing what to say. Finally, she murmured, "You could have awakened me before you left. I was worried." She stared at him and added, "What if something had happened to you?"

His heart melted. Now he knew why she was upset. She was worried about him—and no one had ever worried about him. He did not know what to say. He just put his arms around her and pulled her to him.

"I am sorry. I know how you feel because I worry about you."

"Mitchell, all this scares me. I am way out of my comfort zone. Out of the security of my classroom with things I cannot control and feelings I don't understand and. . . I don't mean to be a bitch." She laid her head on his chest for a long moment before pulling his head down and kissing him long and passionately. Or was it long and relieved? He hoped it was both.

"I do like dogs, and I don't mind being called a country girl. As for the rocks, I am not sure. My life was pretty good before, you know."

Hand in hand they walked to the truck, and Simmons let Dobie out.

"Just scratch him under the chin, and he'll love you."

Elaine did scratch his chin, petted him on his side, and rubbed his head.

"He is a beautiful creature. I haven't had a dog since I was a little girl. I love him already." She pulled Simmons closer as they walked.

"Did you find out who bought them? A dog this well-trained should not be hard to trace."

"Chippernal is working on it. I am supposed to meet him in Tyler this afternoon, and I'll know more then. By the way, have you heard from Penny or Anna?"

"They are still in Austin, meeting with the Security and Exchange Commission, I think, trying to find out how Bradley could have come so close to taking over and selling the Tyler plant. Penny seems to think there were high up officials involved. I really don't understand; business was not my forte."

They walked toward the patio, and Dobie fell in step beside Elaine. She patted him on his shoulder. He looked up and wagged his short tail. She scratched his chin.

"What are we going to do with him? I can't have pets in my apartment, and you are in the service."

"We will come up with something."

Reina was on the patio and, after admiring the dog, said lunch would be ready shortly. After lunch, it was decided that Reina would take care of Dobie while they went to Tyler. On the way, Elaine removed the diamonds from her purse and studied them. "If they are real, how much are they worth?"

"I have no idea, but I'm sure they are real. After we meet with Chippernal, we'll take them to a jewelry store and find out." He waited for Elaine to comment and when she did not, he continued, "Elaine, we found those diamonds in a five-gallon bucket of dirt and rocks. There appears to be many, many more."

He related to her all the events at the cave and at the waterfall. "It's very probable, you are a rich woman."

"I don't know if I want to be a rich woman," she said seriously and laid her head on his shoulders.

Search

After the meeting with Chippernal, they carried the diamonds to Elkmond Jewelry. The diamonds were appraised at between one and three-thousand dollars, depending on the quality after cutting.

They talked little on the way back to the Sanderson Ranch. It seemed each was trying to understand what was happening and how their lives were changing. *Was it changing for the good or for the bad?* Simmons wondered.

CHAPTER TWENTY-EIGHT

BONES

Seventeen ninety-seven

Four years passed, and they panned more and more gold. With the mules, cotton gin, and tobacco, they became even wealthier. Gee's son, Jones, and Saloni were married, and a year later his daughter, Audrey, and Ashwin's son, Jivin, were married. In a couple of years Gee and Mina were grandparents, and nothing could be better. Gee built two houses on the old Johnson place: one for him and Mina and one for Jones and Saloni. They built another house for Audrey and Jivin not far from the waterfall, leaving the big house to Sam, Audie, Ashwin, and Kali. Down the road from Gee's house, they built three more buildings, two for tobacco and one for cotton. Even after spending so much money, the hole in the cave had to be enlarged to contain the remaining gold, totaling now over a hundred pounds.

Gee purchased a section of land adjoining the Johnson place and grew more tobacco. Jones came up with a quicker way to cure the tobacco. Instead of letting it hang until it dried, which took about three weeks, he found if you heated the building, the curing time was less than a week. He did this by building rock furnaces with pipes running throughout the buildings. This also gave the tobacco a golden brown hue, plus it retained more flavor.

Within three years, the tobacco made more money than the gold. Even though Gee did not need more money, he hired more people to raise tobacco.

This changed when gold was discovered farther down Second Creek, which was now called Gilmore Creek. It was not long before the area was flooded with prospectors. Gee was certain some of them came through the split and explored Second Creek in Star Valley, but by now there was little to no gold left. Some prospectors moved their families to Barnes Crossing while they searched for gold, but two years later, the gold was gone and the people had nowhere to go. Gee built houses on the farm next to the old Johnson place and let them live there to grow tobacco. They would farm the land and give a fourth of their crops to Gee. Some families managed to buy land of their own, but most lived on Gee's land or worked for him, either in the fields or in the tobacco warehouses.

His golden leaf tobacco became very popular not only with the locals but with many customers overseas, so Gee began packaging tobacco for pipes, cigarettes, or for chewing—all in personal-sized bags. Soon he employed more than fifty people in his tobacco factory, which he called Gilmore Tobacco Company.

More and more farmers sold their tobacco to him because he offered the best price they could get. The more he purchased, the more people he hired to process it. It was not long before the company employed almost a hundred workers, a lot of whom moved closer to the tobacco company. Altus Ludvig moved his trading post from Barnes Crossing as did other businesses. In less than a year, there was a livery stable, a mercantile store, a pub, a bank, and a church down the road from the Gilmore Tobacco Company. The road at Barnes Crossing was deserted, while new roads came to this new settlement, which the town's people now called Gilmore.

Two more buildings were erected and now the Gilmore Tobacco Company employed almost two hundred people. A school was being built, and it seemed to Gee, no matter what they did, they were successful. The families of Star Valley were happy, wealthy, and well-respected. The falling star had indeed brought them good luck.

    Gee, Mina, Audie, Kali and numerous other people slowly followed a wagon carrying a pine box, driven by Jones. As Gee stared at the wagon, he recalled that had it not been for Sam Stewart, he would not be alive today. None of the people who had overfilled the church, his mother, Kali, Mina—not any one of them would be here. Gee had loved Sam like a father, and now each step he took brought back memories of him. . . like the day he had looked down the barrel of Gee's musket and had not blinked, just warned them about the vigilantes. A million other thoughts ran through his mind; it was so hard to believe he was gone, that he would never see him again, but he silently thanked God for leaving him with twenty-six years of wonderful memories.

    Only a whisper could be heard now and again as they walked the half-mile from the church to a small rise just to the right of the waterfall. The same place they had buried Ashwin two years earlier, and the place where they had planted a garden when they first came to Star Valley. Sam had said many times, "You can plant me there, too."

    Yes, so many wonderful memories, but less than four months later, they were walking behind the same wagon. His mother had just wasted away after Sam's death. "I have had a wonderful life, and I am ready to go and meet Sam, your father, and Jimmie," she said. She had requested to be buried next to Sam, but Gee remembered that she had wished his dad and Jimmie could be here, too. This thought ate at Gee as he walked behind the wagon, hand in hand with Mina, who was crying softly.

"She was so good to me. I loved her like she was my own mother," she whispered softly, her Cherokee accent having long ago faded away.

This also ate at Gee. Mina had lived without her mother and never complained. He knew she must have thought about her mother, her dad, and her brother and sister. Why had he not tried to find them? He had the money to hire people, or he could have tried to find them himself. Even if he had not found them, Mina would know that he tried. Why had he not tried? Her village could have been no more than a two days ride from their cabin. He felt the pain of guilt, as he realized he had not wanted to find them for fear Mina would leave. As they walked, he made a silent promise to his mother and to Mina. I will find my Dad and Jimmie's grave and bring their bones back here and bury them beside Mother and Sam. If Mina's parents or brother and sister are still alive, I will find them, or at least find out what happened to them. If any of her family is still alive, they can come here to live if they would like. I will build a house for them and not allow them to want for anything.

Sitting in the porch swing that night after supper, he told Mina what he intended to do. He saw tears come into her beautiful, brown eyes as she squeezed his hand. "Gee, that would be so wonderful." Tears now streamed down her face. "Your mother would have loved that, and it would mean a lot to me just to know if any of my family is still alive. . . or to know what became of them. My brother would be thirty-nine and my sister forty-two now."

"We will find them."

The next day he told Kali what his intentions were and asked if she and the kids would take care of the business. Kali asked if Mina was going with him, and Gee said he was taking her and two men. That way Mina would have no doubt they did their best to find her family. When he told Mina she was coming with him, she was delighted and hugged him. He said they would leave as soon as Gee could talk to some people who had been up that way recently.

The next day Gee selected two men to go with them, one to drive the carriage and the other would be on horseback. They would leave as soon as he could buy supplies. Two days later, they saddled four horses for him, Mina, and the two men, in case they needed a horse to ride. They harnessed two horses to pull the two-horse carriage, the same carriage Sam had used so many times to transport gold. It had a false bottom beneath the driver's seat. It was here Gee hid five one-pound bags of gold. The seat behind the carriage driver was covered with a fold-down top, and their luggage was tied to the rear. The supplies they would need were loaded onto a pack horse.

They said good-bye to family and friends, and before noon they were on the Great Wagon Road, heading north, stopping at roadside inns to spend the nights. On the fifth day they made it to Ryan's Trading Post. Gee was a little disappointed that Mr. Ryan had sold the post to Alton Griffins and moved to Kentucky.

They left Griffins' Post and crossed into the flatland of Virginia. Gee and Mina were surprised to find there were now only a few trees left of what had once been a great forest. The land had been cleared to make farms of cotton, corn, and tobacco. Gee searched for any landmark he might recognize, but all he saw was one farmhouse after another. They stopped at several farms and inquired about the old Gilmore place or the Grimes place. When no one remembered either, they began asking about Randolph's Trading post. At one of the farms an old man told Gee that he had passed the road less than a half's day back. Old man Randolph still lived there, but he had closed the trading post because no one went that way anymore.

"Look for a row of pecan trees on your left, and the old road to the post will be just past that. Well, it is not a road anymore; it is just a trail. Like I said, nobody goes that way anymore."

They backtracked, found the road, and turned towards the trading post. Gee remembered the trail to his old home place led off this road, and he looked for anything recognizable. All he saw, however, was more farmland.

Two hours later they came to the trading post, which was now a rundown house where Mr. Randolph was sitting on a porch that looked like it might fall any second. Gee could see he was old and very frail as he stood and waved to them.

Gee came and shook his hand, telling him who he was. Mr. Randolph shook his head and began to cry. "I am sorry. I am sorry." Between sobs he said, "I will never forget the look on Mrs. Gilmore face when I would not sell her anything. I have regretted that to this day. I should not have done that. I am ashamed of myself. Please tell her this, will you? Tell her I am sorry."

Gee looked at Mr. Randolph and saw no reason to tell him his mother had passed away. "Mr. Randolph, you did the right thing. I will tell her what you said, but she does not blame you for it."

Mr. Randolph looked at the wagon and saw Mina. "Is that the young Indian girl?" Gee waved for Mina to come. She hugged Mr. Randolph and thanked him for the peppermint stick he had sent her many years ago.

"You were a pretty girl then and you still are." He smiled at her.

"Mr. Randolph, we are now living in North Carolina. We came back here to take my father and little brother's remains back there, but everything has changed so much. I could not find our old home place. Could you help us find it?"

"Gee, I was by your place maybe four or five years back. After you left, some German built a house there. You know the vigilantes burned your house. I know you saw how the land has been cleared for farming. Nothing looks the same; even the road has changed. That's why I had to close the trading post."

He looked at Gee, trying to get the directions in his mind. "If you go back down the main road and before you cross the creek, you will see a trail on you right. You cannot see the house from the main road because it sits in a small valley, close to the foothills. Just follow that trail and you will find it. The man's name is von Carl. Before I closed the trading post, he used to trade with me. He is a good man, I think, but most people don't like him because his son married an Indian girl."

Of course it is where the stream crosses the road, Gee thought. *They would build the house close to the spring the same as my dad. Why did I not think of that?*

"Mr. Randolph, I sure am obliged, but there is one more thing we came for. We want to find Mina's parents or her brother and sister. Her village had to be within a two days ride of here, and we intend to go to every one of those villages. You see, I am also ashamed of myself, because I did not try to find her village after I found her. I guess I was afraid if I did, she would leave, and I did not want that. If it were not for me, she might know where her folks are today." He paused and watched as Mr. Randolph nodded his head. Gee could see he was deep in thought. He added, "Mr. Randolph, I remember you telling me Cain Johnston told someone he had taken the girl from William... Wilburn, or a creek with a name something like that. Do you recall that?'

"Yes, it was Willard Creek. I asked some of my Indian friends about it once, and they said it was about two day's ride towards the foothills—that way." He pointed towards the southeast.

"I don't think it is there anymore; the settlers have pushed the Indians farther back into the mountains." "Do you know of anyone who might be familiar with that area?"

"Yes, if anyone knows this land, it is Hollis Hanson's son, Doug. He hunts and traps the foothills and is friendly with the Indians. Hollis's house is down the main road past von Carl's... I mean your old place. When you get to the place where the road makes a sharp left turn, the road to the right will be the road to his house."

Gee took two twenty-dollar gold pieces from his pocket and laid them on the porch swing.

"This is for the musket you let me borrow. I still have it. Since I did not return it, I guess I will buy it, that is, if you will sell it."

"That old thing was not worth a rotten egg, I won't take your gold."

"That old musket saved my life, so it is worth that to me." Gee smiled and shook the old man's hand. "If we come back this way, we will stop in. If not, you take care of yourself, and I will tell Mother what you said."

"Yeah, come on back and stay a spell. It ain't anybody here but me and ole flea bags over there, and he ain't said a word in years." He laughed, pointing to a red bone hound lying in the yard.

They found the pecan grove and the trail leading to Gee's old home place. They rode up to a small four-room log house with well-kept barns and other buildings. Gee looked at the chimney and immediately recognized it. It was the one he and his dad had built. He was sure his name would still be visible in the stone he had carved when he was eight years old.

They rode up to the house. Gee and Mina got out of the carriage and called to the house. A female voice asked from within what they wanted. Gee explained he had once lived there, and they wanted to visit the graves of his father and brother. There was a long silence. Finally, a door opened, and a woman of about fifty stepped out.

"We own this farm now. We've been living here twenty-five years."

It was Mina who spoke, her voice smooth and charming, knowing the woman feared someone might try to take the land they had squatted on years ago. "Yes, ma'am, we understand that.

The only thing we would like to do is take the remains of my husband's father and brother back to North Carolina, so they can be laid to rest with his mother."

"Are you Cherokee?"

"Yes, my village was on Willard Creek."

"My son married a Cherokee girl. A lot of people around here did not like it, so he moved to North Carolina."

"That is what happened to us. They burned our house and tried to kill us."

"My husband is in the fields, but he will be here before dark. You are welcome to wait on him. You can find feed for your horses in the barn and the water is over. . . oh, you know all about the water. If you like, I will show you the two graves. There were four markers when we moved here, but they rotted away. My husband put up stones to mark them."

They walked past the chimney, and Gee saw his name, "Gaither Gilmore," and pointed it out to Mina and the lady. He stopped and stared at it, trying to recall even the most trivial details of his life back then.

"We saw that when we moved here. The house was burned, but the chimney was still standing. We built our house onto it. Oh, and by the way, my name is Lilly von Carl."

"My wife, Mina, and that's my name on the chimney. My little brother always called me Gee and now everyone calls me that. The carriage driver is Sid and the man on horseback is Arnie. They came along in case we needed help."

Lilly led them to the graves, and Gee knelt by them and took off his hat. He did not say anything for a long time. "Could we wait by the spring until your husband gets home?" Gee asked. She nodded her head and walked back to the house.

A little before sundown her husband came, and Lilly went out to meet him. She explained what Gee, Mina, and the others were doing there and what they wanted. "They seem like nice people, and they are from North Carolina," Mrs. von Carl said to him as he tied the pair of mules to the barn gate, walked over, and offered his hand.

"So, this vas your place. Ven ve moved here, ve vere told all ve had to do was pay back taxes and de land vould be ours. Ve have paid taxes all dees years, and ve have a deed to it. I hope you don't object."

"No, of course not. I don't mind. If we had stayed here, the vigilantes would have killed us. They had already burned our barn and tried to shoot me," Gee said and looked towards the graves.

"All we would like to do is dig up my father and little brother's remains and take them back to North Carolina to bury them next to my mother. That was her wish before she died."

"I am sorry. I don't think there vill be much left, a few bones, if any, after all dees years, but you are welcome to do dat. I vill be glad to help tomorrow." He watched the sun sink below the foothills, the same as Gee had done many, many times.

"You vill spent de night vith us. Ve have our son's room for you and the missus. Ve vill make a pallet in de front room for de other two men. There is feed for your horses in de barn. Ve don't have a lot, but you be velcome to vhat ve do have."

"If there is an Inn close by, we can stay there, or even make a camp by the barn. We don't want to put you to any trouble."

"You will do no such thing. We have plenty of room. Maybe you could tell me about North Carolina? The last time we heard from our son, he was near Salem, but that was five years ago," Lilly said.

"We live only a day's ride from Salem. Maybe we could find him and find out how to send you a letter. I understand that is possible now."

"Would you? I mean that would be wonderful!" Mina could see the hope billowing in Lilly's eyes. "We will try."

The next morning Gee told Mr. von Carl which grave was his father and Jimmie's, how he had placed rocks on top of their bodies before covering them up. "If we dig and hit the rocks, we will know we are at the right place," Gee explained.

They dug into his father's grave and when they hit rocks, they removed them one by one and carefully dug through the soil. They found a bone and Gee was overcome with emotion. He climbed out of the grave, walked to the spring and cupped water in his hands, washing his face. Soon he returned and removed all the bone and bone fragments he could find and put them in a bag he had brought. They found a few bone fragments in Jimmie's grave, put them in another bag, and refilled the holes.

Gee gave Mr. von Carl two twenty-dollar gold pieces for the feed and their lodgings. Mrs. von Carl gave Mina the name of her son and daughter-in-law, and Mina promised she would try to find him and send her a letter.

They said their goodbyes and arrived at the Hanson place, a four-room house larger than the von Carl's, painted white with blue shutters. It was one of very few houses Gee had seen that was painted. Gee introduced his party and told him why he was here. Gee found Mr. Hanson to be a friendly man, about forty, fair skinned, small in stature with long black hair.

Mr. Hanson called for his wife to come and meet their guests. A very thin young lady not much more than thirty came out holding a baby. She had fair skin, hazel eyes, and dark hair that hung almost to her waist. She smiled and welcomed them to her house in badly broken English. She stared at Mina with a questionable look on her face. Mina saw this, but only smiled back. Mr. Hanson also saw how she looked at Mina.

"This is my wife, Eva, and the little one, Daniel. We have been married two years, and she has never been around an Indian except my son, Doug, who is half Indian. I guess she has reason to distrust some of the Indians. Her parents were killed by the Shawnee soon after they arrived from France. My first wife was a Delaware and was also killed by the Shawnee nearly ten years ago. I left Pennsylvania right after that, and I moved Maryville, which is a little town up the main road, and built a mercantile store. Doug hated living in the back of the store so I bought this place and built the house. Now we live here, but work in town. Well, I guess that's enough about me," he said, slightly embarrassed as he looked at Gee.

They made small talk until Gee told him what Mr. Randolph had said about his son and that he might be able to help them find his wife's village.

"Your wife is Cherokee. We never have had any problems with the Cherokee, which is surprising, considering that the settlers have taken most of their land. Doug thinks they are wonderful people. I imagine he will marry one someday."

"I believe her village was on Willard Creek."

"Doug should be home anytime. I'm sure he will be delighted to get the chance to visit his friends in the different tribes. He is only seventeen, but quite a woodsman. Until then, Eva will make supper for us, and you will spend the night. We have a room for you and the missus, and Doug sleeps on the porch most of the time so your two men can have his room. We don't get much company so I will not take 'no' for an answer."

It was almost sundown before Doug rode in. He was tall and muscular with dark skin. His long, black hair was tied in a ponytail. *He looked much older than seventeen*, Gee thought.

Mr. Hanson told him Gee wanted to see if they could find his wife's parents or her brother and sister, who once lived in a village on Willard Creek. Doug informed him there were no villages on Willard Creek, and that most of the villages had moved up into the foothills. They might be able to find some of the elders who would remember it, but he thought the chances would be slim.

Gee asked Doug if he would be willing to guide them to these villages and explained to him why it was so important to him. "I will pay you well for your services," Gee assured him.

Bones

"I would be delighted to take you, but you cannot take the carriage. There are not many roads, just trails, and it will probably take three or four days, especially if we have to visit most of the tribes that once lived around here. Another thing. . . some of the tribes would rather we be a small party," he said, looking at the two men who were now taking care of the horses.

Gee understood what he meant and asked Mr. Hanson if there was an inn in Maryville.

"There is Ms. Sarah's boarding house. It's clean and has great food, but they are welcome to stay here."

"I'm sure the men would be pleased, but I think they would rather be in Maryville. If we could leave the carriage here, they could ride there tomorrow."

The next morning as they prepared to leave, Doug asked Gee if Mina was making this trip.

"It will be long with a lot of riding over rough terrain."

"Doug, she is a Cherokee. I think the only way to keep her from going is to tie her hands and feet behind her back; otherwise she would crawl after us."

The next three days they visited many villages. Gee was beginning to doubt if they would ever find anyone who knew of Mina's village. It was afternoon when they rode into a small village far back in the foothills and immediately Mina stopped her horse. She stared at an old man sitting beside a round house. She dismounted and walked to him.

Mina looked at him intently and asked, "Viho? Viho is that really you?' The old man looked puzzled, but nodded his head.

"It's me, Mina. I am Mina. My father is Oorjit. My mother Avani. My brother and sister are Dinkar and Dali. Do you know where they are?" she asked excitedly in Cherokee.

The old man got to his feet and looked at Mina. He nodded to Doug and stared at Gee for a long time. He came slowly to her, and his eyes said he recognized her as he took hold of her hand.

"We not know you live when white man takes you. Him be white man who took you?" he asked, never taking his eyes off Gee.

Mina shook her head and told how Gee had found her and that he was now her husband. She looked around and saw most of the village had come out of their houses and were now watching, but she did not see anyone she knew. "Is any of my family here?" she asked.

Viho took her other hand and pulled her close to him. With visible pain in his eyes, he slowly shook his head, "Most of Willard Creek die with fever. Only me and three more not die. Now it only me. I sorry."

Mina was stunned. She had expected to find some of her family. She laid her head against Viho's chest as tears ran down her face. After a long silence, she asked, "Where are their graves?"

"So many die, we bury in big grave. White man now farm land," he said, apologizing.

"Thank you." She stood looking at him, gave him a big hug, and kissed him on the cheek. "Thank you. Is there anything I can do for you? We have a big house in North Carolina. If you want to come with us, we will take care of you." He shook his head.

Mina walked to the pack horse, rummaged through the contents until she found two wool blankets, and handed them to him.

"One for you and one for your chief."

The old man removed a strip of leather with bear tooth from around his neck and gave it to her. "Tell your husband I glad he take care of you, or you might be gone with fever, too. It good." With these words, he laid the blankets over his shoulder, nodded to Gee and Doug, then turned and walked away. Mina watched until he went inside the round house. She waited, but he did not come out.

She put the bear tooth charm around her neck, waved to villagers, mounted her horse, and walked him slowly back up the trail. Doug said a few words to one of the men before riding with Gee as he followed Mina. They rode in silence for a long time with Mina leading the way. Gee nodded to Doug, "She needs time alone," so they rode behind her.

It was maybe an hour later before Mina stopped her horse and waited for them to catch up. Gee rode close to her, took her hand, and said he was sorry.

"I have hated the red-haired man many years. I used to lie awake many nights pretending I was killing him. Now, I guess if it were not for him, I would not be here. Maybe I need to forgive him." Her voice trailed off, and she starred at Gee.

"Mina, what he did was wrong, but he paid for what he did with his life, and you are here. But I think forgiveness can sometimes be a good thing."

"Yes, Gee. Let's go home."

It had been ten years since that day. Ten wonderful and happy years. They had three grandchildren and another on the way.

The people of Gilmore erected a statue of a man wearing a buckskin shirt, an old black hat, a black overcoat and holding a flint lock musket by his side. They placed the statue in front of the Gilmore Tobacco Company.

"I wonder where they came up with that idea." Gee looked at Mina and saw her beaming with pride. "That is the way I remembered you the day you found me. The town wanted to honor you for what you did for them, and I suggested the statue."

"I am happy I found you."

"Me, too. I am so happy."

That was two year ago, but in the last four months, everything began to change. They had laid Kali to rest beside Ashwin, and lately all the kids could talk about was moving to

South Carolina or Georgia. They heard stories of rich farmland just for the taking, or you could buy all the land you wanted for as little as a nickel an acre. People were building huge plantations and had Negroes from Africa to farm their cotton. There was a fortune to be made, and Jivin and Audrey discussed this many times with Jones and Saloni. They all wanted to go there.

Since the deaths of Ashwin and Sam, they had stopped farming and concentrated their efforts on Gilmore Tobacco Company, but both couples were restless. They were tired of this tobacco and wanted a new challenge. They talked of taking their share of the gold, which would buy thousands of acres. They wanted to live in huge plantation houses, be southern gentlemen and southern belles.

One day Jones and Jivin left for Georgia. When they returned, they informed Gee they had agreed to purchase a plantation of fifteen hundred acres. It had a huge house, and they had the option to buy an adjoining one with three thousand acres. That would be one for each of them.

"Dad, we have enough gold to pay for both places and live like kings. The tobacco industry is changing, and it won't be long before a big corporation moves in and squeezes us out. Cotton is the big thing now. Dad, you and Momma come with us. We don't want to leave you here, but we have to go. We have to make a life on our own. Please come with us."

Two weeks later, three Conestoga wagons loaded with personal items, two thirds of the gold, and two carriages loaded with Gee and Mina's children and grandchildren left Gilmore, escorted by five heavily armed men. Gee and Mina were devastated. Not only had they lost their children, they had also lost their grandchildren.

"We were once a big family; now it is just the two of us," he said to Mina.

They drove the carriage to their house on the old Johnson place and discussed what they should do with Star Valley. During the next two weeks they came to the conclusion that they should sell it. No way would they be able to work the land when most of their time was spent with the tobacco company.

"What about the graves?" Mina asked.

"What do you think of erecting large headstones and enclosing them with an iron fence? We will not sell that plot of land, nor will we sell Star Valley to anyone who will not agree in writing to give us access to it. We will be close enough to take care of the graves ourselves."

For two years they tried to sell, but found no one who would buy so many acres. During this time, it also seemed that everyone was growing tobacco, making it harder to sell the Gilmore Tobacco Company's product. The harvest came, and Gee could not buy the tobacco from the farmers. His tobacco sheds were full, and he could not sell what he had cured. Gee had no choice but to close half of his company, leaving a hundred men without a job. Gee could see no relief in sight.

Later that fall, with the tobacco rotting in the fields, Salem Tobacco Company offered to buy his company and the land at Star Valley. They offered a fraction of what Gee thought it was worth, so he refused to sell. However, the next year was even worse so when Salem made him another offer, he sold the tobacco company and Star Valley for less money than the previous offer but with the promise that Salem would not close the Gilmore plant. The only things he did not sell were the plot of ground with the graves and the old Johnson place where his house stood.

Later, he moved the gold from the cave, removed boards from the walls of their bedroom, and stacked the bags of gold inside.

Salem Tobacco operated Gilmore Tobacco for a year before closing it and moving everything to Salem, leaving the people in the town of Gilmore without jobs. Without jobs or income, no one could buy from the local stores so one by one the stores closed or moved elsewhere. Without funds the town of

Extending Shadows

Gilmore had no law enforcement; soon, people who were once law-abiding citizens were now thieves.

The only times Gee and Mina went to town were for supplies, and when they did, they were jeered, subjected to threats, and called names. One morning Gee found a bucket of cow manure dumped on their porch. People began to treat them like the plague, calling him "squaw lover," and one lady spit on Mina. Soon there was only one store left in Gilmore, and it would not sell to him.

Once again Gee felt the hate that he had known when they had left Virginia. He knew it would not be long before they would burn the warehouse here, and probably his house as well, because they blamed him for everything that had happened. After discussing what they should do, Gee and Mina agreed they had no choice but to leave. They would move to Georgia and live close to the rest of the family, something they had discussed since selling Star Valley.

Early the next morning, they loaded a few belongings into a trunk and the gold into the false bottom of the carriage. With two horses hitched to the carriage and two saddle horses, they prepared to leave.

"If we cannot live here, no one else will either." Gee set fire to the house and barn. They sat in the wagon and watched the flames engulf all their memories. No one came to extinguish the flames, and no one said good-bye as they left Gilmore and Star Valley forever.

CHAPTER TWENTY-NINE

SUSPECTS
Twenty Ten

Elaine chose to wait in the lobby while Simmons talked to Chippernal. He walked into Chippernal's office and was surprised to see Scott McTune. After greetings, Chippernal filled him in on what he knew and turned a computer screen so both McTune and Simmons could see it. He pointed to a photo.

"Simmons, this is the man you shot at Manny's. His name is Juan Cobel. He is. . . or was. . . a member of a Mexican drug cartel. He was wanted in El Paso in connection with murder and the sale of drugs."

He pulled up another photo. "This is the man Deputy Sheriff Davis shot. We found his fingerprints on several objects at the Simpson place. We are in the process of running them through our database. Also, we have an eyewitness who saw him at Debra Bates's house several times in June. Another witness saw him with Roy Grades in Judge Caldwell's courtroom along about the same time."

Chippernal adjusted his chair, leaned back, and said, "The Dobermans at the Simpson place were two of three purchased by a woman who paid cash on July third of this year from a breeder in Dallas. We had Dallas compile a sketch and fax it to us. Most people here at the bureau believe it is Susie Carter.

"We also have a Dallas Jewelry Store security photo of a woman, identified as Susie Carter, who sold some large, uncut diamonds on the tenth of May that same year for eleven grand. So it's probable she is the woman at the dog breeder because of the time frame. We went to her house, intending to pick her up for questioning, but she was not there. A neighbor said he had not seen her since late Saturday. No one has filed a missing person report on her, so we believe someone knows where she is—or at least they don't think she is missing. We have agents working on this.

"We have not been able to find anything on a Roy T. Grades, so we presume that Grades is an alias and probably the reason he did not practice law, only left the impression he was an attorney for the Tyler Bottling Company. We do have a partial set of prints from a mirror he used to make himself pretty, so to speak, before the TV interview in which he tried to incriminate you in the death of Bradley. We are presently running the prints through our system and awaiting the results."

Chippernal picked up a laptop battery and handed it to Simmons. "This is the battery that was in your laptop. It has a tracking device installed in it. Very clever. . . we almost missed it. It's not the battery that was in the PC when we gave it to you, so someone switched them. We recalled you had said the only times someone could have tampered with the laptop, other than here at the office," he smiled at Simmons and continued, "were when you left the laptop in the chopper with the pilot and while you and Ms. Simpson were at Cracker Barrel. So we looked at their security tapes. A sheriff's patrol car came on the property in that time frame; unfortunately, we could not see the driver. It parked off camera, as was Ms. Simpson's car, and left five minutes later—plenty of time for a battery to be switched in a laptop. We are interested in the patrol car; Sheriff Evans is reportedly a computer guru.

"Deputy Gregg Davis volunteered to check the sheriff's department's vehicle log and found Evans had checked out a cruiser before the Cracker Barrel time frame and logged 6.4 miles on it. It is a 1.6 mile round trip from the sheriff's office to

Cracker Barrel, so that leaves 4.8 miles when the car had traveled elsewhere. There were only two more cruisers in service at that time; both of them were working an accident on FM 1144, each of them logging over twenty miles. We believe Evans was at the Cracker Barrel and are searching for an eyewitness who can verify that it was he."

Looking at Simmons, Chippernal shook his head and said, "Now this was just a hunch, but since we believe Debra Bates may have known one of the dead men, we put her house under surveillance. About three hours ago we picked up a 'cease all surveillance' call made to a throwaway cell number in Houston. We are working on that."

He continued, "The safe at the Simpson cave contained two large bags of diamonds. We are in the process of having them appraised. Ms. Simpson will be given a receipt for them, but for the time being, we are holding them as evidence."

He turned to face McTune and told him, "You can fill him in on what you have if you like."

"I don't have a lot," McTune replied. "We don't have the manpower the Feds do, but we found some 7 mm ammo on Bradley's boat—the same caliber as the ones used by the shooter at Manny's. We checked Bradley's home and found fifteen small diamonds and a scratch pad containing an imprint of a suspicious memo that read 'Shipment Due.' It was addressed to an employee in charge of shipping at the bottling company. We have learned this employee spent a lot of time in Bradley's office. We have him under surveillance and are in the process of running a background check on him."

He paused and gazed at Chippernal, giving Simmons the impression that he wanted to say more but Chippernal's body language suggested he should not. McTune shifted his gaze to Simmons; when the two made eye contact, he looked away.

"Okay, that's it. If either of you find anything, please feel free to call," Chippernal said and turned off the computer.

Simmons stared at Chippernal and at McTune, who was walking toward the door.

"Why the brush-off? Why tell me this, and then tell me to get lost?" Simmons caught McTune in the parking lot. Before he could close the car door, Simmons leaned his body against it, preventing it from closing. "Okay, Scott, spill it." McTune stared straight ahead and said nothing. "I hope you don't make me drag you outta here and beat it out of you. What does Chippernal not want me to hear?"

"Simmons, I wanted to tell you, but Chippernal said no, so I can't say anything."

"He is not your boss," Simmons said, watching him. "Or is he?"

McTune shrugged his shoulders.

"Alright, if that is the way you all want to play. You can bet I will keep whatever I find to myself." Simmons slammed McTune's car door and turned away, seeing Elaine with a stunned look on her face. He did not look back as he walked to where she was standing.

"Simmons, meet me at Cracker Barrel in ten minutes and bring Ms. Simpson with you," McTune called to him.

"Don't play games with me, McTune."

"If you want to know, be there."

"Let's go," Simmons said to Elaine "What was that all about?" she asked.

"I don't know. Something Chippernal did not want him to tell me. I get this investigation out of the gutter and we start to learn things, then he shuts me out."

Elaine drove to Cracker Barrel where they quickly found a booth in the back, ordered ice tea, and waited for McTune. Five minutes later McTune emerged from the men's room and sat down.

"I got here before you did. I wanted to see if you were being followed." He looked around the room. "Simmons, I know you are somewhat of a hot head, so neither of you say a word until I'm finished. Is that agreed?"

Simmons looked at Elaine and both nodded their heads.

"In Bradley's home safe we found deposit slips of 130 thousand dollars from Trinity Saving and Loan in Tidewater. They were deposited into the account of Gavin Gentry. We got a court order to open this account and found one hundred thousand dollars had been transferred to the East Texas Teachers Credit Union to the account of R. E. Simpson in twenty-thousand increments. The last deposit was three days before Lanny's death. The ETTCU listed the address of this account as a post office box in Longview. We got a court order to open this PO box and found monthly statements from the credit union which had never been opened. In the PO box there was also a receipt for a security box in Lanny W. Simpson's name at the Longview Bank and Trust. We were given authorization to open this box and found that it contained over 200 uncut diamonds." He paused and stared at Elaine, noting the disbelief on her face.

"This was what Chippernal did not want me to tell you. But I spent a lot of time yesterday looking into the background of Rita Elaine Simpson and found nothing suspicious, so I'm telling you this."

He looked from Elaine to Simmons and out the window. "Now, even though it is pretty clear Lanny was selling diamonds to Gentry, and that Gentry sold them to Bradley, we have no proof Lanny knew what Gentry did with them. He bought the diamonds from Lanny for 100K and sold them for 130K, and Lanny deposited the money in an account for you. We found no record of Gentry or Lanny paying taxes on this income. So, other than not paying taxes on the diamonds, neither did anything illegal."

He paused and looked at Elaine, studying her face for any reaction. All he could see was disbelief. "Ms. Simpson, were you aware of any of this?" She shook her head, and McTune could see she was still trying to analyze what he had said. "Ms. Simpson, we have confiscated the money and the diamonds until our investigation is complete. Since you are the next of kin, they will be returned to you unless we find you are involved. However, I would strongly suggest that you contact the IRS and explain the situation to them."

Both Simmons and Elaine sat staring at McTune, not knowing what to say or what to do. "Any questions?" Neither said a word.

"Okay. It's up to you if you want to tell Chippernal what I said." He walked to the cashier, paid for the tea, and left, leaving Simmons and Elaine staring after him in utter disbelief.

"What do you think?" Simmons asked tentatively.

Elaine did not answer, but got up and walked outside to her car. Simmons followed her. "Elaine, talk to me."

"Get in," she said and drove to a flower shop, where she walked in, returning a few minutes later with three bouquets of flowers.

"What are the flowers for?" he asked, trying desperately to get her to talk to him.

"I want to take them by Mom and Dad and Lanny's graves."

She drove about three miles past the Longview airport to Shady Oaks Baptist Church. In the back was a small cemetery surrounded by oak trees. A narrow road encircled the cemetery, and she parked beneath one of the large old oaks. She laid her head on the steering wheel, and Simmons saw a tear creeping down her cheek. He wished there was something he could do to console her. Instead he walked around the car, opened her door, took her hand, and helped her out. He wiped the tear off her cheek and gently pulled her close to him. She laid her head against his chest and slumped against him. They stood that way for a long time.

Finally, she led him to a simple, double tombstone with her parents' names, their birth dates and the dates of their deaths with a simple, "You are missed," engraved along the bottom. Next to this tombstone was another with Sergeant Lanny W. Simpson engraved in large letters, below which were his Army information, his date of birth, and the date of his death with "A Special Person" also engraved on it.

Simmons watched as Elaine removed the artificial flowers from the vases on her parents' grave and put in the new ones. She did the same at Lanny's grave, but Simmons noticed that his grave also held a vase of eleven live yellow roses. The twelfth rose lay on the grave without petals. They were scattered over and around the grave. Elaine knelt by the grave, picked up the rose, kissed it, and gently placed it back in the same spot. She stood and leaned against Simmons.

"Penny brings the yellow roses every Sunday morning. She pulls the petals off one rose, reliving a memory for each petal, and lets them fall to the ground. She kisses the bud and lays it on the grave. Over time, it seemed that I needed to kiss the bud as well, so I do."

Simmons stared at the name, Sergeant Lanny W. Simpson, trying to recall every single minute they had spent together. Fun memories, sad memories, life and death memories slammed into his mind and exploded like mortars. Memories of the bond between them made his body cold; he was sweating and shaking. He stared at the name, at the special engraving, and murmured, "He was special. He was like the little brother I never had."

Somewhere in his mind he heard Elaine talking to him and was vaguely aware of her urging him away from the grave, but he could not get his mind off Lanny. *Why?* was all he could think.

Neither said a word as Elaine drove to the Sandersons'.

They sat on the patio, sipping a glass of wine. Simmons heard the sound of a helicopter and watched the Sarkozy circle and softly touch down. Anna and Penny walked from the chopper to the patio. Neither looked happy.

Reina came out to ask if they would like a glass of wine. Both nodded, then sat down and waited for Reina to bring the wine.

"We think we are about to get this mess cleared up—the Tyler plant I mean. The rest raised more questions than answers," Anna said, then took a long drink, and continued, "We hired a firm in Houston to investigate Bradley and Grades. Some of the thing they found were not good." She looked out at the pasture, turned the wine glass up, and drank it all.

"We learned Roy Grades is not his real name. His real name is Charles Sinclair. He was an attorney for the Security and Exchange Commission, but was disbarred for insider trading. He was the one who forged documents giving Bradley majority ownership of the Tyler plant. He is suspected for drug running and money laundering. He has a brother in San Antonio who owns a jewelry store which is thought to be a front for all kinds of illegal activities."

Reina brought more wine and refilled their glasses.

Anna thumbed through her notebook, found the page she wanted, and said, "One other thing we find interesting, and I don't know if it means anything or not, but Judge Caldwell's wife is Sinclair's sister. They married a couple of years ago. She is twenty years or more his junior. The fact that no one here seems to know it, and it was never mentioned is enough by itself to raise questions." She paused and looked at Simmons and Elaine, silently inviting them to fill her in on what they had found.

"Do you mind if I call Chippernal and tell him what you told us?" Simmons asked.

"Not at all."

Simmons dialed Chippernal, who answered on the first ring, and related the story Anna had just told. It was a long time before Chippernal responded, "Simmons, I have some information about the Tyler plant I think both the Gilmores and Sandersons should know. I would like to meet with all of you—

Suspects

tonight if possible. Would you relate this to them and call me back?"

Simmons told Anna and Penny what he had said about the Tyler plant. "I will call my father; if it is okay with him, we could meet at Manny's," Penny suggested.

Thirty minutes later, Penny, Anna, Elaine, and Simmons boarded the Sarkozy, flew to Tyler, and picked up Mr. and Mrs. Gilmore.

On the way, Simmons told of finding the diamonds on Elaine's farm and the man Davis had killed, who had been seen hanging around Debra Bates's house, and Carrie Bates wearing a large diamond that Lanny was supposed to have given Debra. He told about the phone call from Debra and about the expensive house and cars of Chief Bates.

Simmons was watching Elaine as he talked and could see she was unhappy with him labeling the Bates as suspects, but he felt they should know. He waited for Elaine to tell about Lanny selling diamonds.

"Lanny was selling diamonds to Gentry, who sold them to Bradley. Lanny opened an account in my name at the teachers' credit union and deposited a hundred thousand dollars into it. He also has a safe deposit box with more diamonds." She paused, "Penny, I believe if Lanny found that the diamonds were being sold to Bradley, he would have stopped selling them to Gentry. I think this may be the reason he was killed—probably both he and Gentry. I did not know about the diamonds or the money. I knew Lanny always had money not long after he came home from the service, but I just presumed you gave it to him. I am sorry. I was so hung up on me that I paid no attention to anything or to anyone but myself. I am sorry."

Simmons could see that Anna and Penny were as shocked as he and Elaine had been. So shocked, all they could do was sit and stare at her and out the window. It was Penny who broke the silence by putting put her arms around Elaine.

"I know, I know, but you did nothing wrong. I am the one who should have been suspicious. Lanny would never let me pay for anything we did. 'That is a man's thing,' he would say, and we did some things that were very expensive."

They landed at Manny's and found Chippernal waiting on them in their private dining room. He greeted each of them, walked to the head of the table, and opened a yellow legal pad. "On behalf of the FBI, I want to thank you for the info on Sinclair. We ran the Roy T. Grades prints Deputy Davis gave us and compared them to the ones we had on file for Charles Dow Sinclair. They are the same person. We are in the process of running his name through our database, but. . ." He paused and looked at Anna. "This much we have learned already: His sister is the wife of Judge Oliver Caldwell, which you already know. He has a brother, Jack Sinclair, who three years ago opened a jewelry store which we believe is a front for illegal drugs in San Antonio. When we know more, we will share our information with you.

"And now for the reason I asked to meet with you. . . The FBI has a warrant for the arrest of four employees of the Tyler Bottling Plant for the sale and distribution of drugs. Three are already in custody, and as soon as we locate the fourth, the plant will be closed and all records will be confiscated until a thorough search and audit can be conducted. With all due respect, Mr. Gilmore, we do not believe you or Ms. Sanderson is involved, so you will be given the opportunity to make a public statement as to why the plant is closing."

Turning to face Elaine, he said, "Chief Bates and his daughter Debra came forth and IDed the man Deputy Davis shot at your place. His name was Danzi Lopez. He was an Army buddy of Lanny's and the father of Debra's son. Simmons, you were in that unit, so you might recall him."

Simmons mind was racing, trying to recall him, but he could not remember and shook his head.

Suspects

"Anyway, he came back to Longview about three years ago and tried numerous times to see Debra. So many times, in fact, she had a restraining order preventing him from seeing her or the boy. They also hired private security from a firm in Houston for protection. According to some of Debra's neighbors, Lopez was observed knocking on her door, which is probably the reason she very seldom leaves the house. Chief Bates carries the boy to school and picks him up."

He waited for someone to say something. When they did not, he continued, "Chief Bates, his wife, and daughter came to our office earlier today and gave sworn statements. Bates admitted that he knew who Lopez was and should have made that fact known, but was afraid the news media would get wind of it. So, in an effort to protect his daughter and grandson, he did not do anything. He said he will resign the first thing in the morning. I talked to the mayor and some members of the city council who are meeting with him as I speak."

Chippernal looked at his notes for a long moment. "One other thing. . . Simmons, I believe it was you who questioned how Chief Bates could own a big house and expensive cars on a police chief's salary. I am sure the chief was aware of how this looked so to clear things up, he voluntarily told me he was the only heir to his parents' considerable fortune, including a large ranch in South Texas. When his parents passed away, he gave Debra his old house and built another one. He placed an extremely large sum of money in trust for his grandson and also gave a large sum to Debra. She, in turn, gave Carrie the diamond ring Lanny had given her, saying she could not wear it because it reminded her too much of Lanny.

"We asked her about the call she made to a cell phone in Houston, and she said it was to the security firm protecting her from Lopez. We are in the process of checking this out. We have also run a number of searches on Chief Bates and on his wife. So far, all have come back negative and his story about his inheritance checks out."

Simmons looked at Elaine and saw she was staring at him. He could see she was a little annoyed at him and had that "I told you so" look on her face. He could only smile at her. It was a long moment before she managed a small grin and turned her attention back to Chippernal, who glanced at his notes again and continued.

"We have been unable to locate Grades. . . I mean. . . Sinclair or Ms. Carter. We have sent flyers to FBI offices and to other law enforcement agencies for them to be picked up and held for questioning. We feel it is only a matter of time before they are spotted."

"Now. . ." He waited for several seconds before continuing. "Agent Taggart and I have discussed the fact that Sinclair's sister is Judge Caldwell's wife. He agrees it does seem suspicious that no one knew or ever mentioned this. We also wonder why Sinclair spent a lot of time in Judge Caldwell's courtroom. When we have Sinclair in custody maybe we can learn more, but, in the meantime, we have to proceed with caution. After all, Judge Caldwell is a federal judge.

"One other thing. . . I had a hard time convincing our office that it could be beneficial to share our information with all of you. I argued that you have helped us thus far, but I must insist that you not share anything I have said with anyone outside this room—and I do mean anyone! This includes other FBI agents and all law enforcement agencies."

"Mr. Chippernal," Anna spoke. "Bradley's mother called blaming us for her son's death and said she was suing us. I thought nothing of this at the time, because she rambled a lot, but I remember she said Charles knew a judge who would see to that we paid through our teeth. Now I wonder if she was referring to Judge Caldwell and Charles Sinclair."

Suspects

"That is interesting; I will discuss this when I get back to the office. They may deem it necessary to look into this in more detail, especially the part about Judge Caldwell."

There was a long pause as each of them ran all this through their minds. It was Mr. Gilmore who broke the silence. "When would you like me to announce the closing of the plant?"

"We would prefer you do it so it could be reported on the 10 p.m. news."

Mr. Gilmore agreed. Chippernal asked if anyone had any more question. When no one spoke, he had Mr. Gilmore call the TV stations in Longview and Tyler during dinner and set up a news conference to be held at the Tyler Bottling Plant at 9:00 p.m.

They boarded the chopper for the short flight to the Sanderson ranch. The whine of the turbines and the *whip-whip* of the blades seemed to lull Anna into deep concentration. She thought of the many times she had gotten ideas and solved problems while riding. Seemed like it was here that she did her best thinking. She made notes of these thoughts as they ran through her mind.

At one time I thought Roy Grades. . . or I guess I should say Charles Sinclair. . . was most likely the person calling the shots, but now I am not so sure. It could be that Sinclair was a pawn for the Texas mafia or a drug cartel and not a big player in this. However, we have no evidence that the mafia is involved. On the list of suspects, maybe I give Sinclair a five or six and the mafia a three. What about Johnny, Carrie, and Debra Bates? It would seem that they were the ones who would likely gain the most. If Elaine were not around, then Carrie would inherit her sister's farm. But then, considering what Chippernal said about the chief's inheritance, they would not need the money. Another thing that bugs me. . . I don't know how much money we are talking about. How much were the diamonds worth and how many of them have been removed from the Simpson place? Her mind dwelled on this for several seconds as she wondered if there was a way to find out.

What is the value of the diamonds the FBI were holding? If they were worth a considerable amount, then the ones already taken and the ones still remaining might be too much to dismiss. Some people are just greedy. I think I can give a four or five to the Bates, higher if the diamonds are worth a small fortune.

Susie Carter is interesting. Of course, I don't know for sure if she is involved. Even if she is, I am not sure she has the ability to put all this into action. My feeling is that both she and Sheriff Green knew of the diamonds and may have stolen some of them. Maybe it was only Green, and this is why he's dead, but from the way she reacted to Simmons asking questions, I think she knows something. She may have been a player in the drugs at the plant, or maybe a drug cartel could be the main player. Maybe Susie and a drug cartel warrant a five. I am not sure about that. . . could be more, could be less.

So. . . this leaves Judge Olive Caldwell and his wife, Ali, the sister of Charles Sinclair. The judge made headlines a couple of years ago when he married a girl twenty years or more younger than he not too long after his first wife died. Now since she has not told anyone that Charles Sinclair, aka Roy T. Grades, was her brother, it makes me wonder why. Maybe a six or seven simply because of what I don't know. . . But why would a successful judge jeopardize his career? And for what, unless the diamonds were worth millions? That could be tempting to some people, why not him? After all, a judge's salary can't be anywhere near that. On this basis, I think he is an eight or nine, and right now our top suspect.

The chopper set down gently on the Sanderson Ranch's helipad. Anna was the last to disembark. Her mind was still thinking of Judge Caldwell and his young wife. The judge and his first wife had adopted Misty, who was now the wife of Joe Evans and the Sheriff only because Judge Caldwell probably pulled some strings. "Very interesting. . ."

Suspects

She watched the chopper lift off, waved to her parents, and joined the others on the patio. "It's cool out here. Let's all go in and have a glass of wine."

They sipped their wine while Anna told them of her thoughts about Judge Caldwell. Each nodded their heads in agreement.

CHAPTER THIRTY

THE TRUTH
Twenty Ten

A little later Simmons and Elaine walked hand in hand towards the guest house. Both were deep in thought and neither said a word until they were inside. It was Simmons who broke the silence.

"Anna is quite sure Judge Caldwell is involved. He could very well be, but I am not thoroughly convinced." "So you still believe Johnny and Carrie are guilty." Elaine shot a displeasing glance at him.

"No."

"Well?"

"Well," he said as he pulled her close to him, wrapping his arms around her and holding her face close to his and kissing her. She tried to pull away, only to have him hold her tighter and kiss her again.

"No, I don't believe they are guilty. You made your point."

She smiled at him and to his surprise she kissed him and wiggled a little closer. Simmons held on to her, fearing if he let go, he would wake up and find all this to be a dream.

"Who do you think?"

"You. You are the one for me." She giggled and snuggled still closer.

"I mean, who do you think is behind all this?"

"I'm not sure. I have got all kinds of bits and pieces of Lopez and Sinclair running through my head, some of which I'm just starting to remember. Maybe tomorrow, I can figure it out." He looked into those beautiful sea-green eyes and knew he was in love. There was no doubt about it.

"Are you staying with me tonight?" "Yes, in the first bedroom."

Simmons laid on his bed, thinking about Elaine, about Sinclair, and about Danzi Lopez, the supposed friend of Lanny's, who was also in his Army unit. Why did he not remember him? Then it hit him. Lanny and he had met in sniper school, not in boot camp, and Lopez had been kicked out of boot camp. He did not remember Lanny mentioning his name, but Sinclair. He had heard that name before now. But where? He walked into the den, sat down at the desk, and turned on the computer. A couple of hours later he climbed into bed and drifted off to sleep.

He was awakened by a knock on his door. It was Elaine and it was 0545. She came in and sat on the side of his bed. She looked tired.

"Mitchell, I spent most of the night on the Internet, Googling both Charles Sinclair and his sister. I remembered that Lanny dated a girl named Alieah Sinclair before he went into the service and when he came home on leave. At the time, I thought he was serious about her and was somewhat surprised when he began dating Penny."

She lay back onto his bed and continued, "I pulled up a copy of our yearbook and found Alieah Sinclair was a sophomore when I was a senior, so she was a freshman when Lanny dated her. There were over 600 students in our school, so I don't recall ever meeting her. Anyway, I did not believe this girl was Sinclair's sister because of the age difference. Charles Sinclair is fifty-one, and Alieah is twenty-two. That is a lot of years between brother and sister, so I wondered if she was even related to Charles Sinclair. What I found was that she is his step-daughter, so I checked to see if this was the Ali Sinclair who married Judge Caldwell. It was."

She got up from the bed, went to the window, and opened the blinds. She watched as the first rays of the morning sunlight, barely visible behind a dark gray cloud bank, gave the landscape a surreal look with long shadows.

She watched them for a long time before speaking, "Mitchell, I admit that when I graduated high school and went off to college, I was so caught up in my own world that I paid little attention to anyone else. I seldom came home, and when I did, I did not stay long and did not socialize much. But back to last night. . . I thought about the information someone gave Anna about Judge Caldwell marrying Sinclair's sister, when she was really his daughter. This was strange, so for the next three hours I researched the Sinclair's background."

She turned and faced him. "Charles Sinclair was born here in Longview and graduated from Tulane. He finished law school in Dallas and went to work for the Security and Exchange Commission. Three years later, he married Haley Fredrick, a divorcee with two children, James Roger, age six, and Alieah Jean, age two. A year later, Sinclair adopted the two children, but three years later they divorced."

She paused as if she were trying to decide how to relate the story. "Now, get this. In the divorce papers filed by Haley, she claimed Sinclair had affairs with two different men, and she asked for sole custody of her two children. The divorce was never finalized because she was killed in an auto accident. Thus, the children remained with Sinclair. Five years later, he was disbarred from the SEC and moved to Houston where he was employed at a Pepsi Cola plant managed by Arnold Bradley. He came to Tyler when Bradley became manager of Tyler Bottling Company. Now, according to the Tyler Daily News, he and Bradley were golfing buddies and were seen on the course many times with Judge Caldwell. Soon after Judge Caldwell's wife died, he married Alieah, or Ali as she is now called. I could not find much else except that Charles Sinclair listed his address as an apartment in Tyler. According to a gossip column I found in the newspaper, however, he spent a lot of time at the residence of Judge Caldwell."

She turned back from the window and looked at Simmons, "What do you make of all this?"

"There are a lot of unanswered questions. Hmm... what did you find on the son, James Rodger?"

"I found that he and Lanny graduated the same year. I also found that they joined the Army on the same day, but I don't recall Lanny ever mentioning him. Three year later he was listed as missing in action in Afghanistan, but I could not learn if he was ever found."

"What about Lopez?"

"Look, it took me most of the night digging this up. Why don't you try and do something, yourself?" she snapped.

Simmons pulled the blanket from the bed, wrapped it around his waist, walked over, and put his arms around her. "Thanks."

She spun out of his embrace. "Mitchell, the last few years I have lived by myself, and as you can tell, I am used to giving orders—or at least having my students listen to me. I really don't mean to be a hot-head, but I guess that is the way I am, so don't make fun of me."

"Elaine. Elaine, listen to me. Thanks. Thanks for all your hard work. That is what I meant. I would never make fun of you. Never."

She turned and looked at him, suspicion in her sea-green eyes, but she managed a slight smile. "You look kinda sexy in a blanket, but maybe you should get dressed and we can have a cup of coffee."

They were sitting at the kitchen table waiting for the coffee to perk when her cell phone rang. It was Penny. "I saw you at the window, so why don't you and Mitchell come up? Reina is making breakfast, and I have some interesting things to tell you."

The Truth

"So do I." Elaine walked over and turned off the coffee pot.

At the breakfast table, Penny looked at Elaine and observed, "You look like you spent most of the night on the computer like I did."

"Uh-huh."

After a western omelet, Texas toast, orange juice, and two cups of hot coffee, Elaine found they had basically the same information, except Penny had found a James Rodger Sinclair living in Trenton, a small town just west of Tyler. She had not been unable to find much of anything else.

"Did you check on Danzi Lopez?" Elaine asked as she stared at Simmons.

"Yeah, I found he joined the Army the same day as Sinclair and Lanny. He was discharged two months later for bad conduct and apparently came back here. Records show he was arrested for harassing Debra Bates shortly afterwards. Later he was arrested in San Antonio for the possession of drugs. At the time a company called Texas Imports, owned by Jack Sinclair, the brother of Charles Sinclair, employed him. Exactly when Lopez came back to Longview is unknown, but a restraining order preventing him from seeing Debra Bates was signed three years ago."

Penny sipped her coffee and told Simmons, "I am sorry Mother and I will not be of any help today. We have got to up the production of the Texarkana and Longview plants to cover the loss of the plant in Tyler. I hope it doesn't take the FBI long to complete their investigation; we need the Tyler plant."

"I am going to visit Aunt Carrie. She did not seem like herself, and I think something is wrong with her that has nothing to do with diamonds." Elaine stared hard at Simmons.

After everyone left, Simmons sat on the patio, his mind trying hard to analyze all he had heard. He stared at the pasture, now just barley beginning to turn brown, but really did not see anything as different memories were flooding his mind. He finished his coffee and walked to the guest house. He booted the computer and began searching and making notes. Forty minutes later he was in his truck, driving towards Trenton.

Two hours afterward he was driving back to Longview. He called Chief Bates, who reluctantly gave him Debra's phone number. In twenty minutes he was seated on Debra's couch.

It was 1400 when he called Scott McTune and asked him to meet him at Cracker Barrel. "And Scott, bring a Kevlar vest, night vision goggles, handcuffs, and a riot gun with you," Simmons told him.

"Why?" McTune asked.

"Just do it. I'll explain when you get here."

Two hours later they were hiding in a field 300 yards from a white two-story house, surrounded by a six foot cedar fence.

It was almost dark when a black SUV pulled up to the gate. A man got out, unlocked the gate, and drove into a two-car garage. A single light came on inside the house.

They waited five minutes and no other lights came on. They checked the fence, found no surveillance equipment, and had no trouble scaling the fence. Once inside the yard, they studied the house for cameras or other security equipment. There did not appear to be any, but just in case an alarm sounded, they planned for Simmons to crash the back door nearest the light, while Davis hit the front.

"This is my target, Scott. Remember you agreed; you are only my backup." McTune nodded.

They made their way to a window and used a glass cutter to cut out a section of window pane. Simmons reached inside, then unlocked and raised the window so they could both slip inside. They turned on their night vision goggles, and Simmons pointed to a room across from the one where a faint light shined beneath the door. Simmons motioned for McTune to check the rooms on the right side, while he did the same on the left. Assured that no one was there except the person in the room with the light, McTune stepped inside the room next to the one with

The Truth

the light. Simmons made his way to the door with the light and removed the goggles. He tried the doorknob; it was not locked. He turned it slowly and eased the door open enough to peek inside. The only person in the room was a man sitting at a desk on the right side of the room watching TV.

Simmons stepped inside, closed the door softly, and racked a Magnum 12 gauge 00 buck shot into the Remington 870P riot gun. The man jumped to his feet, looked at the shotgun, and down at the desk drawer.

"Don't try it, Lanny."

Lanny froze, looked at Simmons, back at the desk, and back at Simmons, livid hate in his eyes. Suddenly, his mood changed, and a big smile crossed his face. He held out his hand and began walking towards Simmons.

"Lanny, don't make me use it. Pull the chair away from the desk, move it to the TV, turn it off, and sit down." His voice was ice cold, the shotgun rock-steady and pointing at Lanny's midsection.

Lanny stopped, but kept smiling. "Simmons, ole buddy, it sure is good to see you. It's been a long time. How ya been?"

"Move the chair and sit down. Now."

For a brief moment Lanny's smile gave way to a sneer, and Simmons again saw the hate in his eyes. It was the same hate he had seen in Afghanistan, but at the time he thought it was for the Taliban. Now his mind raced back to the days in the mountains, and he understood that the hate Lanny had was for the dead—any dead, even our own.

Simmons tossed a pair of handcuffs on the desk and said, "Move the chair and sit down. Put one on and lock the other to the arm of the chair."

"Aww, come on, Simmons. I am your buddy. Remember? I saved your life. You'd be dead if not for me." Lanny eyed the desk drawer once more.

Simmons pointed the shotgun at the chair and back at Lanny. "You've got three seconds. One. Two."

"Okay, okay." He moved to the chair, pushed it to the TV, and turned it off. He put one cuff on and clicked the other around the arm of the chair and sat down.

Simmons moved to the desk, opened the center drawer, removed a 9mm Luger and slipped it into his hip pocket.

"How did you find me?" Lanny asked.

"Remember the day you saved me from the bomb? You removed the dog-tags and never looked at them. You just said, 'Old J. R. is dead, but he's still trying to kill you.' That meant you knew who he was. Since I did not know him, you had to have known him before we went to sniper school. So I checked the name of those who were with you in boot camp and there was only one J. R. After a little more digging, I found James Rodger Sinclair was missing in action, and his body was never recovered. Penny found a J. R. Sinclair living close to Tyler. I came here this morning and watched you leave, and now, here I am."

Simmons shrugged, still remembering that day in Afghanistan. Remembering things he could not see back then. That Lanny never seemed to care when one of our men got killed. Only when he was forced to remove their bodies did he show any emotions. He remembered the many times Lanny had shot a Taliban corpse in the head, how he would grin, spit on the corpse, kick dirt on it, and laugh. "Now, you've got a proper burial."

Simmons did not like it, but it became such a ritual with Lanny that he overlooked it. In fact he could never see the dark side of Lanny because he admired him so much.

How could I have been so blind? Simmons asked himself.

"Why did you hate them so much?" he asked Lanny.

"Who?"

"The dead. Our dead. . . the Taliban dead. Why Lanny?"

The Truth

"Because they were stupid. Stupid to get themselves killed. Just like you, if I had not been there. They never learned to let someone else stick their head up and get a bullet. Stupid for not letting the other man get killed. Stupid for trying to be a hero. Well, they were heroes, stupid dead heroes. They deserved what they got, but left me to pick up their filthy remains. I would have just left them there to rot. They were too stupid to be picked up."

His eyes were blazing; his fists clenched and his voice was loud, but then he smiled. A smile Simmons had seen a thousand times—and seen a lot of people melt when they saw that smile.

Me, too, Simmons thought.

"Ahh. . . you know, Simmons, that was a long time ago, so let's forget it. Listen, buddy, let's get on with our lives. We can go to Mexico. I have enough money for us to live like kings. You won't have to go back to that stinking Army. Think about it. Simmons, you can have lots of girls, lots of booze, and you would never have to say, 'Yes, Sir' to some glorified, snot-faced lieutenant. You could lie on the beach with a different senorita every night."

"Tell me how you did it. Who did you kill to make it look like you had committed suicide? Tell me about that."

"He was a useless Mexican I picked up in Houston. I looked until I found one about my size and brought him here. He stunk so bad, I made him take a bath, and then I burned his clothes and gave him some of mine. After that, I stuck my ole man's double barrel shotgun in his face and pulled the trigger on both barrels. He was useless, Simmons. Nobody cared about him."

"Why did you need to make it look it was you?"

"Look, Simmons, I don't have to. . ." He stopped when he saw Simmons raise the shotgun. "I asked you a question. Why?"

"I came home thinking my ole man had a tree fall on him, and all Mama did was cry and moan. She kept saying how she wanted to join him, so I gave her a big shot of Anectine—you know, that stuff the bow hunters once used in Mississippi. They

453

used it because if the powder got into the animal's bloodstream, it killed in seconds. So, I mixed some of it with water and gave her a shot. I couldn't stand all that moaning and groaning. After all, that was what she wanted."

He smiled, and Simmons could see he was proud of it. "Then what?"

"I hung around that old farm long enough to find that my parents had spent most of the money they had, and I knew Lain would not agree to sell. I was broke, so me and a girl I dated devised a plan for her to make old Judge Caldwell pay us for not telling everyone he was gay. See, Ali's step-father and the judge had a thing for each other and Ali videotaped them in the act. I've got a copy of the tape. I'll show it to you. Disgusting."

Simmons shook his head, and Lanny continued. "Later, when his old lady died, we decided to make old Caldwell marry Ali. That way she would have a big house and lots of money. Since he was gay, he would not bother her sexually. Once she got all his money, she would show the tape to the media and divorce him. Then we could get married. I was all for that. . . except the marrying part. I was not going to marry her.

"Simmons, I tell you; it was a brilliant plan, and we worked it for two years. It worked until I started dating Penny because she had more money than I could ever have gotten out of Caldwell. I was going to marry her until Gentry told me he had purchased some diamonds from my father and from Sheriff Green after my ole man died. He asked me if I had sent them from Afghanistan. When I said I had not, he said he thought the sheriff may have gotten them from my place. I tore the place apart until I found where the diamonds were and also found evidence that Green was stealing my diamonds. I confronted him about it, and he said if I did not give him half of the diamonds, he would tell the IRS. Well, I got rid of him. After all, I think he killed my ole man. He was so stupid.

The Truth

"I found a lot of diamonds and showed them to Gentry. He said they were worth a fortune—millions, maybe billions—and with that much money, I did not need either Ali or Penny. I was a rich man. Simmons, I was rich. I mean really rich!" He turned on the charm again.

"All that money, you and I can share. I can't spend that much money by myself. Listen, man, we can live high on the hog. We can go wherever we like and do whatever we please. We're rich, man, rich. We won't have to share it with anyone."

"I'll think about it. What went wrong?"

"Think about it, Simmons. We can live like kings."

"What went wrong?" Simmons asked again and raised the shotgun. "Hell, man. Don't you hear what I'm saying? We're rich."

"I'm not asking again. You had someone try to kill me, and I won't mind pulling this trigger."

Once again Simmons saw the livid hate in Lanny's eyes for a few seconds, but he turned on the charm and smiled.

"Well, I had Gentry make a ring for Debra and one for Elaine. He sold some more diamonds for me, and then I found this huge diamond. I asked him to make it into a ring for Penny, but when I found out how much it was worth, I wasn't giving it to her, cause she's got all she wants. Anyway, that story seemed to satisfy Gentry, but I guess he knew that were a lot more where that one came from and he wanted a slice of the pie. I think he suspected I had something to do with Green's death, so he said if I did not agree to give him half of the diamonds, he would tell the authorities about Green and would also inform the IRS that I was not paying taxes on the diamonds I sold. You know what a bunch of crooks that outfit is! They would have taken half of my diamonds. No way was I going to give Gentry, or anybody else, any of my diamonds. So, he had an accident."

"Go ahead."

Lanny looked at Simmons, smiled, and continued, "Well, I needed a way to sell the diamonds. I found out that Bradley was using the Tyler plant to distribute drugs, so Sinclair and I worked out a deal with him. Sinclair would have his brother buy the diamonds, and we would use the money to buy drugs. That way we could double our profit and I'd have a way to turn the diamonds into money without paying taxes." He smiled again and was clearly proud of himself.

"Everything was working fine until Ali got upset about me spending time with Penny. She said she was going to tell Judge Caldwell that I was the one who was blackmailing him and that Bradley was using the bottling company to sell drugs. If Penny found that out, she would fire Bradley, and we would lose the means to trade the diamonds for drugs. I was making so much money, I didn't need Ali or Penny, so I decided to fake my death and get away from them both. It was the best plan I ever came up with, and it worked perfectly until you came and made Bradley lose the diamonds. Sinclair and I went to his apartment and found Bradley packing to leave. At his house we found more diamonds that he had stolen, probably worth a couple of mil, and learned that he had made plans to sell the Tyler plant." He stopped, stared at Simmons, and smiled.

"Simmons, you can have those diamonds. We'll find another way to move the drugs and turn the diamonds into money. What do you say, ole buddy? That's more money than you'll see the rest of your life. I mean, we will be millionaires."

"That is very tempting and I might do it, but I would like to hear the rest of the story." Simmons could see Lanny was so proud of himself he could hardly wait to tell his story.

"Well, Simmons, nobody steals from me, so I carried ole Bradley out on the lake and got rid of him. Sinclair made up that story about you and Bradley going fishing, and Joe Evans was supposed to arrest you." He smiled and turned on the charm again.

The Truth

"Now, ole buddy, don't get mad. You and I have been close a long time. You know I would not do anything to harm you. We just needed you out of the way a few days. With you in jail, we could get the rest of the diamonds. That's all we planned to do."

"Lanny, you tried to have me killed."

"That was Sinclair's idea, and I didn't know about it. He was supposed to just scare you so you might leave, but you didn't."

"What about Elaine? You tried to kill her, too."

"Simmons, I was desperate. I had to protect my diamonds, and with Lain out of the way, Carrie Bates would inherit the farm. Sinclair said we could kill Bates and make it look like a Mexican did it or something. Carrie has cancer and is not expected to live more than a few months. After that, Debra would get the farm."

"How were you planning to get the diamonds from her? You planned to kill her, too?"

"Oh no! This is the beautiful part of the plan, Simmons. See, Debra and I have been lovers since she was ten or eleven, and she is crazy about me. She knew that since we were cousins, we could not get married. Anyway, when her mother dies... Simmons, now listen to this... I go to her and show her I am not dead. Then we can move to Mexico and raise our son. We might even get married since she is not related to J. R. Sinclair." He laughed and rubbed the back of his head.

"Ain't that beautiful?" He smiled and was clearly delighted with the story he was telling. "Miguel is your son?"

"Yeah, we made up the story about Lopez. Debra's parents believed it; so did everybody else."

"Sounds like a good plan, but what about Sinclair, his brother, and Susie? You said you and me could split the diamonds."

"Simmons, do you think I just got off the shrimp boat? I've already taken care of them. I didn't need them since Bradley messed everything up. So, I told them to come here to discuss what we were going to do now that the Feds know about the farm. And, Simmons, listen to this. . . You see, this place here was owned by the owner of Trenton Funeral Home, and it has a crematorium out back. I scattered their ashes up and down the road from here to Trenton. Man, we needed one of them when we were in Afghanistan. Ha, ha, ha. . ." He laughed almost uncontrollably.

"Okay, Lanny, you and Debra will get half, and I get half. Is that a deal?"

"It sure is. Simmons, you know it was always me and you. Man we can live like kings."

Simmons lowered the shotgun, took Lanny's Luger from his pocket, and laid it on the desk. He tossed the key to the handcuffs, and Lanny unlocked them.

"Lanny, it's not that I don't trust you, but why don't you put our agreement in writing?"

Lanny nodded his head, looked at Simmons, smiled, and walked to the desk. He pretended to pick up a pencil, but grabbed the Glock and fired two quick shots.

Simmons felt the impact of the 9mm bullets as they hit his chest. He staggered backwards and saw Lanny smiling. There was pure delight on his face until the 00 buckshot from the riot gun blew it away.

Blood, brains, and hair splattered the ceiling. Bone fragments and teeth ricocheted off the walls like bullets off the rocks in Afghanistan. There was nothing left of his smiling face as his body slammed against the wall, his legs buckled, and he sprawled awkwardly to the floor.

Simmons heard the door behind him crash open and turned to see McTune with a Glock in his hand. For a split second Simmons wondered if he had trusted the wrong man and was relieved when McTune lowered his weapon.

The Truth

"You took a big chance. He could have shot you in the head."

"No, he was a sniper. The only way he would take a head shot is if that was his only target, so I gave him a big chest target."

"Why did you take that chance?"

"I had to know if he would kill me himself. Otherwise I don't think I could have taken him down." McTune nodded his head and stared at the body. "Well, he did exactly what you said he would do. How did you know?"

Simmons said nothing as he unbuttoned his shirt and took off the bulletproof vest. He rubbed the bruises made by the impact of the bullets. He inspected the 9mm slugs embedded in the Kevlar and handed it to McTune.

"After I saw him here this morning, I got Debra's phone number from Bates. I told her I had seen Sinclair and that I believed he was the one who had killed Lanny and the others. She was relieved to think Lanny was dead. I knew she had been scared to death of something more than Lopez; after all, Lopez was dead, and she still would not leave the house. Once I convinced her Lanny was dead, we talked. I soon learned Lanny had sexually abused her since she was eight years old and had raped her many times since he came home from the Army. She said Lanny always used people. She suspected he was the reason Ali married the judge. Also, she said Lanny was so proud of himself, she knew he would not kill himself, and that he had somehow faked his own death. She was afraid he would find out that Miguel was really Lopez's son. If he did, he would kill them both."

McTune took off his shirt and pointed to a spot on his chest. "Hit me hard right here. I need a bruise, too, just in case someone wants to see what happened after the Kevlar stopped the bullets."

Simmons hit him hard. McTune barely flinched and put on the vest.

Simmons took a handkerchief from his pocket, wiped the shotgun, and handed it to McTune. McTune took the shotgun, making sure his fingerprints were on it, especially the trigger.

"I am glad you fired it before we came. Now the powder residue will be on you and your clothes, just in case." Simmons paused, looked at McTune, and added, "Scott, thanks for agreeing to this. I could not bear to have so many people know what kind of person he really was. It would have hurt a lot of good people who truly loved him. What was to be gained, especially since the real J. R. Sinclair died in Afghanistan?

"You can say that Sinclair admitted killing Lanny. That will make Debra truly believe Lanny is dead, and maybe she will get on with her life. From what I have learned about the Sinclairs, I don't think the black mark on that name will make any difference. Davis is the only one, besides you and me, who knows what happened here. I think he will be so pleased to close the file on the drug ring, he will not mind omitting a few details."

Simmons took a long look at the body lying on the floor and shook his head. "I loved him like a brother. I guess that is the reason I could never see what he really was." He stared at the body for a long time.

"Why did you not tell him you talked to Debra, and that she hated him for all the times he raped her. . . that Miguel is really Lopez's and not his?"

"I didn't want him to think he did not have everything under control; otherwise, he might not have wanted to kill me so bad." He shrugged, "You can fill Davis in on all the details."

He took one last look at the faceless body, at a dead body with blood running under the desk.

He always hated the dead, Simmons thought.

"Let's get your cruiser, and I'll walk from there to where we left my truck. When you are finished here, the media will probably have already reported it, but, for the record, give me a

The Truth

call to tell me how J. R. Sinclair admitted to killing Lanny and the others."

He opened the door, took off his gloves, and turned to face McTune.

"Scott, thanks again. I'm sure the others will want to meet you in the morning to hear the whole story." He put the gloves into his pockets and walked out the door, never looking back.

The next afternoon, Anna, Penny, Elaine, and Simmons boarded the chopper, picked up Amos and Marie, and flew to Tyler to meet with Davis and McTune.

McTune related the story in great detail of how J. R. Sinclair had killed Lanny and the others.

"We found enough evidence in his house to leave no doubt about that."

Each of them expressed their appreciation to McTune for discovering the truth and to Simmons for believing Lanny did not kill himself; else Lanny's killer would still be around. They boarded the S-76 and flew to Manny's for lunch.

Later that afternoon they returned to the Sanderson Ranch. Simmons found a shovel and dug a hole below the rear bedroom window of the guest house. He put the boots he had bought for Lanny in the hole and covered them up. He turned and saw Elaine watching him.

"Lanny would have loved them," she said, as she walked to him and slid her arm around his waist. Laying her head on his shoulder, she looked at him with those beautiful sea-green eyes. She smiled, reached down, and scratched Dobie under his chin as they walked to the big house.

The End

ACKNOWLEDGEMENTS

To Margaret, my wife and best friend, with my love and respect

To my daughters, Sandra Wright, Michelle Lomen, and Terri Edwards and their husbands Clay Wright and Kevin Edwards for their unending encouragement

To Dr. Sherman Smith, my publisher and editor. Without him and his staff, this book would still be in Word Processor

To Charlene and Peanut Montgomery. Very few times in a person's life does one meet celebrities who are willing to help others

To Agnes Wilson, a talented singer and song writer, a classmate since grade school and a wonderful friend who introduced me to the Montgomery's

To Holly Ford, a dear friend who always encourages others

To Ruth Harp Vice President, Darrell Harp Enterprises, Inc. for the time and effort of providing me with names of people who could help promote this book

To Scotty Kennedy, Past Chairman of the Bay Tree Performing Arts and owner of Scotty Kennedy Photography, Red Bay, AL, for his never ending patience when trying to make my ugly mug look presentable

To my granddaughter, Lenae McKee Price and her husband Jordan, both talented stage performers, who believed enough to help and tell others

Extending Shadows

    To Lynton Younger. Retired pastor of Providence Baptist Church, for the inspiration to write a book
    To Randy Boyd. House of Representatives, District 19, State of Mississippi, for being a helping friend and a really nice guy
    To Carroll Gates. Itwamba County Circuit Clerk. A wonderful woman and a special friend
    To John R. Leffert, Artistic Director of the Jewish Community of Louisville, KY, for his time and devotion to this book
    To Jimmie Forbus, Past Grand Master, F&AM, State of Mississippi, for his enthusiasm and willingness to help
    To Marilyn Price, Esq. for her help and words of praise
    To granddaughter Kelsey Wright, for the Encouragements and for insisting that I carry her to the car until her legs almost dragged the ground
    And last, but not least. To my other grandchildren, Brandon, Tyler and Cory Wright, Brittany and Amanda Lomen, Price Vanderburg, Lauren and Parker Edwards and Billie Price

    To all of you I wish to express my sincere gratitude. Because of you, I am humbled and a simple thank you is never enough, so I thank you again and again. May I always remember, if not for you I would not be writing this.

    Blessings to you,
    Billy Parker